KHUMBU

Beyond the Summit

To Cindy

by
Linda J. Le Blanc

Linda LeBlanc

PILGRIMS PUBLISHING
◆Varanasi◆

Published by Pilgrims Publishing
An imprint of:
Pilgrims Book House
Varanasi, India
Website: www.pilgrimsbooks.com

Cover design by WebDAKI
Layout by Roohi Burchett

Printed and bound in the United States of America by
CENTRAL PLAINS BOOK MANUFACTURING
Winfield,Kansas

For distribution in the US call (720) 232-7599 or contact
mymingma@yahoo.com Website: www.beyondthesummit-novel.com

ISBN: 0-9785353-0-8

I. Title II. Everest, Mount (China and Nepal) Fiction III. Sherpas (Nepalese people) Fiction. IV Nepal Fiction V. Mountaineering—Everest, Mount (China and Nepal)—Fiction

To my son Mark. Thank you for always believing in me and being there when I needed you most. You have been my strongest supporter and an ever constant friend. You are an eminent surgeon but, more importantly, an outstanding man. Of that I am most proud. Your integrity and honesty, your compassion and genuine caring for others continually inspire me.

INTRODUCTION

After a treaty in 1816 that left the government distrustful of foreigners, Nepal closed its borders to all outsiders and lived in isolation from the modern world. During that period, the Shahs ruled as if it were their private domain. Ninety-five percent of the population, mostly peasants, were no more than slaves serving the needs of the regime. They had no concept that a different way of life existed. No newspapers were published in Nepal and none were imported. Radios were banned until 1946. There was no public education or public libraries. Any expression of the arts or literature was discouraged.

In 1951, the king regained his throne and opened the doors again. Nepal now had to catch up on hundreds of years of development. The country needed telephones, radios, aviation, education, health care and hospitals, money and a banking system, sanitation, business, and manufacturing. To do so all at once was a monumental task. A lot of foreign aid flowed in from around the world, but there was no coordination of programs. Everyone wanted immediate economic returns from business and industry such as the brick works created with Chinese aid and the cigarette factory built by the Russians. Everything else was pushed aside such as transportation and sanitation.

In 1968, this tiny kingdom the size of Iowa contained a population of just over 10.5 million. Composed of 21 distinct tribes who speak as many languages with numerous sub dialects, they cannot understand each other.

Ninety-two percent of the population is Hindu and only eight percent Buddhist, primarily hill tribes such as the Sherpas who migrated from Tibet 500 years earlier bringing Tibetan Buddhism with them.

Nepal contains eight of the world's ten highest mountains. Everest, the tallest, sits astride the border with Tibet. Until 1951, climbers approached the peak unsuccessfully from the north. Then in 1953, Edmund Hillary of New Zealand and Tenzing Norgay Sherpa made an ascent from Nepal and were the first to reach the 29,035-foot summit. During the next 12 years, many expeditions followed until the government placed a ban on all mountaineering from 1965-1969 because of tension during the Chinese Cultural Revolution.

The Sherpa tribe living in the shadows of Everest had a higher standard of living than most due to a flourishing trade industry between Tibet, southern Nepal, and India. Those in Namche served as middlemen with a virtual monopoly since the government allowed no traders to travel further north or south than the Khumbu village. But suddenly the livelihood that had sustained them for generations came to an abrupt halt in 1959 when the Chinese closed the Tibetan border. Fortunately the Sherpas had also gained fame as high-altitude porters after a mountaineer first used them in Sikkim in 1907. They came into demand for all Himalayan expeditions as larger numbers of climbers poured into the country. Having never been interested in scaling peaks, they were now exposed to unknown risks and many perished. When Hillary asked what he could do to help, they replied that their children had eyes but could not see. He built a school in Khumjung in 1961 and a hospital in Khunde in 1966. Anticipating the need to bring in medical supplies, he constructed an airstrip at Lukla in 1964 that reduced the travel time from Kathmandu from two weeks of arduous trekking to a forty-five minute flight. This single event opened the floodgates of tourism as hundreds then thousands of hikers came from all over the world to walk in the Himalayas and see Mt Everest. No longer confined to the dangers of working for expeditions, the Sherpas now found employment leading trekkers through their hills and villages. After 134 years of cultural and technological isolation, the influx of tourism thrust them from the Middle Ages in the modern world and dramatically altered their lives forever.

CHAPTER ONE
October 1968

The plane soared through a thin mist revealing the jagged outline of distant snow-capped peaks and clouds hanging above the mountains like brush strokes of deep red, purple, and pink framed in lapis blue. Suddenly, the captain announced the words Beth had traveled half way around the world to hear. "Ladies and Gentlemen, those of you seated on the right side now have your first view of the majestic Himalayas with their crown jewel, Mount Everest."

"Finally," she shrieked, "after endless years of waiting, I'm here." So excited she could barely sit still, Beth grabbed Eric's arm and pointed, "Look, look there it is! Highest point in the whole world and we're this close to it."

He laughed. "Next you'll be telling me you want to climb it."

"Hey, I'm no dummy and certainly don't have a death wish. What's the matter, you trying to get rid of me?"

Leaning closer, he tickled her ear with his tongue sending goose bumps all the way down her side. "Yep, that's it. I gave up my dream assignment of filming the war in Viet Nam to accompany you just so I could do you in." He laughed. "Crazy woman. Come on, change seats with me so I can shoot through the glass. I know you want pictures."

Indeed she did. He was one of the best photographers around—her intimate companion and co-worker for almost a year. As Beth watched the Kathmandu Valley unfold beneath them surrounded by rolling hills and lush forests, she thought how comfortable she was with Eric. In the past ten months, they had traveled to Botswana, Kenya, and the jungles of Borneo with her writing and him shooting pictures. They made a good team. Although he didn't set her heart ablaze, he was at least gathering firewood and that was good enough for now.

When he was done, Eric leaned back and gazed at her. "I'm proud of you, Babe. All the months of harping at the editor to let you do a story on Sherpas has finally paid off."

Curling her lower lip in a playful pout, Beth muttered, "I didn't *harp*."

He patted her. "Yes, yes, that's right. You simply grabbed his pant leg with your pit-bull tenacity and didn't let go until he surrendered."

"That's right." She grinned. "And the damn story better sell or I may be out of a job."

"True. You did promise him."

She wrapped her fingers over the back of his hand and squeezed it. "Thanks for coming with me."

With a playful grin, he answered, "Hey, I'm only here for the pictures."

When they landed at Nepal's International airport, Beth and Eric climbed into a picturesque taxi with rusted doors and a rope securing their duffels in the trunk. Greedy to experience every sight, smell, and sound, Beth hung out the window like a dog with its ears flapping in the wind. Kathmandu. The very name evoked exotic images and she absorbed every possible one as they drove along potholed, twisted lanes lined with wall-to-wall brick buildings covered with broken tiles and mud roofs sprouting grass.

"Get a shot of those," she exclaimed to Eric as they passed ancient, elaborately carved wooden windows, doorways, and balconies with the decaying figures of gods and goddesses still quietly guarding the houses. Suddenly asking the driver to stop, Beth jumped out of the taxi with Eric and camera in tow. "Look at the carvings on that temple. Are they doing what I think they are?"

He broke out laughing. "If you mean having explicit sex in every possible position, then yes. What a find. You'll never see this in a western church."

"Fantastic," said Beth while he snapped photos of the Hindu worship of carnal love and genitalia. "I'm never giving up this traveling lifestyle and can hardly wait to see the Sherpas tomorrow," she added as they climbed back in the car.

Slowly the taxi threaded its way through cows, pigs, goats, dogs, chickens, bicycles, and rickshaws as a current of humanity flowed past like rapids rushing around a boulder. Twice, they had to wait several minutes while a sacred cow meandered in front of them. It had the right of way. Every side street and alley was filled with years of refuse, and the stench from choking dust and open sewers permeated the air, making it thick, putrid, and suffocating. But who cared? This was the Shangri-La Beth had waited fifteen years to see ever since reading about Hillary's first ascent of Everest in 1953 when she was eight.

Wearing only a shirt, a small boy squatted at the side of the dirt road to defecate. When two chickens immediately scurried over and fought for the droppings, Eric quickly swore he would eat no poultry in Nepal. Minutes later, he swore off all meat when they drove down a street of fly-blackened butcher shops with buffalo heads and hooves lying on the ground next to skinned goats with their legs sticking straight up in the air.

Arriving at their three-story graying hotel, even Beth was a bit put off by the pig and two mangy dogs rummaging through a knee-high pile of garbage only ten feet from the entrance. And the flies! Buzzing from rubbish heaps to steaming piles of shit and back, they were disease magnets.

After laboriously climbing to the top floor, Eric threw himself onto the bed with his arms flung out to the side. "God, I'm tired. Come here, Babe. Let's crash until dinner."

"Twist my arm," she giggled and dropped beside him. Ten minutes later, the exhaustion of two straight days of travel and numerous time changes overcame them both.

Several hours after dark, a howl straight from *The Hound of Baskervilles* pierced the stillness, followed by blood-curdling yelps, growls, and incessant barking. Beth shot bolt upright, heart pounding. Then she flopped back down chuckling as she remembered reading about packs of wild dogs that roam the city. "Eric, wake up," she said gently nudging him. "I'm starved."

Rolling over, he yawned and draped an arm across her. "Will anything be open?"

"Who knows?" She pulled him off the bed. "Come on, Lazy, my stomach's growling."

They wandered through a maze of twisted streets and alleys that opened every so often into small squares containing communal fountains for bathing and doing laundry. Beth washed her hands under a handsomely carved spout pouring a steady stream of water but knew better than to drink from it. Drying her hands, she wondered where everybody was rushing off to. Men clad in white pants with long-sleeved, button-less shirts and the women in colorful saris all headed in the same direction.

"Come on," she said, tugging at her companion's sleeve. "Something's up and I've got to know what it is." Following them, Beth and Eric discovered a crowd gathered at the upper end of Durbar Square where officers in full uniform stood proudly while a military band played and guns boomed. As they politely made their way through the crowd, a sudden rush of warm liquid sprayed over them.

"Jesus, what's this?" Eric growled as he quickly flicked it off his cheek and then stared at his hand.

"It's from the buffalo," answered a bearded American so filthy he must not have bathed in days.

"What buffalo?" Eric snapped.

The American filled a water pipe and handed it to Eric. "Smoke a little of this and you won't give a damn. Don't worry. The hash is plentiful, cheap, and legal. They sell it like spices here."

A young Caucasian woman with pale green eyes and a delicate mouth handed Beth a rag. "Welcome to the Dashain festival."

Wiping her face, Beth asked, "The what?"

"It's the biggest event of the year," said the man, "to worship the goddess Durga who saved them by destroying the evil demon buffalo, Mahishashur. She chopped his head off with her sword and loves to drink blood and eat raw meat. So every year they offer sacrifices by slaughtering thousands of buffalo, goats, and chickens. By the time they're done the square will be ankle deep in blood. They're getting ready to do another one. Want to see?"

"Yes," Beth said eagerly.

When she reached for Eric, he erected both hands in a barrier. "Do whatever you want, but leave me out of it."

"You're kidding. We happen onto the biggest festival of the year and you're not interested?"

"I don't need to watch some animal being slaughtered and I certainly don't need any of this stuff," Eric said returning the pipe.

"It's unique experiences like this that we came for," Beth mumbled under her breath as she followed the man and woman to the front of the crowd where torches dimly lit an open area in the center. Two men were holding a large buffalo, one by the tail and the other by a rope around its neck.

"It must always be a male animal and a perfect one at that," the bearded man explained. "And the buffalo must give his consent by shaking his head. But look, they cheat by dribbling water in his ear to make him do it."

Swinging his sword high in the air, a soldier brought it down with the full force of his body. A mass of blood shot four feet across the square spraying everything as the head dropped to the ground with the tongue and mouth still moving, the eyes open and glaring.

Perfect," said the woman. "He did it in a single blow, releasing the animal's soul to be reborn as a man."

Listening to the terrified cries of the animals and sickened by the smell, Beth's enthusiasm waned. She'd seen enough.

When they returned to Eric who was still irritable, the woman addressed him quietly, "I came here to study the teachings of Buddha. He says that until we can accept life as it is and exist in the present moment, we will never be satisfied."

"I should be satisfied standing here splattered with blood?"

"Yes, if we are to be truly awake like Buddha, we must be unflappable and accept whatever comes along as part of a divine and perfect universe."

When he started to open his mouth again, Beth shot an angry look that shut him up. "Thank you for your kindness and information," she said to the man and woman before bidding them goodbye. Forget about dinner. She was going back to hotel and Eric could do whatever he damned pleased. Beth took off at a swift pace with her arms folded over her chest.

"I suppose you're mad at me now," he said following her.

"You were rude," she shouted over her shoulder.

"Why? Because I didn't want to get high on hash and don't buy into being unflappable and accepting whatever comes along as part of a divine and perfect universe? How perfect was that buffalo's universe?"

"His soul was released to be reborn as a man."

"You truly believe that?"

"I don't know, but the Hindus do and I'm here to experience other cultures and ideas. I thought you were more tolerant."

Eric caught up to her and put his arm around her waist "Let's not fight, Babe. We also came here to have a good time together and do your story."

She let out a long, deep breath. "You're right. And I agree that being sprayed with buffalo blood isn't the most enjoyable experience on the planet. Let's just forget about it."

He gave her a hug. "You'll be euphoric again once we reach Sherpa country tomorrow."

Both too tired to search for something to eat, they went back to the hotel, skirting the pig and dogs still rummaging in the garbage heap. With Eric lying wrapped around her and his breathing growing deeper and longer, she was glad they wouldn't make love that night even though it was the last time they'd sleep off the ground for weeks. Covering her ears to drown out the gnawing sound coming from under the bed, she hoped this distancing that she was feeling would soon pass.

The next day, they waited for the twin otter to Lukla in the Everest region for over three hours. The room was small, hot, and stuffy with urine stench wafting from both bathrooms. Squirming impatiently, Eric mumbled, "This is ridiculous. The plane can't leave because there's too much fog to land when it returns to Kathmandu. So who cares if it sits in Lukla until tomorrow or even next week?"

A few minutes later, a Nepali in a *topi* hat entered and announced the flight to Lukla had been canceled. They must return to their hotels and try again the next day. With disappointment everyone gathered luggage and returned to town. It was not a good omen. After checking for big-toothed rodents under the bed, Beth tried to sleep but couldn't shake a growing uneasiness surrounding the trip. She kept convincing herself that nothing was wrong. Her Shangri-La was simply an energetic, adolescent country growing too fast and struggling to make up for hundreds of years of no progress. To do it all at once was a task that would challenge even Hercules.

After again hauling their duffels to the airport the next morning, Beth and Eric finally boarded for Lukla. Fortunately, the pilot spoke English and explained the sacrificial blood smeared all over the front of the small plane was an offering to the goddess Durga for protection to the vehicle and all its occupants during the year. Leaving Kathmandu, they viewed soft, splayed-out valley walls rising in a series, each a shade darker than before. They glided over terraced fields, bamboo forests, banana groves, and deep gorges with raging rivers. Half an hour into the forty-five minute flight, a gust lifted the STOL and bounced it heavily. The next jolt rocked the plane left and right before it rose again and rapidly plummeted almost lifting the passengers out of their seats.

Eric uttered, "Oh, shit!" and Beth nodded in agreement.

Seated directly behind the pilot, they could see over his shoulders as the aircraft rolled, bumped, and shook on its approach to the 1900-foot landing strip rising at a 9° angle with a mountain at the head and a cliff at the base. Straining against the back of the seat, Beth abandoned breathing as they prepared to touch down. Unfortunately, instead of landing, the plane veered sharply to the right and rose quickly to avoid colliding with the mountain. The pilot completed a U turn, leaving everyone's stomach behind. He flew a short distance before making another attempt. As they flew, Beth glimpsed a downed plane at the base of the cliff and imagined slamming into the face and plunging in flames to join the wreckage. She gripped Eric's hand and waited for the wheels to touch, but once again, the plane rose and turned.

"It's too windy to land," the pilot called over his shoulder. "We must go back to Kathmandu and try again tomorrow."

Nauseated and dizzy, nobody complained of his decision. An elderly lady seated across from Beth vomited into a plastic bag and her companion soon copied her actions. Beth wasn't certain her own stomach would ever return to its rightful place.

In Kathmandu, Eric retrieved the two women's luggage while Beth spoke to them. "What will you do now?"

With her tight, gray curls still shaking, Ruth let out a fluttering sigh. "Keep trying until we get there."

"But how can you after today?"

"Honey, we didn't come this far to be turned back by a little wind," answered Helen, a woman so thin her spine showed like a miniature mountain chain through her shirt. We're here to celebrate my finishing chemotherapy for breast cancer." She pulled a wig off. "See my hair is already starting to grow back."

Still amazed that they were traveling alone and at their age, Beth asked, "But what are you going to do in Lukla?"

"Why go up to the Tengboche Monastery, of course," Helen replied, "to see the monks"

"And Everest," added Ruth. "Don't worry about us, Honey. We've been promised the best guide there is and he speaks good English."

"And is strong," Helen added. "He carried a woman for 12 days, but that won't be me. I'm walking every step of the way."

"Now that's unflappable," Eric whispered to Beth. "Remind me not to complain about anything else on this trip."

Inspired by the women's attitude and pleased with Eric's comment, Beth shoved all portentous feelings aside and convinced herself that everything was going to be just fine. *Sherpas, here I come!*

CHAPTER TWO

Just under 17,000 feet at Gorak Shep, Dorje, ten porters, a cook, and two kitchen boys slept huddled together on the dirt floor of a yak herder's hut. A mixture of yak dung and mud plastered the dry-set stones of the one-story building. With only loose fitting, wooden shutters covering the windows, the wind flicked its icy tongue between the slates and around rough-hewn edges. Shivering, Dorje tugged the wool blanket over his head and reminded himself that he'd survived this cold before. Barefoot and inexperienced, poor Ang Lahkpa snored loudly enough beside him to bring down an avalanche. These m*ikarus,* the white eyes sleeping in their warm tents with foam pads and down bags, treated the Sherpas better than most foreigners Dorje had worked for.

As a biting cold cut through him, he remembered his first porter job four years earlier in the year of the dragon, what the *mikarus* called 1964. Having just returned home at age sixteen after ten years in the warm Solu further south, he awakened to his first snowfall since a young boy. Excited, he ran barefoot outside and stood watching each flake, a silent and glorious thing of beauty, settle loosely on the ground. Half an hour later he ran back inside, his feet red and numb, determined his father must buy shoes for him and his younger brother, Nima. When their mother left with another man ten years earlier and took her boys with them, their father had promised he would come often, but he never did. Unable to forgive him, Dorje wanted to demand warm shoes, but his father's presence as he strode across the room in a blood red, heavy woolen robe intimidated him. The sleeves hanging loosely off the shoulders allowed Mingma to free one arm and adjust body temperature. The high leather boots moved in a whisper but Mingma's square features with high cheekbones and dark, glinting eyes commanded all those who came near. Tall for a Sherpa and strikingly handsome, he wore his long, black hair plaited and tied with a red ribbon, resembling the Tibetans with whom he had traded crossbreeds.

Dorje had hoped for stronger footing before he stood up to him, but this couldn't wait. Cramming the words to the roof of his mouth, he shoved them out hard and fast with no chance for retreat. "You must buy us shoes and do it right now!" he said, astounding even himself with his brashness.

Anger slowly rose through Mingma's body and settled into his shoulders. "I cannot afford them. In winter, farmers don't need dung for their fields or to plaster their walls and my animals aren't producing." In a voice that offered no allowance for further discussion, he added, "When they calve in the spring, I will sell butter, milk, and cheese to buy shoes."

Teetering on the precipice of the rift separating them, Dorje plunged right in. "We won't have feet left by then. You haven't helped us in ten years and I don't need you now. I'll make my own money."

"Doing what? Carrying bags for people who don't belong here? These *mikarus* invade our land, soil our temples with their muddy boots, leave their garbage and toilet paper along our trails, and anger our gods. No son of mine will work for them. As long as you live in my house, you will do as I say and tend the yaks with your brother."

Dorje's confidence faltered. After ten years of waiting and yearning for his father, he wanted to feel like a six year old again. In his head, love, resentment, and fear bickered over who was right and refused to form a single emotion he could grasp. So he banished them to their separate corners. Unable to find words to fill the vast empty space between him and his father, Dorje had no choice but to exit the room in silence.

Frustrated, he turned to the only person he remembered from his early childhood—his father's best friend, Pemba, who had accompanied him on trading expeditions to the north. Standing outside the man's door, Dorje stared at images unlike the lettering in Mingma's Tibetan scriptures. He then entered the lower level reserved for animals at night and climbed a narrow, dark stairway to the large, open room on the second floor used as a living area. As in all Sherpa homes, a bench seat and low tables stood under the front windows opposite a wall of shelves displaying the family's wealth in an assortment of brass pots and water containers. Family life centered around a floor hearth near the door in a room otherwise devoid of furniture.

Small in stature with ears much too large for his face, Pemba stood
erectly and explained that Edmund Hillary had just built an airstrip at
Lukla to bring in supplies for an intended hospital. Tourists could now
fly into the Khumbu in forty-five minutes rather than hiking two weeks
from Kathmandu. "It's easy money. I opened the first teahouse in Namche
with an English sign that says SHERPA LODGE GOOD FOOD GOOD
BED and they come to me."

"How do I get some of that money?"

Pemba motioned toward a man and woman on the bench nearest the
hearth traditionally reserved for the senior-most male member of the
household. "Those two want to see the monastery at Tengboche. Only
the Japanese are foolish enough to come in winter. The porter they hired
in Lukla refuses to go higher in the snow without extra pay and demands
four times as much. With a schedule to keep, they need to go up tomorrow but refuse to give in to him."

"I'll take them."

His eyes nervously flitting from one object to the next like a song-
bird, Pemba lifted himself taller on the bench. "Don't tell your father I
had a hand in this. He blames me enough already."

"Blames you for what? I remember you laughing and sharing *chang*."

"Another time," Pemba answered with a pinched quality to his voice.
"Another time."

To avoid confrontation with his father, Dorje spent the night and rose
early to stuff three cumbersome duffels into a bamboo basket. To put the
doko on, he had to sit on the floor, slip his arms through the leather side
straps, and tip his head back to fit the tumpline snugly over the top. Pemba
helped him to his feet and steadied him while Dorje eyed the strangers.
Their hair was thick and black like his, but their round faces lacked the
distinctive, high cheekbones inherited from his father. They wore matching brightly colored pants, jackets, hats, boots, and gloves. Never had
Dorje seen so many clothes on one person at one time.

In the only shorts and shirt he owned, he started out ahead of them
trying not to grimace under the weight compressing his neck. With the
Japanese chattering behind him, he plodded upward, one foot after the
other over frozen ground. When the Japanese man pointed to a mountain,
babbling something, Dorje gave him the Nepali word for *snow-covered
mountain*. Excitedly, the man quickly wrote it in a book and pointed to the
next one. Chuckling to himself, Dorje gave the Nepali for *another snowy
mountain*. This preoccupation with naming everything made no sense to a
Sherpa whose language didn't even contain a word for summit.

For five hours, they climbed straight up through pine, black juniper, and rhododendron. With every step, Dorje's legs burned and cramped. When it suddenly began to snow again, each flake was no longer a silent and glorious thing of beauty but a cold, wet, and miserable enemy. Gesturing wildly, the woman ordered him to remove the *doko,* untie the ropes with frozen fingers, and unload her duffel, which was at the bottom so she could get out another sweater, heavier jacket, and a wool hat. While she bundled up, he sat there in bare feet that had long since lost any feeling, his entire body shaking so hard he thought it would fall apart.

At Tengboche, they went to the house of Pemba's brother, Changjup. Sitting by the fire in his sopping pants and shirt, his feet searing with the pain of thawing, Dorje watched the Japanese change into dry things. Once the woman was warm, she began jabbering and flailing her arms at the smoke rising from the fire and fanning out along the ceiling. When she opened the shutters and leaned her head out coughing, Changjup shooed her back inside and slammed them shut.

He threw his hands in the air and yelled in Nepali, "What would she do, heat the whole mountainside? Don't they know how scarce wood is?"

The snow ended during the night, ushering in a crisp, clear sky at dawn as the sun rose over the mountains and bathed the monastery in amber light. The penetrating, unearthly sounds of oboes and eight-foot telescoping horns announced the beginning of daily prayer. After leading the Japanese up the wide stone steps, Dorje instructed them to remove their shoes and hoped their feet froze. The dimly lit room smelled of butter lamps and juniper incense. Brilliantly colored images of Buddha, various gods, lamas, and mythological scenes decorated the ceiling and walls while *mandalas* and cloth *thankas* hung from intricately carved rafters.

Sitting in two rows facing the center aisle, sixteen monks recited the *sutra* from long folios open on low prayer tables before them. Their hair shorn close, they wore sleeveless burgundy robes with gold cloths draped over one shoulder. They chanted in a low, monotonous intonation to the quiet insistent beating of a drum and the moaning of long horns, punctuated only by the occasional clash of cymbals. When the Japanese crouched only inches from them snapping photos without their consent, Dorje removed them from the temple as quickly as possible.

In the monastery meadow, the woman started bouncing and squealing, "Everest, Everest," as she pointed to a mountain Dorje knew as Chomolungma. Its triangular peak immense and remote with a long, graceful plume of wind-driven snow, it seemed aloof and formidable with its upper pinnacles of jagged rock rising out of steep glaciers and gleaming ice, soaring above all others. Mesmerized, Dorje knew he would someday stand on the summit like the famous Tenzing did before him.

The Japanese woman pulled him out of his trance by shoving her camera in his face and pointing him towards Everest. Looking through the hole, Dorje watched the mountain move closer. When he used only his eyes again, Everest still loomed in the distance. Curious thing, this black box. She put his index finger on the red button and motioned for him to wait while she stood beside her husband on a rock directly in line with Everest. Thinking how they had left him wet and shivering while they added layers of clothing, Dorje tipped the camera just above the summit of Everest and pressed the button four times, shooting only a brilliant blue sky with not a cloud anywhere.

He carried their duffels three more days down to the small airfield at Lukla and waited for their twin otter to arrive. When they were prepared to leave, he bowed with his palms together and flashed his most engaging smile. "*Namaste.*"

"*Namaste,*" they replied and then did something that blew apart his angry feelings and scattered them over the mountains like gray ash. The man pulled two sweaters, four pairs of wool socks, a pair of long pants, and a wool hat from his duffel and just handed them over to Dorje. More clothes than he had ever owned at once in his entire lifetime. He stared with incredulous eyes as the man removed the coveted, brightly-colored jacket and added it to the pile. Dumbfounded, Dorje flashed another smile and watched as they boarded the plane for a place beyond his comprehension. With the clothes, the agreed-upon six rupees[1] per day, plus a tip clutched in his fist, he forgot about how exhausted, cold and miserable he'd been, how his head felt as though it had been shoved down his spine, how he feared his feet would never walk straight again. His strength, tenacity, and winning smile had gained him a fortune. He was indomitable.

Having spotted boots in a shop that sold used expedition and hiking gear, Dorje raced in and jumped up on the counter. "I want those," he said, pointing to a brown pair with red laces.

The man lifted them from the shelf and handed them to him. Running his finger over the hard, black sole, Dorje wondered how his feet would find their way on the path at night or grip a swaying bridge. "How much?" he asked, thinking he could buy a pair for Nima too.

"One hundred and fifty rupees. They're good quality, all leather."

---

[1] 6 rupees equaled about $1.00

"That's impossible. Nobody has that much!" Dorje shouted, his jaw so tight it hurt.

"Tourists do. And when they need boots, I have the only ones in Namche."

"But what about Sherpas?"

"Sorry," said the shopkeeper. "That's how it is."

That's how it is, Dorje still repeated to himself even now, four years later as he lay in the yak herder's hut at Gorak Shep. Beside him, Ang Lahkpa suddenly woke with a snort, shivered all the way down his spine to his bare feet, grumbled about the cold, and fell back asleep. Soon the snoring resumed and droned on as it had every night. Dorje tucked his blanket tighter and chanted his personal mantra—the only thing that made returning to this horrible, frigid place bearable. *The mikarus pay many rupees so I will simply smile and endure and take them up the mountain.*

CHAPTER THREE

As soon as the first rays of light stole through the shutters and crawled over the mound of shivering Sherpas, Dorje wrapped his blanket across Ang Lahkpa and ducked to exit the hut through a short doorway designed to keep out evil spirits too tall and stiff to bend low. Highest in the Everest region, the solitary building at Gorak Shep sat on a sandy flat at the base of Kala Pattar, an 18,200-foot mountain that looked like a rocky, black mound compared to the peaks surrounding it. Since that first trip with the Japanese four years ago, Dorje had earned the title of sirdar, the highest-ranking Sherpa position in charge of the trek and responsible for decisions regarding Sherpas and *mikarus*. With all but one of the foreigners wanting to climb Kala Pattar for the incredible view of Everest it afforded, Dorje assigned three porters to accompany them on the 90-minute hike. An American named Marty chose to go to the Everest Base Camp instead despite repeated warnings that he wouldn't be able to see the mountain from there and that it was only a dirty glacier covered with rocks and trash from past expeditions. However, Marty was determined to tell his friends he'd stood at the base of Everest and Dorje's job was to keep the *mikarus* happy. Besides, he liked this American. Marty made him laugh.

Dorje grabbed the icy tent flap and shook it vigorously, watching the crystals splinter. "Time to go," he said in English.

"Buck buck?" Marty's favorite expression that rumbled from deep in his throat made Dorje chuckle.

He shook the tent even harder. "You lazy *mikaru*. Get up."

When the door zipped down a few inches, a finger poked through the hole, wiggling to test the temperature. "Brrrr, serious cold-ness," Marty muttered and quickly zipped back up, but Dorje could hear him rustling about inside and knew he'd soon crawl out. Meanwhile, he packed last night's *chapatis* and *nak* cheese for the trek and instructed the cook and kitchen boys to get the fire going for morning tea and a pan of wash water for each *mikaru*. Marty finally emerged in his usual attire: whatever flew out of the duffle first, regardless of color or condition. He claimed life was much too short to worry about whether one's socks matched. His never did. His hair sticking out on all sides and growing down his neck like a mongrel's, Marty held the brim of a bright green hat with writing on the front, clamped it down on his head, and grinned. "Time for some serious fun-ness. Which way?" His voice rose and fell as if playing with each syllable, and Dorje liked this peculiar habit of adding *ness* to words.

With exaggerated marching steps and arms swinging, Marty headed for the right bank of the Khumbu Glacier. "Who lives in that place?" he asked, flipping his hand over his shoulder at the stone hut.

"Nobody. Yak herders use it when they come for summer pasture. There are more huts in the next valley at Gokyo."

A shudder ran all down his body as Marty shot him a stricken look. "You're not a yak herder."

Pretending to swat Marty's rear with a switch, Dorje said, "No. *Mikaru* herder," and erupted in a burst of laughter. "But when you foreigners don't come in the summer monsoon, I take care of yaks to please my father."

Marty hopped onto a rock and stood on one foot, the other leg swinging precariously over a small crevasse, arms waving wildly to keep his balance.

"You cause more trouble than a yak or female *nak*," Dorje scolded and tugged him down. "You are a crazy man."

"No. But a little wacky maybe."

"What is wacky?" Dorje asked, wanting to add this word to his burgeoning English vocabulary. Four years ago, he'd figured out that speaking the language of the *mikarus* guaranteed larger tips and more promotions. He'd been badgering foreigners to teach him ever since. Marty pulled his hair out at the sides and wiggled his tufted eyebrows. *Curious word, this wacky* thought Dorje.

"Life is like a stubborn old mule," Marty said. "So you have to smack it across the head every once in a while just to keep it in line."

Even though he understood the individual words, Dorje had no idea what the American was talking about and changed the conversation by explaining that young people take herds up high to graze at summer camps called *yersas* when summer rains sprout new grasses. Three months of unchaperoned work and play.

Marty abandoned leaping over fragile crevasses and sidled up to Dorje. "You have a girlfriend?"

"Yes," Dorje answered with a grin and swagger. "A most beautiful Sherpani."

"Huh. Well, American women would go crazy for you too. When you want to attract one, just slowly comb your fingers through your thick black hair and flash that big grin of yours."

"You have a woman?"

"Oh, no, that'll never happen. I'd have to grow up!" Pushing his arms out to make himself look larger, Marty drew his eyebrows together in a fierce look and growled. "But I have this really big dog."

After growling too, Dorje started laughing so hard he almost tripped over an ice block, still not accustomed to these boots. Even though his feet were warm now, he missed the connection with the earth he used to have. Chuckling to himself, he remembered his first few days in them. He had earned 300 rupees carrying a French woman for twelve days when she sprained her ankle. After buying boots for himself and his brother, he ran outside and jumped in the mud to verify the footprint matched those of the trekkers. His entire being singing, he swaggered up and down every path in the village, kicked the dirt, crossed over sharp rocks, and stomped in puddles. Running up the stairs to show Nima, he discovered his feet had acquired new dimensions. His toes kept hitting the risers, making him stumble all the way catching himself on his hands.

He glanced at Marty's feet and wondered at what age he had first worn shoes. Noticing the American was now breathing harder, he warned, "You must go slowly, *bistarai, bistarai,* or you will get sick this high."

As they followed cairns up the center, the glacier twisted and undulated in its unrelenting downward progress. Recalling Marty's comments about women, Dorje amused himself with memories of the first time he and Shanti made love last summer at Gokyo. The breeding of yaks and cows all that week had imbued the air with a heightened sensuality. Conversations between the sexes were full of innuendoes and boy/girl roughhousing occurred frequently. With all that excitement surrounding him, Dorje couldn't contain himself any longer. One afternoon when the sun sneaked out between downpours, he ran to the hut where Shanti was churning *nak* butter and asked her to come outside.

The entire pasture had blossomed into a field of alpine flowers glistening from the rain: deep-blue poppies, pink geraniums and wild roses, dark purple bellflower and primrose, pink lilies and dwarf rhododendron. Leading her over a low ridge away from the huts and grazing animals, he intended to gently ease her onto a blanket of yellow buttercups, thread a deep-pink orchid through her long black hair, and whisper sweet things, but she never gave him a chance. Shanti stuffed grass down the back of his pants and took off running with her long skirt sweeping over the meadow. He could suddenly sympathize with yaks trying to mate recalcitrant cows.

When he caught her and pulled her to the ground, they laughed and wrestled until Shanti finally rolled onto her back, threw her dress over her head, and wiggled her bare hips in anticipation. Dorje took her immediately and had the most beautiful girl in the Khumbu the rest of the summer—always robust and playful, ever ready. When summer ended and they returned to their villages, he often sneaked into her parent's house at night to make love. In the fall trekking season, it was hard being away so many nights. He missed her brown, almond eyes and feeling her legs locked around him. Smiling to himself, Dorje decided yak herding provided some benefits but they had nothing to do with those shaggy, unruly beasts.

Three hours after leaving Gorak Shep, Dorje and Marty reached Base Camp, a wasteland of rock and ice strewn with rubbish: used oxygen canisters, empty food tins, frail guy wires, and tent canvas shredded by icy winds. A 2,000-foot icefall at the head of the glacier loomed before them like a torrent of violent rapids frozen in time, silent, its force restrained. However, walking to the base of the frozen river, Dorje discovered it was very much alive, constantly twisting and collapsing on itself in a bizarre and chaotic landscape.

"Now that's serious ice-ness," Marty announced in a flat voice.

"It is the most dangerous place on the mountain," said Dorje. "Many Sherpas have died here."

"Then I must go up."

"Why?"

"To prove that I am not afraid."

"Prove to who?"

"My father," Marty answered with a nervous sweat seeping down his brow. "If you're afraid, wait here, but it's time for me to do some head smacking."

Still confused about *head smacking,* Dorje couldn't let him go alone into this eerie maze of shifting, unstable ice with turquoise pinnacles towering a hundred feet above them.

His voice measured, no longer playing with each syllable, Marty asked, "Have you ever been in a cave?"

"I do not know this word."

"It's cold and so black you can't see a thing. Bats fly into your face. Unseen things slither around your legs and feet. And you never know when you'll step off a cliff and fall into a deep, dark hole."

"I would not like such a place."

Stopping, Marty stared at immense blocks that had tumbled and landed precariously poised to topple again. "When I was seven, my father made me go in the cave first."

"But you were afraid."

"Terrified, same as I am now. I started crying and urine ran down my leg. That only made him madder. He hit me and said no son of his would grow up a coward."

"Did you go?"

"I had no choice. He would have beat me like the day I refused to clean the deer he'd shot when I was only seven."

Feeling a rush of compassion, Dorje said, "You can choose now. Your father is not here."

Marty rolled his eyes. "Oh, yes, he is. He goes everywhere with me."

Walking in the icefall was almost impossible as they stumbled over recent avalanche debris and shattered ice. When they encountered a maze of enormous crevasses threatened on all sides by crumbling séracs, Marty's body started shaking like an autumn leaf barely clinging to a branch jostled in the wind. "I can do this," he murmured. "I can do it."

Dorje didn't understand Marty's invisible demon. "We must turn around. It is too dangerous without the crampons and ice axe climbers use."

"Not yet. I must go another 100 yards."

For what? Dorje started to shout but the words froze on his lips as a sérac suddenly split in half and swept past them in a merciless jumble of ice that rocked the ground before shooting into a gaping crevasse. Silence filled the air as they stared at the ice-strewn slope under the tilting remains of the pinnacle—the only route back to Base Camp.

"I'll show you I'm not afraid," Marty yelled but Dorje waved his arms and pointed to the unstable mass, certain that any noise or movement would bring it tumbling down. "What's the matter? Are you scared?" Marty asked, his voice bounding on the words..

"Yes. If you do not respect Miyolangsangma, the goddess of the mountain, you will make her angry and bad things will happen."

"Nonsense. I don't believe in goddesses except for those in the flesh. Geronimo," he yelled and strutted defiantly beneath the overhanging ice.

"That was a stupid thing to do."

"But we made it past, Buck buck. And now I'll teach you how we ski in Colorado."

Dorje was afraid to unleash his errant voice again. Out of anger, he had called a *mikaru* stupid and that was offensive to his own ears. Never had he spoken his true feelings to them, but Marty was different with an odd fascination and hold over Dorje that made him uneasy. Managing to restrain his tongue, he simply asked, "What is skiing?"

"You wear these long pieces of wood on your feet and go like this." Legs together, Marty bent his knees, held his arms out in front, and leaned forward slightly. Swinging his rear from side to side, he made Dorje laugh and forgo his misgivings momentarily. Suddenly Marty yelled, "Geronimo," again and took off sliding down an ice chute.

Since this reckless and frustrating American had defied the gods of the mountain, Dorje now had to prove himself equally fearless or lose face. With his heart banging in his throat, he took a deep breath and flew down the chute after him, whirling out of control. He crashed into Marty waiting at the bottom and tumbled head over heel. Instead of the expected terror, he felt a wild exhilaration. So that's what head smacking was all about.

When they reached the glacier again and easier footing, Marty asked if Dorje had climbed Everest. "No. But I must someday because Hillary carried me on his shoulders and they called me the Tenzing of the future."

Eyeing him suspiciously, Marty crimped the corner of his mouth. "You met them, Hillary and Tenzing, the first two to reach the top?"

"When I was five." He hoped that would be enough because telling more would stir up memories of how things used to be with his father, but Marty insisted and Dorje's responsibility to keep *mikarus* happy overshadowed all else. So he would relate only the facts of the meeting and not reveal of the emotions of a young boy. Those would remain hidden in his heart.

He began by talking about the day he met Hillary. Dorje's father had been gone many months taking 100 crossbreed *zopkios* and *zhums* over the Nangpa La into Tibet to trade for horses, which he would then drive south to India to barter for goods and grain. As Dorje had done every morning, he ran to the head of the trail and positioned himself to wait for his father. Porters continually arrived carrying loads of grain, handmade paper, and incense from southern Nepal to be bartered for Tibetan goods with the Sherpas of Namche acting as middlemen. Rushing to meet them, he searched for his father's sweeping dark robe and braided hair tied in a red ribbon, but as each group passed, his heart sank and the lonely place inside grew larger.

Late one afternoon, he heard shouting coming from the upper end of the village as men and women poured from their houses onto the narrow dirt paths. Dorje joined them lining the trail as strange men passed, taller than Sherpas with light skin and hair, speaking an unknown language, their heavy shoes leaving peculiar imprints in the dirt.

Tugging on the skirt of an old grandmother, he asked, "Bajai, what is it? What?"

"Men returning from Chomolunga, the mountain they call Everest."

When porters arrived carrying a Sherpa on their shoulders, everyone shouted, "Long live Tenzing!"

"Bajai, who is Tenzing?"

"Tenzing Norgay. He and a white eyes named Hillary are the first to reach the top of the Mother Goddess of the World."

Intoxicated by the fervor and excitement of the crowd, Dorje jumped up and down waving his arms and yelling, "Tenzing, Tenzing."

He froze and stared at a man they called Sahib Hillary arriving amid cheers and clapping; a giant among the Sherpas with a narrow face and long, thin nose unlike the broad Mongoloid features of the villagers. A shock of brown hair hung over his forehead; his skin and eyes were fair. Determined to touch him, Dorje followed the white eyes to a tent camp in the south end of the village and hung by his elbows on a stone wall, toes climbing the rocks. Soon other children gathered to watch too, their arms entangled in a mass of security, faces peeking out from behind each other.

Noticing their eager, gawking faces, one of the men smiled and pressed his palms together, bowing slightly. "Namaste."

Ready to bolt like scared rabbits if he took a step nearer, the children giggled and twitched nervously. He was too new, too unfamiliar, too frightening—but not for Dorje. At five, he already sensed he was different from other children and wanted Hillary and Tenzing to recognize it. To get their attention, he climbed onto the wall and then leapt off with his arms thrown over his head, yelling, "Namaste!"

Preoccupied with getting settled, no one paid attention. Dorje fired an angry look at the children giggling and ridiculing him. More resolute than ever, he marched straight into camp. He could play one game better than anyone else in the village. After nervously rubbing his calf with the instep of his bare foot, Dorje began hopping on one leg. Arms gracefully out to the side lent him incredible balance enabling him to jump forever. Hop, hop, hop. Hop, hop, hop.

His back turned to Dorje, Hillary started towards his tent. "No, don't go. Not until you see," Dorje yelled in Nepali. When Hillary glanced over his shoulder, Dorje's insides scattered like corn popping but he kept his balance and hopped even faster. Then he flashed the smile his father called the most infectious in the village and it spread all the way across his face. Laughing, Hillary scooped Dorje into his long arms and placed him on his shoulders.

"Sahib has the Tenzing of the future," a porter yelled in Nepali and everyone laughed. Perched up there, Dorje was taller than anyone. He bounced up and down and touched Hillary's hair and face. The most auspicious day of his life; Dorje ached to tell his father about it.

Not until a month later during the monsoon did Mingma arrive. Recognizing his stride, Dorje spotted him from afar and raced downhill, yelling, "*Baabu! Baabu!*" He sprang off a rock into his father's arms and wrapped his bare legs and feet around him.

Mingma rocked him gently from side to side. "Have you been good?"

"Yes! Yes! See what I have!" Dorje rummaged in his pocket for the piece of gum he'd saved for his father.

"Hmmm. Even better than sweet yak curds. And where did my young son get this?"

"From the men who climbed to the top of the Mother Goddess of World. I want to see it, *Baabu*. Take me to see where Tenzing climbed."

"Shall we go there now?"

"Yes," Dorje howled and threw his head back, letting sheer rapture flow through him.

With Dorje on his shoulders, Mingma carried him fifteen minutes to the crest of the hill north of Namche. Arms tight around his father's neck and peering over his shoulder, Dorje stared at the triangular peak twenty miles in the distance with its graceful plume of wind-driven vapor arriving from India.

"Is it far to the top?"

"They say that when you stand on Chomolunga, you are higher than anything, higher than birds can fly."

"I will stand there someday because I am the Tenzing of the future."

Marty interrupted Dorje's boyhood story, "So why haven't you climbed it?"

Relieved that he didn't have to dig up memories of what had happened next, Dorje answered, "Because I was gone from the Khumbu for ten years until the winter of 1964. Since then, my government has not allowed anyone to climb because of trouble during what they call the Chinese Cultural Revolution." Seeing the disappointment in Marty's face, he added, "But I hear talk that climbers will return before the next monsoon."

"Huh," Marty said without the usual levity in his voice or expression. "It's October now and your monsoon starts in June. That should be enough time."

"Time for what?"

"For me to join an expedition. Colorado has a lot of serious climbers. I'll find a way to get back here and get you hired too." He hooked his elbow around Dorje's neck and dragged him stumbling along. "We're going to attack life together. You and I to the top."

A riot of emotions fought inside Dorje: to finally climb Everest, to do so with a man who both disturbed and fascinated him, to face his father who abhorred *mikarus* for trespassing on the abode of the gods. Dorje tried gathering all these thoughts up to inspect them, but they were much too unruly and kept slipping away before he could corner them. So he squashed them by telling himself spring was months away and anything could happen between now and then.

When they returned to Namche two days later, Marty wriggled the blue shirt over his head and thrust it at Dorje before he plopped the green hat down on his head and flicked the bill. "It says SKI VAIL and I want you to keep it until I get back."

"But what if..."

"No buts. I'll be here so get ready to climb. You'd better keep these too," he said, hooking sunglasses over Dorje's ears. Leaning back, Marty said, "Yep. You're cool."

"Cool means cold."

"It also means you're the remarkable little kid who hopped on one foot to get Hillary's attention."

Bolstered by Marty's words and the vision of climbing Everest, Dorje raced up the steep terraces towards home with his body always ahead of his feet. He stood outside panting and summoning the courage to go inside. He and Mingma had quarreled bitterly before he left, the usual argument about him not wanting to tend yaks during tourist season. With his heart lodged in his throat, he climbed the thirteen steps representing Buddha's stages to enlightenment and lunged into the room. Mingma sat with a wad of yak wool around his wrist, spinning it as he gazed out the window where he must have seen Dorje coming up from the village and heard him on the stairs. Determined to make his father acknowledge him even if in anger, Dorje pulled a fistful of rupees from his pocket and cast them onto the bench.

"What's this?" his father asked.

"Money for you. Like it or not, status is measured in rupees now, not the number of yaks. So you'd better get used to it."

Mingma pushed off the bench. "Is that why you leave when I need you the most? Two weeks ago, I lost my most valuable *nak* when it fell trying to reach a tuft of grass on a high ledge. And a wolf attacked the *zhums*."

"Nobody told me, " Dorje said with a sinking feeling. He was losing this battle.

"Because everyone, including your brother, knows that Mingma's son cares only about making money for himself."

Mingma had struck him a low blow. "My brother doesn't think this. You have no idea what I want…or who I am. You have made no attempt to know me."

"Nor have you to know me."

His father was right. No matter how hard Dorje tried to resurrect the feelings of a six year old who adored his father, the anger and hurt of broken promises stood in the way like a stubborn old yak refusing to budge on the trail. Since nothing was going to move either of them, all he could do now was turn and walk out the door.

CHAPTER FOUR

Mingma knew his son would soon be bringing the trekkers back down through Namche on the way to Lukla. Waiting at the window every afternoon, he finally saw Dorje racing up the steep terraces from the village after a fourteen-day absence. Every spring and fall his son abandoned all obligations to him and the family when the *mikarus* arrived. Mingma bristled at the sound of Dorje's footsteps on the stairs as his son returned from working for the despised foreigners who were destroying centuries of tradition.

Clad in western clothing, Dorje burst into the room and cast a pile of rupees at Mingma as if to say, *"Here, old man, see how much better I am than you."*

"What's this?"

"Money for you. Like it or not, status is measured in rupees now, not the number of yaks. So you'd better get used to it."

Only then did Mingma realize just how much the *mikarus* had seduced him with their grand ideas and fancy words. What good were these to a Sherpa boy? Nothing. They would only bring unhappiness and tragedy. Of that Mingma was certain, but he would keep his thoughts to himself because his son no longer saw or listened with a Sherpa heart. Like a festering wound that refused to heal, anger had arrived with Dorje four years ago. Perhaps his son still blamed him for not buying shoes that first winter, but it had been impossible then. Abruptly ending generations of trading to the north, the 1959 Chinese closure of the Tibetan border had reduced Mingma to a yak herder selling butter, milk, wool, and dung.

When Mingma accused his son of only wanting to make money for himself, Dorje yelled in a sharp, biting voice, "You have no idea what I want...or who I am. You have made no attempt to know me."

As always, the son's anger and hurt stood between them. So Mingma simply replied, "Nor have you to know me." After a deafening silence, Dorje turned and walked out the door with nothing changed at all in these four years. Mingma had lost the little boy who rode on his shoulders and had fallen asleep nestled in his lap. Someday they would talk of the past but for now the words remained unspoken. Watching Dorje's rage leap over a rock wall and almost collide with a yak on his way down to the village, Mingma feared losing the man too. He knew that each year as soon as the monsoon ended, *mikaru* tents sprouted like wild orange poppies in the open space near the village spring and intoxicated Dorje more surely than even the strongest *chang*.

Perhaps the love of a beautiful woman would bring him back. Having heard rumors of Dorje and Sungdare's daughter, Shanti, at summer pasture, Mingma decided to arrange a marriage that would provide a good alliance for both families since Sungdare owned a large potato farm in Khumjung. Surely selecting a girl for whom Dorje had some affection would please his son. Was this not the way of his *mikarus* whose young people married for love? Mingma had not met Dorje's mother until months after their betrothal. His father an animal trader and hers a farmer, it made a good economic partnership and Mingma had grown to care for her over time. Staring at the bedding they once shared, he regretted not feeling more. Perhaps with Shanti Dorje would discover the passion that had eluded his father in marriage.

With a lighter heart, Mingma resolved to travel soon to Sundare's home in Khumjung to present him with a flask of *chang* and propose a marriage between their children. The acceptance of the beer and proposal would conclude the *sodene*. Knowing that this relationship could be broken by either side with no legal liabilities, Mingma also decided to set a date for the *dem-chang* ceremony to give the betrothal a more solid basis. Crossing the open room to the wooden shelves by the door that contained gleaming brass and copper vessels, he checked the ones with barley and millet. Almost empty! The loss of his most valuable *nak* meant less milk and dung to trade.

Back on the window bench, he sat with his elbows on his knees. His fingers stiff and splayed, he touched and then spread them, trying to picture himself as he used to be—one of the wealthiest men in the Khumbu, a great trader who traveled to Tibet and India and then home again bearing riches. But in the darkest time of his life, the Chinese invasion of Tibet had destroyed everything slaughtering thousands and making refugees of those he loved. Memories from long ago crept from their hiding places and spread through him like smoke from the hearth trapped within a room, enveloping him in such a dark, dense cloud that he could no longer see or breathe. Only prayer stilled the voices and muted the images into shadows. Opening the folio of Tibetan scripture on the table before him, he began the low, monotonous intonations that temporarily numbed his emotions as he once again sought forgiveness.

* * * * * * * * *

After leaving his father, Dorje leapt over a rock wall and almost ran into a yak loaded with tents and sleeping pads. When the large head swung around and grazed him with its curved horn, he smacked it on the rump and yelled, "Get out of here," before heading to the pasture while massaging his sore arm. His father's words, *because everyone, including your brother, knows that Mingma's son cares only about making money for himself,* nagged in Dorje's head. Surely Nima didn't believe this falsehood.

Trudging up the hill, Dorje yelled at his brother, "It's not my fault the damn *nak* died or that you had to fend off wolves. Why didn't you tell me?"

"You weren't here, never are during trekking season." His gaze averted from Dorje, Nima sat peeling a long strip of bark from a branch and flicked it skyward.

"You don't have to be here either." Sitting beside him, Dorje picked up a rock and hurled it at one of the yaks straying from the herd. "Taking care of these brainless, unruly beasts. Come with me to Lukla. I'm the sirdar and can hire you as a guide. All you have to do is walk along with the *mikarus* and keep them happy."

"Doing what? I don't speak English the way you do." Seventeen now with their mother's gentle eyes and a dark brown spatter of freckles across his nose and cheeks, Nima was growing into a man and Dorje hadn't noticed. "Just give them your smile and you'll win their hearts."

Nima stared straight into Dorje's eyes the way he did before pronouncing one of his truths. It was frustrating the way he could see things clearer than his older brother and often felt the need to set him straight. "And who would watch the animals? Both of us can't desert father."

"Like he deserted a three and six year old?"

"That was a long time ago. Forget it." Nima shot him a reproving glance. "And another thing. You know that as the youngest son I'm obligated to stay and take care of him. So don't talk to me of working for your *mikarus*."

Tugging on the denim jeans his brother was wearing, Dorje said, "But you'll take their clothes I bring."

"Especially that hat," Nima yelped and swiped it off Dorje's head.

"No. You can't have that one." Dorje grabbed for it but missed.

Already on his feet and scampering up the hill, Nima donned the hat with the brim turned upwards, and then sashayed behind a large, black yak. "Mine now." On the opposite side of the beast, Dorje lunged for it but Nima jumped back inches out of reach. Circling the irritable, grunting animal as they bantered with one another, Dorje was surprised at how clever and quick his little brother had become.

"What's so special about this hat?" Nima asked.

"I got it from the American I'm going to climb Everest with."

"You...climb Everest! Then it belongs here." Crouching over a pile of steaming yak dung, Nima threatened to smear the precious hat in it. "Have the *mikarus* blinded you so much that you no longer see?"

"I see what a fool you are thinking you can get the better of me." Dorje laughed and dived at him, hurling him to the ground. With Nima's arms pinned over his head, Dorje snatched back the hat before rolling his brother over and using him as a pillow as they had lain together when very young, lazing away the afternoons in meadows where wildflowers mingled with marigolds and begonias had just begun to bloom. Things were better then.

"I don't want you to climb," Nima murmured after a long silence. "You've seen the bodies coming down from the mountain. Our own uncle died up there."

Another of his irritating truths. After all the years of Dorje protecting his younger brother, Nima was now doing the same for him. "I have to go. You know that."

"Yes, yes, the Tenzing of the future. You told me all about that. But it was just some villager shouting at a young boy riding on a man's shoulders. It meant nothing."

"It did to me and I promise not to do anything stupid or reckless."

Nima plucked a handful of grass and tossed it in Dorje's face. "You're as stubborn as the yaks you hate so much." Sauntering towards to the herd, he yelled over his shoulder, "Father will never let you go."

"He has no say in my life. None at all." He slapped the hat back on and marched down to Marty's camp, mumbling to himself.

The American was in the dining tent with a book. "Have you read this *Tiger of the Snows*?" he asked. "One of our group lent it to me. It's about Tenzing Norgay."

Having never seen a picture of him, Dorje glanced at the cover and shook his head. "I don't know how to read."

"You're kidding. How'd you learn to speak such good English?"

"From *mikarus* who talk too much like you," Dorje answered with a grin.

"Well, it's a great story about his climb with Hillary. You and I are going up there. Marty and Dorje to the top like Hillary and Tenzing. Give me five!"

"Five what?"

"Five fingers like this" Marty raised Dorje's hand and slapped the open palm. He tossed the book on the table and stood up. "Here, you need to go to Marty school and learn the hand jive. Just follow me. It's sixteen counts." He gave Dorje a questioning look.

"Yes, I can count," Dorje, answered a little insulted.

"Good. On one, slap your knees like this. Two. Repeat." Dorje mimicked him. "That's right," said Marty. "Now clap your hands for three and four. On five, clap your right hand over your left one, palms down. Repeat for six. Seven and eight, do the same only change hands." After reviewing the first eight counts, Marty continued through sixteen and repeated the whole routine wiggling his body and feet in a hilarious way that propelled Dorje into such a fit of laughter his stomach hurt. When he finally recovered, they did the hand jive over and over, each set progressively faster until it became a coordination and giggling contest. Dorje lost but was determined to practice so he could beat this American when they reached Lukla.

Two days later, the tourists in Marty's party plus another group of five waited all morning and afternoon at the airstrip. When no plane had arrived by 3:30 p.m., Dorje explained they didn't fly if there was fog in Kathmandu. He instructed them to return to the teahouses. Fourteen grumbling *mikarus* shouldered their duffels and headed back into the small village. "Does this happen often, Buck buck?" Marty asked.

"Sometimes we wait for days," Dorje whispered, not wanting to feed the simmering tempers of others.

The next morning, Marty and Dorje competed in twenty rounds of hand jive, the loser being the one who dropped his concentration or timing first. Their crazy body gyrations attracted an amused crowd of *mikarus* and Sherpas, each group rooting for its own. Dorje couldn't bear to lose face, but Marty was just too good, too experienced so he finally conceded and changed the subject by pointing to several *zopkios* and *zhums* grazing on the airfield. "They keep the grass down so planes can land," he explained.

Marty chuckled. "Four-legged lawn mowers."

To pass the time, Dorje told Marty how Hillary had built the strip four years ago to fly in supplies for the hospital he planned to build in the future. "My brother and I lived south in the Solu for ten years," he explained. "We passed through here on our way home and saw fifteen Sherpas running and dancing back and forth across the airstrip to pack down the dirt. Hillary paid them to do this for three days because dragging big, heavy logs did not work. Nima and I ran with them. It was fun."

"I would have earned a fortune," said Marty, "because I'm a great dancer. I do the jitterbug and swing to the great dismay of my father who wanted a football-playing son who would always bully his way through to make extra yards."

"I think I do not like your father."

Hearing the distant hum of an engine, Dorje glanced at the windsock flapping wildly—not an auspicious sign. After swatting the animals to drive them out of the way, he stood at the edge hoping the plane could land because his next *mikarus* were on board and these delays were costing him rupees. The impatient trekkers whistled when the plane came into view and then let out a group moan as it quickly rose and left.

"Dammit!" one of them yelled. "I'm going to miss my flight to the States. It leaves tomorrow."

"Wait. It's coming back," his companion said waving at the pilot. Everyone watched it wobble and shake, rise and dip sharply as it neared.

"Ouch. Rough-ness," Marty chirped in a comment that must have reflected everyone's feelings because no universal moan sprang from the crowd when it turned and headed back down the valley.

Apathy and pessimism permeated the airstrip on the third day until a motor sounded in the distance and the windsock hung limp. Boisterous cheers and whistles drowned out the engine as the plane touched down. "Well, Buck, buck," Marty said, "This is it until next spring."

"Not yet. One more hand jive. I know I can beat you." Locking his opponent in a Mingma stare, he slapped his knees, clapped, put one hand over the other, thumped his fists, and bumped his elbows, wiggling his body and feet like a lovesick worm. Over and over, faster and faster, arms and hands flying, grinning, giggling out of control until Marty finally lost the beat and slapped when he should have clapped. "I did it," Dorje shouted and threw his hand in the air for a final high five.

Watching the passengers disembark, Marty said, "Now that's cour-age-ness," when two old women dressed in baggy pants and silly hats stood boldly in the midst of intimidating confusion: Sherpas stuffing large duffels into *dokos,* strange-looking animals grazing on the field, porters weighed down with pots and pans, folding tables and chairs, baskets of food. Sunburned trekkers waiting to board paced impatiently, their faces gaunt and unshaven, hair grown long, and their clothes covered with trail dust.

"Maybe these ladies are your next *mikarus,*" Marty said snickering.

"Never. I take strong hikers like you. Men who yell *Geronimo* and ski down glaciers. Men who do high fives." He thrust his hand in the air for a slap but Marty's gaze was transfixed on something behind him.

"I'd give up my wild ways and finally grow up for a woman like that," Marty murmured.

What was this crazy American talking about now? Turning, Dorje saw a nerve-tingling vision, honey-golden hair long and straight and eyes like wild blue poppies. Surely he was hallucinating, but could his mind really conjure up such an extraordinary goddess?

"If I didn't have an important case at home, you'd never pull me away from her. I've got to meet this woman and get her number." Marty combed his fingers through his hair, arched his shoulders back, put on a big smile, and casually strolled toward her.

When Dorje started after Marty, Ang Tharkay, the Sherpa in charge of assigning *mikarus* to the sirdars, intercepted him. "You will take the two ladies over there."

Stunned, Dorje glowered at him. "They are not mine. Give them to a weak old man who deserves them, not me. I want the woman with hair the color of honey."

"She and her partner already have a guide and porter. Besides, the office in Kathmandu promised you would take the ladies. You're the only one I can trust to bring them back safely."

Watching Marty take the woman's hand to shake it the way *mikarus* do, Dorje yelled, "Get on the plane now."

With a cocky stride, Marty returned holding a wad of rupees for a tip. He whispered, "Her name is Beth and she lives in Colorado just like me. By the time I come back next spring, she'll be mine."

Jealous, Dorje didn't want his money and told him so, but Marty insisted on stuffing it in the pocket of his Levis. "See you in the spring Buck, buck," he said and then boarded the plane.

While porters packed the duffels, Dorje couldn't take his eyes off the goddess. She was like the sweet mist rising from leaves after a warm rain. When she noticed him watching her, the corner of her mouth turned up in a self-conscious smile and he felt himself soaring above the hills like a giant Himalayan griffon gliding endlessly.

CHAPTER FIVE

On the third day, Beth looked directly over the pilot's shoulder at the runway set on a small shelf halfway up a mountain at 9,350 feet. Noticing it was considerably higher at one end than the other, she wondered how he would ever calculate the correct angle for landing. Eyes closed, she gripped the armrests as the ground rose up to meet them and then felt a slight bump when the STOL touched down. As Eric kissed her cheek and whispered, "We're here, Babe. We made it," all the tension flowed out in one long breath. Never had she been so happy to disembark a plane.

While Eric searched for their contact, Beth watched a string of porters head out on the trail. Their bodies lean and muscled, they stooped under heavily laden bamboo baskets supported by a jute tumpline worn over the tops of their heads that appeared to evenly distribute the load along their spines and minimize muscular strain. Each man carried a short T-shaped stick for balance. Their bare feet toughened with thick, dry calluses were of the earth. Constantly seeking stable footing by slipping around pebbles and conforming to solid ground, their wide-splayed toes had the dexterity of fingers. She surveyed the other Sherpas smoking hand-rolled cigarettes, their hair unkempt and clad in dusty, ill-fitting clothing presumably donated by trekkers. Only half wore anything on their feet, mostly flip flops or light canvas shoes from China that offered no support for tramping over rocks.

Hearing giggling and catching movement out of the corner of her eye, Beth spotted a trekker with frizzy hair that stuck out in all directions and grew down his neck. He and a Sherpa were engaged in a rollicking hand slapping, elbow-thumping contest, their bodies in wild contortions as the tempo increased. Exhilarated, the Sherpa suddenly yelled, "I did it!" and threw his hand into the air for a high five. Certainly not the meditative Buddhist culture Beth had anticipated, yet the man's behavior intrigued her. When he turned and looked at her in his green cap, tight Levis, and blue shirt, a warm flush swept through her and knocked Beth slightly off center.

Finger combing his disheveled hair, the trekker swaggered towards her wearing a ridiculous grin and socks that didn't match. "Welcome to Lukla, the land of perpetual wait-ness" he said in a singular voice rippling across his tongue. "I'm Marty and would remain here for the sheer pleasure of following you wherever you go." His lower lip turned out in a sad puppy-dog expression. "But woefully I have to work to pay for all this fun-ness."

"So do I, but I'm paid to come here and write about Nepal and the Sherpas." Looking back at the man in the blue shirt, she expected the unsettling sweep of emotion to have passed. When she realized he was watching her, a spontaneous smile danced on her lips, one she could not have restrained it if she tried. "Like your companion over there," she said trying to sound casual.

"Oh, I was just entertaining him. The Sherpas are easily amused with so little to do here. They can't even read or write." He inched slightly to the left impeding her view as he asked, "Where are you from?"

"Denver."

"Fate-ness. I'm from Boulder, and we had to come half way around the world to meet."

He was making uncomfortable assumptions. "I need to find out what happened to my gear," she said in an attempt to gracefully end the conversation.

"If you're writing about Sherpas, I could keep a journal about them on my climb up Everest next spring."

Damn. Chin resting in her palm, she thrummed her cheek. "You're really going up there?"

"To the top. I've climbed all the fourteeners in Colorado plus Kilimanjaro two years ago and McKinley the one before that. I would have made it to the top of Kangchenjunga here last year but weather turned us back."

Although doubting if any of it were true, Beth let out a long, disgruntled sigh, knowing she couldn't resist the opportunity for a first-hand account. "Here's my card. Call me if you really decide to do this."

He took her hand and held it much too long. "I promise you won't be disappointed."

"Get on the plane now," shouted the Sherpa, coming to her rescue. So unlike the others in clean clothing and hiking boots and not dangling a cigarette between his fingers, he did high fives and spoke English. Surely he was the sirdar the ladies spoke of—the best in the Everest region. Approaching the ladies, Beth asked, "Have you met your guide?"

Ruth shook her head. "Not yet."

About to state her suspicion, she saw him run his fingers through thick, black, freshly washed hair and saunter towards them. "I am Dorje, your sirdar," he said to the ladies. His dark eyes gazed at Beth before quickly darting back to the other women. Noticing sweat seeping down the sides of his hair on a cool autumn morning, she wondered if she had stirred him too. After another furtive glance at Beth, he continued, "You ladies must not worry. I will take care of you. While the porters pack your bags, we will begin our walk for today. It is not far but you must go slowly, *bistarai, bistarai.*" The taut edges of his face softened as he instructed the women to drink plenty of water and rest often. "We will camp at Phakding tonight," he pronounced so clearly Beth felt he was communicating it to her.

Eric arrived, put his arm around Beth's shoulder, and spoke to the women. "Looks like you're all set. We're about ready too."

"So you found our guide and porters," Beth said.

"The porters don't speak a word of English and the guide's not much better. But I guess that's how it is here."

"I can help if you have questions," Dorje said.

Surprised that he'd been listening, Beth told Eric, "They're stopping at Phakding tonight. Where are we?"

He shrugged.

With an impish twinkle in her eye, Ruth whispered, "I hope we'll see you along the trail."

Both trekking parties consisted of a cook, a kitchen boy, and nine porters: one to carry their personal gear and eight to transport sleeping tents, a dining tent, latrine tent, folding table, two chairs, pots and pans, and food. Everyone started out together. This late after the monsoon, a deep, luxuriant green had washed over the land and trails of delicate white mist floated along distant valley walls. For the first forty-five minutes, the groups descended a gently sloping path. Too steep to cultivate, the contoured hillside rose in flat terraces 20 to 30 feet deep with rock retaining walls that looked like dark wrinkles ascending the mountain.

With most of the land cleared for farming, occasional groves of deep-blue pines still dotted the velvet-green slopes imbuing them with a density of light and shadows. Scattered here and there, dry-mortar stone houses perched like birds nesting on the branches of a large leafy tree with heavy rocks weighting down their roofs made of thin wood slats or bamboo. In the yards stood elevated platforms piled high with maize and on the ground, stacks of wood for the hearth. Overcome with excitement, Beth constantly asked Eric to photograph this house, that mountainside, even the intricate construction of a rock wall.

Meanwhile, she was ever conscious of Dorje's presence, observing how tenderly he cared for the ladies. He retrieved water bottles from their packs when they were thirsty and made walking sticks for everyone. "This is for you, Memsahib," he said, handing her the finest with its rough bark stripped away and then rock-sanded smooth to perfection.

Caught off guard, any composure she possessed turned on its heels and fled. "*Namaste*," she squeaked and felt ridiculous, but it was the only Nepali she knew.

As he gazed at her with huge, dark brown eyes and black lashes, his lips spread into the most infectious smile she'd ever seen, reaching all the way across his broad face. "To help you down steep hills," he added before quickly dropping back to attend the ladies.

When the trail began to climb, Dorje made them rest and drink more water. Shouldering Helen's pack, he headed out again, reminding them to go, "*Bistarai, bistarai.*" With each stride, Beth swung the stick forward and planted it in the natural rhythm of her gait and was beginning to feel like a real trekker. They came upon a farmer turning the earth with a simple wood plow behind a single ox and a woman thrashing grain with a long stick.

"Get their pictures," Beth pleaded with Eric. "Shoot it all—the terraces, the farmer, the porters."

Smiling, he ran a finger along her cheek. "You're loving this, aren't you, Babe. Finally seeing your Sherpas."

Almost on the verge of tears, she nodded. The 15 years had been worth it. While he took various photos, Beth asked Dorje about the grain spread out on the ground cloth.

"It is millet. She must beat it very hard."

Retrieving her note pad from the daypack, she wrote as he explained farmers also grew barley, maize, rye, wheat, and potatoes but not rice because it was too high there. That had to be carried in from the south. Listening to him, she remembered Marty's comment about Sherpas being uneducated. Perhaps this man standing before her couldn't read or write, but a brilliance shone in his eyes and he possessed a charisma that was awakening every nerve in her body. "I'm here to write about Nepal and the Sherpas. You speak very good English. Can I hire you to help me as you did just now?"

With an uneasiness in his shoulders, he shoved his hands into his pocket and looked away, his light brown face taking on a rosy hue. *Is he blushing*, she wondered. "You need not pay me," he muttered, shifting his weight slightly and glancing back.

"No, I insist. That's how we do it in America."

"Yes, Memsahib."

"And my name is Beth. Please call me that."

Eric interrupted with a quick kiss on the cheek. "Ready to go, Babe? I got your pictures." As if embarrassed, Dorje returned to the ladies while Beth politely reminded Eric that open displays of affection between the sexes were frowned upon here.

Half an hour later, they reached the summit of a gentle pass, but the descent was grueling—steep and strewn with rocks too large for the ladies to manage. His shirt soaked with sweat, Dorje moved constantly from one to the other, holding their arms to lift them down. Beth marveled both at their courage and his fortitude. Grateful for the walking stick, she had discovered that transferring weight from her knees onto it greatly reduced joint stress. How porters made it down with those heavy, awkward loads was beyond her comprehension.

*   *   *   *   *   *   *   *   *

Dorje had been furious with Ang Tharkay for assigning these grandmothers to him, but already he had developed a fondness for both and wouldn't trust them to anyone else. Rain the previous night had made the trail muddy. To calm their jittery nerves, he sang the rhyming lyrics he'd learned from porters who joked about conditions they dreaded most. *"Raato maaTo, chiplo baaTo."* Giggling, the ladies asked what it meant. "Red soil, slippery trail," he answered and glanced at Beth whose smile turned his legs to liquid.

"It's slippery enough to ski," she commented and nodded at his cap. Rolling his eyes towards the brim, he remembered it said SKI VAIL. When he was nervous or scared as a young boy, it felt as though little field mice were scampering all around inside him. As he watched the breeze play with her hair and curl it around her cheek, the mice invited all their friends out to play and were running amok around his heart. Hopping on foot as he'd once done for Hillary wasn't going to impress her. Perhaps this would.

Taking a deep breath to calm the mice, he bent his knees, yelled, "Geronimo," and pushed off down the muddy hill. Arms flailing to keep his balance, one leg flying into the air and then the other as he hopped over rocks, he skied with no concept of how to stop other than falling flat on his face. And that was not an acceptable image. He took his eyes off the ground just long enough to see the trail turned sharply to the left with his momentum about to propel him straight off a cliff. With a quick prayer to the god of the mountain, he leapt up and grabbed an overhanging branch with both hands. His legs swung forward trying to tear him loose but he held fast and dropped down. *That wacky Marty made me do this foolish stunt,* he muttered to himself as he brushed mud off his Levis. *Him and all his talk of smacking life in the head. The man's a menace.* But the clapping and cheering behind him soon turned Dorje's mood around. He forgot about the American for the moment and slogged back up the hill with mud sucking and spitting at his heels.

When Beth smiled and said, "That was truly remarkable," in a voice as warm and pure as the first blush of sunlight, it was worth all the aggravation.

Everyone's mood changed when they reached a temporary bridge constructed of branches woven together and spanning forty feet over the water. Rushing wildly downstream, the river swelled in a never-ending torrent, wrenching and twisting at tree roots on the bank while enormous white waves crashed into boulders shooting water high into the air. Due to rain, the water had risen considerably since Dorje and Marty had crossed only four days earlier. Uncertain of the safety of the bridge now, Dorje stepped on to test it. As he watched his feet and carefully placed each step, the rushing water beneath him was dizzying. Instinctively, his toes spread to grip the branches as they had done all of his life but now met only the hard insole of boots that slid on mud deposited by those who had crossed before him. His confidence faltered. "*Om mani padme hum,*" he chanted, praying to *nagi,* the river spirit, to help him. After reaching the other side, he quickly returned, noting the most slippery spots.

As he told the ladies he would take them one at a time, his gaze wandered to Beth, wanting to be her hero and lead her safely across too. Like a male dog guarding his bitch, Eric stepped between them. "I'll go with you, Babe. Let the Sherpa take the women."

The Sherpa. Not Dorje or the sirdar, but *the Sherpa.* With those two words, Eric had reduced him to a non-entity, stolen his individuality and dignity in front of her. Dorje would not forgive him for that.

By late afternoon they reached camp in a farmer's field and Dorje was glad to see Beth's guide had chosen the neighboring one as he had suggested at Lukla. Dorje quickly made sure everything had been taken care of: water boiled for afternoon tea, the latrine pit dug and draped with a tarp for privacy, dining tent and folding chairs in place as well as two-person sleeping tents. When the ladies seemed relaxed and content with tea, biscuits, and popcorn, Dorje's thoughts returned to Beth. In the next field, she was sitting outside writing in a notebook while Eric took pictures of the camp. As if she sensed Dorje was watching her, she put her pen down and looked in his direction. Her unwavering gaze caressed his face as surely if she had trailed her fingers along his cheek. In all the moments of intimacy with Shanti, he had never experienced this feeling. He couldn't move, couldn't turn away for fear of losing it. Once again as if asserting his possession, Eric finished shooting, sat beside her, and took her hand. What an idiot Dorje was for thinking she could ever feel anything for him. Just *The Sherpa*, he had no right to consider her as anything other than just another *mikaru*. Tomorrow he would take the ladies to Namche and erase her from his thoughts.

CHAPTER SIX

After a long, restless night with Eric fussing with his sleeping bag trying to get warm and comfortable, Beth woke to the voice of the kitchen boy outside their door. "Tea, Memsahib?"

"Yes, thank you," she answered and unzipped the flap so he could slide two saucers and cups inside before quietly disappearing.

"What time is it?" Eric mumbled through a yawn.

Beth looked at her watch in the light of the doorway. "Six thirty. Here, they brought us tea."

Rolling onto his back with his arm over his eyes, he moaned, "You know I need coffee in the morning."

"Well, don't think that's an option, Sweetie." Resting on her elbows, she sipped slowly, trying not to burn her lips while awaiting the kitchen boy's return with two shallow pans of warm water for bathing. Knowing the importance of Eric's daily rituals, she whispered, "Your morning shower just arrived," and then broke out laughing.

"Oh yeah? Want to join me?" He rolled on top of her in their double bag. "Let me help you off with those clothes."

"What brought this on?" she whispered.

"I'm damn horny, that's what. We haven't made love since Denver."

He was so eager that it happened fast, and fortunately Eric didn't seem to notice she wasn't 100% there. Score one for horniness. It eased her guilt. As he was dressing, Beth told him about hiring Dorje to work for her.

Stopping in the middle of tying his bootlaces, Eric stared at her. "When did all this take place?"

"While you were taking pictures of the farm."

He yanked the knot tight. "Guess he's good for something, so you might as well use him" Then he shoved his duffle through the door and crawled out after it.

While they dined on porridge with *nak* milk, a flat unleavened bread called *chapatti*, and fried eggs floating in oil, the porters loaded the duffels and tents to head out. Watching Dorje cater to the ladies in the next camp, Beth wondered why this Sherpa make her breath catch every time she looked at him? Was it some romanticized notion of experiencing a different culture? No. She'd traveled all over the world and met thousands of men, even had a brief foreign affair, but this was different. A natural fluidity in his movement exuded confidence but not arrogance, and that irresistible smile traveled all the way up to his eyes and thick, black hair.

When they set out, the air held a lucid apple freshness with golden orioles and rose finches flitting from branch to branch, singing to greet the morn. Shadows danced and leapt through thick-leaved trees and then sprawled across the ground like lazy children. Looking for a way to initiate conversation with Dorje, Beth asked, "Where happened to our guide?"

"He left early to find a good camp in Namche tonight because my village is too crowded with tourists."

Namche, the social and political capital of the Sherpas, through which most expeditions passed. If he'd said Paris or London, she wouldn't have been more elated. The story she'd come for was walking right beside her, and she could tell it through his eyes and words. Her job secure now, she had a thousand questions to ask. "Where did you learn English?"

"It is easy. I listen and speak with tourists like you."

And how many others have you charmed? she wondered. Yesterday she had caught him gazing at her several times but today, nothing. Only initial curiosity perhaps. "Other Sherpas haven't learnt English. Why you?"

"Because I do not want to be a porter or yak herder all my life. For a Sherpa, sirdar is the best a man can do." With that, Dorje raced up a row of steep rock stairs to join the ladies who had made a water stop at the top. Instead of helping them with bottles from their packs, he herded them to the hill side of the path gesturing wildly.

"What's going on?" Beth asked catching up to them.

"There," he answered, nodding downhill. "You must always stand away from the cliff when they pass because they swing their horns and knock you off."

Hearing the steady, rhythmic clang of bells all pitched differently, she turned and watched a caravan of yaks loaded with baskets of vegetables and large bolts of cloth slowly winding up the stairs. To maintain speed, they hunched their massive back muscles and thrust themselves forward with their heads lowered. Everyone hugged the hill as the snorting animals passed. Her first yak sighting! Beth found them humorous—these shaggy, lumbering beasts with short hairy legs, bushy tails, shovel-shaped heads, and long curved horns. They resembled little kids bundled up in too many sweaters with their woolly undercoats covered with a coarse outer coat of wiry hairs giving them a bulky look. The beasts' large, sure-footed hooves scuffed trail dust into small clouds that stung her eyes.

Blinking for clarity, Beth asked, "Where are they going?"

"To the Saturday market in Namche. Tomorrow they will return with empty baskets."

"And those too?" she asked, pointing to a string of gaily-decorated donkeys following a lead animal sporting a bright red plume on its head and seemingly without a human escort.

"The donkeys are small and cannot carry much but they move quickly and often travel for eight days to get here. Yaks only go in the high places. It is too hot for them below."

Beth's voice leapt into the air excitedly. "Eric, get pictures of the donkeys." Bouncing back onto the trail and walking backwards to search for more caravans, she yelled, "And go in front to get the one with a plume on its head. The yaks too."

While Eric squeezed past the animals, she walked with Dorje, feeling more comfortable in her role as interviewer. "Were you born in Namche and have you always lived there?"

Eyes straight ahead and his jaw tight, he answered, "Yes, but I left at six and came back four years ago."

Her journalist tongue was dying to ask why he'd left and how old he was now, but for once she kept her mouth shut even though she was famous for prying more information from people than anyone else. Those questions could come later. For the present, she'd concentrate on impersonal topics such as the significance of the lofty poles bearing colorful flags.

"Those are *Lung Ta,* the wind horse," he said loud enough for the ladies to hear too. "Prayers are printed on cloth with a horse in the middle and four sacred animals in the corners. When the wind blows, the horse carries the prayers to the gods. All who meet the air or breathe it, even a bird flying by, receive the blessing of the prayers,. They bring good luck and happiness. When things are not going good for you, your *Lung Ta* is down. When life is easy, your *Lung Ta* is up. You can see flags on mountain tops, bridges, temples, roof tops, and outside of every Sherpa house."

Hurriedly making notes, she asked, "And the five colors?"

"They are for the sky, clouds, fire, water, and earth."

What an adrenalin rush. "Oh, thank you, thank you, thank you," she said scribbling it all down. "I never would have figured that out on my own."

Looking bewildered by her enthusiasm, he seemed amenable to more questions. When they passed a fifteen-foot boulder with symbols carved in relief and painted black, he explained it was a *mani* stone, or prayer stone, to protect travelers. "Most have the Buddhist words *Om Mani Padme Hum*. We repeat them many times when we pray to the gods."

"And what do they mean?" she asked, flipping to the next page in her notebook.

"I do not know your words for them," he answered simply and then politely extended his hand to persuade the ladies to pass the *mani* stone on the other side. "You must always go on the left. When you return, you will make the circle of life."

The four tourists giggling and scooting backwards while looking over their shoulders to keep from running into each other reversed direction and marched forward with exaggerated strides. Pen in hand, Beth corrected a common misconception that the Everest region was covered with ice and snow year round. Rhododendron painted the dark green hillsides in red, pink, yellow, and mauve and the waxy, white flowers of giant magnolias bloomed high beyond reach. Bearing small orange and purple blossoms, bougainvillea climbed naked tree trunks while delicate pink and white orchids festooned the oaks. Lining the path were rocks covered with colorful lichens and mosses, patches of pale yellow and pink primula, clumps of bright dahlias, and dark azaleas. The exquisite aroma of sweet daphnia filled the air.

Pointing to the cliffs above the river, Dorje said to watch for musk deer and wild Himalayan goats with dark brown coats and a long shaggy manes. So intent upon spotting one, Beth almost missed her distinctive blue and green duffel in a *doko* at the side of the path. Had all their gear been abandoned? Stopping suddenly, she asked, "Where are our porters?"

"There," Dorje said pointing to a group of Sherpas crouched around a small fire. "They drink only tea before leaving camp and now must rest and eat."

"And what are they cooking?"

"*Tsampa.* Roasted barley flour." Dorje spoke to a porter who gave him a brown mass that literally looked like a piece of shit. He palmed it in his right hand, rolling it into a ball, and then made an indention with his thumb and dipped the *tsampa* spoon into a bowl of chilies and garlic. "It is very good and healthy. Sherpas who work for expeditions make a *pak* ball with *tsampa*, sugar, and nuts to give them strength. You try it?"

An elderly porter with creases in a face folding around a toothless mouth dropped a warm, brown mass into her hand. Terrific. She was stuck now. With a thank-you smile and bow, Beth began rolling it between both palms as she'd done with cookie dough as a kid. But the look of horror on the man's face told her she had just committed another cultural offense. Now what? Her eyes pleaded with Dorje who graciously explained that in Nepal one never touched food with the left hand, which was used for toilet purposes and considered unclean. Grateful that she was at least right handed, Beth made a Sherpa spoon and gingerly dipped it in the sauce. Dorje's lips were trembling as if trying to suppress a smile and a whimsical look danced in his eyes. Having gotten herself into this mess, she couldn't back out now. Taking a deep breath, Beth plopped the *tsampa* in her mouth—the most god-awful thing she'd ever tasted and Dorje knew it. Smiling, she could play this game too. "It's great...unique," she told Eric. "Try some."

With a raised brow, he took some from the toothless porter who was not nearly as adept as Dorje at hiding his amusement. Obviously all of them knew tourists didn't share their love of this roasted barley flour. When Eric frantically looked for a polite way to dispose of it without being rude, the porters and Dorje burst into unrestrained, innocent laughter. Beth remembered Marty's comment about them being easily entertained. Finding this an endearing quality, she laughed right along with them. Grinning, Dorje offered some *tsampa* to the ladies who took note of Beth's rapidly shaking head and politely declined.

Less pleased with their childlike humor, Eric seemed to need to prove himself. Walking over to the heaviest-looking *doko,* he asked Dorje, "Can I try it on?"

The laughter-containment quotient doubled. As usual, the porters were squatting on their haunches with their feet flat on the ground—an impossible position for Beth who toppled backwards every time she tried it.

Elbows on their knees and chins cupped in their hands to hide smiles, they watched with mirthful eyes. This would be Eric's shining moment. At 6' 1" and an ex football player in college, he towered over them. Other than Dorje who was about 5' 9", the tallest porter was no more than 5' 2". Slight and wiry weighing little more than 110 pounds, they seemed no match for Eric. Dorje instructed him to sit on the ground and slip the woven straps over his arms. Adjusting the hemp tumpline on top of Eric's head, he said, "This is the *naamlo* and this a *teko*, walking stick, to help you up."

Wearing a smug expression, Eric dismissed him with a backhand wave. As soon as he tried to stand, the *doko* shifted to the right and he caught himself on an outstretched arm. In a semi-squat and leaning 45 degrees with all his weight on one arm and the *doko* slowly sliding toward the ground, he had to do something fast. Eric pushed off and tried using that momentum to stand upright, but the basket swung the other way and tossed him on the ground. Dorje and three porters came to his rescue.

"Jesus Christ, this thing's going to crush my spine," Eric groaned.

Afraid she'd break out laughing, Beth didn't dare look. Fingers to her tightened lips, she said, "Try walking with it."

Listing heavily to the right, he took three steps, winced, and yelled, "Get this damn thing off me. It's obviously a two-man load."

Snickering, the porters relieved him of the basket and realigned the load. Embarrassed for Eric, Beth whispered, "I'm sure that's right because you're the strongest guy I know."

"Oh yeah?" he said as the old man who had served them *tsampa* walked past carrying the same *doko*. In bare feet with quarter-inch calluses, he climbed up from the river with a steady stride, seldom pausing for breath. "And look at that!" A porter was hiding several large rocks in another man's *doko*.

Beth laughed. "I bet they're rivals for the heart of some Sherpani." She alerted Dorje, but instead of rushing to squash the inevitable conflict, he asked her to quietly point out the two porters involved so he could observe the fun. She stood agape as he explained they often played such tricks. It was expected and relieved their boredom. Shaking her head, she whipped her notebook out and wrote. *The people are even more incredible than the mountains. I'm ashamed of myself for grouping them all as porters and not seeing individuals. They are what I will carry home in my heart, not pictures of Everest.*

After cautiously crossing two wire suspension bridges and a narrow cantilever bridge with no handrails, they headed along the stony bed of the valley until they came to the confluence of two rivers below the mountain wall upon which the unseen Namche perched. "It is very steep from here and very high," Dorje warned as he relieved the ladies of their daypacks. "You will get sick if you do not go *bistarai, bistarai* and drink much water."

Eric's ego apparently still suffering, he announced, "I'm going ahead and will meet you in Namche."

Despite Dorje's warnings, he took off at full speed and Beth didn't see him after that. Thirty minutes into the walk, her thighs and calves were burning. Feeling slightly nauseated and with a pounding headache, she collapsed against a boulder and watched the barefoot porters pass with a steady gait, eyes to the ground, no surfeit of breath for conversation, but a shared rock joke that turned up the corners of their mouths. Perhaps that's what kept them going. She was still exhausted when Dorje arrived with Ruth and Helen.

"You two are incredible," Beth said, wiping her brow with the bottom of her shirt. "I didn't think it would be this hard." As soon as she uttered the words, the last porter bearing rocks trudged past. She just shook her head in disbelief. "How much do they get paid for this torture?" she asked Dorje and found the answer unfathomable: six rupees a day for 60 kilos.[1]

More notes for her journal. *Porters are supermen.* Ashamed and feeling like a whiner, she pushed off the wall and plodded on up the trail.

"Most porters are farmers," Dorje explained walking beside her. "They cannot grow enough to feed their families. So when tourists come, they leave home to work."

Beth was embarrassed. An educated woman who traveled the world, she had come here with a mindset that was quickly unraveling. "Is it worth leaving their families?"

Staring at the ground, Dorje rolled both shoulders inward with a kind of shrug. "Most go back with very little. Every day, they must pay for food and a place to sleep. Their only hope is to get tips from trekkers."

"Were you ever a porter?"

With a defensive glance out of the corner of his eye, he replied, "Yes, at sixteen when I came back to Namche and spoke no English." As if she had criticized him, he left and walked with the non-judgmental ladies. Damn. Her offending tongue had struck again. She'd better get control of it soon because Dorje was an important element of what she'd come for. She'd sensed that from the first moment in Lukla.

---

[1] 60 kilos = 132 pounds

CHAPTER SEVEN

Out of self-defense, Dorje dropped back to Ruth and Helen. Walking with Beth was too stimulating and uncomfortable. When she wiped sweat from her forehead, the top of her shirt had ballooned out giving him a full view of her breasts, soft and white like fresh *nak* cream. Not that he was looking. But the longer he remained beside her, the more fixated on them he became. Even discussing the plight of porters hadn't provided enough distraction and he had to erase her from his thoughts. Her question about whether he'd been a porter opened doors he couldn't shut now anyway, so he hauled images from the corners of his brain that should return any man to a flaccid state.

Climbing the Namche hill reminded him of returning home at sixteen. After fighting one more monsoon flood that washed away their crops and destroyed the terraces, he couldn't face starting over again and had to leave the Solu even if it meant being separated from his mother who refused to go without her husband. But Nima was like his other half and could not be left behind. Taking his brother, Dorje simply headed north. Hungry and cold, they slept in the woods with no destination in mind. "Back to Namche?" Nima exclaimed when Dorje suggested it one night.

"Haven't you ever wondered about father?"

"I was only three when we left. I don't even remember him."

"And I was six but I remember everything, like him promising to come to the Solu and see us as often as he could."

"Maybe he couldn't for some reason."

"What was more important than his sons? You're too soft and forgiving like mother. The truth is he simply didn't love us enough."

"If that's how you feel, why do you want to see him?"

Rolling onto his side away from Nima, he answered, "Because I have to." He moved his hip off a stone and pillowed his hands under his head. "Because I have to."

As they headed north the next day, Dorje pondered Nima's idea that Mingma couldn't come for some reason. For ten years he'd gone over every possibility and always arrived at the same conclusion. His father simply didn't care. The emptiness created by Mingma's absence was so immense that Dorje was lost in it and couldn't find his way out. A young boy's yearning for his father had waged a ten-year war with his feelings of abandonment and anger. By the time he and Nima started the final climb to Namche, his emotions were in tatters.

Rounding the last hill, they stared at the collection of seventy houses built on terraces. "Which house is it?" Nima asked.

Dorje remembered it being up high but which one? The two-story, rectangular buildings all looked the same. After dreaming about returning home a thousand times, he felt like a stranger in his own land. He glanced at the white jagged peaks thrusting into the sky. Snow. He hadn't seen that since they left. Near the spring where their mother had washed clothes, light-skinned tourists inhabited a forest of orange and blue tents. Watching young children ready to bolt at a stranger's move, he wondered if any of them could hop on one foot as well as he had.

Thinking about that day with Hillary, he suddenly heard Nima shout, "I know where he is." With a quick grin displaying the whistling space between his two upper front teeth, he added, "I asked somebody."

Trying to quell the riot in his stomach, Dorje hooked his arm around his brother's neck and took a large shaky breath. "Let's go find him."

"He's in that teahouse playing cards but I don't recognize him."

As soon as they stepped under the low doorway, Dorje knew his father. Seated at a long table, six men were playing cards. Although others had adopted short hair and western clothing from tourists, Mingma sat in his blood-red robe, his long, black hair still pulled back and secured with a ribbon, as striking and handsome as ever with his perfect square features and glinting dark eyes. At the shock of finally seeing his father again, Dorje's entire being grew faint.

"So which one?" Nima whispered.

Taking a tremulous breath, Dorje acted as though he wasn't sure. He needed a few more minutes to absorb Mingma's presence unobserved.

One of the men dealt cards. As Mingma slid each one into his hand, his eyes skimmed the room, passing over Dorje and Nima with no sign of recognition. He picked up the cards and sorted them. The first player tossed one to the center of the table. Each player in turn slapped his harder than the one before until the last man stood and threw his card down so hard it bent in the middle. Apparently Mingma had won. While shuffling for the next hand, his gaze settled on the boys momentarily.

"Well?" Nima insisted.

His thoughts and words still too fragmented, Dorje wasn't ready yet. He tried to gather them up but they scurried in confusion. Before he could corner them, his brother grew impatient and spoke. "Mingma?"

Everyone turned in their direction.

"Yes," answered their father in a voice so full and round it filled the room. "Who wants to know?"

"Your sons," replied Dorje, his heart drumming painfully in his chest.

Leaning back in his chair, Mingma studied them a moment. "I knew you'd come some day. I've been waiting."

If his father hadn't said that word *waiting,* Dorje might have held himself together. All the years of standing by the path, aching to see that robe sweeping towards him, could not be forgotten. "What do you know of waiting?" he said, his voice gnarling around the words. "I watched and waited ten long years. Where were you?"

Quietly studying his son's face, Mingma said nothing.

The silence bolstered Dorje's courage. "Do you remember a three and six year old being dragged down the stairs crying?"

"Yes."

Although he'd practiced the speech a hundred times in his head, it stumbled out in clumps of words with pauses, jumps, and starts. "And do you remember telling us how we must be brave? You said you loved us and you promised to come see us as often as you could."

The card players quickly moved to the door and crowded to get down the stairs. Mingma's face remained rigid, his gaze unwavering. "What do you want from me?"

"Something to eat," Nima answered before Dorje could utter another word.

Their father nodded, looking only at his younger son. "And a place to sleep?"

"Yes. We're tired."

Relieved the two of them had shut him out for the moment, Dorje knew he would have said more hurtful things and this wasn't how he wanted it to be. He wanted to feel like a six-year-old, loving child again.

Mingma rose from the table. "Let's go home."

Home! Dorje's last moments there had been in his father's lap, crying and begging to stay. Their house stood atop the highest terrace on the east side of the village. As Dorje climbed the narrow, steep path lined with stone fences, all the smells flooded back: barley roasting, snowflakes falling, warm steam coming from the animal's nostrils, the dust churned up by their hooves. Reaching the house, he paused in front, hearing voices from the lower storage room next to the animals.

"Who's that?" he asked after having remained silent since leaving the teahouse.

"Tibetan refugees," his father replied. "They arrive hungry and cold with nothing but a few clothes. Many of their children died while crossing over the Nangpa La. I let them stay here until they have recovered enough to move on to other parts of Nepal or India, as far from the Chinese as they can get."

Dorje's anger softened thinking his father may have sheltered hundreds in the nine years since the uprising. Entering the dark, lower room where animals were kept at night, he felt the familiar warmth of their bodies. He'd missed nuzzling against their dense outer coats and tasting their sweet *nak* curds. Brushing against them, he worked his way to the winding staircase that led to the living quarters on the second floor.

As he ducked under the doorway, he discovered something unexpected. A heavy woman with a bulbous growth on her neck as thick as an arm was making *chapattis*. Mingma introduced their aunt, Droma Sunjo. "And this is your cousin Dawa," he added when a short, squat body that seemed all out of proportion ambled out of the corner, tilting awkwardly left and right. A large, bloated stomach forced the truncated limbs outward. It was a boy of about twelve with thin hair and dry skin of an odd yellowish hue. The puffy face, with thick lips and flattened nose crinkled into a vacant smile.

Nima tugged the back of Dorje's shirt and whispered, "What is it? A *pem?*"

"Don't know," Dorje whispered back. "Maybe a witch cursed them."

Mingma spoke. "There's salt tea and *thukp*a on the hearth. Take what you want."

After two days of hunger, the promise of noodle dumplings in potato stew flavored with sheep fat overrode fear and revulsion. They agreed to eat and stay the night. When the hearth fire burned out, Droma Sunjo put mats on the floor for Dorje and Nima. Mingma didn't join her in the sleeping alcove but lit a butter lamp and sat on the window seat with two piles of Tibetan scripture on the low table before him. Reciting the text in a low monotone, he moved the pages with both hands from one pile to the other. Although Dorje lay in the familiar room, it wasn't the same with these two strangers. He no longer knew the father he had longed to see and couldn't jump into his lap to soak up his warmth or feel him gently stroking his forehead. As Dorje watched Mingma, the flame from the butter lamp cast shadows across his father's face, making him appear more distant and removed. If only Dorje could take back those first few words in the teahouse.

Lost in memories, he plodded up the hill until Ruth's scream jolted him back to reality. Whipping around, he saw Helen on the ground inches from a 500-foot cliff. "What happened?"

Trembling, Ruth said, "She was complaining about feeling awful and just dropped."

Her face pale and listless, Helen whispered, "I'm sorry."

Scared and not knowing what to do, Dorje helped her sit. "Do not worry."

"I feel a little better now. I think the chemo just took more out of me than we realized."

He didn't know this word chemo but sensed it was a bad thing. "Do you want to go back to Lukla or on up to Namche?"

"Namche. I came to see the monks."

"I will carry you." With no *doko* available, he squatted and told her to hang onto his neck with her legs around his waist, the way he'd carried Nima when young.

"I will be too heavy."

"No. Much lighter than a porter's load." He rose and shifted her weight to make them both comfortable and continue upward.

Assuming the slow but steady gait adopted by porters, Dorje and Ruth arrived with Helen. As he walked into Namche, he realized nothing had changed since his first day back four years ago. Neither he nor his father had bridged the chasm created that night and probably never would. The two ladies waved their walking sticks over their heads with such bravura that Dorje swallowed the proud tears welling in his throat. He took Helen to her tent and instructed the cook to boil water for tea and biscuits because she wasn't doing well.

When Beth joined them and asked if there was a doctor nearby, his groin reacted immediately with the image of her soft white breasts still vividly in mind. Struggling to keep from glancing at them, he stared straight into her wild blue-poppy eyes while explaining about the hospital in Khunde built by Hillary just two years earlier.

"Is it far?"

"Sherpa time or yours?"

"Mine."

"I can go in thirty minutes. You are a good walker. Maybe one hour if not too tired."

"So you'll take Eric and me? He's got a horrible headache and nausea and I want to talk to the doctor about Helen."

Having warned Eric about going too fast, Dorje contained the chuckle gurgling in his throat. The man deserved to get sick but Helen didn't, and she was his priority. Here was a chance to be alone with Beth for several hours. Of course he'd take her but not with Eric tagging along. "Eric is sick from going too high too fast. Khunde is even higher. He must rest here today and tomorrow, but I will take you to ask about Helen."

While Beth talked to Eric and prepared to leave, Dorje rushed down to the spring. Two Sherpanis slapping clothes against the rocks giggled and flirted with him as he dunked his head in to wash his hair and splashed ice-cold water on his face. Another time, he might have returned their attention, but not today. The American with honey-golden hair consumed all his thoughts.

CHAPTER EIGHT

Crawling into the tent, Beth found Eric face down on his sleeping bag, breathing heavily as if struggling for air. "Still feeling rotten?"

"I want to puke."

"Dorje says you're sick because you went too high too fast."

"Good for him. Mr. Know-it-all."

"I'm sorry, Sweetie," she said and lightly ran the back of her hand down his cheek. "Rest and keep drinking fluids." If she told him about planning to hike higher yet today, he'd throw an understandable fit. Best to just let him sleep undisturbed.

She waited outside for Dorje as he walked up from the spring with glistening, wet hair. Watching his confident stride, Beth thought about her teenage fantasies. On nights when her mother had made life unbearable and Beth needed to escape, she daydreamed about Tarzan swinging down, swooping her into his arms, and carrying her deep into the jungle. And when that story grew old, Omar Sharif from *Lawrence of Arabia* with his dark, sultry eyes rode up on a white stallion and whisked her off into the desert. Now Dorje was leading her into the mountains.

Her first time truly alone with him, she wanted to know everything. What was his childhood like? Was he married or did he have a girlfriend? What drove him to despair and what brought him happiness? Rarely hesitant about probing into someone's personal life, she had offended a number of people with her directness. So once again she had to wrestle her brazen tongue into place and stick to cultural and historical inquires, the stuff she was paid to do. Asking about the hospital, she learned that before Hillary built the one in Khunde, the nearest doctor had been eight days away. Slightly nauseated and plagued by a headache by the time they reached the long stone building overlooking the village, she was much too stubborn and independent to admit to such weakness. She'd survived her mother's hell and would endure this mountain too.

When she announced she was doing a story about Sherpas, the volunteer doctor from New Zealand proudly showed her the facility and said that during the smallpox epidemic of 1963, Hillary had donated medicine to eradicate the feared scarring disease. The doctor was a tall, lanky man with a bulbous nose and receding chin. He explained that yak caravans had made the yearly arduous journey to Tibetan salt fields until the Chinese closed the border in 1959. Landlocked and many miles from the sea, both lands contained iodine-barren soil. "So for generations, thyroid conditions such as goiters and cretinism infected the entire Khumbu. Hillary gave iodine injections but some still won't take them."

A curious wrinkle crawled across Beth's face. "Why on earth not?"

His voice slid to a murmur out of Dorje's hearing. "Because they still don't trust our medicine. Some believe needle holes create openings for an evil being, a *pem*, to enter."

"But surely you've explained everything to them."

"Of course, many times over but to no avail. My sole success has been adding *cretin* to their vocabulary. A large percentage of the population in the isolated village of Phortse suffers from both conditions." Frustration settled in his eyes. "I guess I can't blame them. Tuberculosis is rampant here. I treat them but as soon as they feel better, they stop taking the medication, get sick again, and frequently die. My explaining they have to continue the full course falls on ears as deaf as those of a cretin."

Aware of Dorje's eyes on her while she took notes, Beth wondered what he was thinking. Was her hair a mess? An old habit, she toyed with the ends, curling them around her finger. When he stretched after leaning against a table, she decided he was tired of dealing with tourists and impatient to leave. She quickly thanked the doctor for the interview and the pills to help Helen adjust to the altitude.

"If it means so much to her and she's feeling better after two day's rest in Namche," he added, "she could probably be transported to Tengboche."

Dorje was standing outside with one foot on the rock wall leading to the hospital, his arm resting on his knee, the Levis tight across his rear. "If you are finished, Memsahib, we will go back now a different way."

Hands deep in his pockets and staring straight ahead, he didn't appear open to conversation. And for once in her adult life, Beth restrained her tendency to strip someone bare of all his secrets. Notepad out again, she described Khumjung's *chorten* at the village entrance as Dorje explained it contained sacred items or the ashes of lamas. The square base was the earth, the bell-shaped dome was water, and the spire at the top with thirteen pieces was the thirteen steps leading to Buddhahood. Biting her lips to suppress a smile, she realized he didn't know the word *enlightenment* and she didn't want to humiliate him with a correction. Instead, she recorded images of the sacred Mount Khumbila that formed a dramatic backdrop to the village and the ice-chiseled mountain, Thanserku.

"Can we see Everest from here?"

"No, but I will show you." Knees bent, his head and shoulders always level, Dorje seemed to glide down the rocky slope without touching the ground. When they arrived at the crest of a hill overlooking a valley, he announced, "This is where *mikarus* come to take pictures of Everest."

"*Mikarus?*"

"White eyes. That's what we call foreigners."

"But mine are blue," she purred, hoping for a reaction.

As if he hadn't heard, he jumped onto a low, flat rock. "They stand here with Everest behind them."

She stepped there too, facing him so close she heard him gasp. "Which mountain is it?" she asked casually as if she'd done nothing to precipitate this condition.

He turned towards the distant mountains and held his hands in the shape of a triangle. "The one that looks like this behind the wall of Nupste. That is Lhotse on the right and over there Ama Dablam. It means mother's jewel box because the ridges look like a mother's arms reaching out. Tomorrow Eric will come and take pictures of you and the ladies."

"And you? Will you stand here beside me for a picture?"

"Many *mikarus* want pictures of Sherpas."

But you're not just any Sherpa, almost escaped but she snatched the words as they raced towards her lips and said simply, "Because you are all so kind to us." Like Eric, she had gone too far too fast and must turn down a different path now or risk scaring him away. As the sun crept below the ridge of the western mountains, Beth sat down and hugged her knees to her chest. "For years I've dreamed of being here and seeing Everest. This is a very special moment for me." From below the horizon, the sun glowed in distant clouds, infusing them with a flaming orange tinged with purple along the frayed edges. As the color slowly faded to copper, the peaks took on a golden hue.

Seeming a little more relaxed, Dorje sat beside Beth maintaining as much distance as possible on the narrow rock. "I like to watch Everest too. I came here with my father when I was very young."

A hint of his past? She couldn't let that sneak by unnoticed. Knowing full well that he had left Namche for ten years, she still asked, "Didn't you come often while growing up?"

"I left when I was six."

"Where did you go?" she asked, finding it impossible to stay out once his door was ajar.

"To the Solu." Another curt reply with his foot pressed firmly against it.

She'd seen the area on maps: the southern region of the Solu-Khumbu. Namche was in the north. "How many days walking…Sherpa time, not mine," she asked with a smile.

"Four days adult steps. Seven for small, tired children of three and six."

She waited for more but the air was silent. Even the birds had stopped singing. Years of gleaning information from people had taught her the most effective way to get someone to open up was to reveal herself showing she wasn't afraid to be vulnerable and was willing to talk of the dark places she'd been. Sensing a nonjudgmental ear, most people bared their souls willingly. An expert at body language, Beth had recognized an uneasiness when Dorje spoke of his father. So she headed in that direction, uncertain of the cultural boundaries she would have to cross.

"It's hard when life turns your childhood upside down," she murmured and paused to gauge his reaction. Leaning forward with his elbows on his knees, he stared ahead, hands clasped in front. Had she touched something or was this a Sherpa's way of politely telling a *mikaru* enough conversation? Every nerve tingled inside as she studied his long back with the contours of his muscles visible through the T-shirt. How would it feel to run her hands over them? As the glow on the mountain dimmed to silver in the dying sun, the sky darkened and she knew she might not have this chance again.

"My father left when I was seven." His face a mixture of doubt and surprise, he looked back at her as Beth continued. "And he never returned. I used to sit at the window every day waiting for him to lift me into the air saying I was his sweet lovebird and we would fly to all the places we dreamed of. But it never happened."

"So now you fly with Eric," he answered with an insight that caught her completely off guard. This job, all the men in her life. What a revelation and coming from someone she was trying to penetrate. How could she have not realized she was still waiting and searching for her father? Perhaps she was too close to see.

Suddenly a high-pitched, piercing yell ripped through the air. Beth jumped a foot, leaving her stomach still in her throat when she landed. "What was that?"

"Yeti!" he exclaimed with terrifying urgency.

The Himalayan abominable snowman? "Really?" A second unearthly yell sent her flying off the rock without waiting for an answer. "What do we do?"

"Run to Namche."

On a moonless night, bone-shattering darkness lay in ambush at her feet. "But I can't see a thing."

He took her hand. "Come. I know the way."

The direct way to her heart. Following him was like riding the middle of a current down a rock-strewn stream, passing smoothly around and between the boulders. "What if it catches us?"

"The yeti carries men into the high mountains and they never come back."

"Have you ever seen one?"

"No but I…" A shrill whistle cut him off. His hand at her waist, he quickly turned her to the right. "This way. It is waiting on the path." The gravity of his voice broke her rhythm and a second later she was heading face first for the ground. Catching her, he yanked Beth from the grasp of phantoms lurking in the darkness.

"But you what?" she asked with an indigestible lump of fear in her stomach.

"I saw a yak's neck broken by something that took its horns and twisted the head. Only a yeti is strong enough to do that."

Balance completely deserted Beth as she imagined a Yeti ripping her apart. The current that only minutes ago flowed smoothly around boulders was now crashing her into them. Struggling to keep her upright, he said, "We must hide."

Shit, I can't believe I'm doing this, Beth grumbled to herself as she climbed over a stone wall after him. Hearing another yell, she hurried and snagged her butt on a sharp rock. *Damn.* Hitting the ground, she reached behind and discovered that not only did it hurt like hell but her most expensive trekking pants were ripped. Explain that one in camp.

Eric wouldn't believe her anymore than she believed the grunting yak now charging her. In their haste, they had dropped into a farmer's yard and his attack yak was on a rampage.

"Run," Dorje yelled.

Hopping awkwardly to avoid putting weight on the sore hip, Beth raced across the yard with the animal's hot, moist breath close behind as Dorje grabbed her arm and hauled her onto the wall out of horn's reach. Hah! Add scraped elbow and one enraged yak to the evening's journal entry. The darkness offered no reprieve from terror; every sound grew more ominous as it became apparent something was shuffling towards them, but what? A true yeti, boys chasing a large yak, or some mischievous porters playing a prank on Dorje? Beth couldn't make out a thing, but he seemed convinced that a yeti was dangerously near and they must scale yet another wall and hide behind it. He went first to help her but she was getting good at this; a regular rock climber. As soon as she was over, he grabbed her arm, pulled her down, and placed his fingers to her lips. Crouched only inches apart, his hand still firmly on her arm, she hoped he couldn't hear the loud stirrings inside her. But how could he not? He had awakened every nerve and cell in her body. In the dim light of the stars, he entranced her with his eyes and all thoughts of yaks and yetis vanished. It was as if they were suspended in a different time and space. She wanted him to lean forward ever so slightly and kiss her. It would have been so easy, yet she was afraid to make the first move, to let him know she was willing. His hand gently stroked her arm only once before letting go, but it was enough to arouse her more than Eric's most competent foreplay.

"We are safe now," he whispered and helped her rise.

Face to face, hands still touching in an awkward silence, she looked at him with the passion she'd seen in the eyes of other lovers. So this is what it felt like. The confident, articulate writer who had a word or phrase for everything went suddenly speechless. If only he'd say something, do something, but he merely studied her face a while longer before whispering, "We must go now."

The moment had passed but the sensation of his hand on her arm lingered. With eyes now accustomed to the dark and without a howling yeti in pursuit, she felt more sure-footed as they made their way down the rocky path.

As if he knew her thoughts, Dorje said, "I have never heard a yeti this low before."

"So other people in Namche haven't seen one either."

"Usually much higher. Climbers see them and many big footprints, very wide with a large toe. You know Tenzing Norgay who went up with Hillary? He saw a yeti and there is the skin and hair of a yeti's head at the *gompa* in Khumjung."

When they reached camp, Dorje left her at the dining tent where Eric was reading by flashlight. "Where have you been?" he said, shining it on her. "And what in the hell have you been doing, Babe? You're a mess."

Beth pulled a chair out and collapsed on it. "You'd never believe me," she said, letting both arms drop to the table and resting her forehead on them.

"Try me." Closing the book, he sat back against the chair, arms folded over his chest, staring at her. "Was it just you and the Sherpa out there?"

From the table, she peered up at him. "Yes, just the Sherpa and me."

He leaned forward again and wagged a finger at her. "You're gone for hours and come back looking like shit. What were you two doing out there?"

"I asked him to take me to a doctor because I'm worried about Helen and it's a long climb to 12,600 feet. I was dragging after today." With exaggerated movements, she swung her body out of the chair, lumbered towards the tent door, and turned. "And by the way, coming down, I was set upon by a screaming yeti and enraged yak."

"Please," he said, flopping back against the seat. "Give me a little more credit than that."

Pushing her hip towards him, she displayed the torn-pants. "I did this scrambling over a rock wall trying to save my ass. Now I'm going to bed." That said, she limped outside. Of course he didn't believe her. She hardly did herself. The whole scene on the mountain had been surreal, but what a fantastic story for her publisher. She grumbled to the moon now above a snow-clad peak, "Where were you when we needed your light. It would have been nice to see what was out there. Now I'll never know."

CHAPTER NINE

From outside the dining tent, Dorje heard Eric ask, "Was it just you and *the Sherpa* out there?" And her response, "Yes, just *the Sherpa* and me," said it all. What a fool for thinking her sidelong glances and subtle smiles meant anything and a complete idiot if he had tried to kiss her. A shudder started at his head and shook him all the way to the ground. He had to get her out of his system. To save the few rupees earned that day, the porters and kitchen boys would sleep huddled together on the cold floor of the dining tent, but Dorje had a warm retreat. Remembering their last argument, he stared at Mingma's house on the highest terrace. His father's words, *"Nor have you to know me,"* had echoed in his head a hundred times since then. If he returned home tonight, what would he say to Mingma or he to him? His emotions already in an upheaval over Beth, Dorje couldn't deal with that too.

Instead, he went to Pemba's house because they understood each other. His father's old friend had converted the second-story living area into a place for dining, reading, chatting, and playing cards plus added a third story dormitory and two private rooms. "Business is good," Dorje commented in reference to the six empty bottles of beer at the guest table.

With a crooked smile, Pemba spoke freely in Nepali. "These *mikarus* have too much money and don't value it. They are willing to pay whatever I ask, so why not take it?" He sliced a piece from a compressed block of Tibetan tea, dropped it in hot water, and set the pot on the hearth to finish boiling. "From my window," he said in a deliberate voice that meant a fatherly lecture was on the way, "I saw you walking towards Khunde with a woman whose hair is the color of sun shining on wheat."

"Just another tourist."

"One you walk alone with and who makes you uncomfortable on your seat even now."

"She wanted to see the hospital."

After pouring the tea into a slim, wooden cylinder, he added butter and salt and then used a wooden piston to churn the mixture. "You're an ignorant cretin if you get involved with this woman. I've seen it before and nothing good ever comes of it. These foreigners meet a young, handsome Sherpa like you and decide to have a little fun while they're here, but it means nothing to them."

"Many Sherpas sleep with tourists just to keep them happy. Foreigners think we are always smiling and desire to please, so we keep that image if we want to make good tips."

Pemba poured the brew now served only on special occasions because Tibetan tea was difficult to obtain after the border closing. "Sleeping with the tourists is not your job."

Slowly turning the cup in both hands, Dorje trusted this large-eared man barely five feet tall but with the wisdom of a god. "You don't have to worry."

"Stay away from her because these women fall in love with the idea of being with a Sherpa more than the Sherpa himself. You'll only get hurt."

To shove Beth out of his mind, Dorje changed the subject by relating stories of the old women and their courage. When he finished the tea, Pemba started to pour another. As was the custom, Dorje politely refused, shaking his hand that he couldn't possibly; then with seeming reluctance, he gave in to a second. A guest must never leave without allowing his host to serve at least three.

When the trekkers went upstairs, Dorje lay on the window bench with a blanket wrapped tightly around him. Exhausted from the day, he tried to sleep but it was impossible with images of Beth invading his thoughts. Beth tasting *tsampa* and pretending to like it, Beth hiking to Khunde with such vigor after having just climbed the Namche hill, Beth hopping onto the rock so close he could smell her hair, Beth asking him to pose with her the next day. But Pemba was right. She merely wanted a picture to show off to her friends at home; she didn't care about *the Sherpa*. Rolling onto his side, he pulled the blanket over his head to block out the visions swarming over him like ants over a piece of fruit. Finally surrendering, he dreamed of her nestled among blue gentian and purple bellflower with her golden hair splayed beneath her head. Lying propped on an elbow beside her, he lightly traced the contours of her cheek and lips. When she rose to meet him, her kisses lulled him into a deep sleep.

* * * * * * * * *

Mingma sat in his place nearest the hearth, a place he would never relinquish to strangers for any amount of money as Pemba had done, but his son cared nothing about such traditions. Dorje's ways angered the gods and would only bring disaster. Having lost him once, Mingma couldn't suffer that again. This time he would fight for his son. Marrying a beautiful woman like Shanti might clear the boy's head and bring him back. In the dim light of the butter lamp, Mingma finished reciting a page of the *sutra* and turned it over. His eyes were tired and his mind, distracted. For two days, he'd been waiting for Dorje to return from Lukla and had seen him walking into the trekker's camp that afternoon carrying a woman on his back like a lowly pack animal. But it was late now and his footsteps had not sounded on the stairs. Gazing at the dark camp below with only embers remaining of the cook fires, Mingma decided his son would rather sleep on the cold, hard ground than come home. He looked at Nima dozing on the floor mat and remembered how entwined the brothers had been as young boys, always running and hopping together, claiming they were two legs of the same frog. Such a bond they shared. But Mingma also recalled the wrenching pain of his separation and could still hear their cries. If only he had gone to them as promised. Having made a lot of wrong decisions, he couldn't change the sins of the past now but would atone for them through prayer and hope the gods would forgive him even if Dorje couldn't.

The next morning, Mingma went to the Saturday market for grain to brew *chang* for the *sodene* proposal. Namche teemed with excitement in the bright hustle and bustle, full of color, noise, and smells as hundreds of buyers and sellers jostled each other for space and haggled over prices. Round, bamboo trays overflowing with rice, vegetables, and fruits impossible to grow in the Khumbu carpeted the upper terraces at the entrance. The aroma of fresh herbs and spices filled the air as Mingma wound his way past squawking chickens in reed enclosures and bleating goats straining at their tethers.

Meandering wide-eyed through the crowd, foreigners examined colorful bolts of cloth from India, yak wool rugs, yak bells and tails, brass pots, jewelry, and fruit. Seated on the ground with a foot-powered sewing machine, a Tamang tailor from Kathmandu was making pants to order for two tourists who would pay ten times what anything was worth and push prices beyond Mingma's reach like smoke spiraling into the sky. How things had changed. He remembered the flourishing salt trade with yak caravans bringing the precious commodity over the Nangpa La from Tibet while he traveled north with his crossbreeds. Life was good until the Chinese shattered his world.

Knowing he could never afford rice brought all the way from the southern Terai, Mingma found a Rai farmer with a flat bamboo basket heaped with millet. Since neither understood the other tribe's tongue, Mingma asked in the national language, Nepali. "How much for two *pathi*?"[1]

"Twelve rupees."

At first Mingma was stunned; then he decided the man couldn't be serious. Surely he was getting back at him for all the times fun-loving Sherpas had convinced Rais that rupees flowed from the Everest ice field. The numerous accounts of shivering Rais going to the mountain in search of the legendary cash had provided many nights of humorous gossip. So 12 rupees was a fine joke. Throwing his head back laughing, Mingma asked, "But truly, how much?"

"Twelve," the Rai repeated, his voice unyielding. Arms folded, Mingma rocked back on his heels waiting for the farmer's lips to quiver suppressing a smile or even a tiny tuck in the cheek. But the man never flinched. "Do you want it or not?" the farmer asked impatiently.

No longer amused, Mingma could feel himself tightening up. He needed grain and this man was robbing him. "Not at that price. I'll give you one fourth the amount."

"I came all the way from Jubing because you pay more in Namche." Flicking his hand towards something behind Mingma, he added, "I heard the man with the big ears will pay much for his tourists, so why would I sell to you for less?"

Mingma spun around and saw Pemba strolling through the market attended by three heavily-laden porters. Blood pounding in his ears, he started to turn away before he lost face in front of other villagers. But seeing his oldest son assist the enemy in bargaining for rice that he, the father, could not afford enraged Mingma. So that's where Dorje had spent the night. Suddenly all the anger from past months hurled itself from his lips. "You pestilence-ridden, mangy cur rolling in dung to mask your own foul odor," he yelled striding towards Pemba with both arms in the air, the

---

[1] A *pathi* equals 8 *manas*. A *mana* is 10 handfuls. A *pathi* is also the brass or copper vessel which contains a *pathi* of grain.

large sleeves of his robe flaring out like bat wings. "Your greed pollutes you and everything around you. You're not even worthy of wiping the soles of my feet."

Pemba's eyes narrowed. "And your soles will never be clean as long as they wade in yak shit and you're either too ignorant or too stubborn to give up your old ways."

Trembling with anger, Mingma tapped the side of his head, the spiritual center of his body. "I will not corrupt my soul with money that destroys our ways and brings death to our people. You were once my friend but some things cannot be forgiven. Never enter my home again. You are not welcome at my hearth." Glancing at his son, Mingma saw such resentment in his eyes that he had to turn away before saying something he would regret. Striding defiantly through the crowd of onlookers, he knocked down a damn *mikaru* trying to take his picture.

* * * * * * * * *

Dorje gawked in amazement at Pemba who had not only rebuffed his father's overpowering presence but called Mingma ignorant and stubborn. Maybe wealth bought courage and power. But w*hat can't be forgiven?* As he started to ask, Beth and Eric intervened questioning what the scene was all about.

"Nothing. Just two old friends having an argument."

"The hell it was," Eric said brushing dirt off his shirt and pants. "The Tibetan had real hatred in his eyes."

"He's not Tibetan," Dorje snapped. "You should not take pictures without permission. Now go spend your rupees. The market will be over by noon and Sherpas will pass the day drinking *chang* and talking about everyone in the village." *Especially my father,* he thought, turning away from them. What had provoked Mingma's outrage? Something to do with the Rai selling millet. Standing over the farmer, Dorje demanded, "What did you say to the man in the robe?"

"He wanted two *pathi* but refused to pay."

"Pay how much?"

"Twelve rupees."

"You're a thief. That's two days of porter wages."

"And I walked three days to get here."

"With many *pathi* to sell, not just two."

Shoving the brass container towards Dorje, the farmer added, "I say the same to you. The man with big ears will buy it all at that price and I won't take less."

So that's how it is, Dorje reminded himself. Since the Saturday market began three years ago, he had watched prices rising as more Sherpas earned money from tourists, but he hadn't understood the impact until now. Men who didn't profit from them were being left behind. Frustrated as he was with his father, he couldn't let him be humiliated like that.

"Give me four." He hefted the bag over his shoulder and hauled it all the way up the steep terraces and narrow, winding stairway.

As usual, Mingma was reciting the sutra when Dorje entered. He glanced up and frowned. "What is this?"

Dorje dumped the large bag at his feet. "Millet."

His father stiffened and squared his shoulders in a defensive posture. "From who?"

"Me."

"And why would you do this?"

"Because you wanted it."

Heaving himself off the bench, Mingma pushed the bag aside. "Take it away."

"I was there and know what happened," Dorje said in a carefully measured voice, trying to remain calm and repair the damage of their last meeting. "Accept it as a gift from me."

His robe sweeping the floor, Mingma strode to the end of the room and turned with fiery eyes. "I don't need your charity and want no part of their death money."

"Then starve because that's what will happen if you don't quit being so damn stubborn." Waving his arm around the room, he shouted, "Build a teahouse like Pemba or...or..." Searching for the cruelest barb to provoke his father to action, he added, "Hire on as a porter. You're strong. Then maybe you can take care of your family."

As Mingma stormed back towards Dorje, his eyes bore right through him impaling him to the wall. "I'm an educated man, not one of your pack animals."

"Educated?"

"Eight years I studied in Tibetan monasteries while my father traded there."

"But you learned nothing. You can't speak English, can't read or write Nepali like young children in the Khumjung School. You read Tibetan but can't even write that."

"I don't need to compose scriptures, only read them."

"And you do that all the damn time," Dorje dragged out imitating the monotonous droning that went on day after day. "You must have a thousand sins to atone for."

"Don't talk to me of sin," Mingma muttered and swung his hand across Dorje's face. "You know nothing of these matters."

Paralyzed by the blow, Dorje said nothing but simply watched his father exit the room. But what could he know? There were no words to make up for his dishonor. Never meaning to go that far, he'd been caught in a word avalanche tumbling out of control.

"He'll come back when his pride heals," said a quiet voice behind him. Dorje whipped around and saw Droma Sunjo. He hadn't noticed her when he came in and rarely spoke to her when he did because he was jealous of the attention and sustenance his aunt and her son took from Mingma—things his father had denied him and Nima for ten years. As far as he was concerned, they merely existed in the house, nothing more.

She lowered her head as if trying to conceal the goiter. "Why do you always fight him?"

Who was she to ask? He owed her no explanation but the question demanded an answer in his own heart. "I don't know," he heard himself saying aloud. "I don't mean to, but when I open my mouth, harsh, ugly words rush out and I can't stop them."

"They hurt him."

All of a sudden, Dorje needed this woman who understood his father better than he did. "How do you know that? What does he say?"

"Nothing. Your father doesn't speak to me of such things, but I see it in his eyes as he watches for you at the window every day."

No. Impossible. The man who had just hit him didn't care. "He watches for me?" Exasperated and confused, Dorje sank onto the bench and kicked the bag of millet. "So what do I do with this thing?"

"Leave it. He will bury his pride because he needs the grain to brew *chang* for a *sodene*."

"*Sodene*? Whose?"

"Yours."

His emotions in complete shambles now, Dorje fell against the seat and closed his eyes to make the room stop spinning. So what other surprises did Mingma have? Was he planning to marry him off to some cretin from Phortse? The village was full of them. Or maybe a girl with a twenty-kilo butt, the daughter of someone who could benefit Mingma economically so he wouldn't have to change his old ways. Whoever she was, Dorje didn't want any part of it. He leaned forward again with his elbows on his knees, his fingers plucking at each other. What to do? Confront him again so soon?

Looking back at Droma Sunjo, he really saw her for the first time—a woman whose disfigurement isolated her from the eyes of strangers and most likely kept her from his father's bed. Dorje had never witnessed any sign of affection between them. "I'm sorry," he said as if she could read his mind. She blushed and little pleats formed in her cheeks, the first smile he'd seen on her face. It was then that he realized she was pretty in her own way. He would bring a gift and tell her so the next time he returned, but for now he was too preoccupied with thoughts of Mingma.

The hive of market activity had already diminished. After *chang* and the exchange of weekly gossip, sellers would begin the long journey home with their empty baskets. Where was Mingma? Dorje knew he should wait until he cooled down, but his anger was quick and hot like flames roaring through dry grass. He ran to Chotari's home where his father often played cards. After taking several deep breaths to still the rioting inside, he stepped through the door having no idea what to expect from Mingma or himself. His father's cold, hard stare had removed all earlier thoughts of forgiveness.

Deciding he had nothing more to lose, Dorje released his mouth in a rampage of words. "If you think marrying me off to some twenty-kilo butt is going to turn me into an ignorant, shit-gathering fool like you, you're dead wrong. Things are changing here and you can't control me like one of your belligerent yaks. So forget about the *sodene*. I won't do it!"

Mingma bolted from the seat and began that annoying pacing again. "Never did I show my father such disrespect."

"Because he was a better father," Dorje replied and winced, anticipating another blow.

Only inches from Dorje's face, Mingma's eyes blazed and the dark blue veins in his forehead pulsed like worms inching along his scalp. In a bitter, commanding voice that forbid any response even in Dorje's agitated state, Mingma announced slowly and clearly, "You will do exactly as I tell you. If Shanti's father accepts my offer, you will be wed before the summer monsoon. Now get out of my sight."

Once again, Mingma had taken Dorje's emotions and twisted them inside out and upside down. Not a cretin or twenty-kilo rear but Shanti whom he had lusted after and loved all summer long, Shanti with the large brown eyes and strong back who giggled and teased him in the meadow. Did his father know of this? Struck as mute as Droma Sunjo's son and possessed by the same vacant stare, Dorje envied Dawa because he could exit a room with his awkward ambling gait and no one would blame him.

CHAPTER TEN

By noon the baskets lining the terraces at the entrance to Namche had been cleared away. Only scattered grain remained, strewn by the wind. Gone too were the squawking chickens and bleating goats, the loud haggling and arm waving. Donkeys eager to return home trotted down the hill relieved of their loads. Beth had recorded all the sights, sounds, and smells and Eric had shot four rolls of film. Now she wanted to document everyday village life. Passing them coming up the hill was a Sherpa lumber truck: a porter with nine two-by-eight boards ten feet long strapped to his back. His face deeply furrowed, his short, wiry legs all muscle and sinew, his feet, bare, the man navigated a sharp corner by pulling on a rope attached to the top end of the boards and turning them. Racing ahead to photograph, Eric followed him to the delivery area at the north end of the village where two men were sitting on the ground with crude hammers splitting and shaping rocks by hand with machine-like precision. The corners of the new house were perfectly square and wood for the trusses and windows had just arrived.

Heading back, Eric said, "Slap me across the side of the head if I ever complain about bringing groceries up from my garage again."

"No such thing as free delivery here. He probably made a whole $1.00 or $1.50 a day to transport it and has never even seen a truck." Hearing children's laughter, Beth jumped out of the way as two young boys raced past rolling a large tire with a stick on either side to control the shorter axle through the center. "But I could be wrong," she laughed. "Look at that."

Giving her shoulder a quick hug, Eric said, "No, Babe. I'm sure that's off a plane. They must have retrieved it from the wreckage at Lukla. Very industrious boys though, future CEO's if they were born in America. It's all in the luck of the draw. Thank God, I was a winner. Otherwise, I wouldn't have met you and that would leave a huge hole in my life."

"Mine too," slipped out, taking her by surprise, but it was true. Eric was a known entity, comfortable, and secure.

Interrupting her thoughts, he asked, "What do you think she's doing?"

"Huh?"

"Over there. The little girl making mud patties and plastering them all over the house."

Her turn to tease now, she gave his shoulder a quick hug. "No, Sweetheart. I'm sure that's dung. She must have retrieved it from a yak."

"Cute, real cute. And the plastering?"

"Probably drying it for fuel. Look around. There aren't many trees."

While Eric took more pictures, Beth wandered down the narrow street. Larger than other villages they had passed through, Namche reminded her of a giant horseshoe-shaped amphitheatre rising steeply on all sides. The center buildings packed tightly together along single-file, dirt paths all looked the same. Passing an open doorway, she was noting the all-purpose mud/dung floor when Dorje startled her by emerging from the next building and turning north, so engrossed he didn't notice her. Besieged by the shortness of breath and fluttering in her stomach that Eric never quite aroused, Beth tried to get control of herself. For a few moments last night, it had felt as though she and Dorje were the only two people in Namche and Beth didn't want to let go of that. She had to know whom he was with just now and what they were doing. Stepping back, she peered at the second-story window expecting to see a woman but met instead the gaze of the man from the market.

Even more intrigued now, she joined Eric and they continued roaming the village to document life at 11,300 feet. He took pictures of a woman sweeping the entrance to her home with a yak-tail broom and a Sherpani bathing her babies in a shallow pan on the stone step. As in Kathmandu, there appeared to be no mingling of the sexes. Girls walked hand in hand with girls and boys did the same. Women washed at the spring while men sat in the village center gambling and drinking *chang*. For half an hour, Beth and Eric watched four men playing on a raised, four-foot-square carom board and concluded it was similar to eight ball pool except using chips flicked with the index finger.

Back in camp in time for tea and biscuits, Beth noticed two chickens caged near the makeshift kitchen: the evening entrée, chicken hacked into small squares making it almost impossible to separate the bones from meat. The color back in her face, Helen was sitting on the ground playing a kind of jacks with two village girls while Ruth blew up balloons for three boys.

"Anyone seen Dorje?" Beth asked.

"Not since morning," said Ruth.

Making notes in her journal, Beth kept a constant eye on the trail to the north and finally saw Dorje arrive just in time to instruct the cook about dinner. Something had made him that late. The myriad questions brought up by the village excursion provided an easy entrance to a man who had eluded her all day. Concise and informative, his answers allowed no opening for further discussion. Without making eye contact, he explained lumber came from a Sal forest in the Terai of southern Nepal, twelve days on foot. Curious about all the syaks wandering through the village, she asked if they were sacred like the cows in Kathmandu. Yes, he told her but unlike the Hindus, Buddhists never killed a living thing, not even the ant under one's foot. Only eating meat slaughtered by someone else, the Sherpas paid low-class Khambas from Tibet to perform the task. Also allowed were animals that died by accident. A subtle smile spreading across his lips, he confessed that an unusually high number of yaks appeared to commit suicide by falling off cliffs.

While jotting notes, she'd tried to think of a tactful way to approach the subject of the man in the window. "Why were those two men yelling at each other in the market this morning?"

Dorje shifted from one foot to the next as if anxious to leave. "I told you. Just two old friends having an argument."

"About what?" Forging ahead with her usual directness, she probed further until she had the whole story of friends who were now at odds because one refused to change. He was being left behind because he couldn't afford the prices set by tourists and those who profited from them. Precisely the story she'd come for with visions of selling a million copies to seal her career forever.

Excusing himself, Dorje said he must leave now and would answer more questions tomorrow. As she watched him head north again, it seemed he didn't share the connection she'd felt last night. Aware of more cultural changes unfolding than she had envisioned and a Sherpa who had a firm grasp on her heart, she lay awake that night contemplating a longer stay in Namche.

*   *   *   *   *   *   *   *

Trekkers usually reached Khumjung in an hour but Dorje could do so in under thirty minutes. Racing up the hill, he groused about Beth all the way. Last night he had tried to remove her from his thoughts. And today, hearing of Mingma's intention to arrange a marriage, he had rushed immediately to Shanti's village and learned of a party tonight for which he would now be late because of Beth's incessant questions. If only she hadn't sat there in that blue top that made her eyes even more brilliant. Just thinking about her aroused him. Plus the woman had a way of squeezing information from him like a fist around *chapatti* dough and not the least bit shy about giving out her own. Imagine a stranger talking about missing her father and waiting for him, almost as if she knew he had waited for Mingma. But that was impossible unless she was some kind of witch and had peered inside his head. Females could alter their form at night and often appeared as a blue light. Perhaps American witches cast love spells on men. A shiver ran through him and he climbed faster, his eyes darting warily in every direction.

In Khumjung, he listened for a conch announcing the location of the party. Then he wound along a narrow path lined with stone fences until he reached a house with lights and laughter streaming from the upstairs windows. Entering an open living space identical to Mingma's, he headed for a table filled with *chapattis*, potato cakes with ground spices, vegetable and yak *momos*, hard *nak* cheese, fried Tibetan bread, and plenty of *chang*. Dorje dipped a *momo* in hot chili sauce and searched the room. Shanti was standing with a group of young women who were whispering and casting furtive glances at the men on the other side. When she looked at him, the same seductive smile and large brown eyes she had used on him all last summer totally encompassed him and shoved all thoughts of Beth aside. Whipping her head with the thick black hair flowing over her shoulder, Shanti turned back to her friends and left him gazing at her and remembering how they had made love in the meadows at Gokyo. A strong and bright Sherpani, she would make a good wife and mother.

The room stirred with excitement when two musicians arrived with hollow cylindrical, wooden drums 18 inches long and covered with parchment on both ends. Sitting on the window bench, the musicians strapped the *madals* around their knees with the drums resting on their thighs and then began slapping the ends while singing. Dorje joined the men in a line down the center of the room, arms locked around waists, moving forward a few steps and then backwards. Lining up opposite them, the women moved in unison. When the men sang several lines from a song, the women responded with the next verses. After they had alternated a few times, one of the men sang to a woman in a bright red blouse, "If you are so beautiful, why do you spend your days gathering dung cakes?"

The other men sang his refrain and the women responded. "If you are so handsome, why do you only have *naks* for girlfriends?"

After the women repeated the refrain, the first man continued, "And where is the rich *mikaru* who will carry you off to America? Do you hide him in your goiter?"

As the two sides matched wits and bantered with playful insults, the tempo increased. Their footwork quickened to a rhythmic stomping and kicking until the dancing became so frenetic that everyone was giggling and panting too hard to sing. The faster Dorje's feet moved, the more his heart raced with desire. His gaze never strayed from Shanti. Her tantalizing eyes and lips promised the same rapture he had shared all summer, and it had been too long since he had held her in his arms. Consumed with the thought of making love again, he hardly noticed when the music stopped and everyone broke for refreshments. As ladles of *chang* with fermented grains floating on top filled everyone's cups, the party livened into the playful wrestling and sexual innuendos common at summer pasture.

Other musicians entered, one with a hand drum and the other a *sarangi.* Playing the small four-stringed instrument with a horsehair bow, the musician sang a love song, and the dancing resumed but not in lines. Men and women danced alone, turning and swaying with their arms upraised, their hands dipping and rising, circling in and out. Dorje watched Shanti's body undulating in a continual, sinuous motion, gliding with effortless grace, her feet barely grazing the floor. Teasing him, she parted her lips just slightly with her tongue until he couldn't stand it. Longing to be inside her again, he inched close enough to whisper, "Come with me."

She cupped her hand around his rear cheek to give it a squeeze and then sashayed to the door tossing a mischievous smile over her shoulder. As soon as they were out of sight, Shanti whipped her skirt up giggling.

"Not here," he laughed, "I want to lie with you. "I'll..." Before he could finish, her tongue was tracing his lips and she was snuggling up to him. "Quit that," he said, pulling away. He wanted time to explore and relish her entire being. "Open the shutter a crack when your parents are asleep and I'll come to you."

"Now," she purred, drawing his hand to her thigh until laughter coming from the doorway swept a frown across her face.

Dorje yanked her skirt back down, turned her, put one hand on her waist to direct her towards home. "My father will be coming soon with beer for a *sodene*."

Shanti stopped so quickly his stride carried him past. He spun around and pulled her to him. Burying his face in her hair, he whispered, "Will you ask your father to accept?"

"I shall tell him that if he does not, I will run off to Kathmandu with you." Slipping out of his arms, she ran along the path, yelling, "Watch for the shutter."

Dorje waited on the rock wall opposite her house as he'd done the first few weeks of fall before the tourists arrived. Trekking season had separated them as it did many families in the Solu Khumbu when husbands left their wives and children to work for two to three months each fall and spring. His leg bounced nervously. At great risk sitting here alone with Beth's bewitching ways trying to depose Shanti, he had to fill his head with her brown eyes and full, warm lips. *Hurry up and open the damn shutter.* Finally a playful hand crawled out the window and beckoned to him. Groping his way up the dark stairway, he paused outside the door to the living area, knowing her parents were in the same open room. The first time he had come, her father coughed loudly as Dorje tiptoed to her place on the floor just to let him know he was aware of his presence. But nothing was said that night or any other. With nowhere else to go, it was accepted that boys would visit girls. Tonight her father rustled in his bed as if to say, *so you finally came back to see my daughter after these many weeks.* But no words were spoken as Dorje's feet slid in a whisper across the floor. Loving her was fun and exciting. Teasing and tickling his most sensitive parts, she sent goose bumps all the way to his toes. When he came, his entire body shuddered in a wild explosion.

Afterwards, Dorje lay with her head in the hollow of his shoulder and stroked her hair and cheek. The most beautiful girl in the Khumbu and he knew how to please her. But he also feared he could never stay in one place raising yaks or farming potatoes as their fathers did. The restless shadow that had chased him all summer would always be in pursuit. Closing his eyes, he held her tight, planning to stay until the misty light of dawn slithered through the shutters and crept across the room.

CHAPTER ELEVEN

Lying awake for over an hour, Beth couldn't ignore her bladder another minute. After carefully lifting Eric's arm from around her waist, she opened her side of the bag leaving the other still zipped to his to maximize body heat. She crawled through the tent door and arched her back like a cat stretching in the sun and yawned. This sleeping on the ground, even with a foam pad, killed her back. Shivering, she hugged herself and lumbered to the latrine tent mumbling, "What bothers me most is I'm getting used to this." Inside the tarp, the awkward and unglamorous Asian toilet awaited. The most workable position was squatting slightly and straddling the hole in the ground.

As she exited, Beth watched dawn seeping down the hills with a gentle apricot glow in the still air. Embraced by the solitude, she stood a long while in the sleeping camp with her eyes closed. Having given up on an all-seeing, protective God many years ago, she still wondered if this was a spiritual experience. Finally opening her eyes, she saw someone hurrying down the path from the north. It was Dorje. As he neared and their gaze met, he quickly turned away as if she were a stranger.

Back in her tent, Beth waited for the tea and warm wash water that announced the beginning of another day. "How do you feel?" she asked Helen at breakfast.

"Okay but really disappointed because I wanted to walk all the way to Tengboche and now I won't even get to see what I came for."

"I'm not so sure. The doctor said you could probably go if transported."

Fifteen minutes later, a *doko* appeared at the dining tent door with the top half of the back cut out and stuffed with Helen's bag and pad for a seat. Eric laughed. "Methinks your taxi has just arrived, My Lady." And so had the driver. After getting Helen settled and reassuring her she was not too heavy, Dorje adjusted the *naamlo* and slowly rose to his feet with her on his back facing away from him. The air resounded with cheers from everyone. Although Beth was also pleased at Helen's good fortune, her presence precluded any personal conversation with Dorje on the trail. Since he had avoided her since the night of the yeti, perhaps Dorje planned things this way.

The trail led them to the very spot where Dorje had brought Beth two nights earlier. She wanted some acknowledgment that they had shared a moment there, but he never looked in her direction. Instead he focused on the ladies, identifying Everest, Nuptse, Lhotse, Ama Dablam, and a speck on a dark ridge that was Tengboche. When he showed them the photo rock, Beth wanted to say, *but that's ours where we sat together.*

Posing them with Everest in the background, adjusting his lens, teasing to elicit just the right smile, Eric was very good at what he did and Beth admired that. They could build a comfortable and exciting life around work and travel. So why did her entire being grow faint when she glanced at Dorje and caught him watching her? Not turning away this time, he fixed his eyes on hers as if to say, *I remember our night together. It meant something to me too.*

Eric broke the moment when he asked Dorje to take his picture with Beth. Standing with her arm around Eric's waist and his on her shoulder, Beth felt something was missing as if the photo would develop in black and white. When Dorje returned the camera, Beth couldn't let go of that night. "Dorje," she said quietly as he started to help Helen into the *doko*," I want a picture with our sirdar to take home."

"Good idea," said Eric. "You two get up there." On watery legs, Beth posed beside Dorje, not touching, barely able to breathe, but knowing the photo would print in blazing color.

Continuing the trek, they headed out on a contouring trail high above the Dudh Kosi, called the milk river because of its glacial flour. Then they moved along a steeply plunging hillside through forests of blue pine, fir, black juniper, and colorful mountain rhododendrons. Sparkling micas, mosses, lichens, and azaleas lined the path. Ruth spotted two Himalayan tahr and Eric shot half a roll on the national bird, the Impeyen Pheasant. Gleaming in the sunlight, the male revealed its iridescent, multicolored plumage while Dorje explained they were downhill flyers and could only walk uphill. Overhead a lammergeier with a ten-foot wingspan soared on thermals.

Descending 1,100 feet to the river, the group reached the small village of Phunki Tenga next to a series of water-driven prayer wheels with the mantra *Om Mani Padme Hum* carved on the outside and printed on parchment inside. Dorje explained that all who touched the wheel receive *sönam* or merit towards a better incarnation. Sitting in front of her house, an elderly woman spun a hand-held prayer wheel made of a hollow metal cylinder attached to a handle with a lead weight on a chain to aid rotation, each turn equivalent to reciting one mantra. Simultaneously with her other hand, she fingered rosary beads counting her recitations with each prayer earning merit.

After resting half an hour, they began the 2,000-foot ascent on a trail that initially climbed steeply along the right flank of the ridge, narrowing to single file at times above cliffs that dropped hundreds of feet to the river. Dorje regularly urged them to go *bistarai, bistarai* and drink more water, so they rested often. Eventually the trail grew more gradual and the trekkers marveled at the lush canopy of scarlet rhododendron, pine, magnolia, birch, and spiky even berberis shrubs. The dark forest contrasted sharply against the soaring white mountains.

Three hours from Phunki Tenga, they reached a covered gateway alight with brightly painted scenes of local deities and forms of Buddha adorning the walls and arched ceiling. Built by the monks, the *kani* cleansed people of evil spirits before entering the sacred grounds. Passing through and then around a large *chorten*, the group entered a clearing surrounded by dwarf firs, sweet smelling incense scrubs, and colorful rhododendrons. Perched on a ridge at 12,700 feet and ringed by spectacular peaks, Tengboche sat in the most stunning natural setting Beth had ever seen. To the left, a broad stone stairway led to the main *gompa*, its whitewashed walls and red shutters rising against a stark blue sky where yellow billed choughs and black ravens played on the winds.

While the Sherpas set up camp in the clearing, Eric took photos of the ladies and Beth with Everest and Ama Dablam, the Matterhorn of the Himalayas, in the background. "That has to be one of the most photographed mountains in the world," he said, pointing to the latter. "Look how the steep slopes and curving ridges draw your eyes to the glacier on the summit."

Their work done for the day, one of the porters with both hands behind his back sauntered to the center of the clearing, grinning. When Dorje finished setting up the dining table, the porter yelled something in Nepali, whipped one arm out and flicked his wrist, releasing a blue Frisbee that sailed high over the sirdar's head. Dorje raced after it, leapt several feet off the ground for an incredible one-handed catch, and spun around tossing it hard and fast to another porter. Three more joined in all playing with the energy and precision of professional athletes.

"Get pictures," Beth told Eric excitedly. "Pictures of Sherpas playing our games." Her reporter self took over with a flood of questions. *What other western ways had they adopted? Were we altering their culture and beliefs? Their economics?* As she watched their faces and body language, different personalities emerged and they were no longer collectively *the porters.* Enamored of these gentle men and boys who every day hauled gear up and down the mountain and crossed swaying bridges in bare feet or flip flops without complaint, Beth wanted to know their names and called Dorje over. Pointing to each one, he identified Pasang, Phurbu, Lhakpa, Gyeljen, Jamgbu, Tuchi and explained that many parents name children after the day of the week when they are born: Nima for Sunday; Dawa, Monday; Mingma, Tuesday; Lhakpa, Wednesday; Phurbu, Thursday; Pasang, Friday; and Pemba, Saturday.

"And you. What does Dorje mean?"

"Thunder bolt."

Her eyes traced his lips and perfect white teeth. "So you are very powerful and can light up the sky."

"And knock down large trees with one blow," he said grinning.

Where had this man with an enticing smile that could win the heart of any Sherpani gone last night and stayed until just before dawn? "What else do Sherpas do for fun?"

His eyes searching for an answer, Dorje shrugged. "We dance and sing, drink *chang.*"

"Where?"

"Sometimes outdoors. Most of the time in our houses."

"And if a man and woman want to be alone?" Dorje shifted his weight to the other foot and appeared on the verge of departure. Once again, she'd gone too far. *Damn prying tongue. Change the subject.* "Will you show us Sherpa dancing?"

"We don't have a drum," he answered simply before turning away. A few minutes later, she saw him talking to the porters. The youngest, a boy of fifteen named Gyeljen, and Phurbu, who was very proud of his Snoopy T-shirt, left immediately. She thought little of it until they returned an hour later giggling and concealing something. Dorje, the other porters, cooks, and two kitchen boys quickly gathered around them and advanced as a unit towards the tourists. Beaming with pride, they presented Ruth with a birthday cake baked at 12,700 feet using a crude rock oven and firewood.

The little lady with tight gray curls who was first across the perilous bridges and had climbed the Namche and Tengboche hills with such courage and gusto broke down and wept. This, her sixty-ninth birthday, would be the most memorable of her life. "Tell them, Dorje," she said through her tears. "Tell them I will never forget this day with my new friends. I am so happy to be here."

Watching Ruth and seeing the joy in the Sherpa faces, Beth blinked to keep tears from rolling down her cheeks too. Dorje had to be responsible for this. No one else could have known. Even she didn't. "Thank you," she told him. "We will all remember this night. Do Sherpas have birthday cakes too?"

"We do not know the month or the number of the year. I only know I was born in the year of the rat, so I am either eight, twenty, or thirty-two."

While a kitchen boy sliced and served the cake, young Gyeljen revealed another surprise, a *madal*. Sitting on the ground with his legs crossed, he supported the drum between his knees and began slapping the parchment ends. By now the other porters had consumed a fair amount of *chang* and were in a giddy, singing mood. Dorje and Pasang pulled the most outgoing porter, Topkie, to his feet and pushed him to the center. Shooting nervous glances at Dorje who returned a stern look, the porter began to dance with his arms upraised and flowing freely. Another couple of swigs of *chang* and he lost all inhibitions, swirling and dipping so loosely it seemed as though his limbs weren't connected to his body. After ten minutes of this continuous motion, the other Sherpas started giggling and then erupted in riotous laughter that lasted another five.

"What's happening?" Beth asked Dorje who was barely in control himself.

He explained that Gyeljen had finished the song but Topkie wouldn't sit down so Gyeljen had to keep singing. "He is making up funny words about weak *mikarus* who cannot carry a *doko* up the hill."

Observing the activity, Beth became aware that her journal notes were merely those of an outsider looking in, which anyone could do. Exploring the intimacies of the Sherpa heart and soul would take time. While she watched Dorje summoning the others to form a line, Beth spoke to Eric. "I'm fascinated by them. They're quite amazing, don't you think?" He nodded with a look that said he knew she was heading somewhere. "I'm especially curious about what influence we're having on their culture."

"So get to the point."

"I want to stay longer."

"What?"

"Only a few weeks...a month at most. That's the only way I can get to know them."

"And what about me? You know I have to shoot that job in the Galapagos. We've been planning the trip together ever since I got the assignment."

She placed her hand on his. "Yes, Sweetie, I know. But we're here together now, and it's been good, hasn't it?"

Removing his hand, he crossed his arms and stared straight ahead, his knee bouncing.

Beth rubbed her leg up against it. "Please try to understand. It's only for a short while."

"No public displays of affection allowed," he said in a reproachful, dispassionate tone and then rose. "Do whatever you want. You will anyway...always have." Eric marched to the line of Sherpas and pushed his way in beside Dorje. "So what are we doing here?"

"Follow me," said Dorje.

Arms linked around their waists, the Sherpas shuffled forward a few steps and backwards, ending each phrase with a stomping motion. Eric looked tall and awkward among them. Beth hoped he wouldn't humiliate himself as he'd done with the *doko*. She imagined the porters singing about the clumsy American who can't carry a basket or dance. Seeming intent upon humbling Eric, Dorje added more complicated footwork until even the Sherpas struggled to keep up. Eric didn't stand a chance and was lost in a flurry of dust churned up by Dorje's flying feet, but he refused to concede. It became a duel with only two men remaining—one of them touching heel and toe, moving forwards and back, stomping the ground as hard as he could with split-second timing; the other staggering and lurching off balance like a drunken giant. Angry at Dorje and embarrassed for Eric, Beth wished he would walk away before falling flat on his face. Finally, at least Gyeljen was kind enough to end the song.

Eric strode past her with sweat coursing through his dust-caked face. "That bastard. I'd love to get him on my turf. You think they're so damn interesting. Then stay here. Sleep on the ground, wash with a cup of water, and piss in a hole. But not me; not any longer." He dragged his sleeve across his forehead to wipe his face before throwing open the tent flap and crawling in.

Beth was furious at Dorje now. There was no excuse for this aggressive behavior; he had just refuted all western images of Buddhist Sherpas as smiling, enlightened people desiring only to please. When she glanced back at him, he immediately turned and walked away with no apparent regrets, and she would not forgive him for that.

Beth and the ladies drank hot tea and chatted until it was too cold to stay up any longer. Shivering and hoping Eric had settled down by now, she joined him in the tent. "Are you all right, Sweetie?" she asked and began to remove her boots.

Lying on his back with one arm folded under his head, he said, "Leave them on. We're going outside."

"Now? Why? It's freaking cold out there."

"We won't be long. Come on."

Eric led her away from camp to the far end of the clearing. "Look at that moon. There, beside your favorite mountain."

Still shivering, she inched closer until completely enveloped in his arms. The moon hung just above Ama Dablam illuminating the glacier. "It's beautiful. Thank you for bringing me out to share it."

His thumb massaged her neck. "I want to apologize for earlier. I admit to being upset when you first told me. You caught me by surprise and I was thinking only of myself. Of course, you have to stay. Your career is on the line and I can't stand in your way. Besides, it's your nature to do everything the best you possibly can. It's one of the things I love most about you." Leaning back to look at her, he added, "And I do love you. I hope you know that."

Almost out of habit, she answered, "Yes, and I love you too."

"Good. That's what I needed to hear. Sometimes I'm not sure."

She nodded, knowing that she hadn't always expressed great passion for him, but right now she felt warm and comfortable in his arms. And perhaps that's what love was all about. Her head resting against him, she listened to his heart beating faster as his chest rose with a deep breath before he spoke again.

"I was so upset because I've been saving something for our Galapagos trip, thinking it would be a romantic interlude." Curious, she looked up at him and Eric laughed quietly. "But hell, you probably think this place is more romantic. Standing before a Buddhist monastery at 12,700 feet in the freezing cold with Everest and Ama Dablam as your witness."

She drew back and stared at him. "Witness to what?"

"My proposal. I've wanted to marry you from the first day I met you on that ferry going across to San Francisco."

"It was cold then too and oh so windy."

"You're evading the question."

"And just what question is that?"

With one finger, he tipped her chin up to look at him. "Will you, Beth, marry me, Eric?"

It all seemed to flow so easily and naturally that she heard herself saying, "Yes," without really thinking about it. But maybe that's how it was supposed to be, just responding and moving forward with one's life. No more questions or searching. "Yes," she repeated, "I, Beth, will marry you, Eric."

CHAPTER TWELVE

Shortly after midnight, a loud cry ripped through camp, shattering the silence. Beth grabbed Eric's arm. "What was that?"

"Don't know, Babe. Probably a drunken porter." He yawned. "Go back to sleep."

Propped on her elbows, she unzipped the door and peered into the darkness, listening to other sounds: someone vomiting, another cry, scurrying feet. A ray of light stole along the ground and disappeared into the ladies' tent. Watching shadows play on the wall and hearing muffled voices, she feared something awful had happened. On her hands and knees outside the ladies' door, Beth whispered, "What's going on?"

Dorje almost bumped her on his way out. "Helen is sick this high. I must take her down."

"Right now? In the dark?" she asked as he prepared the *doko*.

"It is too dangerous for her to sleep here. I have seen stronger *mikarus* die." After wrapping Helen in a warm bag, he lifted her into the basket, strapped the *doko* on, and pushed to his feet. "The cooks know what to do. They will take you back to Namche tomorrow."

"But how will you see?" she asked as he quickly strode away from her. "*And what if a yeti…?*" she started to add but realized he was already out of earshot. Feeling helpless, all she could do now was attempt to comfort Ruth left alone and scared on her sixty-ninth birthday.

After a fitful night, Beth woke to a crisp, cloudless sky and watched the sun rise over the mountain bathing the monastery in amber light. From the main *gompa* came the penetrating, unearthly tones of a pair of ten-foot, telescopic horns, *dung-chens*, calling the monks to Morning Prayer. The deep and powerful sound of the long horns resembled the singing of elephants. Eager to see Helen, Ruth chose to stay just long enough to visit the monastery so Eric could take pictures for her ailing friend. One of the cooks led them up the wide stone steps and signaled for them to remove their shoes and remain quiet. After bowing and presenting a white silk *kata* to the presiding lama, he showed them into a dimly lit room permeated with the aroma of butter lamps and juniper incense.

"Amazing," Eric whispered as he quietly took photos of the ceiling and walls decorated with brilliantly colored images of Buddha, various gods, lamas, and mythological scenes. From intricately painted rafters hung rectangular, cloth *thangkas* of intense colors and incredibly fine detail depicting deities and other elements of the Buddhist cosmology. Creating a visual safe place, a large square *mandala* illustrated a cosmic fortress filled with gods and goddesses. At the far end of the room hung two parasols and a large flat drum. As they walked the perimeter, Eric photographed the different meditative poses of Buddha set in recesses alongside shelves containing hundreds of Tibetan scriptures.

Sixteen monks sat cross-legged in two rows facing a center aisle as they recited from the single sheets of scriptural narrative lying on low tables in front of them. Under the soft light of butter lamps, they chanted prayers in a sustained monotone. The close-throated and deep-pitched sounds appeared to emerge from the depths of the soul rather than mere vocal chords. An ensemble of wind and percussion instruments accompanied the intonations with the moaning of a pair of *dung-chen* and the quiet insistent beating of a drum acting as an undercurrent. Punctuating the music, cymbals, hand-held bells, and smaller drums of indefinite pitch marked off sections of the service. Having heard the monks at dusk the previous night, Beth had learned from Dorje the importance of chanting aloud so that the gods living in the trees, rocks, houses, streams, and mountains can benefit from Buddha's teachings.

Reluctantly, they slipped away and started back to Namche accompanied by the cooks. On Dorje's advice, they had left shopping in the small villages for the return trip rather than add weight to the climb. In Sanasa, they enjoyed a short stop to examine the Tibetan souvenirs laid out beside the trail: turquoise and silver jewelry, yak tails and bells, woolen mittens and scarves. Eric squatted to examine a collection of rings. Calling Beth over, he asked, "Which do you like best?" She selected a silver one with a small turquoise inset. "Then it's yours." After much bargaining with wild hand gestures and facial expressions, Eric made a grand display of placing the ring on her third finger.

"Are you engaged?" Ruth exclaimed.

Looking at Eric, Beth saw the love radiating from his eyes and hoped it was strong enough to hold them together if she faltered After living through her mother's four acrimonious divorces, she didn't know if she had what it took to make a marriage work. "Yes," she answered with a quick kiss on his cheek. "Casanova proposed in the moonlight last night." An expert negotiator now, Eric purchased two more pieces of jewelry for Ruth and Helen.

Waiting for them at the north entrance to Namche, the small man with large ears from the market place managed to convey through gestures and a handful of English words that Dorje had taken the sick old lady lower. Beth, Eric, and Ruth were to rest for the night and meet Dorje and Helen in Lukla in two days. Beth saw no reason to accompany Eric and Ruth all the way back to the airstrip and have to climb the Namche hill again. In those four or five days, she could record more village life, visit the Hillary School in Khumjung and the Khunde hospital.

After retiring early because it would be their last night together for weeks, Eric held Beth close with his lips to her ear and whispered, "I don't feel right leaving you here alone. Too many things can happen."

"I'll be fine."

"But look at Helen. We don't even know if she's still alive"

Rolling onto her side to face him, Beth said, "She's seventy and just finished chemo. Nothing is going to happen to me. I saw a sign in English advertising a place with a good bed and good food. I'll stay there."

"Promise you won't do anything stupid."

"Trust me. I'll be back before you know it and we'll share tales of our adventures. I hope you understand that this story will not only save my career but earn me a reputation as a premier student of cultures." As a long exhale brushed her cheek, Beth knew she had disappointed him. "Sweetie, we have an entire lifetime together. Please give me these few weeks."

Eric put his finger to her lips. "Hush. Enough already. It's obvious I'm not going to change your mind."

When his tongue tickled the inside of her ear sending goose bumps all the way down her leg, she raised her shoulders in defense. "Promise you'll contact my boss and tell him what's going on. There's no way I can from here."

"I will." He kissed the hollow at the base of her neck. "Now let's celebrate the beginning of the rest of our lives."

As Beth surrendered to him, she wanted to share his confidence that they'd be together forever, but there were always doubts. Having never experienced love as a child, she wasn't sure how it felt, giving or receiving. Whenever past lovers got too close, they accused her of retreating to an emotional closet like the broom closet she used to hide in from her mother. Perhaps they were right.

The next morning, she accompanied everyone to the south end of the village. It was hard seeing Ruth go. "I'm sure Helen is fine and waiting for you. Eric will send pictures as soon as they're developed. You two are my idols. I hope I'm half as strong, courageous, and adventurous when I'm your age." After giving Beth a tight hug, Ruth donned her daypack and started down the hill, waving her walking stick in a farewell.

Now for the most difficult parting. Eric, because she was genuinely sad to see him go. He'd been a part of the last year's planning and given her much-needed support. Ignoring all rules of cultural propriety, Beth gave him a long, deep kiss. "I should be home by the time you're back from the Galapagos. I'll call and let you know as soon as I reach a phone."

"I still don't feel good about this but it's who you are and I can't change that...wouldn't even try. It's what makes you unique."

A mixture of sadness and excitement filled Beth as she watched them descend and finally disappear. Alone in the Himalayas and about to embark on a new adventure, she turned and headed back into Namche with Eric's little gnats of uncertainty flapping their wings in her head. *What if...what if...?* To drive them out, she needed the comfort of a warm bed and good food. Having never been inside a Sherpa home, she wasn't sure what to expect as she climbed the winding stairway. The same small man from the market place led Beth to the third floor quoting the rates for the ten-bed dormitory versus a private room, the US equivalent of $.12 versus $.36. Time to splurge. Hardly the luxury she hoped for, the seven by seven room contained two small beds along the sidewalls with barely enough space to pass between them, no heat, and a half-burned candle on the sill. The instant she sat on the foam mattress, it sank to a wooden plank. As the commotion of trekkers arriving in the adjacent dormitory carried through paper-thin walls, it seemed the sole benefit of sleeping indoors was the ability to dress standing up, not having to crawl through a tent door, and arranging gear on a second bed instead of living out of a duffel. That task accomplished, she wandered down to the second floor to check out the food situation. From a menu bearing the marks of weary trekkers soiled with trail dust, she chose *aalu*, having no idea what it was. Thirty minutes later, a plate arrived piled with fifteen tiny, boiled potatoes still in their skins. Staring at the steaming mass, she wondered if she was supposed to pick them up and eat them whole or what?

Beth dumped them in a plastic bag from her pack and started out for the Hillary school in Khumjung with no directions other than about an hour up the hill. Nibbling on a hot potato, she chose a path to the left, figuring she could always turn around and come down if lost. Thirty minutes later while searching the bag for another potato, Beth hiked around a large boulder and suddenly came face to face with a yak charging straight at her chased by an adolescent boy. All three panicked with Beth scrambling up the rock and the boy grabbing the tail and digging his heels in while the animal careened to the right. Pulling out of his grasp, the yak grunted and joined the rest of the herd leaving the boy with nothing but a handful of long, shaggy tail hair. Spotting Beth sitting on the rock, the boy slapped the hair onto his head, grinned, and shouted, "*Namaste.*"

"*Namaste,*" she yelled back and slid down. Sauntering toward him, she opened the bag and tossed a potato at him.

Crouched with knees bent and heels flat on the ground in the familiar Sherpa position, he patted the grass beside him and said, "*Basnos.*" Having observed this posture with great admiration ever since arriving in the Khumbu, Beth had even secretly practiced with zero success. Embarrassed by her complete inability to achieve his squat, she pretended not to comprehend what he wanted. When she didn't move, he repeated louder, "*Basnos.*" Determined to give it one more try, she bent down with her heels flat against the ground. Either her seat was too heavy (a quality no man had ever complained of) or her ligaments too short. Either way, she fell backwards onto her butt to his great amusement and hers.

"Sit," she said with her rear firmly planted on the grass.

He lay down. "*Sutnos.*"

She sprang to her feet. "Stand."

"*Ubhinos,*" he shrieked and jumped up. Then arms out to the side, he fell straight backwards, wild with laughter. "*Khasnos.*"

Even though it would be painful, she couldn't let him show her up again. "Fall," she cried and hit the ground. "Ouch!" The latter needed no translation.

They lay among the wildflowers munching boiled potatoes and watching clouds swell into giant, fantastical shapes and then disperse to form anew. He babbled and pointed, naming imaginary creatures she presumed, and Beth did the same knowing he didn't understand a word. As she was describing Pegasus galloping across the sky carrying lightening bolts to Zeus, Beth felt something tug her hair. She tipped her head back and encountered a mobile upper lip and long tongue. "Yikes!" she yelped and dug her heels in to scoot downhill and roll away.

The boy exploded with laughter. "*Nak.*"

She must have looked confused because he reached under a coarse coat of outer wiry hairs covering fine woolly fibers to reveal a teat. So it was a male/female thing. Beth crawled back up to him to continue sharing a delightful afternoon with this boy of sixteen or seventeen with a gap-toothed grin and tiny dark freckles across his cheeks and nose. The trip to Khumjung could wait. Touching herself, she said, "Beth," and then pointed to him.

"Nima."

Indicating both of them together, she walked her fingers up the hill. "Khumjung?"

He rocked his head slightly to one side and back to the other in a manner she had learned meant *yes* but still found a bit confusing and too much like a western *no*. If only she knew the word for *tomorrow*. The sun slowly slid behind the snow capped peaks leaving a sky dappled with pink clouds. Gathering the smaller animals, the *naks*, Nima drove them onto the trail with Beth in the rear choking on dust churned up by their hooves. Between that and smoke from unvented fires, it was no wonder half the population suffered from lung disease. When they reached Namche, she smiled and repeated, "Khumjung?" Another head-swaying affirmative left her uncertain of their plans. Her hands clasped together, she bowed and said, "*Namaste.*" He replied with a smile puckering the freckles on his nose.

At breakfast the next morning, two fried eggs floating in oil and fried potatoes convinced her that only climbing up and down these mountains kept Sherpas lean. Sipping the last of her morning tea before departing, Beth heard footsteps as if someone were taking the stairs two at a time. Nima raced into the room with his usual boyish grin and hopped onto the bench beside her. With no words to express how pleased she was, Beth started to tousle his hair affectionately but remembered it was an insult to touch an adult Nepali's head—the most sacred part of the body. Smiling, she asked once more, "Khumjung?"

This time, Nima's entire body swung from side to side in an emphatic *yes*. He leapt off the seat and ran to the door like a dog eager to go outside; she could almost see his tail wagging. Like the beagle she used to own, Nima covered twice the ground by climbing onto rock walls and prancing along the top with his arms out for balance, hopping down, and racing to the other side. He wore her out. "Nima, *bistarai,*" she called to slow him down.

An hour later, they arrived in Khumjung at 12,507 feet. Unlike the close-quartered houses of the traders in Namche, barley and potato farms spread over a wide area on the southern slope of the 19,000-foot holy Mt Khumbila. A long *mendan* with three-foot prayer stones stood outside the schoolyard. Constructed in 1961 of aluminum sections with translucent panels on the roof to admit light, the building was cold inside. When they entered, Nima spoke to the teacher who then addressed Beth in English and invited them to stay.

Lopsang came from Darjeeling, India, and had been here five years. "Edmund Hillary asked the Sherpa people what he could do to repay them for their help in climbing Everest," he explained. "They said they wanted a school. Their children had eyes but could not see."

Staring at the rows of smiling children seated on a dirt floor behind low tables, two or three sharing a tattered book, and most without shoes or sweaters, Beth shivered involuntarily thinking how cold and dark this would be in winter with no artificial light or heat source. "And what do you teach them?"

"At first to read and write the national language, Nepali. Then English. It is their only hope for a future in the tourist industry."

"But what of their own Sherpa language?"

"It is not a written language and there are far too many dialects. A Sherpa from the Khumbu cannot even understand one from the Solu in the south. It would be impossible."

"How long do they attend school?"

Frustration and disappointment spread across his face. "Most only a year or two until they learn basic communication and enough math to barter. Then their parents want them back working to support the household."

"What about Nima here," Beth asked, glancing at her cheerful companion whose eyes never left her.

"Their father wouldn't let either boy attend. He said yak herders don't need to speak English or read and write. But his older brother, Dorje, is the most brilliant boy I've encountered in many years of teaching. He came to me four years ago begging to enter school, but he was too old at sixteen. We only have primary grades. So he stood outside my door every day just listening and refused to go away."

"Dorje and Nima are brothers?" Beth asked in shock.

"Yes, yes." Lopsang's body swelled with excitement. "Dorje comes often to talk when I am so lonely for conversation, and he learns everything I teach him." Lopsang asked the children to sing. As Beth stood at the wall listening to a chorus of happy voices filling the air, her eyes watered. It was a new generation of Sherpas with the promise of a better life tugging at her heart—a moment she'd never forget.

After leaving the school, she and Nima returned via the Everest look-out. From her pack, Beth dug out two apples, several slices of nak cheese, and four chapatis for lunch. Seated flush against her on the rock she and Dorje had shared, Nima grinned, his knee gently rocking against hers. She wanted to adopt him as her little brother and give a big sisterly kiss but knew it wouldn't be appropriate. What a shame that such loving people couldn't openly express affection for the opposite sex. Instead, she chose to tease him by secretly picking up a rock and flinging it behind them. When it hit the ground and clattered, she jumped and screamed, "Yeti!" Nima whipped around, dropping his cheese, obviously saw nothing, and stared at Beth who couldn't keep a straight face after observing his stricken expression. He caught onto her game, threw his arms in the air making himself as large as possible and began a high, piercing yell. Pretending to be terrified of this horrific, hairy monster, Beth grabbed her pack and raced downhill, her arms flailing wildly with Nima right behind her giggling be-tween yeti screams.

Spending the entire afternoon and next two days together, they played Frisbee and tag. He showed her how to use the carom board and she taught him yo-yo basics, the latter requiring many patient hours because she had observed earlier that Sherpas appeared to have no natural talent for it. Even Dorje hadn't been able to master a yo-yo in camp. In the afternoons, they lay watching clouds, drawing pictures, and teaching each other new words such as *zopkio* and *zhum*. She learned the latter two referred to the yak/cow crossbreeds used at Namche and lower. Larger, with shorter hair, and less pronounced horns than yaks, the male *zopkio*s were not as likely to dump their loads or knock travelers off a cliff while the female *zhums* gave richer and more plentiful milk than *naks*.

Nima seemed giddy at times and always smiling, always watching her every move. He was the childhood she never had—carefree and innocent, intoxicated with pure joy. And things were so easy with him, none of the complexities and intellectual or emotional games of the modern world. She was free to just experience life in its most elemental form for the first time in her memory. And it felt good.

CHAPTER THIRTEEN

On his way down, Dorje had stopped in Khunde where the doctor assured him Helen would be all right if he immediately took her even lower and gave her plenty of water. To pass the time while waiting for Ruth, he sat with Helen on a bench outside a teahouse in the village of Lukla. They chatted about Helen's son who had moved to New Zealand, Hillary's home. When she explained the first man to climb Everest had been a beekeeper, Dorje couldn't believe it. A beekeeper turned god! If Hillary could do that, Dorje could be the Tenzing of the future.

In the early afternoon, a woman with tight gray curls strode boldly down the village path waving a walking stick. Screaming with joy, Helen ran to her and they laughed and hugged as if they were children again. Watching them, Dorje knew the physical and emotional demands of the trip had given both renewed confidence in themselves. Seemingly, ten years younger than when they had arrived, these loving grandmothers would take part of him with them. He'd fetched their sweaters when they were cold, knew how they liked their tea and who wanted her egg scrambled instead of fried—the little, personal things of life.

While the ladies chatted, Dorje wandered up the trail a short way wondering if Beth and Eric were taking the next day's plane also. Their cook and kitchen boy passed, followed by Eric ten minutes later who shot a threatening glance. "You'd better take good care of her."

"Take care of who?"

"Beth. I know this is all your doing."

Catching up to him, Dorje asked, "What are you talking about?"

"She's staying two or three more weeks to study you Sherpas and will want you to translate."

"I knew nothing of this and have no time for her. You should make her go home."

"Won't happen. When Beth gets something in her head, she's tenacious as a pit bull and doesn't let go."

Not knowing the word *tenacious* or anything about pit bulls, Dorje intended to stay far away from this dangerous woman. "I am taking three Norwegians to Gokyo and over the Cho La to Everest Base Camp. She must watch after herself."

"We plan to marry when she returns home so I'm warning you. If anything happens to Beth, I'm coming back after you." Then Eric headed for the village leaving Dorje distraught but also more at ease. Since she'd given her heart to Eric, *The Sherpa* was no longer in danger of her stealing his.

The next morning, the ladies boarded after Eric following a final round of teary-eyed farewells. Dorje watched the plane roll down the dirt runway and then lift and soar before disappearing behind rows of hills that seemed to fade into nothingness. Feeling unsettled with too many people and emotions crowding into his life, he turned to the next strangers wondering what challenges they would bring. Eyeing the tall men in their early thirties, strong and eager looking, he sighed *easy trip* as he clasped his hands in a greeting. "*Namaste.*"

"*Namaste,*" they replied and he suddenly wondered what language they spoke. "Do you know English?" he asked, envisioning far fewer tips if they didn't.

"You have to if you're Norwegian," answered Kirk, a square-jawed man with a toothpick protruding from the corner of his mouth.

"Because when you come from a country of less than 4,00,000," added Royd, "you wouldn't have anyone to talk to otherwise." Dorje chuckled and immediately liked these Norwegians.

"Today we hike to Phakding and tomorrow to Namche for two nights," Dorje explained.

The Norwegian named Hamar was bouncing from one foot to the other. "When do we see Everest?" he asked eagerly.

"Not until tomorrow and only a short look."

"So why are we waiting? Where's the trail?"

When Dorje pointed the way, the man quickly took off, his large, awkward body appearing to move in sections rather than as one coordinated mass. As if in competition with him and each other, Royd and Kirk immedi-

ately followed at the fastest pace Dorje had ever observed in a foreigner.
Right behind them, Dorje kept shouting, "Go slowly. *Bistarai, bistarai*,"
but no one listened. Racing past smiling children who rushed out to greet
them, and past the terraced fields cloaked in muted shades of green, and
even past women thrashing millet, the Norwegians could be more trouble
than the ladies. Hamar, an unusually large man with his upper and lower
body constantly at odds, screamed and purposely bounced the first suspension bridge as if he were possessed by a *shrindi* ghost.

Scratching his cropped, red beard, Royd said, "He gets a little too
enthusiastic at times."

"To run across with such noise angers the river god. Bad things will
happen," Dorje grumbled.

Removing his toothpick, Kirk winked at Royd and slowly walked onto
the bridge composed of two iron-link chains hanging in a deep U. He
carefully sidestepped large holes in the rotted planks lining the bottom.
After four more such irreverent crossings, the group reached the base of
the 2,000-foot Namche hill. "Half way up is your first view of Everest,"
Dorje explained, trying to maintain his helpful-Sherpa demeanor.

"I'm there," Hamar announced and took off with long, loping strides.

Staying right with him, Dorje kept repeating, "*Bistarai, bistarai*, or
you will get sick."

"Not me." The Norwegian raced ahead but was soon stopping every
few minutes, breathing heavily with sweat pouring down his body.

He would have missed the viewpoint if Dorje hadn't muttered, "There
it is." The glow that spread across the man's face almost made it worth
putting up with him. And when Hamar's eyes watered, Dorje couldn't
resist liking this ungainly Norwegian who cried upon seeing his beloved
mountain. Hearing the others, Hamar quickly wiped his cheeks and gave
Dorje a look that begged silence.

Kirk and Royd arrived, glanced at the mountain, and doubled over
with their hands on their thighs, gasping for breath. Dorje stuffed the
desire to say *I warned you*. His ego riding a little higher, he announced,
"We must go," when the first large, wet, snowflakes began to fall.

Royd laughed and held his hand out, palm up. "Looks like we angered
your gods by not paying proper respect on the bridge."

Knowing they considered him an ignorant peasant and were mocking
him, Dorje kept his mouth shut and simply smiled. Arguing with tourists
didn't earn tips.

Snow fell during the rest of the climb and while they set up camp. Then
it stopped abruptly and the sun came out melting everything. After in-

structing the Norwegians that they would remain in Namche two nights in order to acclimate, Dorje left amid complaints of headaches and nausea. Perhaps now they would listen to him, but the satisfaction of being right diminished as soon as he left camp.

The scathing words he had flung at Mingma during their last meeting crawled out of the recesses where he had stuffed them. All quarreling was a sin and he had dishonored his father. Westerners spoke of a loving god who forgave sins and offered salvation, but the fate of Dorje's next reincarnation depended solely on the balance of merit (*sönam*) and guilt he accumulated in this lifetime. Every act of virtue added to his store of merit; every negative action decreased it. Before facing Mingma again, he needed to replenish his supply. At the end of May villagers would celebrate the Niungne rite to cleanse themselves of sin and earn *sönam,* but Dorje's soul was too edgy and restless to wait. To perform his own Niungne, he went to the great stone *chorten* and *mani* wall at the south end of the village and removed his hiking boots to show penance by walking barefoot as he circumambulated the wall clockwise three times. In the village temple, he sought forgiveness by reciting 21 prayers beginning with an invocation of the serpent deities of the four quarters and then paying respect to fierce, man-eating spirits. He asked that his mind and body become one with the great god Pawa Cheresi and obtain release from the effects of all sins. During the recitation, Dorje prostrated himself 90 times by kneeling and sliding his arms and hands along the floor until his forehead touched. Tomorrow, he would repeat the entire ritual and again the following morning before departing Namche with the Norwegians.

Taking deep breaths and exhaling slowly to expel any negative emotions about to erupt, he climbed the hill from the village center. "Father, I am humble before you," he began rehearsing a speech. "At our last meeting, I spoke too soon and out of anger. For that I am sorry. As your dutiful son, I will gladly marry Shanti." Pausing at the base of the final twisted, rock-strew path, he struggled with *humble* and *dutiful.* How could he sound convincing when his heart was ever proud and headstrong?

Reaching the lower room, he anticipated the warmth and odor of Droma Sunjo milking *naks* but found it strangely empty. He dismissed it, needing to focus solely on his contrite demeanor. "Lower your shoulders and bow your head," he told himself as he climbed the stairs. "Say, 'Thank you, my honorable father. I am forever dutiful and humble.'" Pausing on the landing outside the door, he tried to calm his stomach.

Facing the window, Mingma didn't acknowledge Dorje's presence even though he had surely seen him coming. His cousin Dawa made up for it as he did every time Dorje returned. The short squat body ambled across the room with its awkward tilting gait and pressed so close he seemed attached to Dorje. This proximity made Dorje uncomfortable but he'd given up trying to explain that to Dawa who simply didn't understand such things. With Droma Sunjo at the hearth preparing dinner, a private reconciliation wasn't possible and it was too late to turn back. Mingma was already striding across the room with an upraised arm and that damn loose sleeve waving like a vulture's wing. Anticipating a possible blow, Dorje gently pushed Dawa aside

"Must both of my sons betray me now?"

Dorje didn't know what was going on but the wrath in his father's eyes and voice implied that every grievance in the world was somehow his fault, and he resented the accusation. *Honorable, humble, and dutiful* wouldn't pass through his lips.

"You sold your soul to foreigners," Mingma said with his sleeve waving in Dorje's face. "And have corrupted your brother too. Four days now he hasn't brought the *naks* home in time for milking. And yesterday, Phuri from Khumjung returned my most valuable yak—the one that will bring the most rupees at market because of it prized light coat. He found it trying to reach grass on a dangerous ledge. If he hadn't intervened, I would have lost a second one in a few weeks. I'm not a rich man and won't tolerate this negligence."

At a complete loss but pleased he wasn't the target for once, Dorje promised to find his brother and take care of things. After a quick sweep through the village, he headed for the meadow and found the herd scattered all over the place and with some missing. "You catch me," from his brother's voice in English astounded him. Impossible. Nima, who had refused to learn a single word, was shouting to someone? Whipping around a boulder in Dorje's favorite shirt that showed off his muscles, giggling, and covered with grass, Nima stopped cold when spotting him.

"What are you doing?" Dorje growled.

Glancing nervously over his shoulder, Nima replied, "Just playing. It's boring up here with the yaks. You won't do it."

"Who are you talking to?"

"Just a friend."

"Who speaks English?" As the question left his mouth, Dorje glimpsed Beth racing around the boulder with a handful of grass and then darting back out of sight. Struck dumb, he wrestled with the words but they fell flat at his feet with no shape or meaning. "Huh. How? I…?"

Grinning, Nima brushed is shirt and pants off. "I met her four days ago. Isn't she wonderful?"

His face wrinkled in disbelief. "Much too old for you and going back home soon."

Nima rocked on his heels with a satisfied grin and combed his hair back. "Maybe not."

"For sure, yes. She's getting married soon."

Red with anger, Nima yelled, "You're lying. You don't know anything about her."

"I shared their camp for many days and just put her boyfriend on a plane in Lukla."

When Nima started pacing like their father, Dorje knew it was designed to infuriate him. "Why didn't she go too?"

"Because she wants to study us," Dorje answered, "like the Japanese who come to study our glaciers. We're just another hunk of ice."

Water forming in the corners of his eyes, Nima yelled, "That's not true. She likes me."

Dorje held his brother's arm to reassure him. "I know how you feel. I liked her too. She lets you think she cares, but it's only a way of amusing herself. Ask Pemba. He's seen it often and warned me of such things."

Nima jerked free, picked up a pile of fresh dung, and hurled it at Dorje. "You want her for yourself just like everything else. You go wherever you want, do whatever you want, and leave me to take care of the yaks. When I find someone who makes me happy, you want to take that away too."

"That's not fair. I tried to get you to come with me." Dorje reached for him again but Nima stayed out of reach with tears rolling down his freckled cheeks. "Father's right. You think only about yourself and don't care about us. You are no longer my brother." He turned and ran with Dorje behind him.

"You're wrong, Nima. Two legs of the same frog, remember?" Ignoring him, Nima left with Dorje's words hanging like dark, gloomy clouds. As Dorje realized this was the first time anything had come between them, an immense emptiness opened inside him.

Only a very powerful witch could have caused such pain and separated them. Dorje strode back to the rock where Beth had disappeared and found her sitting ashen-faced and slump-shouldered among a field of purple asters. Before he could amass enough scathing, biting words to spew at her, she said in a voice coming from deep inside, "I heard you fighting with Nima and know it was about me. I'm sorry for any problems I caused."

Temporarily disarmed, he had to bolster his anger and fire back. "Don't ever go near my brother again."

"I did nothing but spend several afternoons with a most pure and gentle spirit."

"You possessed his heart and made him fall in love with you."

She straightened up and slowly shook her head, eyes closed. "I only provided company to a lonely boy who wonders why his beloved brother has forsaken him."

"I've done no such thing and would never hurt Nima."

"Nor would I."

Dorje then accused her of being selfish and insensitive to his culture, all in self-defense against those poppy-blue eyes. He thought he had cleansed her from his heart, but being this close aroused that uncomfortable stirring in his loins again and he needed to escape. As a final shot, he told her to leave the Khumbu and never return. Before she could seduce him with any more words, he turned his back to her and headed for Khumjung in desperate need of fortifying his resolve by making love to Shanti that night.

Pacing outside her house until dark, Dorje waited another half hour after the butter lamps dimmed. As he tiptoed across the room, Shanti's father gave the usual cough announcing; *I know you're here.* That irritation plus all the negative feelings of the day dissolved the instant Dorje felt her warm, comforting body next to his. "I missed you so much," he whispered, burying his face in her silken, black hair to inhale every part of her being. "I want to celebrate our *dem-chang* as soon as possible and make you mine."

"I'm yours already. Now quit talking." Always playful, her giggling elicited a cough from across the room and Dorje had to kiss her to hush her. He made love with the same passion they had shared last summer and fell asleep wrapped tightly around her. She was his salvation.

CHAPTER FOURTEEN

Dorje left just before dawn after making love to Shanti again. Always ready to receive him, she was the perfect lover and they would have a good life together. As the darkness of night dissolved to gray, silhouettes emerged like goblins. In spite of their menacing appearance, Dorje felt indomitable strolling back into the Norwegian camp—confident of his immunity to Beth and his ability to make amends to both his father and brother.

His first test arrived when Beth approached him at breakfast wearing a blue top that matched her eyes and revealed her hard nipples in the cold morning air. "I know you're angry at me, but Nima was like the little brother I never had. Nothing more. I still need your help and won't leave until I'm finished."

Ready for her this time, Dorje announced, "I am taking three Norwegians to Gokyo and over the Cho La to Everest Base Camp. You must find someone else."

"But you're the only Sherpa in Namche who speaks good English. I'm willing to pay very well."

Using a foreigner's most powerful weapon, money, she was tempting him with visions of enough rupees for an early *dem-chang* with Shanti "How much?"

"Three times what they're paying if I come along too."

"That is too far, too difficult, too high for you, and they will not want a woman."

Arms folded firmly across her chest, she said, "Ask them."

So that's what *tenacity* meant. Dorje calculated the pay and decided it was enough for a grand *dem-chang*, one that would heap honor upon his father in the eyes of the villagers. For that reason alone, he would do it if the men agreed.

Royd peered around Dorje at Beth. "Hmmm, I wouldn't mind having a body like that to keep me warm going over the pass."

"You're always looking to get laid," grunted Hamar. "But I don't want her slowing us down. I came to see Everest and won't take the risk."

"He's right," added Kirk with the toothpick slowly traveling across his mouth as if it were a permanent appendage. "A woman would be a liability."

"What does *liability* mean?" Dorje asked.

"That she won't be able to keep up and will endanger our trip."

"And the three of you live at what elevation?" Beth interjected without being invited.

"Sea level," Hamar mumbled.

"Well, I come from Denver, a mile higher than you, and have climbed twenty Colorado peaks above 14,000 feet. So tell me who's better suited for high altitude?" A pit bull had them by the pant leg and they couldn't shake her off. Fifteen minutes later, all three threw their hands in the air and surrendered. She was going.

At least removing Beth from camp would allow Nima to resume his duties. The added promise of money for an early *dem-chang* should lighten Mingma's mood. Feeling less anxious now as he climbed the stairs, Dorje still paused on the landing to clear his throat and shake his arms out. He wanted to be casual and loose upon entering. Dawa's absence was a relief, but Droma Sunjo rarely left the house because of the goiter. Seated on the window bench, Mingma's intonations droned as usual.

Easing into the conversation, Dorje said, "Father, Nima was simply weary and regrets neglecting the herd. It will not happen again." Now the hard part—telling him of yet another absence. Approaching with drooped shoulders and bowed head, an unfamiliar bearing for him, Dorje continued, "It is auspicious that I marry soon. I spoke too quickly after hearing of the *södene* and regret my harsh words. I'm happy you chose Shanti and want to celebrate the *dem-chang* within a few months."

Mingma stiffened on the seat. "I can't afford it for at least two years."

Arching his shoulders back and raising his proud head, Dorje said, "But I can. In two weeks I will earn enough for a grand party that will honor our family."

"And what will you do to get this great fortune?"

Shifting his weight to the other foot, he avoided eye contact. "Take three Norwegians to Gokyo and over the Cho La to Everest Base Camp."

Mingma rose and slowly circled Dorje, studying his face. "You've done that before for less money. What else?"

"I will also be a translator," Dorje answered, trying to maintain a steady voice.

"For who?" Mingma was directly in front of him now with those dark eyes that tethered him as if he were a wayward yak.

Trying to quickly come up with another story, his brain failed him. "An American writing about Sherpas who will pay three times what Norwegians do to come along."

"Toe ye!" his father yelled and spit at Dorje's feet. "This American is even more reckless with money than the rest of them...to pay for words from a boy who knows nothing and has abandoned his beliefs." Mingma poured a cup of *chang* from the barrel on the far wall. "I will accept none of their rupees." He touched the beer with his sacred ring finger and sprinkled upwards three times repeating, "Che che," as an offering to the gods before taking his first drink of the day. Without another word, he simply exited the room and left Dorje reeling inside.

Peeling potatoes at the hearth, Droma Sunjo whispered, "Control your anger and give him time. He's a proud man."

Proud of what? Dorje felt like asking but didn't want to open the way for words that might temper his indignation. Instead he focused on Droma Sunjo pitying her isolation and loneliness. Remembering the red scarf from the bundle of clothes the old ladies had given him, Dorje carefully removed it from his pocket and draped it around her neck. "This is for you."

She closed her eyes, fingers trembling as she touched it.

"It's beautiful on you." A tiny smile stole across her face. He liked the way her mouth turned up, creating little tucks in her cheeks, and the way her eyes wrinkled at the corners. "You look pretty when you smile."

Giggling, she covered her mouth and peered at him over her hand. He figured no one had said that to her in a long while, if ever. Indeed, she did look pretty.

Droma Sunjo quietly slid a steaming cup of tea across the floor to him. Holding it, he warmed his fingers as he walked to the window. His resentment still simmering from the day he and Nima were forced to leave Namche fourteen years ago, Dorje understood conflict with Mingma but not with his brother. They had never suffered a rift. Dorje had always taken care of

Nima and his brother looked up to him. Making him cry yesterday was unforgivable and must be resolved. Climbing to the meadow and finding the animals scattered over the hillside again disappointed him. "Nima," he yelled. No answer. Dorje scrambled over rocks to bring those on the fringe closer to the herd before leaving to search for his errant brother.

Taking the stairs two at a time at Pemba's, he asked out of breath, "Have you seen Nima?"

"He was here, looking for her and angry at you. I've never seen your brother so upset." Pemba cleared the tourist table and set the cups behind a counter displaying beer and candy for sale. "Never thought anything could come between the two of you until she arrived."

"I don't need a lecture. Just tell me where he went."

"Don't know, but I suggest you find him soon."

If not on the mountain, where would he go? Surely, his brother wasn't foolish enough to return to the Solu or go to Kathmandu. Roaming through the village, Dorje finally ran into Nima coming out of the shop that sold used expedition gear with a sleeping bag draped over his shoulders and a thick pad under his arm. "What are you doing?" Dorje asked.

"Helping Beth get ready for her trip to Gokyo. I want to go too."

Having come to mend their hurt, Dorje wasn't prepared for this and knew he was reacting too quickly but couldn't stop the words. "Don't even think about it. You're staying here to help father."

"Not this time. You do it."

When Beth exited the shop, Dorje shouted, "What have you been telling him?"

"Only that I'm going to Gokyo. He wouldn't understand much more."

"Does he know you're going with me?"

"No."

"And why does he think he can accompany you?"

Agitation creeping into her voice, Beth answered, "I have no idea. Don't blame me for everything. Nima found me and I let him come along like a little brother."

Dorje was still mad at her for teasing him with her eyes and smiles but would not tolerate her toying with his brother's heart. "Can't you see he doesn't feel like your little brother? I told you to stay away from him."

"I've done nothing but make friends with a young Sherpa. Why don't you look at what your anger's doing to him."

The sweet, freckled face that had always adored and depended on Dorje now stared at him through glacier-cold eyes. Afraid of losing the one constant in his life, Dorje tried putting his arm around his brother's shoulder the way he did when walking together, but Nima recoiled. With the same icy stare, he asked, "What are you arguing about?"

With Nima in such an emotional state, Dorje didn't want to admit he was accompanying Beth so he lied knowing it was a sin he must atone for later. "I told her you want to go too, but she said it wouldn't work. She's traveling with three Norwegians. After Gokyo, they're going over the Cho La to the Everest Base Camp and will be gone too long. Father needs you here."

"So why can you walk away any time you please and I have to stay?"

Closing his eyes, Dorje let out a long, quavering breath and admitted a painful truth. "Because he already resents me, and I don't want him to turn against you too."

"You lie," Nima yelled, wrestling the sleeping bag off his shoulder and throwing it to the ground. His eyes brimming with tears, he glanced at Beth once more before running away.

"Don't, Nima," Dorje cried after him, feeling as though his insides had just been ripped out, but his brother never looked back. Dorje was bleeding and needed someone to blame. He turned on Beth ready to accuse her of being the most vile witch.

Her compassionate eyes and gentle voice diffused his anger once again. "I'm sorry if I'm the cause of all this. I really didn't understand but can see now how selfish I've been. I didn't have much fun growing up, and with Nima I felt like a child again. We were just two kids playing."

Remembering Pemba's warnings, Dorje didn't trust her words or the uneasiness he was experiencing standing this close to her. Needing to untangle the bits and pieces of emotion tied up inside so he could understand what he was feeling, he said, simply, "We leave after breakfast tomorrow. I will send a porter for your things."

Not having the courage to go home that night and face the brother who had twice run away in tears, Dorje hoped time would take care of things. With Pemba's out of the question because of Beth, he threw his sleeping bag on the floor of the dining tent next to snoring porters. It didn't matter. He couldn't have slept anyway, thinking about how he and Nima had always lain shoulder-to-shoulder and rump-to-rump, feeling the connection all the way down their bodies, keeping each other warm. Through everything, they had been inseparable, jumping and laughing, running barefoot along dirt paths. When their mother and her new husband, Kushang, took them to the Solu, three year-old Nima was scared and crying. From that moment, Dorje vowed he would always care for his younger brother. He gave him piggyback rides, played in the stream, and made up stories about a yak and mouse that were friends. And in the afternoon, he gathered leaves to make a soft place for Nima to nap while he squatted, elbows on his knees, chin in hands, watching and waiting for their father.

Dorje flipped to his other side and pulled the bag over his head to drown out what had mushroomed into a cacophony of lip-smacking snorts and wheezes. Maybe he never should have brought Nima home to the Khumbu. He was too innocent to resist the temptations of the outside world. Dorje laughed at himself. Maybe he shouldn't have come either, but there had been no other choice. It was here or Kathmandu and he'd heard too many stories of villagers moving to the capital with visions of great opulence and fortune only to end up starving on the streets. As a small boy, he had sensed there was something special inside him that couldn't thrive in the Solu. Lying on the tent floor, Dorje remembered what had finally driven him away.

After an oppressive heat that had hung over the village for months, his mother and stepfather rejoiced when the first big of drops of rain struck the ground and flattened into thin sheets of water pouring into every crack of the dry crust. Within a few days, the brown earth was transformed into softly waving fields of green. Later that week, the sky which had been a rich blue softly streaked by veins of mist all morning grew heavy with an ominous feel. Thick clouds scudded along the horizon, and suddenly lighting flicked its jagged tongue turning the backsides a pale gray. Then the torrent unlashed itself. Dorje, Nima, their mother, and her husband watched the land on which they had toiled all summer quickly turn to a quagmire of crops drowning in a sea of mud. Since their only hope was to save precious topsoil, they frantically created damns. Yet water cascaded over a hundred murky waterfalls causing the village terraces to lose their topsoil to the Hongu Khola that would ultimately carry it to India. Helplessly, Dorje stood watching months of backbreaking labor roll over his feet, ankle deep. There would be no fall harvest.

His mother picked up a tender rice shoot that hung lifeless across her finger. A rain swell struck her hand and washed the shoot away. "Must you take that too?" Dorje watched her trying to swallow the tears in her throat, but she couldn't contain the exhaustion and despair any longer. She began to sob, her shoulders heaving and falling with each gasp. Realizing he hadn't seen Nima for a while, Dorje found his little brother collapsed below a terrace with mud pouring over his face and his thin body shivering with cold. He lifted his brother in his arms and slowly slogged back to the house.

When the monsoon ended, they'd have to start over again this year and the year after that for the rest of their lives. He couldn't do it again and nor could Nima. They would leave in the fall when trails were passable again and the downed bridges had been repaired. Dorje begged his mother to come, but she claimed at thirty-five to be too old to start over. Ten years of struggling to survive on that pitiful plot of land had aged her. Once youthful and strong, she now walked bent forward under the weight of her doko, her gait slow and heavy and with her hands gripping the straps to ease the load. Even her feet revealed the toil. Her heels had grown thick and cracked from walking barefoot on the parched earth in the dry season and through ankle-deep mud during the monsoon.

Her image followed Dorje everywhere as Marty's father went with him. He would never forgive himself for leaving her and now wondered if he'd made a horrible mistake in bringing Nima here. Worse yet, maybe he should not have come himself. The air had the same ominous feel it did then.

CHAPTER FIFTEEN

Unable to sleep with so many thoughts racing through her head, Beth tried everything, even visualizing them stuffed in a box with the lid shut. Unfortunately within minutes, a corner rose and guilt about Nima slipped out and crawled down the side. Had she subconsciously flirted with him for some unknown reason? A boy six years younger? Surely not. She was simply experiencing the childhood she'd never had. Kick that one out of the way. From under another corner slid the anxiety specter about keeping up with those strong, healthy Norwegians. Get rid of that too. Coming from Colorado, she'd probably walk them into the ground. Beth beat her parka into a pillow, buried her face, and tried again. Then Eric demanded his time. Was he all right? Did he really understand her need to stay? When and where would they get married? Then there was the big question not so easily disposed of: did she really love him? That was a permanent poison-ivy-like itch under the skin. Beth pounded the parka again, pulled the sleeping bag over her head, and tried clearing her brain by picturing nothing but a wall of flat, blue ice. It worked intellectually. What kept her awake the next two hours was an unsettling sensation that had begun when she stood close to Dorje that afternoon.

The next morning when Dorje appeared instead of the expected porter, she momentarily forgot how to breathe. Pemba met him with an angry exchange, most likely a diatribe against this woman who destroyed lives. *Please don't listen to him,* Beth whispered to herself as her eyes traced the lean, muscular body of this twenty-year-old Sherpa genius.

"My bag is there," she said when he stood before her with a slight flush to his brown skin. She rose weak kneed and took a long, deep breath before heading out behind him. "Where are the others?" she asked when he took the trail north instead of returning to the Norwegian camp.

"I sent them ahead to take pictures with Everest behind them."

"Where we sat together that night," escaped unexpectedly, but she didn't care if he knew the memory lingered.

His mouth turned up in a roguish smile. "And were chased by a screaming yeti."

"Was there really a yeti or were you just teasing me?"

"You heard the yells and footsteps."

Yes, but they could have been anything, she thought. Rather than impose western skepticism on his beliefs, Beth changed the subject. "The Norwegians look strong and eager."

"But they are more trouble than the old ladies, especially the big one, Hamar."

Dorje unloaded her gear onto a Sherpani porter who was already carrying a huge duffle. Beth felt pathetic next to this hardy girl with a square face and dark almond eyes, an equal to any of the men whom Beth already considered super heroes.

"Here, take a group picture," Royd said handing the camera to Dorje before pulling Beth to the photo rock. Standing beside the Norwegians, she felt more allied with the Sherpas after being here this long. Royd told her to stand still, insisting on a picture with the Sherpani and *sirdar.* Her insides a bit quivery, Beth stood beside Dorje and took another deep breath. "Closer," Royd ordered, waving his hand. "And now, Dorje, put your arm around both girls," he added with no concept of cultural impropriety. Dorje obliged. The warmth of his hand sent a flush all the way through her. Another photo in blazing color.

Before departing, Dorje lectured the Norwegians about not straying from the trail, going *bistarai,* and drinking plenty of fluids. Beth wondered how many times he'd said the same thing and how many times foreigners who thought they knew it all had failed to listen. Hamar's seemingly disjointed body left first with arms and legs out of sync. The other two followed. Beth watched Dorje herding them to the uphill side of the path when a yak train approached. As he pointed out a pair of wild Asian goats and an Impeyen pheasant with its iridescent plumage, she became so immersed in Dorje's world that she momentarily forgot about Eric and home.

Intrigued by the Sherpani, Beth dropped back to walk with her and learned that Lhamu lived in Khumjung. Although that was extent of their verbal conversation, Lhamu's expressions suggested a young woman full of life. At the first rest stop, she leaned back with her basket resting on a rock shelf designed to take the weight off porters' backs forcing them to remove the *doko*. When Hamar shambled over and offered her a bottle of water, the Sherpani giggled with a smile flirtatious enough to drop the strongest man to his knees. Tipping her head back, she drank by pouring rather than touching the bottle to her lips. Then she offered some to Beth who gladly accepted, having been too caught up in thoughts of Dorje to bring enough that morning. When Hamar's companions yelled at him to come, he reluctantly departed. Even more fascinated now, Beth pointed to Lhamu and Hamar with a questioning look of attraction. The young woman rolled her eyes in a *yes* and astounded Beth by indicating the same about her and Dorje. How could she know? Caught completely off guard, Beth smiled and rocked her head slowly from side to side forming a bond between two women who shared a secret.

When they reached Sanasa where Tibetan refugees were selling jewelry and wool, Royd insisted on shopping. Waiting for them, Beth unconsciously ran her thumb over the empty ring finger. Eric's purchase here a week ago was too tight and uncomfortable, or maybe it was just the idea of marriage that was a little too snug. She should be missing him more right now. Observing how Lhamu's eyes followed Hamar, Beth realized she rarely looked at Eric that way. He was comfortable and supportive but didn't elicit the same response as this hulking, lumbering man who offered to carry part of the Sherpani's load. Smiling, Lhamu wiggled her hands side-to-side, palms down.

"It means no," Beth explained. "She's probably afraid of not getting paid."

"Now look who wants to get laid," Royd said nudging Kirk in the ribs.

After an angry look at his companions, Hamar started out with Lhamu, both of them chatting and neither understanding a word. Suddenly realizing their departure, Dorje ran after the pair to turn them back because they had missed the left-hand trail out of Sanasa. Instead of dropping to Phunki Tenga and crossing the Dudh Kosi to Tengboche, he intended to remain on the west side of the river all the way to Gokyo and visit the monastery on the way down.

Curiosity about Hamar and Lhamu gave Beth an excuse to walk with Dorje and ask about Sherpa marriage customs in order to continue her research.

While climbing a steep ridge, he explained in a limited vocabulary what she paraphrased in her notes. Parents arranged most marriages and the first step was a *sodene,* or asking, where the boy's father presented *chang* to the girl's family. Acceptance meant the couple was engaged and could sleep together, but both were still free to have other relations. Children born to them were illegitimate, but no one considered it a disgrace. The second step, the *dem-chang* or beer tying, put the relationship on firmer footing even though the couple continued to live with their parents. Since it required a great outlay of cash, the ceremony generally didn't occur until several years later. Although the partners still had no exclusive rights, children were considered legitimate. The third step, the *zendi* or final wedding rite, might not occur for several more years because it required an even greater expenditure. After the *zendi*, if either partner strayed, the other was entitled to collect a fine from the person known to have slept with his or her spouse.

Hearing about the sexual freedom and long periods between rites, Beth wondered how anyone reached the third step and if they stayed married. She explained divorce and asked if such a thing existed in his culture. After having rambled on so fast she could barely take notes while walking, he grew silent. His fluid gait turned awkward as if his mind and body were no longer communicating. She had touched something deep inside and for once had enough sense to leave it alone.

"My parents divorced when I was five," she said, deflecting the subject from him. He merely glanced at her before moving forward as if needing to speak to the Norwegians. Left alone, Beth hiked accompanied only by memories of her fifth Christmas Eve. For weeks, her mother had spent the days slumped in a chair with the curtains drawn, one cigarette dangling from her fingers with long ashes about to fall, another still smoldering in the tray. In a dirty robe tied loosely at the waist, eyes red and swollen, no makeup, hair unwashed, she just stared for hours. At times like this, Beth tried coaxing her out into the sunlight. That failing, she made up silly stories to make her mother laugh, but nothing worked. It was the same day after day. Alone and feeling her childish helplessness, Beth played by herself waiting for her father to come home.

Arriving later than usual he picked her up and swung her in circles with her head back and arms out to the side. "How's my sweetheart? Have you been good?"

"Yes, very, very good so Santa will bring me presents." She giggled and wrapped her arms around his neck, playing with his thick, black hair as he carried her to the living room.

He stood before her mother with Beth's cheek pressed against his warm, light-brown skin. "You could have at least dressed for tonight. It's Christmas Eve, for God's sake."

Hands clenched with restless fingers, her mother cried, "You don't understand how hard it is, how hard I try."

"You're right. I don't get it. And now I suppose you're drinking again?"

"No. I promised I wouldn't."

He set Beth down and gave her a kiss on the forehead. "Go, Sweetheart, it's time for bed. The sooner you sleep, the sooner Santa can come."

Afraid of the angry words and yelling about to erupt, Beth wanted to leave but her stomach ached from not eating all day. "I'm hungry."

He glanced at the clock and back at her mother. "Eight thirty and you haven't fed your daughter? Get out of the damn chair and go fix something." When her mother didn't move, he yanked her out and a bottle hit the floor. "You goddamn liar. Twice I've spent a fortune trying to dry you out and this is what I get?" He grabbed the bottle and another from behind the seat cushion, marched to the kitchen, and began pouring their contents down the drain.

"No," she screamed, running after him. "Those are mine. You can't do that."

"The hell I can't. I'm sick of this crap. I can't keep going through this. Not again." When she grabbed for the bottle, he threw it in the sink where glass shattered. "I'm getting rid of every damn drop in this house if I have to tear the place apart. Where are you hiding it? In the toilet tank like last time?" He flung open the cabinets and swept his arm across the shelves knocking dishes and glasses on the floor, exposing hidden bottles. Tears running down her cheeks, Beth covered her ears.

"Bastard!" Her mother rushed at him with a skillet, swung, and grazed his head.

Reeling against the counter, he yelled, "You're insane, a mad woman. And if I stay here any longer, I'll go crazy too. That's it. I'm done with it. I can't take this anymore."

"I know there's another woman. If you leave, I'll take everything you've got and you'll live on dog food the rest of your life."

"I'd eat maggots before spending another night in this house." He went to the bedroom, threw a suitcase on the floor, and started packing while Beth watched in horror.

Her mother ran at him, screaming, her fists raised. "You can't leave me."

"Watch me." When she struck him, he grabbed her wrists and held them, glaring at her. "Careful, woman."

"Go ahead, hit me, hit me!"

After pushing her away, he threw clothes into the suitcase until it barely closed. From the dresser, he unloaded socks and underwear into a paper sack and retrieved a few toiletries from the bathroom. Standing in the bedroom doorway with the most awful pain in her stomach, Beth watched the person she loved most in the world preparing to abandon her. When he headed for the door, she barred it with her thin five-year-old body and cried, "Daddy, please don't go. Don't leave me."

"I'll come back for you in a few days, Sweetheart. You're my beautiful, special girl." He lifted her and held her tight as he whispered, "We'll go explore the world together, just the two of us. Okay?"

Lips trembling, Beth looked into his dark brown eyes and nodded. Nausea shot acid-tasting into her throat as she watched him haul clothes out to the car, slam the door, start the engine, and drive away. Remembering that night, Beth was again on the verge of tears as she caught up to the others waiting at the crest of a 13,000-foot ridge. A change in weather distracted them and saved her from embarrassment.

"Snowing again?" Hamar exclaimed and tipped his head back, flicking his tongue.

"It does not matter," said Dorje. "It will melt by afternoon."

"What's a little snow to you anyway," teased Kirk with his toothpick traveling across his mouth left to right. "We've probably endured more of it than anybody here."

Grumbling, Royd pulled a wool cap out of his daypack and zipped his jacket to the collar. "You'd better be right. I didn't come here to freeze to death."

They quickly descended 1,000 feet to the river and set up camp as soon as the porters arrived with tents. Beth spread her sleeping bag out on the pad and wadded some clothes into a pillow because she would need her parka tonight. Dorje was right about the snow stopping and rapidly melting, but it would be her first time alone in the tent without a warm body to snuggle next to. She missed Eric's emotional and physical warmth but questioned whether that was enough to create an enduring relationship.

Since the days were growing shorter, they finished dinner around 4:00 p.m. as night smothered them in darkness. The Norwegians retreated to their sleeping bags to read by flashlight. Thirty feet away, porters crowded around a small fire, smoking *bidis* and casting occasional glances at Beth sitting on a large rock before the main cook fire, hugging herself. She should run to the tent as the Norwegians had, but Dorje was still about and she badly needed a connection tonight. The shadows stretched long and thin, and indigo hues deepened as daylight waned over the hills. As the fire turned to embers, Beth shivered and tucked her arms tighter.

A sleeping bag dropped around her shoulders and Dorje uttered in a matter-of-fact tone, "This will keep you warm."

Wondering if he spoke merely as a *sirdar* taking care of a client or a man with feelings for a woman, she said, "Sit with me."

"I cannot." Turning his back to her, he added wood to the fire and started to leave.

"No, wait. Don't go away. It's early yet." Feeling very much alone and sad, she desperately wanted him to remain. "We didn't finish our discussion. Do you remember my last question this afternoon?"

He waited so long to respond that she was about to repeat it when a reluctant voice answered, "Yes. My parents had a divorce too."

Realizing that he had probably struggled all day with what to tell her, Beth wanted to take his hand and say she understood but didn't dare. "Please sit and tell me about Sherpa divorce…for my story, of course."

Standing with his toe digging at the dirt, Dorje said, "Before the Chinese closed the border my father traveled every year to Tibet to trade *zopkios* and *zhums* for small horses that he took to India to trade for silk, brass, tea, and spices. The year that I was six, he was many months late returning. My mother usually sang and laughed like birds in the trees. Now that her husband was home at last, she was quiet. I watched her making *chapattis* and didn't understand. My father said the snow was much deeper this year and taking 80 animals over the Nangpa La had been difficult. 'No more excuses,' my mother told him. 'I know enough.'"

"What did she know?"

"I was too young to understand," he answered and turned toward her. "Nima and I slept on the floor not far from our parent's bed. He was only three and fell asleep but I was too excited about Father being home to let go of his voice yet. I heard them moving under the blankets and my mother said something in a voice that sounded like it was drowning inside her and my father came back hard and cold. They threw words at each other, words that had no meaning for me." He squatted to stir the fire and rested his arms crossed over his knees, staring straight ahead. Neither of them speaking for a long while, Dorje finally added, "A week later, all of my mother's family arrived one morning. The men took their seats on the window bench and the women sat on the floor. My father poured glasses of *chang* for everyone. My insides that had been all tied up like this," he said, knotting his hands to show her, "finally relaxed. Everybody was laughing and smiling. The anger between my parents had gone away and I was happy."

"I'm glad." Feeling the connection she had sought and wanting him closer, Beth opened the bag. "Come sit and get warm."

As though lost in his own memories, Dorje didn't move but continued with a slight snag in his voice. "But then my father stood in the middle of the room, holding a glass of *chang*, and said things that hurt in my child's brain. I kept shaking my head and crying, but his words wouldn't go away."

"What words?"

"He said that he and my mother were no longer married and that he was no longer their son-in-law. To show that they were breaking apart, he stretched a thread between himself and her brother and asked her father to cut it. I watched the ends of the thread drift slowly to the floor and felt they had cut me in two. I could not believe this was happening. Someone had made a terrible mistake. I yelled, 'Stop it! Stop it!' but no one listened. They drank more *chang* like nothing had happened, visited a few minutes, and left. I searched my parents' faces. What did this mean?"

Hearing the pain in his voice and wanting to rescue him from embarrassment just as the weather had done for her, Beth interrupted with a neutral reporter's question. "Is this how Sherpas get a divorce?"

He was rubbing his hands down his thighs over and over, his voice thin. "Yes. The ceremony is called *nia-tongu* and it means to get rid of a problem in a bad marriage. The wife must give her husband one rupee to pay for the beer his father brought during the *sodene*."

"And that's it? A much better way than ours where everyone hates each other and fights."

"There is more. My father was on the bench with Nima beside him carving trails in the thick wool rug with his fingers. And my mother stood at the window like she was waiting for someone. My stomach got all tied up again when a man entered wearing loose trousers and a shirt. The heavy folds in his lids made them look like snake eyes. I did not like him. He walked across the room to my father and laid some rupees on the low table. My father picked them up and both men bowed to each other. Then they sat drinking *chang* and talking."

"What was that all about?"

As Dorje gazed at her with his dark brown eyes, her heart skipped a beat. "If a man wants to marry another man's wife and she agrees, he must pay her husband a fine."

"And can a wife claim a fine if another woman wants to marry her husband?"

"No. A man has the right to bring a second wife into his house."

She couldn't resist entering the door he had opened. "And what does your wife think of that?"

His body jerked upright. "I have no wife. Who told you this?"

"Nima. While we were in the shop, he said Dorje *zendi*."

"My brother likes you too much and does not want you to think I am free."

"And are you?" slipped out before she could grab it to examine the consequences of what she was asking.

"My father promised me to a girl named Shanti. With money from this trip, I will soon have the *dem-chang*."

Beth wanted to retreat and crawl inside herself because now there was a name attached to this faceless woman she'd been envisioning. "So we are both engaged," she said, trying to comprehend fully her own feelings.

The fire had reduced to embers and the air was biting cold. It was late by Sherpa standards, although probably no more than 6:00 p.m. At home, she and Eric would not have begun dinner or would be on their way to the theatre. Here she was confused and shivering in the dark. She needed time to sort her feelings and certainly couldn't keep her head on straight with him only two feet away. "I should go to bed now, and where will you sleep?"

He nodded towards the large tents. "With the porters."

"I can't imagine sleeping in such a pile of snoring humanity."

"It is warm there."

He waited until she was in her tent and had zipped the door shut. Shivering with her sleeping bag pulled up over her head and ears, she lay questioning what on earth she was doing. If Dorje had asked to join her in the tent, she would have been tempted—and that was insane. Being this far from home was no excuse for her behavior. She was marrying Eric in a few months, and Dorje was betrothed to this woman named Shanti. The intellect that had always ruled her life, and done so quite nicely, said to stay miles away from him. But her emotions were crying out for more.

CHAPTER SIXTEEN

Walking to the porter's tent, Dorje wondered how he could be so aroused in this cold, but when she asked where he would sleep tonight, he had sprung to life. What did she mean by that and the three offers for him to sit with her and even share the warmth of her bag? Probably just bored or lonely without Eric and wanting a Sherpa to play with. Knowing this, it still took every bit of self-control not to move onto that rock and wrap himself up or follow her into the tent. As Dorje looked for the best place to squeeze among the porters, he wondered how it would feel to make love. He'd never be bold enough to suggest it. Instead he would lie here awake all night recalling every word and movement, wondering why he had told her things he'd never shared with anyone, not even Shanti.

The next morning, Dorje wished he hadn't taken this job, sensing the Norwegians would be a problem to the end. The pay was good, however, and it meant ten days with Beth. He could put up with anything, even knowing she would break his heart when she left just as Pemba had warned. At breakfast he could hardly take his eyes off her and when she looked up at him, his entire being resounded. Every muscle and cell desired her. Needing to concentrate on something else, he watched Kirk push his eggs from one side of the plate to the other and finally shove it all out of the way and drop his forehead to the table, almost jamming the toothpick through the roof of his mouth.

"What's wrong with him?" Dorje demanded, taking advantage of the distraction.

"It's called a hangover," explained Royd.

Dorje glanced at Beth who explained, "It means he drank too much and feels lousy."

"You should not drink up this high." Dorje next turned on Hamar and Royd. "And you two go *bistarai* today or you will be as sick as he is."

Royd removed an aspirin from his pocket and took it with tea. "Norway's covered with rugged mountains and glaciers. I've walked them all my life and know what I'm doing."

"How high are your mountains?"

"The highest is only 8,100 feet," Kirk moaned. "Lower than we landed at Lukla. Plus we all live at sea level."

Point made, Dorje removed their plates and announced they would depart in half an hour. They climbed a steep, forested slope on the left bank of the river with waterfalls cascading from above and then passed through groves of rhododendron and birch trees with occasional glimpses of Cho Oyu at 26,748-foot on the Tibetan border. When they reached timberline at 13,175 feet, it started snowing again. Frustrated by the weather, Dorje looked around for Hamar.

"He and Lhamu were right behind us awhile ago," Royd said.

Angry at himself for being so absorbed with Beth that he could lose track of someone that large, Dorje grumbled, "Wait here," and charged back down the hill. He returned twenty minutes later with a wet Norwegian in tow. "He was trying to drink from the river and fell in. I warned you the first day to only drink boiled water or you will get sick. Why don't you listen?"

"We ran out," Hamar complained. "Lhamu needed some too."

"More trouble," Dorje grumbled to himself as he started up the hill. They climbed four more ridges and finally looked down on Machhermo spread out in the wide valley below. By the time they made camp that afternoon, all signs of snow had disappeared and Dorje hoped they were done with it. During afternoon popcorn, biscuits, and tea, Beth asked about the three small stone buildings.

"This is a *yersa*," Dorje explained. "We bring animals here to graze during the warm summer months while the lower meadows rest."

"And people actually live in those places?" Royd asked disgustedly wrinkling with his face like a desiccated old potato.

Dorje wanted to grab the man by his short red beard and shake him for disparaging his culture in front of Beth, but no Sherpa would carry out such a violent act against a tourist. So he gritted his teeth and donned his customary affable smile. Beth must have sensed his anger because she intervened with, "Can I go inside one to describe it for my story?"

To go with her would challenge his composure; to not go was impossible. He wished Pemba were here to get him through moments like this. Taking a long, shaky breath, he tried to send the field mice scurrying back to their burrows and answered, "Yes." Hands in his pockets, he casually walked to the hut furthest from camp, removed the block wedged behind the door handle, and opened it. Entering first to check things out, he tapped the low header reminding her to duck. The room was chilly and dark with only the light of two small, shuttered windows.

With her arms folded over her chest, Beth walked further inside. "It's just a much smaller version of Pemba's."

"With the same soot on the ceiling," Dorje said, coming up behind her. "From the smoke," he whispered, inhaling the aroma of her hair.

She went to the window bench covered with yak-wool rugs. "Where do you sleep?"

"Where you are sitting or on bamboo mats on the floor."

Arm resting on the sill, Beth twined a finger in her hair and gazed at him with her lips parted slightly in a smile. A slow tingling sensation crawled up his neck and spread across his face. *Don't go there*, he told himself as he took a step forward.

Suddenly a noise came from outside and Royd entered, banging his head on the doorjamb. "Jesus," he said rubbing it. "You guys are all too short."

"Or maybe you're too tall and don't know how to duck," Beth said and winked at Dorje. He smiled back and the field mice rejoiced.

Later as the sun lowered casting a pale haze on the mountains, the temperature dropped precipitously at 14,500 feet. Immediately after dinner, the Norwegians sought the warmth of their bags and the porters and cook staff piled into their tents. "I'm not used to going to bed at 4:30 p.m.," Beth said, her teeth chattering. "But I guess above timberline we don't have wood for a fire."

"We have to save what little we carried for cooking," Dorje explained. "We will use kerosene going over the Cho La."

"Guess I'd better crawl into my tent, but I was hoping we could talk more like last night."

The field mice sat up, their ears perked and tails twitching. Dorje didn't want her to leave but wasn't bold enough to suggest joining her. "We could bring both bags out here and try to stay warm."

"Uhhh, huhh," she said, her teeth hitting so hard he could hear them.

"Wait here. I will get yours." He raced to her tent to retrieve the bag, unzipped it, draped it tightly around her shoulders, and then ran for his.

They sat on a rock inches apart, wrapped in their bags. "Have you been this high before?" he asked

"Yyyesss," she answered, shivering. "We have 54 peaks above 14,000 feet in Colorado but I've only hiked to the top during the day, stayed an hour at most, and come down. Nothing like this."

"Sleeping high is what makes foreigners sick, and the Norwegians don't listen to me."

Moving a little closer, Beth observed, "Kirk's already coughing and Royd's chugging aspirin like candy."

When she gently leaned against him, the mice raced in circles and bounced off walls. Trying to ignore them, Dorje said, "And that fool Hamar drank stream water. Tomorrow will not be a good day."

"Did you come here to graze animals in the summer?"

He could simply say *yes* and let it pass or relate the worst moment of his life. By continuing to talk, he was less likely to respond to her touching his side. He sent the field mice scampering to their holes and with a tremulous breath began the rest of the story, confident she would understand the emotions of a six-year-old.

"While Father and snake-eyes, Kushang, drank *chang*, my mother packed her clothes in a *doko*. I was afraid she would leave with this awful man. Then she put my clothes and Nima's clothes in another *doko*. 'No!' I screamed and pulled them out of the basket. Holding them tight to my chest and swinging side to side, I would not let loose. But Mother said the clothes had to go, that we had to go. 'Not without *baabu.*' I cried. Every day for six months I had waited by the trail for my father to come back from Tibet and I was not going to lose him again. He was the most important thing in my life. I dropped to the floor, face down, and curled in tight ball. When mother tried to lift me, I yelled and swung at her. That made Nima start crying."

"We're so helpless when we're young," Beth said as she slid her hand inside the bag and took his. "It's the most terrifying feeling in the world."

Not nearly as terrifying as the feel of her soft, white skin. Disturbed, his words stumbled over themselves on the way out. "Mother, no I mean Father, no Mother yelled at him to come get me. I tried digging myself into the floor so he couldn't pull me out, but Father was too strong. He picked up a screaming, kicking boy and carried him to the bench where he held me in his arms saying, 'It will be all right, Dorje.' But it was not all right. I grabbed his robe and buried my face in it. 'Promise me that you will always be brave,' he whispered. 'And promise you will always take care of Nima. He is not strong like you.' I was trembling and clinging to him. When Mother touched my back and said it was time to go, I wrapped my legs around Father and held on. When she touched me again, I swatted her hand away."

"Didn't you like your mother?" Beth asked holding his hand tighter.

"Yes, yes. I loved her but I could not leave him. He was everything. Father reached for Nima crying beside him and held us both in his arms. 'You are going to live with your mother and Kushang,' he said. Then his voice caught like a piece of cloth snagging on a branch, and I knew he was sad too. 'She loves you both very much and will take good care of you,' Father said. I shouted that I was not going. I would stay here with him. He could take care of me. 'I am sorry,' he said, 'but this is how it has to be.' I yelled that was not how it had to be. Father lifted me higher and held my face to his. His cheek was hot and wet; his arms were trembling. He whispered, 'Don't ever forget how much I love you. I will come see you as often as I can. I promise.'"

Beth was gently rubbing the back of his hand causing Dorje to break out in a sweat. "A promise never kept, I think."

"Never," Dorje uttered from the darkest part of his heart. "Father put me down and stared at me through wet eyes. 'You have to go now.' I dug my bare heels into the floor while Kushang dragged me out the door. Father told me to be brave and offer prayers every day. And then I was gone."

Beth was shuddering uncontrollably now and it scared him. Remembering the *mikaru* who almost died two years ago from what they call hypothermia, Dorje's *sirdar* instincts overrode all else. This was business. Knowing she would never get warm enough with just her bag, he rose and said, "Stand up. You must get warm before you go to your tent alone." Facing her, Dorje extended her bag around him and told her to hold it closed behind his back. He did the same with his, creating a double layer to trap body heat. "Is that better?"

"Much. You feel good."

You feel good summoned every tail-twitching, whiskered creature in Nepal to run amok inside. When she nestled against him with their bodies flush, he was lost and gave up all hope of saving himself. His mouth next to her ear, such things he wanted to whisper but didn't dare.

She spoke first. "When was the next time you saw your father?"

"Not until ten years later when I came back to Namche," he murmured with the aroma of her hair permeating his entire being.

When she ran her free hand through the back of his hair, he leaned into it like a cat longing to be rubbed. "I waited at the window every night for years," she whispered so close he felt her the warmth of her breath on his cheek. "But my father never came back as he promised."

Not wanting to let go of her, Dorje had to keep talking. "I know about waiting. Every evening in the Solu at age six, seven, and eight, I ran to the end of village looking for a man in a Tibetan robe with long, black hair tied back in a ribbon."

"Then that was your father in the market place," Beth said pulling back to look at him.

"Yes." In the moonlight, his eyes traced her nose and lips. How he yearned to kiss them. When he continued, Beth buried herself in his warmth again. "At nine, I watched for him every afternoon while I hauled firewood from the forest two miles away. So certain that he would come, I glanced at the road every time I raised a stick over my head to beat the grain. At ten, eleven, and twelve, I looked for him while I threshed millet in the winter, barley in the spring, wheat in summer, and collected rice and maize in the fall. But by thirteen, I was angry and used to stand in the middle of the field yelling at him. 'You lied. You never came. You do not care if we are sick or hungry…or dead! You do not love us!'"

Her fingers toyed with the hair along his neck. "Are you still angry?"

"I don't want to be, but it always gets in the way when I am with him. Before leaving Mother I promised I would try to look past my anger, but I fail every time."

"I watched your father with Pemba at the market. He's not like other Sherpas. He has what we call a presence that is intimidating."

"What does this word mean?" he whispered into her hair.

"A bit frightening."

Still shivering but not as violently, she seemed content so he didn't want to risk doing or saying anything to alter that. After a long silence, Beth murmured, "I thought about my mother while hiking today. She was frightening too but in a different way. The night my father left, a noise woke me. It was a holiday we celebrate where children believe a man called Santa will bring presents. Thinking it was the puppy I had asked for and he was scared in a strange place, I slid my legs over the side of the bed and dropped to the cold floor. I was so eager to see him that I forgot to put slippers on. The living room was dark except for twinkling Christmas lights. 'Here, Puppy,' I whispered, tiptoeing toward the tree. 'Don't be afraid.' Something wet squeezed between my toes and I giggled thinking my puppy had peed on the floor. My eyes were finally used to the dark, so I knelt to check how much mess I'd have to wipe up. That's when I saw her lying only a foot away, her arm stretched out. 'Wake up,' I said. 'You shouldn't sleep here.' I shook her but she didn't move. Now my knee was moist too and I saw it wasn't pee but blood oozing from her wrist. I was all alone and scared so I ran to the next house and banged on the door until the old man answered. 'Mommy's hurt,' I cried. He told his wife to watch me while he checked. Fifteen minutes later, a loud siren screamed in the night and a red light kept flashing through the curtains onto the wall. I wanted to go see but his wife made me stay inside. Climbing onto a chair, I watched through the window as men in white coats hurriedly pushed my mother down the walk on a cart. Her body was limp and not moving. I was certain she was dead. When they loaded her into the ambulance, closed the door, and drove away, I started sobbing thinking both parents had left me that day."

Feeling her tremble and her breathing change, Dorje knew she was crying. He leaned back and gazed at her. "Did she die?"

Beth sniffed her tears back inside. "No. But she had tried to kill herself and everyone kept saying how lucky it was I found her. I became my mother's keeper that night and was always afraid I wouldn't find her the next time."

Dorje held her. The woman he had feared wasn't a witch but a lonely little girl who had related her worst night too. Sharing such emotional intimacy gave him courage. An orange gibbous moon had risen over the 20,000-foot peaks surrounding Machhermo. Gazing at her skin that glowed like white silk in the light, he gently wiped a tear away. Sensing no resistance, he took a chance and gently brushed his lips against her cheek. When he felt her breath catch and she melted into him, he slowly kissed the nape of her neck, her ear lobe, her eyes. Feeling her heart beating rapidly against his chest, he lightly ran his finger along her lips and held her for their first embrace. Her lips parted easily, inviting him to explore, and her tongue was warm, sensual, and full. She tasted sweeter than the precious Himalayan honey gathered from the highest cliffs. Wanting her to know how much she aroused him, Dorje slid his other hand down her back and pressed her to him. With a sudden inhale, she threw one arm around his shoulder and the other around his waist and kissed him with a passion greater than he'd ever experienced before.

Untended, both bags had fallen to the ground. Beth noticed first. Teeth chattering again, she threw her head back and laughed. "At least our feet are warm."

He gathered the bags and wrapped his cherished butterfly back in her cocoon with him. For another hour in the moonlight, they stood nestled in each other's arms, kissing, laughing, hugging, kissing, laughing again until Royd shouted to be quiet and let everybody else get some sleep around here.

"He is jealous," Dorje whispered in her ear.

A temperature drop of another ten degrees persuaded Dorje and Beth to go to bed. After making sure she was zipped up to her chin, he zipped the door and headed to the porter tents. Tomorrow they would be at the Gokyo *yersa* at with five huts spread fairly far apart and a supply of dried dung left from summer. He would suggest everyone move inside and build small fires. And he would offer to light Beth's.

CHAPTER SEVENTEEN

The next morning, it seemed everyone in camp was aware of the sleeping-bag tryst. Beth only wished she'd given them more to gossip about. If Dorje had asked to stay when he took her to the tent, she wouldn't have hesitated a second. Of all the men she had dated, no one kissed her the way he did. Certainly not Eric. With all his fine qualities and creative talents, economic potential, and undying love for her, Eric simply didn't stir things up inside and make her feel totally alive. She'd been clothed in a shroud of sadness since childhood with only momentary glimpses of light, and now suddenly the sun was blinding. Maybe it was the altitude or exotic setting and foreign culture. Whatever the cause, when she looked at Dorje this morning, nothing mattered except being with him. Her ever-rational-self whispered, *You're crazy. It can't possibly work*, but she didn't care. It was the happiest she'd ever been and that was good enough for now.

Since everyone had retired at 4:30 the night before, they all rose early with the Norwegians eager to set out for Gokyo and climb the peak that would afford an unobstructed view of Everest from the west. Camp broke at 6:30 and they began the four-hour trek by climbing a mountainside to the ridge encompassing a view of Cho Oyu and the mountains surrounding the Ngozumba Glacier, the longest in Nepal. After a gentle descent to its terminus, they hiked along the rough, rocky moraine above the boulder-strewn surface of the glacier. They reached the first small lake and then a second at the junction with the path that crossed over the Cho La.

Finally arriving at a large, emerald-green lake, the party walked along its eastern bank past a *mani* wall to the Gokyo *yersa* at 15,583 feet. Empty and cold, the stone huts with slate roofs stood waiting for young herders to arrive during the summer monsoon. Stone walls divided the barren, rocky landscape into parcels. Dorje explained that in the spring and summer thousands of alpine flowers surrounded the lake in a carpet of delphiniums, gentians, poppies, germaniums, asters, wild roses, saxifrage, potentilla, buttercups, bellflower, primula, colorful dwarf rhododendron shrubs, mint, and other low-growing plants trekkers hadn't identified for him yet.

Pointing to the peak rising above the northern edge of the lake, he said, "We will rest here today and climb Gokyo Ri tomorrow for the best view of Everest in all the Khumbu."

"Looks simple enough just walking up a long hill," said Kirk. "How long does it take?"

"Two to three hours up."

"And a lot faster down," Hamar shouted, his whole body swaying like an elephant's trunk. "I want to go now."

"No. You will get sick going too high too soon. We came 1,000 feet already and that is another 2,000."

Royd checked his watch. "It's only 10:30 a.m. I don't want waste an entire day just sitting around in this god-forsaken place."

Wanting to smack the Norwegian on the side of the head, Beth glanced at Dorje who signaled it was okay with a small, downward motion of his hand. "You can go to bed early and rest for tomorrow," he told Royd.

"Bed at 4:30 again," Royd muttered, "because it's too damn cold to stay out here unless of course you're sharing someone else's body heat."

"I agree," said Kirk. "We've got good weather. Let's use it. Who knows what tomorrow will be like. It's snowed twice already."

"Only very little," argued Dorje. "That happens many times and it means nothing."

"The point is, I don't want to sit around here all day and do nothing," said Royd.

"You could read, write, or play cards," Beth suggested, managing to restrain the angry words lined up on her tongue.

"Boring," said Hamar who hadn't stopped swaying and fidgeting since they arrived. "I'm going up," he added and took off with his curious shambling gait.

"Me too," said Royd. "Dorje, if it's too much elevation gain for you, just wait here and keep Beth company. I'm sure you'll find some way of entertaining yourselves." Royd motioned to Kirk. "Coming with us?"

Twirling the toothpick in the corner of his mouth, he answered, "Sure, why not."

Dorje threw both hands up in frustration as the three headed out on stepping-stones in the small stream flowing into the lake. "I have to go with them," he told Beth, "but you stay here."

"I'd probably do better than they will since I've been here longer and live higher."

"I do not want you to get sick too. Stay and tell the porters not to set up tents because we will use the huts tonight. There is some dried dung for fires. Now I will show the Norwegians what a real mountain is like instead of those hills they are proud of."

When they disappeared from view, Beth gave a giant shrug and flapped her arms at her sides. *Oh my. What to do?* Standing alone in a cold, rocky wasteland surrounded by snow-capped peaks, she hoped Lhamu and the other porters would arrive soon. After surveying the place, Beth decided that as the sole guardian of five yak herders' huts she might as well pick the best one for herself. All were dank and reeked of smoke odor. The first thing to do was air them out. She threw open the shutters on glassless windows and used rocks to prop the doors. "No shortage of stones around here," she laughed as she rolled a boulder towards the last hut.

Finally done and with arms akimbo, Beth smiled proudly and was wondering what to tackle next when Lhamu strode past the *mani* wall well ahead of her male companions. Finally! Running toward her, Beth waved her on to the huts and signaled to drop the *doko* there. Now the real test was convincing the string of weary porters, cook, and kitchen boy who arrived ten minutes later not to put up the tents. Spotting the *doko* with her duffle, she kept motioning for the porter to follow to her chosen hut and pantomimed his removing it and leaving it there. She repeated her performance for the unloading of the Norwegian gear in the hut furthest away. Beth hoped they'd figure out that the three remaining open doors were invitations to them.

Once the porters understood, Lhamu sauntered over to Beth and showed her a silver pendant bearing a small photo of the Dalai Lama inside. Having seen it among the Tibetan items at Sanasa, Beth smiled and asked, "Hamar?" Giggling, the Sherpani closed the pendant and slipped it inside her long-sleeved blouse worn under a floor-length, wrap-around tunic. She lacked only the striped, multicolored apron worn exclusively by married women. Unlike men who had adopted western attire, none of the

Sherpanis appeared to have given up their traditional attire, even those working as porters.

Anxious to finishing preparing the huts, Beth pinched her nose and waved her hand in front of one, hoping to indicate the foul odor. Smoke wasn't the only offender. One by one, she and Lhamu hauled yak wool rugs outdoors. Each holding onto an end, they shook vigorously in a laughing contest to see who'd lose her grip first. Eyes closed and head turned aside, Beth felt like the Peanuts character, Pigpen, who walked around in a cloud of dust, sprinkling dirt on all he came in contact with. The rock walls separating pastures were soon elegantly draped in wool.

Returning to the huts, Beth studied the hard-packed floors and finally concluded that they were made of the usual mixture of mud and dung. Easy to sweep if one had a broom. She thrummed her cheek, pondering, until Lhamu pointed to a yak tail resting in the corner. Beth picked it up gingerly with only her thumb and forefinger, wary of creatures residing among the thick hairs. A few hefty shakes dislodged only a couple of multi-legged beasts that scurried too quickly to identify. As the women swept the last lodge, it struck Beth that she was getting used to this too! Being immersed in another culture was intriguing and challenging and she had adapted too frightfully well. Now heat. Faced with the reality of spending a night this high in Gokyo, she remembered Dorje's comment about dried fuel for a fire. The floors swept, benches wiped, rafters cleared of cobwebs, the women went in search of the sacred dung.

But first Beth needed to pee and in private, away from curious porters who had assumed she meant no tents were to be erected including the *charpi.* Feeling pretty cocky about having accomplished so much this morning, she swaggered over to a three-foot wall, planted her hands, and threw her legs over with the grace of a gymnast. When her feet hit the ground sliding, Beth grabbed the top stones and held on desperately trying to remain upright because a quick glance revealed she wasn't the first to choose this location. A summer's worth of excrement softened by yesterday's snow had created a viscous mire of unbelievable length and breadth. Clinging to the wall, she managed to pull herself back over by sheer arm strength alone. To heck with it, she was dropping her pants behind the nearest rock.

Resurfacing, she discovered Lhamu had unpacked Beth's duffle and was holding her sleeping bag around her shoulders, wiggling and kissing and saying, "Dorje, Dorje."

It cracked Beth up and she couldn't let it pass without pretending to pull a pendant from her blouse and swooning, "Hamar, Hamar."

Taking the bag inside, Lhamu pantomimed Beth and Dorje making love. Not to be outdone, Beth ran to the Norwegians' hut, found Hamar's duffle, and dragged it to a separate hut. "Lhamu and Hamar." Agreed. Both women would seduce men into their huts tonight.

However, the elusive question of dung remained and Beth wasn't about to act that one out. Not in any of the huts, it had to be somewhere sheltered from the elements. Searching all the rock structures, Beth discovered a kind of root cellar housing hundreds of dried patties. After her recent incursion over the wall, she wasn't thrilled about handling them. But weighing *Do I want to be cold or do I want to touch shit,* she chose the latter. Her eyes to the ground and carrying a load stacked to her chin, she trod across the rocky terrain to her hut and ran straight into Royd and Kirk who looked like walking cadavers. "What happened to you?" she exclaimed.

Kirk mumbled something incoherently and Royd said they just weren't feeling too well and needed to lie down. Where were the tents?

"We're using the huts tonight. Your gear's in that one over there." Royd's skin was sallow and his eyes had sunk in deep hollows. "You look dehydrated," said Beth. "You should drink more water."

He smirked, his body unsteady. "A woman standing with an armload of shit is telling me what to do."

"It's going to keep me warm tonight," she answered with a crisp edge to her voice.

Kirk mumbled something else and tugged on Royd's sleeve. Watching them stagger toward their hut as if drunk, Beth wished Dorje would return. After stacking the dung by her hearth, she found the Norwegians stretched out on their window bench wrapped in their bags. "Where's Dorje?" she asked.

"Hamar insisted on going to the top and he went with him," Kirk groaned. "We turned around half way."

"Wasn't Hamar sick too?"

"Worse than us." Kirk was holding his forehead and breathing rapidly. "He threw up and had diarrhea the first quarter mile. Dorje said it was from the water yesterday."

"Then why...?"

"Don't ask," said Royd. His arm dropped to the side of the bench and he pointed. "Just get us some water. Our bottles are over there."

She started to snap back with, *Get your own damn water,* but figured she wouldn't add to their misery. More concerned about Dorje and Hamar, she and Lhamu watched for them while the cook filled bottles with boiled water that had cooled rapidly. To keep from worrying about the men, she and Lhamu finished the household chores: replacing the rugs, closing the shutters, moving the rock doorstops, and lastly hauling dung to Hamar's hut and then Royd and Kirk's. The snide remark about her being a shit bearer was no longer forthcoming; nor was a thank you. With a shallow pan of warm wash water, she closed the door to her hut, stripped down and took a very small shivering sponge bath. Rifling through her duffle, she pulled out clean clothes and quickly felt rejuvenated.

Almost three hours after the arrival of the two Norwegians, Beth spotted what appeared to be a single large form at the base of the mountain, lurching and falling, and then slowly and awkwardly getting to its feet again like a wounded bear. Panicked, Beth yelled at the porters, waving her arms excitedly and motioning for them to come. As they neared the specter, she could see that it was not one but two beings, the smaller struggling to keep the ponderous, ungainly one afoot. Lhamu ran to Hamar and supported him through two rounds of dry heaves.

"He has already thrown up everything else," Dorje said. His eyes blurred as if he were about to faint. Beth grabbed his arm and steadied him. "Why did you let him go to the top?"

"Could you have stopped him?'

"No, I guess not."

With Lhamu's help, Hamar lumbered and staggered across the stepping-stones in the stream while another porter carried the daypacks.

"What about the other two?" Dorje asked.

"They'll survive if I don't kill Royd first."

"Don't be angry at him. He doesn't want you to see his fear."

"Afraid of what?"

"That he's not as strong as he wants to be."

"Or as appealing."

The cook prepared *thukpa* with extra broth to re-hydrate the Norwegians. At dinner Dorje announced they would not be crossing the Cho La in the morning. None of them was well enough. To go higher could mean death. After a day of rest, liquids, and aspirin, he would determine whether they were fit to continue or to return to Namche. This time, no one complained about the prospect of spending a day with nothing to do but sleep or read.

Beth helped Dorje settle Royd and Kirk in their hut and build a dung fire to take off the chill. As they walked back to Beth's hut, Dorje asked, "And Hamar? Where is he sleeping?"

"With Lhamu in another hut. She'll take good care of him tonight." *As I will of you*, she thought as they arrived at her door. Leaning against the cold stone wall, Beth reached under his jacket to massage his back. "You must be tired and sore after today."

Eyes closed, he leaned into her hand. "That feels very good. No one has ever done that for me."

Pressing harder on his large, lower muscles, she said, "If you want to come inside and sit by the fire, I will rub your whole back. We call it a massage and it's so relaxing you will probably fall asleep. Maybe you should bring your bag here just in case."

Dorje had the eyes of a cat because he was gone and back in minutes with the moon not yet risen and no flashlight. She shone hers while he built the fire after making small offerings to *phug lha*, the god of the home who dwelt in a pillar of wood, and *thab lha*, the god of the hearth who tolerates no impurity. The smoke fanned out along the ceiling—a dense, stagnant cloud of acrid, pungent dung fragrance that infused everything. She would smell like this for days, but so would everybody else. "It is better to sleep on the floor by the hearth," he said, "and let the smoke go above you."

"And what happens when the entire room is filled?"

"The wind calls to it through tiny holes in the roof, windows, and door."

"Then I will not block its escape." She moved her pad from the bench to the floor near the fire and pulled his beside it. "Now sit," she said, "and I will soothe away all your cares of the day." As he sat leaning forward with his arms wrapped around his knees, Beth slowly worked the tension out of his muscles. She wanted to explore every inch of his smooth, flawless skin. When finished with his back, Beth ran her fingers up through Dorje's hair and massaged his scalp. Slowly rolling his head from left to right as if asking for more, he responded to her every movement.

Kneeling behind Dorje, Beth slowly wrapped her arms around him with her head resting against his shoulder. "Sleepy yet?" she whispered.

He turned and held her face between his hands, gazing at her. "You are so beautiful in the firelight. I like your blue eyes." He kissed each closed lid, her cheek, and lips.

So ready to make love with him, she barred all other thoughts and sensations. No gnats of doubt or guilt allowed tonight. "Stay with me" she whispered. "I can zip our bags together."

After removing his shirt and jeans, Dorje crawled in beside her. "I want to make you happy," he said. And please her he did with a slow, gentle touch over every part of her body, taking his time, caressing her with his lips and tongue—his breath warm and sensual. She remembered the first day at Lukla when he turned and looked at her in his green cap, tight Levis, and snug blue shirt. A warm flush had swept through her and thrown her slightly off center. And she'd been atilt ever since. Afterwards, her head spinning and lips tingling, she was too enervated to move. Beth stepped outside of herself and with amusement looked at the woman lying on a mud-dung floor with a suffocating smoke cloud overhead and below zero temperature. How could anyone feel this complete or be this happy in such circumstances?

CHAPTER EIGHTEEN

Thin shafts of light slipped through the shutters and spilled across the floor, washing over Beth's white skin that felt as soft as the finest Indian silk. Like a sweet mist rising from leaves after a warm rain, her body had responded quickly to his touch last night. And now they were lovers…but for how long? To think about her leaving in a week or two cut through his every nerve ending making him raw and vulnerable. Wrapped around her, he would carve this moment into his heart like a prayer chiseled in a *mani* stone and use it as his mantra forever.

The hollow-faced Norwegians didn't reach the dining tent until after 10:00 a.m. and then only had a breakfast of tea and watery hot cereal designed to replenish liquids. Graced by an exceptionally warm afternoon, they basked in the sun, read, and played cards. By dinner, they boasted of no more headaches, nausea, or shortness of breath and were eager to start over the pass to the Everest Valley the next day. Dorje announced that he would make that judgment at breakfast and his word was final. There would be no taking off without him this time.

Eager to set out, the Norwegians awakened early the next morning. After two days of perfect weather, the skies still remained clear. Dorje agreed it seemed an auspicious time to travel. While everyone prepared to leave, he constructed a stone altar for a short *puja*. From his pack, he placed a prayer flag on top and lit two juniper boughs at the base for incense. Scattering rice and *tsampa* offerings, he and the other Sherpas chanted prayers to the mountain gods asking for their blessing, continued good weather, and success in crossing the pass. At the conclusion, they spread *tsampa* powder on their faces to mimic graying hair—a blessing for a long and fruitful life.

When the Norwegians were ready to depart, Hamar announced, "I'm going to walk with Lhamu and the porters."

Grabbing his arm to pull him along, Kirk said, "Oh, no. You're coming with us and letting her do her job. You can hump her again tonight."

Like a wild animal, Hamar shrugged him off. "Don't talk that way about the woman I love."

Royd howled. "Love? You've known her...what? —a few days...and don't even speak the same language. Are you crazy?"

"I know what I feel. Now leave me alone," Hamar snapped and ambled past him.

Certain that Beth had overheard the conversation, Dorje wondered what she was thinking and feeling. Yesterday and last night, he had experienced with Beth the most intimate emotional and physical connection of his life. The two of them had been like beautiful gold eagles that soar in pairs high above the Khumbu, gliding endlessly on wind currents with their broad wings touching. He never wanted to part from her and tonight would again share her tent whispering words of love.

He waited for her to join him before they departed for the trail over the Cho La. The group crossed the rock and sand debris on the surface of the Ngozumpa Glacier for an hour before climbing a deep, narrow valley that eventually opened out on an ancient lateral moraine. After hiking more than three hours, the Norwegians and Beth were flushed and breathing heavily.

"We will rest here," Dorje announced. Removing their daypacks, they lay down with their arms across their foreheads to shield their eyes. Dorje climbed a large boulder from where he could identify the pass and fix the route in his head, but he was reluctant to leave before spotting the porters. Only one had crossed the Cho La before and knew the trail. Fifteen minutes later, he saw them slowly making their way up the valley. Anxious to get over the pass, Dorje waved to the lead porter, a man in his fifties who had crossed several times. When Sangbu waved back, Dorje felt it was safe to move on.

Sliding on loose rock and gaining only two steps for every three on a talus slope slowed their progress. It was laborious work requiring frequent stops to catch their breath. Bent over with her hands on her thighs, Beth rolled her eyes up at Dorje and gave a little nod saying she was okay. She only needed a minute. The Norwegians plodded upward dragging one foot after another until they reached the glacier at the base of the pass. This cold and intimidating challenge seemed to revive them.

"This calls for a fresh toothpick." Pulling one from his pocket, Kirk brandished it like a sword before neatly slipping it into the corner of his mouth. "Now onward over the pass."

Singing a drinking song, the men tramped up the glacier ahead of Dorje and Beth. But after twenty minutes of boisterous marching, the pace slackened as altitude and the effort of moving in ice and snow eroded their spirits. When they reached a steep, icy traverse with a 300-foot drop, morale plummeted.

"There was a path last time," Dorje explained. "The snow has covered it. I will go first and make a new one."

To Dorje's great surprise, Royd stepped in behind him. "I'll help pack it. We men from above the Arctic Circle should be good for something. I'm sorry we've been a nuisance."

Battling a sudden headwind, Dorje made his way across grateful for Royd's help and regretting his earlier hostile feelings. Negative emotions polluted the mountain, which in turn polluted those who walked on it. Touchy and inclined to anger, the gods demanded respect and veneration. If he failed to nourish and worship them, they would seek revenge. As Dorje and Royd returned widening the path, he asked the gods' forgiveness for any offensive behavior.

Kirk removed his toothpick and tossed it muttering, "This will take concentration." Hamar followed, arms swinging and legs splaying out to the sides.

Beth was next. With a large, shaky inhale, she repeated, "I can do this. I can do this," and started out. Half way, a gust knocked her down but she rose again with Royd's help and slowly made her way across. Dorje was proud of her: truly a woman worthy of the mountain.

With the wind howling and battering them now, Dorje yelled into it, "We must get over the pass and down out of this. The top is not far. Royd, will you take them while I make sure all the porters are with us?"

"Yes," he shouted back with the wind whipping his clothing. "We'll find shelter on the other side and wait. Don't worry, we'll take good care of Beth."

"And I will take good care of Lhamu," Dorje said. Confident in the Norwegians now, he held Beth before saying good-bye. "I will join you in a few minutes," he promised and kissed her on the cheek. Watching them stagger up the hill into the wind, Dorje hoped the day would end soon and he'd be back in her arms tonight.

The cook and kitchen boys arrived first, wearing their cheap Chinese tennis shoes traded with the Tibetans. The smooth rubber soles immediately slid on the ice. "Lean against the hill," Dorje yelled, "and stay in the tracks." Each praying to the god of the mountain, they crossed safely and were almost out of sight before the long string of porters came slogging up the glacier with Lhamu in the lead. All had carried in snow before and picked their way across in spite of slippery shoes and awkward loads. "That makes nine," Dorje counted as they passed, but where was the tenth? Frustrated that everyone was getting too spread out, he stormed back looking for the last porter and found him dragging at his own pace. "Hurry up. You must stay together."

The man simply looked at him and trudged past. No amount of scolding quickened his step. One speed only, slow. At the traverse, the porter removed the *doko* and dropped it.

"What are you doing?" Dorje yelled. "Is the Sherpani stronger and braver than you?" No answer. "You won't get hired again," he threatened in a wasted breath.

After crossing, the porter stopped as if waiting for Dorje to pick up the basket. What choice did he have? It contained the greater portion of their food. He hefted it onto his back, stomped across in a show of superior balance, and slammed it at the man's feet in a sweaty rage. "Now you carry!" The porter flinched and Dorje had him. Finally, he was as intimidating as his father.

After spewing moist clouds across the sky, the wind finally died allowing only veins of sunlight to seep through. His jacket zipped and hands buried deep in his pockets, Dorje headed for the Cho La. Overtaking the porters first and then the cook and kitchen boys, he said, "Keep moving so we can get down by early afternoon." With the temperature dropping as he climbed, his breath condensed. Out of sight of both groups now in an unearthly quiet, he felt strangely alone. Beth and the Norwegians were somewhere ahead but he didn't know how far. He was but a speck in a vast whiteness and beginning to doubt his decision to cross today.

Dorje found them slumped against the rocks laboring to breathe on the 17,880-foot summit. Beth wilted at the sight of him, shivering violently. He kissed her cold, bluish lips and rubbed her arms and hands to keep the circulation going. "You will feel better once we are lower."

Doubled over and gasping for air, Kirk said, "I'm used to cold and snow, but this damn altitude is a killer."

"And I'm freezing just standing here," moaned Hamar. "I need to keep moving."

"We all do." Dorje zipped Beth's collar up to her chin and took her daypack. "Come on. The porters are not far behind."

"Did you see Lhamu?" Hamar asked.

"Yes, and you don't need to worry. She's stronger than any of them." Dorje glanced at the sky before departing. No streaks of sunlight, only the heavy, gray mist from which the first large flakes drifted slowly to the ground.

"Not again," Hamar laughed, sticking his tongue out to catch them.

"You must have really pissed the gods off," Royd snorted.

"Me? What about you?"

Walking with his arm around Beth to keep her warm and listening to their boyish banter, Dorje momentarily took his mind off the weather. Over the pass now, travel would be easier. But within half an hour, the wind picked up again bringing wetter snow that fell thick and heavy onto their hair and clothes. Royd's red beard turned white. "You are a grandfather now," Dorje laughed, pointing to his chin. Running his hand over his face, the Norwegian shook the snow off, but within minutes he aged again. The snow and cloud merged into one making it difficult to judge where the mountain ended and the sky began. "We must get off the ice before setting up camp," Dorje said. "It is too cold."

"This is just one of those little snowfalls like we've been having, isn't it?" Beth asked, her teeth chattering.

"Yes," he lied to keep her spirits up, knowing too well that this wasn't the light flurry of the previous days but a rapidly developing, full-blown storm. No one had anticipated or dressed for it, including him. With the temperature continuing to drop, wind whipped through the tiniest openings in their clothing making them dangerously cold. Already noticing Beth's stiffness, he said, "Keep walking. Do not stop." With each step growing more difficult, they could only move between gusts and were frequently forced to stand for long periods huddled together with their backs to the wind.

Shaking and with her arms tucked tight against her body, Beth snuggled closer to him. "I'm so cold, I can't feel my hands or feet anymore."

More slender than the Norwegians, she couldn't take this much longer. He had to get her inside a tent with dry clothes and a sleeping bag and do it soon. "We will camp here," he said regretfully because they were still too high. Then came one of the hardest decisions he'd ever made. "I must go look for the porters with our tents and bags. Maybe they cannot find us or they have stopped already." Wanting to pull Beth inside himself and keep her warm, Dorje stayed wrapped around her to the last minute before instructing Royd, "Find a place out of the snow, maybe under a large boulder, but do not go far. In thirty minutes call my name so I can find you." After kissing Beth long and hard, he pulled her hands from under her armpits and clapped them. "Do this to keep your fingers moving." He turned to Royd. "Take care of her."

The Norwegian nodded. "I promise."

Shaking and bouncing from one foot to the other, Hamar said, "I'm going with you to find Lhamu."

"No. You are too cold and tired and will slow me down. It is better if I go alone at Sherpa speed."

Pulling the collar over his nose and mouth to breath his own warm air, Dorje started out with the wind to his back now. Not prepared for this weather, the porters could be far behind or may have already set up camp to get warm. Accumulating quickly, the snow had covered his tracks. He tried noting markers to lead him back to Beth, but huge boulders disappeared into nothingness as visibility shrank to five feet. In the flat light, it was impossible to judge the unevenness of the ground, and he tripped over a rock, banging his knee. Pain shot up his leg. Getting back to his feet, he stumbled on, moving only by instinct for he could see nothing. "Sangbu," he called out to the senior porter, but the wind snatched his voice and buried it in thick clouds. He stopped to listen for a reply but heard only his heart pounding in his ears. Shouting again and again, he forced himself back up the pass. Still no answer. They could be lost or seeking shelter somewhere. What if he couldn't find them? Beth was back there freezing. He would try fifteen minutes more and then return to her. Shouting until his breath felt torn, listening, shouting again, he trudged toward the summit of the Cho La. At last a muffled reply. "Sangbu," he cried and heard the old man's voice. Slowly, one by one, the porters stepped through a veil of snow like ghostly apparitions

"How many are you?" Dorje asked, shuddering with cold.

"Nine porters, the cook, and kitchen boys," Sangbu answered. "The last porter is far behind. We haven't see or heard from him in over an hour but we had to keep moving."

"I know the one. If we leave him, he may die, but without tents and bags the others will."

Buried under a mantle of snow, Lhamu asked, "Is Hamar all right?"

"Yes. Except he misses you."

Phurbu who had worked for Dorje on the ladies' trek said, "We don't want to go on. We'll put the tents up here and wait for you to bring the others."

"No. You can't stay here," Dorje shouted at them through the howling wind. "She won't make it. It's too high and too far for them to climb back up in the cold. You must go down."

"But our hands and feet are numb," said another porter. "We don't have good shoes or warm clothes."

"I know," Dorje hollered back. "Nobody does." Watching a porter remove his *doko* and drop it, Dorje begged, "Please just one more hour. And if we don't find them, I'll go on alone."

While the Sherpas talked among themselves, Lhamu stepped forward. "I'll come."

"So will I," said Tashi. As the nephew of Mingma's former best friend, Tashi had known Dorje all his life. Unlike his uncle, Pemba, he was tall and rangy for a Sherpa but with an intellect that couldn't match the size of his body or enormity of his heart.

"And me," added Phuri, the youngest porter. Soon the rest agreed to one more hour. Bowed under their loads, they started out once again unable to see where to place their feet. Driving snow and wind buffeted them until at times they could do no more than crawl.

"Just a little further," Dorje pleaded each time he pulled someone to his feet. "Ten minutes, only ten minutes more." He was afraid that both groups would die: one waiting for him, freezing and terrified; the other, fighting to get there. In a complete whiteout, he lost all sense of direction and had no idea whether he was walking toward Beth and the Norwegians or away. Soon it would be dark and the temperature would plummet further.

Coming up to him, Sangbu said, "It's been more than an hour. We can't go on."

"I understand." Seeing the disappointed look on Lhamu's face, Dorje added, "You are too tired and must stay here. I will find Hamar and bring back the others."

In one last attempt before setting out alone, Dorje called to Beth but only the wind answered in a mournful whisper. He yelled again and again until his throat was raw. Terror had a firm grip on him now, its icy fingers strangling all hope that Beth and the others would survive the night.

"What's that?" Sangbu asked suddenly.

Dorje's heart leapt. "What?"

"I'm not sure."

Holding his breath to prevent any distraction, Dorje heard only fear throbbing in his throat. He shoved his cries through the heavy cloud and waited, listening. Finally a sound so faint it didn't seem human. "Set up the tents," he ordered the porters. "I'm going after them. I'll find Beth if I have to look until my fingers and toes turn white with frostbite. And when I can no longer walk, I'll crawl like a baby. But I *will* find her."

Alternately calling and listening, he plowed blindly through knee-deep drifts, guided only by distant shouts swallowed by the storm and spewed out in muted whispers. As the cries became clearer, Dorje thrust his entire body forward desperately trying to reach them before it was too late. Finally, he spotted a gray figure lurching toward him.

"At last," Royd said, his legs buckling under. "We thought you'd never come."

"Where's Beth? Is she all right?"

"She's with Kirk and Hamar on a narrow ledge under an overhang. It was the only shelter we could find. I came looking for you."

Dorje and Royd alternated shouting to his companions until they reached them fifteen minutes later. Shivering with icicles frozen in their hair and clothes, the two Norwegians were holding Beth tightly between them. "She fainted almost two hours ago," Hamar explained.

"And has gone in and out of consciousness several times since," Kirk added. "We gave her all the water we had."

"But I carried her here," Hamar boasted. "Have you seen Lhamu?"

"Yes. She is fine and waiting back in camp for you."

As they spoke, Dorje was checking Beth's hands, nose, and ears for frostbite by touch only because night had enveloped them in such darkness that he could only feel not see her snow-encrusted face. "We have to get her back to camp."

His large body resembling a white yeti, Hamar said, "I'm too sick to carry her any more."

"Me too," Kirk added. "I can barely stand and am not thinking clearly."

"It's as you warned," Royd admitted. "The altitude and cold. Have them bring the tents and bags here."

"No," Dorje shouted. "It would take twice as long to go and come back and I might not find you again. They have already set up camp and have warm tents and bags waiting for us." He lifted Beth's limp body and held to him. "Do as you like, but I'm taking her back."

It hurt simply to breathe as frigid air seared his lungs and ripped the lining of his throat. With the Norwegians lagging and stumbling behind him, he walked, fell, staggered to his feet, tripped, and rose again. In his haste to get off the Cho La, he had neglected to honor the deity residing on the pass, not offered enough prayers, placed no stones on the pile. He must appease the angry gods. "*Om mani padme hum...Om mani padme hum*," he repeated quietly, hoping the deity of this lower place would hear and protect them.

Between mantras, he told Beth that she must stay with him, not let go of life, because hers was more important than his own. "I love you. You are my goddess," he repeated over and over, warming her face with his breath.

"I'm soooo cold," she whispered back. Her first words gave him courage to continue. Walking as a blind man in the thick, heavy snow with nothing to guide him, he was suddenly, ambushed by an unseen boulder. Tumbling, he instinctively folded his arms over Beth's head to protect her.

As Hamar and Royd helped him up, the large Norwegian with the gentle heart said, "I will carry her now."

Dorje brushed the man's arm away. "No. I must take her and I will not fail."

CHAPTER NINETEEN

Holding Beth pressed tightly against his body, Dorje carried her past the point where his legs became numb, calling to Sangbu and trusting that the gods would lead him there. In the distance, he saw a faint blue light. A witch? That's how they appeared in the dark. Shaking off that thought, he had to believe there were no evil spirits, no restless *shrindis*, wanting to torment him tonight. Otherwise he wouldn't have the strength to go on. "*Om mani padme hum.*" Coming closer to the light, he saw Sangbu standing in the snow holding a lantern. How long had he waited there?

"Is she alive?" the old man asked as he helped move her into a tent.

A shudder of relief rippled through Dorje. "Yes. Buddha willed it so." Beth was still shaking uncontrollably as he laid her on the pad and carefully removed her wet jacket, shirt, and pants while Sangbu went for hot tea. After changing Beth and himself into dry clothes, Dorje crawled into the sleeping bag with her for body heat. He tucked her dead-cold hands in the warm spot between his legs and gently massaged them. Did the gods think his love for her was so fleeting they could take her away? Not this woman who made his heart sing. They could not have her. He would die himself before letting go.

When Sangbu returned, Dorje whispered to her, "Open your mouth for hot tea."

Teeth chattering so hard he could hear them striking, she answered, "I'm too coldddd."

"But you must drink." After two cups, her shivering subsided enough that she could sit holding a bowl of hot soup. Satisfied that she would be all right for a few minutes, he left to check on the others.

"We're still damn sick and frozen, but we'll survive," said Royd.

Giddy as a child, Hamar called from his tent, "Lhamu is keeping me warm."

In the dining tent, the other porters were sitting on the floor, shoulder-to-shoulder, wet and shivering, sharing a pot of *tsampa*. Dorje joined them. Wanting out of there too, no one argued when he said they must rise very early and get everyone lower. Since the wind made it too difficult to erect more tents, the porters moved all the gear to the outer walls of the dining tent and crowded into the center to sleep together.

Dorje crawled back in with Beth and wrapped his bag over them. With full body contact and two covers, they should stay warm. The storm hammered them for hours with a howling wind driving its icy breath through the canvas. As the cold penetrated clear to Dorje's bones, he pulled the bag over Beth's head and held her tighter. Through the constant flapping of the walls, he heard the creak and moan of distant avalanches and won-dered if this nightmare would ever end. Finally emotionally and physically spent, he drifted into sleep. As wind bombarded the tent, the canvas groaned and one of the tethers ripped out of the ground slapping the roof and jolting him awake. Expecting the other tethers to go also, he ran his fingers along the ceiling and found it intact. The outside of their bags was covered with a fine layer of snow driven through the walls. He brushed it off before surrendering to sleep again, dreaming of the porter left behind.

Alone in heavy snow, the man was trudging toward the pass when strange yells and whistles shattered the silence. He stopped and listened. There they were again. When a rock glanced off his pack, the terrified porter dropped it and ran, sinking deeper and deeper until his legs couldn't move. An enormous creature covered with shaggy, red hair grabbed his neck from behind, twisted him to the ground, and dragged him to its home to bury him alive. The porter screamed but no sound escaped his lips.

Waking suddenly, Dorje gasped for air, unable to move. The roof and sides of the tent had collapsed under the weight of the snow and were burying them alive like the porter in his dream. "Wake up!" he yelled at Beth as he wriggled his arm out of the bag into a narrow space between the roof and floor. With aching lungs, he searched for the door and fumbled with the zipper, desperately trying to pull it with stiff, awkward fingers. Dizzy and almost out of air, his face tingling, Dorje tugged once more and ripped the door open. Freezing air shot into the tent and he gulped convulsively as the cold burned his lungs. He quickly enlarged the hole to let air travel down to Beth who gasped as the icy air struck. "It is okay," he said trying to calm her. "The roof fell. That is all." He kissed her forehead. "Are you all right?" When she nodded, he whispered he would return soon.

Reaching back through the hole, he dug with bare hands, gradually widening a space large enough to crawl through, and pushed to his feet against powerful gusts threatening to blow him over. While yelling at the others to wake up, he quickly scraped snow from the roof and sides to take the weight off Beth. Then he searched for the Norwegians and dug with numb fingers until the men slowly emerged quite shaken. Roy, Kirk, and Hamar followed him to the dining tent that was covered with a thick, powdery blanket that had broken loose and tumbled from a rock above. With a flurry of hands, the rescuers created an opening and pulled out the gasping porters, cook, and kitchen boys. After clearing all the roofs and sides, everyone was too exhausted to think of anything other than their beds.

Although it was still snowing heavily as night faded into a gray dawn, the wind had died when Dorje cleaned the tent again. With enough light to survey the camp, he discovered that their frequent assaults on the roofs had packed the area next to the tents, but surrounding their small camp was a five-foot snow barrier and still growing.

"Jesus!" Royd exclaimed when he stuck his head out the door. "Would you look at that."

"Oh, shit," Kirk added. "How in the hell are we going to get out of here?" He looked at Dorje. "You do know where we are, don't you?"

Not having the faintest idea, Dorje answered, "No problem," and strolled casually to the dining tent. "Do you know where we are?" he whispered to Sangbu who had crossed the pass many times.

"Not until it clears and we can see the way. Never in my memory has there been such a storm this time of year."

All day the snow fell. Dorje sat with Beth through a fitful sleep. Breathing heavily and shuddering, she frequently woke screaming as if hallucinating or having a nightmare. He'd seen it before and knew it was a bad omen. She'd been too high too long and had to go down. Every hour as he swept the roof, he searched the sky for signs of clearing. Meanwhile the Norwegians read and wrote in journals while the Sherpas joked, played cards, and smoked *bidis* that filled their tent with fumes. By nightfall, everyone was bored, despondent, and cold. To cheer them up, the cook prepared a special meal he'd been saving to celebrate reaching Base Camp: SPAM, the precious canned meat that arrived by plane all the way from Kathmandu.

After making sure everyone was settled for the night, Dorje stepped outside to return to Beth. By now so accustomed to snow pelting him in the face, he didn't notice its absence at first. Then the realization that he was gazing at stars in a clear, black sky returned his stomach to its resting place after its having been perched at the back of his throat for more than thirty hours. All was well now and tomorrow they would go down to a safe, warm place.

Morning sunlight danced on the roof and shimmered along the walls: the first warmth in days. Dorje gently lifted a wisp of hair back from Beth's cheek. More radiant and beautiful than ever, her face was softer around the edges and her body more comfortable and relaxed in his arms. He kissed her softly and lay holding her while she slept making a gentle purring noise that delighted him. Yawning, Beth snuggled closer with her arm across his chest and her head nestled in the hollow of his shoulder. "Good morning," he whispered into the top of her hair. "You slept well last night."

"And how do you know that?"

"I can feel you move even in my dreams."

"And are they of me?"

"Always. And do you dream of me?" he asked.

"You are in my thoughts every day and night."

"And when you are gone?"

Playing with his hair, she whispered, "Hush, I'm here now and want only to be with you." Though she seemed content, Dorje knew he could never offer the life Eric did. She would soon grow bored and yearn for the excitement of their world. "Why so quiet?" she asked.

"Nothing." Giving her a hug, he decided to simply enjoy the moment and not think about the future. He faced more immediate problems now. Hearing others rustle about in camp, he said, "I hate to leave this wonderful, warm place, but I must prepare for us to leave."

As he pulled his jeans and shirt on, she ran her hand down his back and along his thigh. "And I will stay a few minutes longer daydreaming about making love tonight."

He was surprised at how quickly his body reacted to a few simple words. After he exited the tent, Phuri and Tashi shot knowing glances at each other when he walked past. Not a cloud anywhere. A perfect day for traveling. If they started early and kept moving, perhaps they would reach Periche by nightfall. Dorje searched the sky. When he had crossed the pass once before, the sun warmed his back in the afternoon, so he must go toward it in the morning.

"I think that way," he told Sangbu and received the confirmation he sought. Walking the perimeter of the now seven-foot snow barrier, Dorje wonder what was just beyond. Wanting to show off for Beth, he took a small wood axe to chop stairs. However, instead of the grand ascent he envisioned, he was quickly clambering on all fours as the soft snow caved under him. Only sheer agility got him to the top where he immediately sank with a loud whoomph!—and disappeared. An outburst of laughter skidded across the snow. Humiliated, Dorje chopped his way out sending powder flying in every direction and causing big clumps of it to cling to his hair and face as he emerged.

"Does this mean we won't be walking out?" Royd asked, not even attempting to hide his amusement at Dorje's appearance.

The porters were already snickering. When a wet clump dropped from Dorje's hair and slid down his cheek, he too chuckled and then started laughing to hide his concern from Beth's eyes.

When the joke had passed, Royd stood with his back to the others and quietly asked, "What did you see up there?"

"Nothing but snow and too soft to hold us."

"Then we'll pack it down to make a path, but we need something large and flat."

"The six-foot dining table." Questioning Girmi who had carried it, Dorje learned the porter had left it outside the first night of the storm and couldn't remember where. Everyone dug through the surrounding area until Hamar finally uncovered it.

Sliding the table into Dorje's escape route, Royd jumped on, but the snow sank only a few inches. Kirk joined him with little more success. At Hamar's turn to show off, he pushed the others away and gave Lhamu a glowing smile. Like a baby trying to climb onto a cabinet, he threw first one arm onto the table, and then the other, his legs kicking until Royd gave him a shove. Finally on top, Hamar jumped up and down, waving his arms and hollering as his great body weight compressed the snow. Everyone cheered, especially Lhamu, and he took a bow before hopping down to push the board forward another six feet and climb back on. When he tired, the others took over, working in shifts while he sat with Lhamu teaching her to say, *I love you* in English. Progress was slow and by late afternoon they had only cleared a path that took ten minutes to walk.

Dorje returned to camp exhausted and in despair. Unless the snow melted, it would take days to go a distance normally covered in a few hours. Tomorrow they must start at first light. His only consolation was having more time with Beth. Their lovemaking was nothing like he had with Shanti. She was eager and playful, but Beth made his entire being quiver with every touch and every breath. She had crawled inside and carried his heart away when he would have given it freely for it had truly never belonged to anyone. While he cared deeply about Shanti, Dorje realized that lust had driven him to her bed most nights. With Beth it was different. Such things he had wanted to tell her that night standing wrapped in their bags at Macchermo but didn't have the courage.

Now passion warmed their naked bodies wrapped in bags zipped together. Using all five senses, he explored every inch with his fingers and tongue: her full breasts, flat stomach, slender legs, and firm rear. Her sinuous responses and their bodies flowing in perfect unison took Dorje to realms never experienced before in an explosive orgasm that left him trembling and light headed. When his heart quit racing and he could breathe again, he pulled her on top of him to retain their heat. His mouth at her ear, he longed to tell her he loved her but was still afraid. They had ridiculed Hamar's love for Lhamu saying it was too soon, but the big Norwegian had recognized his feelings immediately just as Dorje had known from the moment Beth gazed at him in Lukla that he would fall in love with her.

Trailing her fingers ever so lightly over his face, shoulders, and chest, she had a mesmerizing touch that cast him under her spell. He would do anything for her. Beth kissed his lips, eyes, and cheeks and whispered, "I love you."

She'd struck him with the thunderbolt that was his name and sent his insides sprawling with unhinged, uncontrollable joy. "And I love you. I love you," he repeated over and over like a prayer he was sending to the gods. Rolling her onto her back, he lay on top with his weight on his arms and gazed at her. "I was afraid to tell you before."

"And I was scared too. I didn't think I could ever really love someone. When my father left, I stopped feeling and let my mind take over my emotions because it was safer. But when you turned and looked at me that day, I toppled off center and have been at risk ever since."

Nuzzling her ear, he whispered, "You smiled at me."

"Couldn't help it. That was all physical and emotional, nothing mental about it."

He pulled back to read the expression in her eyes. "And are you sorry you did?"

"Not one bit. And you?"

"What do you think?" he said smiling and lowered himself to begin exploring her again.

The next morning, Dorje wanted to stay with Beth reveling in their love but the cook hastened him outside. "We're getting low on fuel," he said.

"How can that be?"

"We brought only enough kerosene for one night on the pass and were supposed to use dung we find in the Everest Valley. I tried melting snow in the sun but it takes too long."

"Keep all the water for drinking. We can eat the potatoes raw."

"There are no potatoes," said the cook. "Most of our food was with the lost porter."

"The canned fruit?'

"That too."

"And the cheese, sausages, tomato sauce?" The cook rocked his head after each one. "So what do we have?"

"Three packages of biscuits, some rice, and barley."

"And almost no water to boil it," Dorje said. "Four trekkers and twelve Sherpas to go another four or five days. Ration it," he ordered. His head throbbing, Dorje found Sangbu and instructed him to break camp in the late afternoon and move it to the end of the day's path. They must sleep lower that night.

The Norwegians were already at work. To buoy his spirits, Dorje asked them about America. When they explained it had 50 states and half of them were larger than Nepal, he spent the rest of the day trying to grasp the size of it and wondering how one could find his way in such a place. The sun beating down in an unrelenting glare, Dorje removed the sunglasses Marty had given him and wiped sweat from his forehead. Putting them back on, he estimated four more hours of daylight.

After a dinner of boiled rice for Beth and the Norwegians, the cook confided to Dorje that all the kerosene was gone. Ashamed of his earlier outburst, Dorje whispered, "Keep melting snow in the sun and do the best you can."

When he made love to Beth that night, something was wrong. It was subtle and intangible but not quite the same. He hesitated to question her because it was nothing she said or did; only a feeling he had. Afraid that she was too scared and had changed her mind, he decided to let it go and hoped it would pass.

CHAPTER TWENTY

After a restless sleep, Dorje rose before dawn and started work on the path. He could no longer distinguish between gnawing hunger and the queasiness of worry. With the trail dropping steeply into a long ravine and no place wide enough for a camp, they would have to push all the way through or sleep high one more night. Dorje explained this to the porters who until now had refused to help, saying it was not their job. But having not eaten yesterday or today, they finally understood his urgency and worked feverishly, especially Lhamu who tended to an ailing Hamar and never left his side now. A merciless sun reflected off the snow. Squinting painfully, the porters complained about not having glasses. Sangbu showed those who still wore their hair long how to wrap it across their eyes to filter the sun. Those who had cut theirs short like the *mikarus* were cursed with swollen, weeping vision. Having seen the clouded eyes of old yak herders who spent winters on snowy slopes with their animals, Dorje feared his porters were going blind and prayed to the gods for cloud cover.

Late in the morning, they heard a noise like a plane. Searching the sky, Dorje spotted a round machine with a long tail like the one he'd seen land at the small police checkpoint just above Namche when Hillary built the hospital. The Norwegians started yelling excitedly and waving their arms.

"What do you call this thing in English," he asked them.

"Helicopter," Royd shouted and took his jacket off to whirl it over his head. They all held their breath as the machine hovered over the Everest Valley. When it turned northeast towards Base Camp, a barrage of Norwegian words spewed from the men's mouths as they stared in disbelief while it disappeared over the ridge. "They know trekkers are out here but they can't see us in this damn hole," Royd said. "Surely there are others like us."

As a glum silence settled over the group, enthusiasm for path clearing waned. Most of the porters turned back to camp saying they needed water. Everyone did. When Lhamu remained with Hamar who had been feverish during the night, Royd and Kirk teased him relentlessly about his Sherpani girlfriend. The sun had softened the snow making work easier. The Norwegians relaxed a little and joked about the long cigars and tall drinks they would enjoy on the French Riviera on their way home. Forty-five minutes after the first sighting, the helicopter reappeared flying toward them this time. Dorje grabbed Hamar's red jacket and scrambled to the top of the snow bank. Waving it wildly, he watched the helicopter pass farther north over the Cho La.

Stunned, he wondered if they could be that far off the trail, but it was impossible to tell with everything snow covered. He wiped the sweat from his face, grateful for the glasses hiding the disappointment in his eyes. Having heard the dull boom so often in winter, he almost didn't look up as a fresh layer of soft snow separated from the rock wall a hundred yards ahead and plummeted down its face, exploding like a giant rapid striking a rock and shooting enormous white walls into the air. A second crack and another piece tumbled with a horrendous roar and filled the sky with impenetrable white powder. Then deathly silence. Scanning the high ridges ahead, Dorje saw heavy cornices wind-shaped into giant waves hanging precariously above them. The snow and ice having thawed enough to become unstable by afternoon, it was too hazardous to go on. After a long argument with himself, he reluctantly shoved out the words, "We must turn back."

The cook met him coming up the path. "What's happening? We can't stay here without food and water. The Sherpas are sick and half have swollen eyes. They will go blind. The longer..."

"Think I don't know that?" Dorje muttered as he strode past. Feeling guilty, he turned to apologize but the understanding cook motioned him on. Going to Beth's tent, Dorje was surprised to see her lying on top of the bag with her eyes closed. He gently lowered himself beside her.

"You're back early," she murmured and rolled over toward him.

"I could not stay away from you."

"So promise you'll never leave me," she said with a strange timbre to her voice.

How could he? With Beth in his arms, he could block out the boom of a falling cornice, hunger, pain, and glaring sun. Only she mattered. He tipped her chin to kiss her, tongues teasing and playing, building to the fervor of rapids hurtling downstream as they made love. Completely spent afterwards, he drifted endlessly as the slanting evening light cast the tent in shadows and the air chilled. Shivering, he knew she must be cold too, but when he started to cover Beth, her skin still felt warm—too warm. Puzzled, he touched her shoulders and arms and then laid the back of his hand on her forehead.

"You feel hot," he whispered, not certain that she was awake.

"Yes. Have been all day and with a bad headache since last night."

So that's why it felt different, he thought. "Why did you not tell me?"

"I was afraid we wouldn't make love, and I don't want to miss a moment with you."

"You need water. I will be right back."

When Dorje talked to the cook, he learned she had eaten little of the small meal offered that afternoon. "I want her to have water before anyone else," Dorje told him. "Melt as much as you can tomorrow."

"I already did today."

Taking the last two cups from the dining tent, Dorje returned to Beth. Even though the cold had lowered her temperature, she still felt warmer than on other nights. Headaches were common at high elevation, but she had been free of them and was now sleeping lower. None of his clients suffering from altitude sickness ever had a fever. Something else was going on and it scared him. The next morning, he found her sitting slump shouldered. "I'm not doing too well today," she admitted and looked up at him with eyes that seemed less blue as if the poppies had wilted.

Needing to get her lower yet, he instructed Sangbu to break camp immediately, move to the head of the ravine, and wait until they had cut through to the end. Then they must pass under the cornices quickly and before the afternoon sun made the snow unstable. Needing to work on clearing the path, he asked for a volunteer to carry Beth in a *doko* seat when the camp moved, but no one was willing. The long walk would be difficult enough without food and their eyes burning. Dorje repeated the urgency and finally Pemba's nephew stepped forward once again agreeing to take her.

The repeated melting during the day and freezing at night had packed the snow, creating a hard crust impervious to the table. Without it, Dorje, the Norwegians, and Lhamu took turns forging a trail. Again progress was slow with Kirk only advancing several feet before breaking through and sinking to his waist, hauling himself out, advancing several steps more, and falling again. With a deep growl, Hamar hurled himself forward, arms flying like a great clawing beast, a feverish sweat dripping from his face.

"Hush," Dorje whispered pointing to the fragile lip looming directly overhead but he was too late. A cornice broke free and tumbled towards them with great powdery plumes shooting skyward as the avalanche roared and crashed down the ravine.

"Run!" Dorje yelled, turning back towards camp.

The snow thundered past Royd, the last in line, who barely escaped by diving forward face down. "You oversized moron," he screamed at Hamar. "You just buried an hour's work. We'll never get out of this fucking place!"

Ignoring them, Dorje immediately started breaking trail again, but Hamar dragged him out of the way and charged with the ferocity of an angry bull. With everyone working, they finally created a channel wide enough for porters to pass. Once they were clear of the cornices, Dorje announced he was going back for Beth and the others.

"I need to rest a bit," said Kirk.

"Me too," added Royd. "We'll follow in a minute."

The snow already soft under his feet, Dorje warned, "Don't take long."

Seeing Beth at the head of the ravine and feeling the nightmare about to end, he breathed for the first time all day without his stomach trying to exit through his mouth. Not caring who watched, he kissed her long and hard, whispering his love even though no one else understood English. Her face still felt too warm. Dorje glanced at the cook. "Have you been giving her water?"

"All that we had," he answered with a haggard expression, and Dorje realized the others were sacrificing for her. The magnitude of that guilt did not override his need to save Beth. At least he could relieve Tashi of carrying her any farther, but the affable, lanky porter would not be dissuaded and insisted on following Dorje. Shouldering a pack with his own bag and pad, Dorje headed out with Tashi babbling about wanting to prove he was strong enough to work an Everest expedition and could Dorje help him get a job.

Pointing to the cornices, Dorje whispered, "Hush. No talking till later." They proceeded with eyes constantly searching the ridge. The sun dancing on ice crystals in an array of formidable beauty kept Dorje in awe as they walked silently through the ravine. Fifty yards after passing the Norwegians on their way back to Sangbu, Dorje heard the chopping of helicopter blades again. Suddenly rising up from the valley as if out of nowhere, it hovered a quarter of a mile away. The Norwegians became hysterical, shouting and waving their jackets once more. Dorje tried to still them but they were too caught up in the promise of rescue.

"Please see us?" Beth whispered and Dorje gripped her hand as the helicopter circled the area as if trying to locate a landing area. Then they gazed in horror as it turned north toward Lobuche and Everest.

"Wait," Kirk yelled. "We're here! We're here in this fucking hole where you can't see us." Royd and Hamar hollered too hurling their jackets in the air;.

Hearing the first ominous rumblings and seeing the snow pucker on the ridge, Dorje yelled, "Look out!"

Fifty yards from him, Royd cried, "Oh shit," and began running towards camp with Kirk, Hamar, and Lhamu right behind him.

Tashi started after them but Dorje caught his arm and pulled him the opposite direction, unwilling to lose the ground they had gained.

A crack followed by a terrible pause, and then a horrendous boom as the cornice broke loose. Sweeping slowly off the top at first, it thundered down in a violent mass. Dorje tried dragging Tashi and Beth beyond its reach, but the first wave hit with an agonizing jolt slamming them into a boulder and tossing Beth out of the *doko*. He grabbed her arm but the snow savagely wrenched her from his grasp and consumed her. Like a pebble carried downstream, Dorje tumbled head over foot until he didn't know which end was up. Suffocating in darkness, he fought by instinct for the surface, thrashing and whipping his body but the snow's power was unrelenting. His lungs on fire, he let his breath out slowing, conserving it to the last second. Then it was gone and blackness filled his head. In a dizzying final thrust, he kicked his way through to daylight and gasped for air like a baby's first breath. Having spent its fury, the avalanche now lay motionless. "Beth!" Dorje screamed. His side in horrific pain where he'd struck the boulder, he clawed his way onto the surface and quickly searched for a landmark where he'd last seen her. Guessing about ten yards back, he clambered over the surface, frantically uncovering every mound. Expedition porters caught in avalanches had survived if found in time. But how long? A few seconds, minutes?

"You can't have her," he shouted at the gods. "Not here, not like this!" Spotting a strand of golden hair, he used his arms as shovels, shooting snow into the air with the fury of a dog digging after a rodent. She was lying upside down, folded over. He pulled her shoulders free and lifted her head. Beth's breath exploded in a loud gasp as she gulped the air convulsively, her entire body shaking, her face terror-stricken. The seated position she'd been riding in had created a small air pocket in her lap—enough to keep her alive the precious minutes between life and death.

The pain in his side reminded him. "Are you hurt?"

"Don't think so, but I feel awfully sick." Looking around, Beth asked, "Where's Tashi?"

The porter had to be nearby but time was running out. Again Dorje scoured every mound and depression for a sign of life. Finding the blue corner of Beth's sleeping bag, he dug wildly. More bag, the *doko*, black hair, and then Tashi's face staring at him with vacant eyes. A deep shudder coursed through Dorje. Was it the will of Buddha that this tall, rangy Sherpa with an enormous heart should die so young?

Hearing Beth empty her stomach made it even more imperative that he get her to the Khunde hospital. He climbed to the crest of the avalanche and yelled, "Are you there?"

"Yes," Royd shouted back. "It missed us. No one hurt? And you?"

"Tashi is dead and Beth is sick. I am going to take her down. Tell Sangbu to follow my trail. We will all meet tonight."

Dorje returned to Tashi and placed in a fetal position to prepare him for rebirth and then prayed to the gods to guide him to the heaven of boundless light. But having died in an accident on the mountain without proper funeral rites, Tashi's soul risked becoming a restless *shrindi* spirit doomed to wander endlessly without entrance to one of the six realms.

When Beth wasn't looking, Dorje lifted his shirt to check his side, expecting to see a wound, but the skin was unbroken. He touched where it hurt and almost screamed but didn't want to alarm her.

The snow's weight had crushed the bamboo *doko* beyond use. "Can you walk?" he asked.

"I can do anything I have to. I learned to survive long ago."

Admiring her courage, he added her pad and bag to his pack. Then they slowly worked their way off the avalanche and continued down the ravine, constantly alert for any sound or movement of melting snow. Beth could not survive another fall. The intense glare of the sun burning his eyes, he reached for his glasses and with a jolt realized they were missing, lost in the avalanche. At the end of the path, Dorje looked back for Sangbu and the Norwegians. Nowhere in sight. It must have been harder to get through than Royd anticipated, but Dorje couldn't risk waiting with Beth still too hot. She needed fluids badly and he had neither water nor a container, so he insisted she eat snow even though it would take ten cups to produce a single liquid one. With perhaps three more hours of sunlight, he could get her lower yet.

Thirty minutes later, they reached a steep slope covered with fresh, loose snow—optimal conditions for an avalanche. At the base loomed a rocky cliff. Folded over with her elbows on her thighs, Beth was breathing heavily and still feverish. "I will cross first," Dorje said.

"Oh, no, you don't. If you get swept off that mountain, I'm not staying here alone."

"Sangbu and the others will come."

"I don't care. I'm going with you and you can't stop me."

He remembered Eric's comment. "Are you being a pit bull?"

"Yes." Beth laughed for the first time in days. "My teeth are sunk in your pants leg and you can't shake me loose."

That image he understood. She was coming with him. Knowing his weight could trigger a slide, Dorje stepped gingerly and motioned for Beth to remain a few feet behind and not speak. Watching the slope above them, he prayed it would remain stable. A silent, thin line at first, the fracture widened and the ground slowly moved beneath them. Too far across to turn back, Dorje signaled Beth to run. Gathering speed, the avalanche tossed him with such ferocity it was impossible to stay upright. She was down too, swept along by the current. Another thirty feet and they would be hurled off the rocky precipice. "Swim," Dorje shouted as he scrambled on hands and knees trying to reach the edge of the slide. Snow lashing his face, he couldn't see a thing but suddenly he felt the ground stop moving. He'd made it. Turning, he thrust an arm out and grabbed Beth seconds before she went over. With his last strength, he dragged her to him and held her, panting as they watched the avalanche disappear in a valley 500 feet below.

"My hero," she said gasping and touched his face, rekindling all his passion.

"I want Sangbu to bring the tent so I can make love with you tonight," he whispered.

"Me too." With a grin, she added, "At least we moved all that snow out of his way."

He was pleased she could find some humor. Leaning forward to kiss her, Dorje felt how hot she still was. Though exhausted, they had to keep moving lower. He insisted she eat more snow to cool her temperature. His hand applying pressure to his side, he rose and stepped onto the crust hoping it would hold them, but it was too soft in the late afternoon. He succeeded in staying on top only momentarily before it caved and he sank thigh deep. The constant, excruciating pain in his side having become a part of him now, he yelled for Sangbu and Royd every fifteen minutes, praying they would arrive with tents. To go back looking for them was too dangerous and time consuming.

Shadows stole across the landscape as ominous clouds forebode another storm. It would soon be dark. With no trees for shelter and finding no overhang, Dorje dug a small snow cave and spread the pads and bags on its floor. Twice in the late afternoon Beth had experienced bouts of dry heaves and was now shivering uncontrollably in spite of her fever. He crawled in the bags with her and zipped them together. She had eaten only a few crackers two mornings ago, and he couldn't remember when food last crossed his lips. Everything was becoming a daze. Although their snow consumption hadn't replenished as much liquid as they lost in the heat, to eat more after dusk would drop their temperatures dangerously low.

"Hold me tighter," she shuddered. "And never let go."

Confident that their body heat in the confines of a small cave would keep them warm, he tried to reassure her. "If we leave early while the snow is still frozen from the night, I can move much faster. And soon we will be making love in a warm bed with full stomachs."

With her wrapped in his arms, Dorje tried to stay awake prolonging the feeling of closeness, but physical exhaustion claimed his thoughts and emotions. With a tremulous breath, he closed his eyes and allowed himself to drift into sleep thinking of the Norwegians, Sangbu, and porters. His travel had been slow with Beth and they should have caught up by now. Hearing the wind howl, he dreamed of his companions struggling to reach him, perhaps dying in the cold. Trying to ignore the pain in his leg, he prayed for clear skies and help in finding Sangbu and Royd.

At dawn, the first shafts of snow-filtered light stole through drifts surrounding the door. Leaving Beth still sleeping, Dorje crawled through the opening to search for the others. Struggling against violent gusts that knocked him onto his injured side, he shouted repeatedly to Sangbu and Royd and waited for an answer. After 30 minutes of digging himself out of one hole after another, he decided to turn back, afraid of never finding them and risking the loss of too much time. With the wind pushing from behind, he had only gone a few yards when it cast a muffled cry over his shoulder. He stopped and listened but heard only his heart echoing in his head. Yelling their names again, he waited and still heard nothing. Dehydration, exhaustion, and hunger must have made him delirious. *Forget it. Keep going.* He lunged forward again in the ever-deepening drifts. A second cry, louder this time, made him turn around and spot Royd moving toward him. "Are you all right?" Dorje gasped.

"We're all sick and weak. Two porters were killed in a fall."

Not more deaths. It was too much. "Who?"

"I'm sorry. The only name I know is Lhamu and Hamar would turn back an entire avalanche for her."

Dorje was not surprised. "And the rest?"

"An hour or two behind. I came ahead to find you. Where's Beth?"

"In a snow cave, not far."

Beth was coughing uncontrollably when they reached her. Royd felt her forehead. "She's severely dehydrated and burning up. We can't wait." While Dorje prepared the bags and pads for travel, Royd asked Beth if she could walk.

"I'll try."

Despite her effort, she was too weak and dizzy to bear her own weight. Supporting her on both sides, the men departed in a whiteout with nothing to guide them other than continuing in a slow and cumbersome descent. An hour into their trek, Royd tripped on a rock lurking beneath the snow and tumbled downhill pulling Dorje and Beth off balance in a head-over-heel, arm-and-leg sprawling freefall behind him. Striking his back, shoulders, and injured side, Dorje fervently sought to grab anything that would stall his descent, but it was all happening too fast in a dizzying blur. "Beth, Royd," he screamed and heard nothing but the swish of his sliding parka. Suddenly the pack with sleeping gear tore loose and whizzed past, disappearing only seconds before Dorje's legs were airborne after it. In a desperate reach, he caught a rock on the edge of the precipice and hung on as his legs slammed against the wall.

"Watch out," he yelled clinging to the rock. "There is a cliff."

"I missed it," Royd called from Dorje's right.

"And Beth?"

"I don't know."

Shaking with exhaustion, pain, and cold, Dorje slowly pulled himself on top and collapsed trying to get his breath. "Beth," he shouted into the dense white surrounding him.

"Here," came back, the most beautiful sound ever heard.

"Do not move." Once again testing the ground before each step, Dorje followed her voice. "Are you hurt?" he asked before taking her in his arms.

"Not too bad, but I'm getting a lot sicker." Her face was hot against his shivering cheek.

Royd joined them. "We should wait for the storm to clear. It's insane to go on."

"I am afraid for Beth and want to go down now."

"But we can't see a damn thing. I don't intend to die falling off some mountain in a whiteout."

"And I don't intend to die freezing up here," Beth murmured. "Stay if you want, but we're going."

"Then you're both mad." When Beth's body crumpled as Dorje lifted her, Royd added, "Oh, what the hell. I'll come too. You'll never make it alone."

He led as they picked their way down the boulder-strewn face of the cliff never knowing when the next step would cast them into an abyss. Holding onto Beth, Dorje carefully handed her down to Royd on the steepest sections. Again progress was slow and treacherous, the rock face never ending. Hours later, the clouds gradually thinned to a blue-tinged, gossamer sky. They rested on a ledge trying to get their bearings with Beth beside them still feverish and weak.

"Looks like a valley over there," Royd said pointing to the left. "Probably where we should have come down."

"I did not know where to go," Dorje answered. "I could not see."

"Hey, I'm not blaming you. None of us could."

But Dorje blamed himself. He had failed Beth and everyone else: two porters dead and perhaps more by now. Sitting with his hands clasped around his knees, he closed his eyes and silently recited, *"Om mani padme hum."*

"We'd better go before it gets dark," said Royd.

As he repeated one more mantra, Dorje heard a sound from far away—the gentle chiming of yak bells, all at a different pitch. "Do you hear that?"

"Hear what?"

"Yak bells."

"It's just the wind. You've been out here too long and are going crazy. We all are."

The chiming—so faint. Thinking he could be hallucinating like *mikarus* who are sick from being too high, Dorje stopped breathing and listened harder. Five or six different tones. He got to his feet, trying to determine which way. Rising from the valley below, the bells clanged with the slow, steady rhythm of yaks plowing through snow. In a frenzy, he half stumbled, half crawled to the edge and searched the valley. Nothing but glaring white. In the distance, a red spot moved. Heart pounding, he watched it move again—the blood-red robe he had waited for as a boy. Surely he must be dreaming. The unmistakable form of a yak train was climbing toward the Cho La but far to the north of them just like the helicopter.

With a dry tongue that felt swollen and his throat frayed, Dorje screeched, "Father, we're here!" but his cries scattered like leaves rustling in the wind. "No! You're going the wrong way!"

"Who are you talking to?" Royd asked.

"My father is down there. We must get to him." But between them and Mingma lay a steep, snow-covered slope. Dorje glanced at Royd. "You can ski?"

The Norwegian laughed. "We invented the sport."

"And Colorado is famous for it," Beth added to his surprise that she was aware of their conversation. "But you'll have to hold me up."

Dorje lowered her over the ledge to Royd waiting below. With one on either side of her again, Royd counted, "One, two three, go."

"Geronimo," Dorje shouted and pushed off with his knees bent Marty style. Arms flailing for balance, he discovered skiing on steep snow was harder than he thought. But of the three, he remained upright the longest with Beth and Royd sliding on their seats and backs behind him. Then hitting a bump, he flew ten feet and landed face down before finally skidding to a stop. Are you okay?" he shouted and got a nod from each one.

He could see the procession better now: two men with six yaks breaking a trail through deep snow, the animals' thick coats impervious to the cold. Father!" he yelled. "Fa...ther!" The animals stopped; their bells stilled. Dorje yelled again, waving his jacket. Mingma turned toward the mountain and raised both arms, the full sleeves hanging like enormous red wings ready to enfold his son.

"They see us," Dorje cried. The schuss having drained her strength and spirit, Dorje's announcement seemed to give Beth the freedom to surrender to fatigue. Carrying her on his back, Dorje made his way down by stepping in the deep prints created by Royd ahead of him. When the two groups finally converged, Dorje expected to be reprimanded for dishonoring the gods by trespassing on their abode.

When instead Mingma commented, "My son is brave and strong to survive this storm," Dorje suddenly felt like his six-year-old self wanting his father to make everything all right.

"Beth is very sick. I must get her down."

"And what about the others—my nephew?" asked a third voice.

Pemba? How was it that these enemies came together? "Tashi's dead," tumbled out like rubble in the sweep of an avalanche. "He was carrying Beth and got buried alive."

"I knew she was a curse," Pemba grumbled. "I warned you to stay away."

"It wasn't her fault," Dorje said, too exhausted, cold, and hungry to argue. "He insisted on carrying her so he could prove himself worthy of working on Everest."

Pemba hurled and spat the words at Mingma. "Just like your brother. You blame me for his death, but he chose to carry a double load that day; he chose to cross the ice field at night."

All Dorje could see was a red blur as the pendulous sleeve rose and Mingma struck back with the vengeance of an angry god. "You corrupted him with your cursed blood money and sent him onto Everest."

"Wasn't me. He saw where the future is and wanted it. Lhakpa wasn't like you, a stubborn old dog with its tail curled so tight it can't straighten out."

Dorje covered his ears and yelled, "Stop it! Stop it! I'm sick of your fighting. Beth needs to go down and the others are still up there. They all need your help now!"

"I will show them the way," Royd interjected, "while you and your father take Beth."

After consuming the first water in days, the Norwegian left with Pemba and four yaks. Squinting into a bright sun now, Dorje watched steam snorting from their nostrils as they plowed up the hill in his jagged path. With visions of Sangbu and the others screaming from the icy depths of some chasm, he retreated from guilt and despair by turning his thoughts to Beth and his father.

"Your woman is shivering but her skin is hot," said Mingma. "My most gentle yak will carry her to the monks at Tengboche. But tonight we must stop at a *yersa* where we stored food, water, dung, and blankets on the way up. Many trekkers are lost."

"And you came for me," Dorje said, incredulous that his father had risked the cold.

"Now perhaps you will stop all this nonsense and I won't have to worry about you so much."

Worry about you so much? The words halted Dorje in his tracks. He was grateful and didn't want trouble with his father, but fourteen years of anger and disappointment bubbled into accusing words that appeared on his tongue and would not be silenced. "Why do you worry now when you never did before?"

"What are you talking about?"

"How...how can you ask that when you abandoned your sons and stopped loving them?"

Eyes averted from Dorje, Mingma continued with an unbroken stride. "I never stopped loving you."

The anger had smoldered too many years for Dorje to let go. "Then why did you never come for us?"

Mingma's voice hardened. "It's too cold now. You must wait until tonight, my angry son, and we will finally speak of this."

CHAPTER TWENTY-ONE

With one yak for Beth and another for gear, Dorje and Mingma returned using the animals' earlier path and reached the sole hut at Phulong Karpa just as the setting sun cast a pink wash across the white landscape. No one spoke. Only the clanging of yak bells and Beth's persistent, deep-throated cough broke the silence. After building a dung fire and supplying the young people with dry clothing, wool blankets, and water, Mingma went outside to give them time alone.

Sitting next to the hearth, Beth was still shivering uncontrollably. "I'm soooo cold. Hold me."

"I will as soon as you are out of these wet clothes." As he unbuttoned her shirt, Dorje noticed flat, rose-colored spots that had not been there before. Not wanting to alarm her, he distracted Beth by pulling a shirt over her head while he checked for more and discovered the rash covered her entire lower chest and abdomen. A scrap of fear attached itself firmly to his ribs and wouldn't let go.

Wrapped in two blankets, he was holding her by the fire when Mingma knocked and entered. "How is she?" he asked in Nepali.

Dorje tightened his jaw to keep his voice from wavering. "She has red spots all over her chest and is still too hot. What does that mean?"

"That a *shrindi* or witch has possessed her. We'll leave at first light for Tengboche."

Staring at Mingma, Beth said, "Is your father really here? I thought I was dreaming."

Dorje wanted to give her only good news. "Yes, and he just told me you are the most beautiful woman he has ever seen."

"Thank you," Beth said, nodding at Mingma. "Does he understand?" Dorje chuckled. "No. Not a word of English. We can speak of love all night and he will think we are talking only of yaks and the storm."

As Beth giggled and nestled closer to him, Dorje tried to ignore the nervous field mice who had again invaded him, scurrying about in a fearful frenzy. In order to squelch them, he would hold onto Beth all night and believe the monks could exorcise her demons. After a meal of *tsampa, nak* cheese, cold *chapatis,* and tea of which she ate very little, Beth lay on the bench wrapped in her sleeping bag, her head in Dorje's lap.

To keep from thinking about the rash, fever, and coughing spells, he looked at his father lying on the other side of him—the closest they had been since Dorje's return to the Khumbu. "You promised we would talk later," he said quietly, not wanting to wake Beth.

Mingma shouldered himself upright and closed the blanket over his chest. "I have started to tell you many times, but your anger always comes between us. Can you put it away long enough for me to explain?"

"I will try."

Hands folded in his lap and eyes to the floor, Mingma said, "Sometimes, especially when we're young, we don't always make the right decisions. And so much was happening when you were six and seven that I..." He paused and opened his thumbs in a kind of shrug. "But none of that matters to you."

"None of what?"

Mingma was silent as if he didn't want to go on.

"What was happening that was more important than your sons?" Dorje demanded.

"I didn't say more important."

"You watched us being dragged away, crying for you, and did nothing about it."

"Your mother wanted to leave me and I couldn't talk her out of it. Away for months at a time on trading trips, I couldn't have taken care of two young boys. I had to let you go." His shoulders arched and his back stiffened. "I don't know where to begin. As a boy, I was educated in Tibetan monasteries while my father traded there."

"You could have done that with us," Dorje said, as if pleading his case now would change the past.

"No. Things were different then. And you are very impatient," his father added frowning. He shifted onto the other hip. "I knew early on that

I didn't want to be a monk, so at fifteen I disrobed and gave back my vows. When I was seventeen, my father needed an alliance with a wealthy salt trader, so he arranged a marriage with his daughter."

"My mother?"

"Yes. She was from a different village. And although we had never seen each other before, we learned to care. But there was never real passion or love. I found that years later...with a Tibetan woman."

Stunned, Dorje suddenly didn't recognize the man next to him. Mingma was no longer the pacing, indomitable figure whose eyes could impale him to the wall but a man desiring the same depth of passion he felt for Beth. Of all the possible explanations he'd conjured up over many years, this was not among them. "What happened to her?"

Hands clenched tightly between his knees, Mingma stared at the fire. "I've made some bad decisions in my life but none as terrible as that one. For years Nimputi begged me to bring her to Nepal. She was scared of what was happening around her. Chinese troops occupied the cities and claimed Tibetans must return them to the Motherland." Still gazing into the fire, Mingma pressed his fingertips together. "I was young and ambitious, too absorbed in trading animals to really understand what was happening—not the way she did. Then one year, she told me rumors of Tibetans in Kham fighting back. The Chinese retaliated by destroying villages, torturing and executing thousands. This region was far to the east, away from Nimputi's home. I didn't believe she was in immediate danger, but I promised to return for her and our children as soon as I finished trading in India."

"Children?"

His fingertips splayed together, Mingma tapped them lightly against his lips. "Yes, two young girls."

Tibetan sisters. Unprepared for this, Dorje didn't know what to feel: anger, jealousy, curiosity! "But what about us?"

His father turned to him with a surprised look. "My feelings hadn't changed. I loved you as much as always and planned to take care of you and your mother. Many Sherpas have two wives, especially those who travel, but I waited too long. She had heard stories of Nimputi before I asked her permission, and that caused her to lose face. Feeling disgraced and betrayed, she walked away from me and took you with her."

Understanding now the angry voices in bed the night his father returned and the raging silence the following days, Dorje couldn't condemn him for having wanted love. If he were married to Shanti now, would he not be guilty of the same? Dorje ran his hand along Beth's sleeping body, feeling the curve of her hip, the slenderness of her waist. The thought of anyone taking her from him sent a chill through his bones. With unexpected compassion for his father, Dorje asked, "What happened to her?"

Mingma's chest rose and then let out slowly as if the air were too heavy to breath. "I don't know." Leaning forward with his elbows on his knees, he buried his face in his hands. "I never believed the Chinese would commit such crimes. I never…" His voice faltered. "Never thought they would harm women and children." When Mingma lapsed into silence, Dorje waited, trying to imagine the visions haunting his father.

"I went back for them right after India, but when I arrived in her village …" He folded his hands as if squeezing them would mitigate the pain. "It had been destroyed. The buildings were in rubble, broken glass and wood everywhere. From a large open grave came the sickening stench of death. Searching through hundreds of decaying bodies, I prayed I wouldn't find them. I wandered for months, half crazed, asking everyone I met what had become of the others in her village. And it was always the same. No one would talk to me. I was a stranger—someone to be feared. The Chinese had created so much distrust that people were afraid of their own neighbors betraying them.

"Anyone accused of believing in the old ways before the Chinese *liberated* Tibet was subject to *thamzing*, what the Chinese called a struggle session. I witnessed one of these horrible scenes where people were brought to a courtyard and questioned about the old society. Any kind of wrong answer resulted in immediate beatings and execution. I stood helplessly while soldiers wrapped a man in a blanket and set him on fire, and I watched them behead and disembowel another." Shaking his tightly clenched hands, Mingma stared at the ceiling with a strange laugh. "All this time the Tibetans thought I was spying for the Chinese while I was in constant fear of the Chinese thinking I was Tibetan."

Dorje sympathized with the urgency and pain of Mingma's search, but a young boy aching for his father didn't care about Tibetans or Chinese. He simply wanted him back. "Then you should have left them and come home to us."

"How could I?" Mingma sat back with the color draining from his face. "All around me, Tibetans were starving because Chinese troops confiscated their crops and shipped them off to the Motherland. I knew my wife and children were hungry somewhere. I couldn't abandon them."

"You did us," answered the angry man-child.

Dropping his hands in his lap with an impatient look, Mingma said, "I had hoped my oldest son would have more compassion. You and Nima were safe with your mother, but I didn't know the fate of Nimputi and our children. I had been without food for many days and my stomach was eating away at itself. So I finally gave in and joined others scavenging through refuse thrown to the pigs. But I still couldn't bring myself to break apart the manure of soldiers' horses looking for undigested grain."

When Mingma paused again, Dorje thought of the debilitating hunger and thirst of the previous days and couldn't imagine enduring it for weeks and months. His father continued a few minutes later. "As always, I asked if anyone knew of the people from Nimputi's village and got no reply. Remember I was a stranger and not to be trusted. But late one night as I lay shivering in a rocky ditch, a man quietly approached in the cover of darkness and whispered that he'd been there when the soldiers came."

"Been where?"

"In Nimputi's village. The Chinese had taken all the valuable religious objects and packed them off to the Motherland. They removed the carved pillars and beams for use in their own construction and then burned the scriptures in a great bonfire in the temple courtyard before destroying the buildings. While the ashes still glowed, soldiers forced the monks at gunpoint to have sex with nuns and made the villagers watch. Anyone who protested was immediately executed. Then they ..." Mingma took a long breath and closed his eyes as if he couldn't bear to look. "Marched the women and young girls naked through the village ..." His voice came from a hollow, dead place as he uttered, "And raped them."

It couldn't be true what his father was saying. Men couldn't be that savage, that barbaric. Even animals didn't rape their young. Dorje clung to Beth and vowed no one would ever touch her. Finally understanding, he relinquished all the resentment, all the accusations and hurt he had so carefully tended and nourished for fourteen years. His father wasn't a cold, unloving man. He simply loved too much. "Did you ever find them?"

"The man confiding in me said all were taken to a labor camp. With only barley mixed with sawdust for rations, thousands died of starvation, cold, and exhaustion. He had escaped by pretending to be dead. He was dumped in a mass grave to be cremated the following day. He might as well have been dead when I met him. Every bone shone through his thin skin; his eyes bulged; his teeth were hanging from their sockets; all his hair had fallen out. He was a walking skeleton bearing a greater curse than a *shrindi*."

"And Nimputi?"

Covering his face, Mingma wept quietly. "She had died only two weeks before and not far from the place we talked. I hadn't arrived in time. If only I had come earlier...not gone to India...if only..."

"There was nothing you could do," Dorje offered but knew his words were of no solace. "And your daughters?"

Mingma closed his eyes as the energy flowed out of him. "I wanted to search longer but was too overcome with grief. Maybe I was afraid of learning the truth. I couldn't have endured more. Since then, I have questioned every refugee coming through Namche and no one knows of them." After rising and putting more dung on the fire, Mingma stood watching Dorje and Beth. "You love this woman?"

"Yes as you loved Nimputi." Brushing her hair back, he felt Beth's cheek. Still too warm. "And if I lose her..."

"You will be like me, alone and surviving on memories of what could have been."

In the dim light of a flickering fire, they sat talking of love, and Dorje forgot about the pain in his side and the years of watching and waiting. He knew now that Mingma had never deserted him. He had only gone away for a while.

CHAPTER TWENTY-TWO

Mingma stayed awake all night to tend the fire for his son and this woman with eyes as blue as the sky above a snow-capped peak. Lying beside her on a bench barely wide enough for two, Dorje clung to Beth as if afraid her spirit would flee in the night. Watching them, Mingma knew his son would give his life for her as he would have done for Nimputi. They were both men who loved too deeply, and he didn't want Dorje to suffer the same cavernous feeling that consumed him. When dawn came seeping down the mountainside, Mingma touched his son's shoulder and whispered, "We must go now." He waited outside while Dorje readied Beth for traveling, but when his son joined him ashen-faced, Mingma knew the rash had spread.

Claiming Dorje was too weak now, Mingma insisted on lifting Beth onto the yak and leading the animal, but in truth he was acting selfishly. Every step that he bore the burden of this young woman helped atone for leaving his own daughters behind. "I desperately wanted to keep looking for them," he said, his thoughts forcing themselves in words. "But I was starving and as sick as the man who had confided in me. In a few more weeks I would have been dead and of no use to anyone. Already monsoon snows were falling on the high plateau and soon the Nangpa La would be impassible in my condition. Plus, I had two sons waiting for me in the Solu. I came home determined to see you and to regain my strength for another journey into Tibet when the snow melted."

"Then why didn't you come?"

The sadness in his son's voice clutched his heart. "Too much happened at once. I almost died coming over the high pass in snow just as did so many of the refugees and their babies who followed the Dalai Lama when he left. In Namche, I arrived at an empty house where a young boy used to jump into my arms and hug my neck, yelling, 'Baabu!' Now the room was barren. Happiness no longer resided there, only my lifeless, mangled spirit lying in despair. I was alone and dying when Pemba entered."

"Pemba? What does he have to do with this story?"

"He staggered into the room, and I was pleased to see my best friend who had left Tibet eight months before I did, but it wasn't the same Pemba I knew. The waist-length braids were gone. Short stiff hair shot in all directions when he pulled a wool cap from his head, and his face was sunburned around an outline of the goggles *mikarus* wore. In climbing pants and a foreign jacket, yet barely five feet tall, he was a strange crossbreed. 'What sort of specter visits me?' I asked, thinking my illness was hallucinating again. Not a ghost, he told me, but a man wise enough to know our trading days had ended. Tibet was no longer ours. The future was in the mountains and the men who came to climb them. He had gone to work for an expedition."

"He started that quickly?"

"Yes. I called him their pack animal, a small, belligerent yak, and said I was ashamed of my friend trading his soul for rupees."

The rest was harder for Mingma to relate because it had altered the rest of his life, yet he had to make Dorje understand. "Pemba's hands were trembling and his eyes were jumping from one thing to the next. I knew something was wrong, but I wasn't prepared. He said three expedition porters had become ill and were forced to go down. That left the climbers three porters short for moving loads higher to the next camp."

Watching his son, Mingma wondered if he could grasp the enormity of what he was saying. "I didn't know why Pemba was telling me this or why in a cold room, beads of sweat were curling on his brow. He explained that the climbers saw a storm moving in and wanted to reach the top before it arrived. They couldn't go further without supplies and didn't want to lose days waiting for the remaining porters to haul them up. I knew bad news was coming and I couldn't bear any more right then. I told him to stop but he was determined. His whole body drooped and his voice became thin and tight as he explained the climbers offered double wages to anyone who would carry twice in one day. His nervous eyes narrowed on me as he asked if I understood that double wages were more than I could make in a year."

Stopping to shift Beth's weight on the yak, Mingma took a few long breaths before continuing. "He said three porters volunteered and tried to make two trips in daylight but it was impossible with such loads. Then Pemba backed away and his eyes never settled on me as he spoke of my brother and another porter never returning. My brother? The words whipped and cut me like an ice storm. My brother was a simple man living in the isolated village of Phortse. He had no contact with expeditions. 'You killed him,' I yelled at Pemba. 'You and your talk of easy money killed him.'"

"What did he say?"

"The same as you heard yesterday. That Lhakpa chose to carry the extra loads, not him. Twice Pemba betrayed me, first by telling your mother about Nimputi and then by taking my brother on the mountain. When Lhakpa died, I assumed the responsibility of his wife and child forever because Droma Sunjo and Dawa can't survive on their own. My life no longer belonged to me. I couldn't return to Tibet or go to my sons. I could only hope you would come home."

"And I did, angry and hurtful. I'm sorry for all the awful things I've said and done."

"So am I. Things would have been better if I had told you sooner."

"But I didn't let you, so we are both at fault. But now it is done."

As Mingma strode on toward Tengboche, he wanted to lift a six year old into his arms and erase all that had happened. Perhaps taking care of his son's woman as if she were his daughters would temper a few regrets.

As they dropped 5,100 lower, the snow depth diminished until by Tengboche the accumulation was no longer excessive and walking became much easier. But by the time Mingma climbed the stairs to the main gompa of the monastery, his legs were aching. *I'm too old for this*, he thought as Dorje lifted Beth from the animal's back.

She looked at Mingma and smiled. "Thank you."

"What is she saying?" Mingma asked his son.

"It is their way of expressing gratitude for something you have done or given them."

"Oh," he answered and bowed. With her beguiling charm that tugged at his heart too, Mingma could see why both sons loved her. Relating all he knew of her illness to the head monk, he said he could only afford eight lamas to pray for her recovery.

After conferring with Beth, Dorje explained, "She says she is very ill and must see the doctor at the Khunde hospital right away."

"But we can't get there by dark and it's too dangerous traveling at night. Explain that the lamas will pray for her." Watching them, Mingma hoped their love was strong enough to bridge two such different worlds. His had not been so very different from Nimputi's.

After spreading her pad and bag in the center of the room, Dorje stayed with Beth while four lamas sat cross-legged on either side murmuring prayers in low intonations accompanied by a pair of *dung-chen*. The low constant tone of the long horns resembled the sound of dragons mating to Mingma's ear, but at last the sustained notes lulled Beth to sleep. Pacing the room, Mingma recognized the sorrow in his son's eyes and could not allow him to lose this woman. When Beth showed no improvement by nightfall, he decided to summon other forces. Mingma sent a young lama for a shaman to exorcise the evil spirits causing her illness and told Dorje to warn Beth so she would understand and not be afraid.

An hour later, the shaman entered with long garlands of bells, beads, and snake bones hanging from his neck. As he strode across the room, strings of feathers and ribbons whirled from a headdress bearing paintings of the five Buddhas in meditation. Sitting beside Beth, he took her pulse at her wrist and her stomach and began chanting in a low, resonating voice while playing a *damaru* made from human half skulls. His right hand rotated the hour-glass-shaped drum making its clappers strike the membranes while his left fingertips cupped rice and held it to Beth's face before pretending to pull it from her ear and toss it over his shoulder. Taking her pulse again, he announced with great assurance that a *pem* had caused Beth's illness.

Removing two large brass cups from his basket, he told Dorje to fill one with water and the other with flowers and leaves. While performing a circular hopping dance, he beat a two-headed drum, the *dhyangro,* with a long snake-shaped drumstick. As the drumming intensified, he shivered and sweat simultaneously, his breathing became labored, and his body shook violently. The clanging garlands of bells mimicked the rhythm of his body as his head thrashed back and forth with his lips flapping and sunken eyes closed. The timber and quality of his voice changed into deep guttural sounds and strange hissing sounds emanated from his mouth. "It's coming! It's coming!" he shouted and circled Beth to seal her in a protective ring.

When Beth started crying, Mingma told Dorje, "Tell her what's happening and hold her tight. Don't let her be afraid like Nimputi."

The shaman's face twisted and grimaced as he alternately hissed and moaned. His guiding deity spoke through him in a high screeching voice announcing it had seen the face of the *pem*: the spirit of a woman who had drowned and taken possession of Beth. When the shaman slumped forward, his guide departed and a sudden chill filled the room. Moments later, the shaman poured the container of leaves and flowers onto the floor and a small cloth bundle rolled out holding a tiny scrap of cloth which he said came from Beth's shirt and mud from the sole of her foot. The witch had created the bundle to bring harm, and the invoked spirit had retrieved it to remove the curse. Kneeling beside Beth, the shaman placed his mouth over hers and sucked the evil in one long breath. Her body shuddered and grew limp.

After Mingma agreed to pay in *chang* and butter as soon as he returned to Namche, the shaman packed his things and left. Exhausted from being up all night and making the long, difficult trip to Tengboche, Mingma took a blanket and curled up on a bench near his son and Beth. He'd done all he could for now and hoped the gods had listened.

*   *   *   *   *   *   *   *   *

After the monk and lamas had departed to their rooms, Dorje lay holding Beth who still seemed frightened. To reassure her that faith healers possessed supernatural powers, he recounted the story of when his brother was sick. When prayer had failed to remove the swelling and pain in his stomach, their mother had called for a shaman whose personal deity said they must build a *torma* and fool the *shrindi* ghost into thinking it was Nima.

"What's a *torma*?" Beth asked, gripping him tightly as if afraid to let go lest some evil spirit whisk her away.

"*Tormas* are made from barley dough painted with colored butters, usually in the shape of gods or demons. We use them in many ceremonies. It is a sin for a Buddhist to kill a living thing, so we sacrifice them instead of animals the way Hindus do. My mother and I made the torma and dressed it in Nima's clothes. We put cheese, *chapatis*, apples, and *chang* around it and then waited at the end of the room. The shaman ordered the demon to leave Nima and move into the *torma* that offered much good food and drink. He repeated this many times."

"And did it go there?"

"Yes. When the shaman felt the ghost had left my brother to eat and drink our offerings, he placed a protective spell over Nima and whispered to me, 'Now!' I grabbed the *torma* with the *shrindi* in it, ran downstairs, and threw it to the dog outside. He was hungry and loved this rich dough filled with creamy butter so much that he gobbled it up and destroyed the ghost in it."

"That's an amazing story. And did Nima get well?"

"Yes," Dorje answered feeling confident he had put her mind at ease. "Tomorrow I shall make a *torm*a as beautiful as you and color the hair bright gold."

"I would like that," she whispered and he felt the tension gradually slipping from her as she drifted into sleep.

CHAPTER TWENTY-THREE

Dorje awoke to Beth heaving in his arms, her body dripping with sweat. She pushed away from him, rolled onto her opposite side, and vomited. As if suffocating, she took long, gasping inhales and began trembling uncontrollably. Dorje panicked. "Father, what can I do?"

Off the bench and at his side immediately, Mingma felt her skin and looked at his son helplessly.

"This demon's too powerful for our gods and healers," said Dorje. "We must take her to the doctor in Khunde and do it now."

"Get her ready while I prepare the yaks."

When Dorje started moving again, the pain that had lain silent while he slept screamed, but he stilled the cries. The only voice Beth would hear was his reassuring love. Dawn was struggling with heavy, black-tinged clouds veiling the sun. Watching his breath puff and blow back in his face with each step, Dorje knew the journey would take them more than four cold hours.

They arrived in Khunde just before noon. First the New Zealand doctor questioned Beth about her activities and contacts the past few weeks and then checked her pulse, skin, eyes, mouth, and chest. The rash and high fever alarmed him the most. "Are you sure you haven't had unboiled water?" he asked a second time. "Maybe a handful from a stream on your way up?"

"Positive. I've been very careful."

"Well, your symptoms indicate a severe case of typhoid but I can't be certain without a blood test."

While awaiting the result, Dorje sat tracing Beth's long, slender fingers and telling her everything would be all right. Suddenly, a familiar voice in the outer room pulled him from his seat and into the hall as Hamar pushed past the nurse demanding to see a doctor. He was hot and felt miserable all over.

Hearing him, Beth slowly drew her hands down over her face. "Of course," she said with a sigh. "How could I have forgotten or been so stupid. One day, he gave water to Lhamu and me. He must have filled his bottle in a stream."

Mingma waved a menacing red sleeve at Hamar in a gesture that said *Sit down and be quiet.* To Dorje's surprise, the big Norwegian complied. "I will never have that power," Dorje confessed to Beth. "Look at him. Without a word, he can do more than I can yelling."

"Hush. You possess the power of my love," she whispered, her lips stretching into a smile that took the edge off the interminable waiting.

Twenty minutes later, the doctor confirmed his typhoid diagnosis in English. "Both of you are also suffering from severe dehydration, malnutrition, and exposure. Rest here until evacuation arrangements can be made, hopefully by helicopter to Kathmandu tomorrow. You can't make the long trip down to Lukla. At home, check into a hospital for a fluid and salt drip plus antibiotic treatment."

"Will we be all right?" Beth asked.

"I think so. Most cases are cured, but there is always a risk of complications such as bleeding of the intestines and kidney failure. I'm not equipped to treat those."

The roar of an avalanche paled to the words emanating from the doctor's mouth. Dorje glanced at his father who had not understood. It had taken the rape of an entire country to separate him from the woman he loved but only a few sips of bottle of water to wrench Beth from Dorje's arms. In shock, he didn't know whether to scream, curse the gods, blame Hamar's recklessness or worse yet himself for allowing her to go up there.

Absorbed with guilt, Dorje wasn't listening until the doctor shook his arm and brought him back to consciousness. "You have what's called a flail chest," he said in Nepali. "Many ribs are broken in several places. The whole side of your chest is floating free with broken bones acting like sharp knives. That's why you've experienced so much pain."

"Can my son die from this?" Mingma asked.

"Not if he's careful. Eventually the ribs will heal by themselves, but I want to keep him here to make sure his lung doesn't collapse or he doesn't get pneumonia."

Dorje only half listened because without Beth he didn't care anymore. Holding her with his mouth to her ear, he whispered, "What am I to do? If you stay or go, either way I risk losing you."

She ran her fingers up the back of his hair and pulled him closer. "I came half way around the world to find you and I'm not letting go."

"But if you don't get help…" He paused, unable to voice the unspeakable.

"I'll come back if you'll wait for me."

In words that seemed to come from far away, the doctor spoke to his father in Nepali about getting a helicopter for Beth and the Norwegians. "I know a man in Namche who has such connections," Mingma said, "and will go to him immediately." Hearing his proud father offer to seek the help of his greatest enemy told Dorje of the sacrifice he was willing to make. He vowed to never utter an angry word to him again.

Hamar remained at the hospital in one room with Lhamu while Dorje and Beth shared a bed in another. Lying on his back with Beth against the full length of his healthy side, Dorje felt her heart beating and the rhythm of her breathing. He gently stroked her hair and inhaled its aroma to saturate all of his senses for recall when she was gone. Dreading the first blush of dawn, he held her through the night fighting sleep so he wouldn't miss a moment of their time together. Sadly, it arrived much too soon with its pale light filtering through smoky clouds. Dorje watched it steal through the window and along the floor whispering, *I've come to take her away*

No! You can't have her, he yelled in a silent scream.

But dawn was heartless and cruel. She lit the way for his father and doctor to enter. "We must go," said Mingma. "Yesterday, Pemba radioed Kathmandu from the police post above Namche. A helicopter will be here in two hours. He and the other two Norwegians will meet us there."

"Give us just five minutes." After Mingma exited, Dorje lightly kissed Beth's forehead and watched her slowly emerging from sleep. "They have a helicopter and are waiting for us."

"I hoped it wouldn't be so soon. I can't believe this is happening." She held her hand to his cheek. "But we'll be together again. I'll return in the warmth of spring after I finish writing about you."

The Norwegians and Pemba were waiting with everyone's belongings at a level stretch of ground near the photo rock. "You look like shit," Royd told Hamar. "I don't understand what Pemba was saying but got the message we have to leave today."

His face still flushed with fever, Hamar said, "I have typhoid and the doctor wants me to go home, but I'm staying here."

Removing his toothpick, Kirk asked, "What the hell are you talking about?"

"I love her Lhamu and she loves me."

"For God's sake, how do you know that? You don't even speak the same language."

"Love needs no words."

"You big dumb Norwegian," said Royd. "You're in lust not in love. Now get on the damn helicopter."

Feet planted firmly and arms folded across his chest, Hamar said, "No. I'm staying. You know how much I wanted to come here. This is my home now."

Turning to Beth, Royd said, "Don't tell me you're caught up in this insanity too."

Dorje squeezed Beth's hand wanting her emotions to rule, but her old rational self reigned. "No. It's too risky. I'm going back to recover and write my Sherpa piece. I'll return in the spring."

It was time to board. Turning to Dorje, Beth said, "One last picture together?"

"Not one last, just one more," Dorje replied. He handed her camera to Royd before helping Beth onto the rock. Then he took her in his arms for a long, passionate embrace. "I want you to look at this picture and remember how good it feels so you'll come back to me," he whispered before letting go.

As they approached the helicopter, Nima stepped from the crowd of curious onlookers that always gathered when the flying machines arrived. Releasing Dorje's hand, Beth said. "Let me go say good-bye to him."

Dorje had hoped time would erase Nima's hurt and anger, but they still loomed in his brother's eyes. And when Beth returned, Dorje watched Nima erect a wall as impassable as the Nuptse Ridge standing between them and Everest. After a last, lingering kiss, Dorje reined his emotions by performing a traditional farewell. He placed a white silk *kata* around the necks of the two Norwegians and finally Beth, biting his lips as he gave hers a little tug. "*Namaste*," he whispered. "I love you."

"Me too," she whispered. "I'll be back."

When the door closed, Dorje clung to himself to keep from splintering further apart. The blades spun, churning the ground into great whirling, dust clouds, and the helicopter magically lifted into the air with a deafening noise. He walked to the end of the ridge and gazed as it flew past soft-splayed hills and finally disappeared. The anguish in his heart was like a glacier scouring a valley and leaving behind only a cold, rocky moraine where once marigolds mingled with wildflowers. His life had just been stripped of lush meadows and left in muddy debris.

CHAPTER TWENTY-FOUR

The pilot gave Beth and the Norwegians cotton for their ears and hard candy to suck on. Biting the insides of her cheeks to keep from crying, she pressed her face to the glass and watched Dorje as they lifted off. She wanted to grab his thick, blowing hair and pull his mouth to hers. Such rapture resided in his kiss. As he became smaller and smaller and finally disappeared, her eyes clouded over. Hamar had the courage to remain. With her body and heart aching for Dorje, why didn't she? Because it was a foolish, irrational thing to do and those words had never defined her, but nor had passion and love until a few weeks ago when she felt fully alive for the first time in her life.

Below her lay the serpentine valley of the Dudh Kosi with trees clinging to the sides and edged by huge, precipitous peaks that seemed to be leaning inward. As they flew over Lukla, the muscles in her face strained to ward off tears as she remembered Dorje's first gaze. Beyond the landing strip, terraces unfolded like dark wrinkles across the mountain face. Fifty-five minutes after leaving the snowy depths of the Khumbu, they reached the verdant Kathmandu Valley with the ancient cities of Bhaktapur, Patan, and the capital itself. Seeing the city now after being in the hills, Beth was in awe of the achievements of this medieval, fairy-tale kingdom struggling to come of age.

Pemba had contacted the American consulate who sent a representative to assist Beth in getting a flight home that departed just two hours after her arrival. After thanking Royd and Kirk for their help and wishing them good luck, Beth boarded the plane that would whisk her away from Shangri-la. Still feeling nauseated and feverish, she took a pill for motion sickness and slept intermittently, waking for meals and the frequent cups of hot tea advised by the doctor. Stepping off the plane in New York, groggy and blurry eyed, Beth felt quite disoriented. For weeks, the Himalayas, Buddhist temples, avalanches, Sherpas, yaks, and yetis had been her world. Suddenly plopped down in the 20th century again, how could she move from that reality back into this one? Standing in line at immigration beside men in pinstriped suits and carrying brief cases, Beth felt strangely alien to them. And later, gazing at the drinking fountain, she couldn't force herself to turn the handle and drink until someone impatiently demanded she hurry up. Never before had she immersed herself so completely in another culture. It was disquieting.

She called Eric to ground herself. "I'm in New York," she said yawning, "waiting for the plane to Denver. Can you meet me?"

"Of course, Babe! How are you?"

"Okay. Just a little feverish from drinking some water, but I'll be fine after checking into a hospital for a couple of days."

"How'd that happen? You're always so careful."

"It's a long story but I don't want to go into it now. We'll have plenty of time in a few hours."

"I can hardly wait. His voice softened. "Still love me?"

"Of course," she said not having the strength or courage right now to tell Eric the truth—that she loved him but was not *in love* with him. For now, her recounting of the trip to Gokyo and the storm on the Cho La would have to exclude any mention of her relationship with Dorje.

Meeting her at the gate with an armload of flowers and a shower of trembling kisses, Eric pulled Beth to the nearest chair and sat staring at her. "I just need to look at you for a minute. It seems like you've been gone forever."

Beth held his hand and smiled, telling herself that fatigue and illness were dulling her emotions and a week from now things feel different. "So tell me about the Galapagos," she said when they started for the car. "I want to hear all about it."

He boasted of landing at 9300 feet in Quito with no ill effects after being in Nepal and raved about the giant tortoises weighing up to 550 pounds and living 100 years, the iguanas, and hundreds of land and sea birds. "I missed you so much and wanted you with me. I would have taken better care of you."

"I missed you too," she murmured with her heart whispering, *'Be kind and don't hurt him.'*

Beth spent five days in the hospital, resting and organizing her notes. Before going to Nepal, she had read numerous anthropological studies on the Sherpas but found the works dry and too analytical. She wanted to offer an intimate portrait of their lives that would engage readers. During visiting hours, the Denver world closed in on her, usurping her thoughts and emotions. Eric came every day with pictures of Galapagos and Nepal, saying she could keep the latter to choose which ones best illustrated her work. Friends from the Colorado Mountain Club seemed to come in designated shifts to ask about trekking in Nepal, a goal many of them shared.

When finally alone, Beth placed two pictures side by side: one with her standing on a rock next to Eric and the other with Dorje. Such different emotional realms. In the still of the night with only occasional hushed voices coming from the nurses' station, Beth nestled her head in the hollow of Dorje's shoulder, clasped her arm around his neck, and slid her leg snugly between his as they had slept in another hospital bed. Then she quietly escaped into the deep cavern of her loneliness where dreams yearning for his reality echoed off the walls. Was he thinking of her too? If only there were some way of letting him know how much she loved him and that she planned to return. When she promised to write, he explained that letters never made it to Namche. So she could only fantasize about the moment they would reunite and hoped those images would pull her through the cold winter of writing.

Beth finished the longest work of her career in early February after spending the holidays with Eric's family. They were kind and caring people who treated her well. His sister Carolyn and her husband became the siblings she never had. Since her father had never resurfaced, Beth didn't know whether he was dead or alive and holidays with her mother and the current live-in sugar daddy and lesbian lover were insufferable and generally a designated time for the annual suicide attempt. Having resigned from the post as her mother's keeper a year ago, Beth was now alone with painful memories of other holidays that even Eric's loving family couldn't expunge.

By mid March, the accolades for her work were overwhelming. It was the best she'd ever done and Beth glowed with satisfaction. "It belongs to you too," she told Eric at dinner the night she received an award. "You're an amazing photographer. I admire you tremendously."

"And love me too," he said smiling but with the faintest inflection at the end—not really a question but a glimmer of doubt.

"But of course," she gave as her stock answer and added a playful kiss on his cheek. How handsome he looked in his tuxedo and so debonair as he led her onto the dance floor.

"You're radiant tonight," he whispered in her ear, "and seem much more present than you've been since returning from Nepal."

"Really?" she said leaning back to look at him. "And how is that?"

"I don't know. I can't define it, just something that I feel."

Moving to the slow dance of lovers, she rested her cheek against his and wondered if she'd been away from Dorje too long. Was it possible to return to the harsh reality of his world after being at home these past months? Or could he feel comfortable here? She imagined him sitting at one of the tables dressed in a tux and trying to converse about politics or religion. Most likely, he'd be miserable and feel out of place. In the Khumbu, he was a high-ranking sirdar who shone brilliantly among the other Sherpas, but would he garner the same respect here sitting among her cohorts? And would she feel the same about him? At times, the whole Everest experience seemed a distant dream now.

Eric's hand interrupted her thoughts as it moved along her side and brushed the fullness of her breast. She hadn't rejected his advances since her return but had often feigned the throes of passion. As long as the orgasms shook his whole being and he fell asleep spent and satisfied, the little gnats of doubt and guilt left her in peace. Feeling giddy with success tonight, she appreciated who he was and what he meant to her. When they returned to the table, she slipped her hand under the cloth and along his thigh. He jumped and glanced at her, his mouth agape. "Let's go home," she whispered. Thirty seconds later, he was out of his seat and seeking the waiter for the bill. Who cared that the main course had not yet arrived.

Instead of falling asleep immediately afterwards, he turned onto his side and faced her. "We haven't moved forward with wedding plans except to set a June date and that's not very far off. My family keeps asking, but I told them you needed to get well first and finish the piece."

"And now it's done," she confirmed and tried snuggling up to escape his gaze, but he kept her at a distance studying her face. How did she say *No* to someone with such love in his eyes and who might be the very man she should or would marry? "Maybe we can look into some places this weekend."

"I think Carolyn already has," he admitted. "She wants to show you."

The next morning, Eric's sister drove them to a place on top of Lookout Mountain with an incredible view of the city and suburbs. "What do you think?" she asked.

"It's perfect," Eric answered and looked to Beth for confirmation.

"Yes, just perfect."

"Oh, I'm so relieved you like it," said Carolyn. "But you have to make a deposit today. It's only available because of a cancellation. I've had your name on a long list ever since Eric came back and told us you were engaged." She threw her arms around Beth and hugged her. "Welcome to the family. We love you."

"I love you too," came out so naturally it surprised Beth because she'd never said that to another woman. The relationship with her mother had shrouded most female interactions in distrust.

"If you're free next week," Carolyn said walking back to the car, "I could help with the arrangements. You're running short of time and there's so much to do."

Caught up in Carolyn's enthusiasm and enjoying the sisterly affection, Beth allowed herself to be carried along the next few weeks picking out the wedding gown, a dress for Carolyn as the only maid of honor, the invitations, cake, flowers, a photographer, and caterer. With everything suddenly taken care of and the reality of an impending marriage looming near while part of her heart was still roaming in the Himalayas, Beth panicked and called her editor seeking a momentary reprieve.

"John, what do you have for me?"

"I've got a month in the outback of Australia with an Aboriginal tribe but not until June. It's too freaking hot now."

Her leg bouncing nervously, she insisted, "I need to go right away."

"They're looking for someone to do a story and photograph this tepui in Venezuela."

"And what in the hell is a tepui?"

"A kind of table-like mesa. Mount Roraima's the tallest one, about 9200 feet." Beth slumped forward with her forehead in her hand, picturing Dorje standing at the same elevation in Lukla. "Sure you really want to do this?" John asked.

"Yes," she answered, fighting back a well of tears. "And as soon as possible."

"I guess you could go this week but only if Eric is willing."

"He'll go."

"Then see if you can also talk him into taking the Nam job.

"What Nam job?"

"Right now there's the largest number of troops since the war began. We think something big is about to happen and we want Eric there."

"He knows about this?"

"Yes and turned us down again. He's lucky to get this second chance."

"I'll speak to him."

After carefully researching Roraima, Beth waited until Eric was in a romantic mood. "Now? You've got to be kidding," he said.

"But I thought you loved exploring new places together," she whispered snuggling up to him. "It's one of the most spectacular mountains in South America and like nothing you've ever seen. There are 2,000 plant species found nowhere else in the world and endemic wildlife too" With a crooked smile, Eric leered at her out of the corner of his eye as she continued. "Sir Arthur Conan Doyle imagined prehistoric beasts roaming this fantastic landscape and wrote a book about it. Ever hear of *The Lost World*?"

That stretched his lips into a broad smile. "I've always been a sucker for dinosaurs," he said and rolled her onto her back with her arms pinned over her head. "And beautiful women."

At breakfast the next morning, Beth brought up Vietnam as promised. "It's too damn risky right before the wedding," he answered.

"But it's what you've been dying to do."

"You're more important and I'm not going. So drop it. End of discussion."

She'd never seen him this resolute. It was flattering but drove the guilt gnats into a frenzy. With the wedding sweeping her along like a pile of wind-blown leaves and no more escaping to Venezuela to climb a tepui, she'd have to settle back to earth soon.

Six days later, they reached the base of the stunning, sheer-sided mountain. Vertical walls of bronze sandstone skirted the huge plateau lifting it a mile above the rolling landscape. The next morning, Beth and Eric climbed through an ancient cloud forest inhabited by an abundance of orchids, prehistoric tree ferns, palms, and delicate flowers. On the summit, they crossed a black, craggy surface of naked, slippery rock and explored the quartzite plateau belonging to the oldest geologic formation in the world. Any guilt Beth had about bringing Eric here rapidly disappeared when he started shooting pictures of the endless labyrinth of surreal sandstone sculptured by sun, wind, and rain and blackened by a rock-encrusting lichen that covered every bare surface in all directions. "This is astonishing," he exclaimed with the biggest grin she'd ever seen on his face.

When a swirling cloud descended with little warning and closed around them, they quickly learned the high summits of tepuis create their own weather. Caught in an electrical storm with heavy winds and pelting rain, they retreated to their tent under a rock-ledge shelter and closed the flaps behind them.

Eric zipped their bags together and crawled in with Beth who was shivering. "Shit, this is almost as bad as Nepal. Come here, Baby, I'll keep you warm. I don't know how you survived the cold in that avalanche."

"Wasn't easy," she said, treading water to keep her head above the memories suddenly flooding in.

He opened the dam even wider. "Did you miss me all those cold nights alone?"

Seeing the words floating by, she couldn't answer without time to line up her emotions and examine them. After skillfully avoided doing so for months, she again took the coward's way out. "Of course I did."

Even under the overhang, the temperature dropped as the wind whipped the tent walls. Shivering and listening to their incessant flapping brought back images of lying in Dorje's arms. Engulfed in hot, choking tears, she could barely breathe. As Eric spoke lovingly of their future and how they could do the Australian job as a third honeymoon, Beth pretended to fall asleep. But her thoughts turned to Dorje, wondering what he was doing during the winter months when few tourists arrived. With no word from her, did he think she'd forgotten him, that he was only a diversion? Perhaps he sought the warmth and comfort of Shanti's bed again or had even celebrated their *dem-chang*. The thought of making love with him again aroused every cell in her being, but doubts were gnawing at the back of her ever-too-rational mind. When caught up in the romance of the Himalayas, she thought she could stay forever. But this was her life: travel, exploring the far reaches of the world. It's what brought her here and she couldn't give that up. The man quietly dozing beside her was a good choice, but Dorje still had a firm grasp on her heart and wouldn't let go. Rolling over, she buried her face in the pillow to muffle her tears.

Exploring Roraima's summit the next day, they took a circular route to the junction of Venezuela, Brazil, and Guyana. Thousands of white crystals littered sparkling pools of clear water and lush meadows stood among the stark rock outcroppings. Often shrouded in fog or mist, Beth and Eric spent three days documenting the landscape's otherworldly feel. Totally fascinated by the enormity of the landscape, Beth was able to keep her feelings about Dorje in check but knew she'd have to confront them soon.

Back in Denver, she hadn't even unpacked yet when the phone rang. "Hi, I'm ready to go. Want to come along?" asked a voice that rose and fell in the most peculiar places. She'd heard it before but couldn't place it.

"Who is this?" she demanded, too tired to play guessing games.

"Marty!" he chirped. "Ready?"

A vague image of this strange man who had accosted her in Lukla popped into her head. "You're talking about Everest."

"Yup. I signed on with an expedition and am going to the top. Told you I'd give you the real dope on the Sherpas."

Beth sank to the bed holding the phone to her ear, too stunned to speak. "You still there?"

"Yes."

"So are you coming with me? We'll have great fun-ness. I'll be going back and forth from Base Camp, but you could stay there and I'll bring frequent reports."

With a long, shaky exhale, Beth asked, "When are you leaving?"

"Twelve days."

"I...I don't know if I can be ready that soon."

"I've been calling for weeks but nobody answered."

"I've been out of town." Still dazed, she opened the desk for a pencil. "Give me your number. I'll have to think about it."

When he hung up, Beth fell backwards onto the bed and stared at the ceiling. Decision time. The intellect that had kept her sane through childhood and ruled her life ever since had done a perfectly good job, but she didn't want to listen now because her life had been painfully void of any real emotion. In Nepal, she had found missing parts of herself and learned she was capable of loving someone. Since her return, however, the damn intellect had been questioning whether she had simply been caught up in the romance of the place and time. This odd character with the crazy hair had just given her the opportunity to discover whether her love was real and capable of lasting. And she could do so without telling Eric about Dorje.

Her stomach too bound up to eat at dinner, she dabbed at the mashed potatoes. "Got a phone call out of the blue today," she began, forcing the words to march boldly out.

Checking the movies, Eric didn't look up. "Oh yeah?"

"From this character at Lukla."

He slowly put the paper down. "Who are you talking about?"

"I'm not sure you even saw him. You were off searching for our guide and porter."

"And how did this *character* get your phone number?"

"Ohhh, I gave him my card because he said he was coming back to climb in the spring and would give me the inside story of Sherpas on Everest."

Hands folded, Eric leaned forward on the table across from her. "So is he going?"

"Yes."

With an unwavering gaze fixed on her, he asked in an agitated voice, "And you?"

She wanted to simply disappear and not have to go through this. "I told him I'd think about it." Her stomach clutched waiting for his response. When he just sat there staring and not speaking, she felt like throwing up.

Finally in a deliberate voice as if he were calculating each word, he asked, "When are you going and for how long?"

"I haven't said I would. I wanted to talk to you first. But if I did, we'd leave in twelve days and return around the first of June. Climbers use a window just before the monsoon arrives."

Leaning on his elbows with his hands still clasped, Eric tapped his thumbs together impatiently. "Just two weeks before the most important day of your life and then assuming you don't get sick again."

Eric was a good man but she had to listen to her heart too. Still not having the courage to call off the wedding, she said, "I won't get sick and I'll be back in time. This will cement my career forever. No one has described the climb from a Sherpa point of view other than Tenzing Norgay and his story was unique."

"I turned down the biggest shoot of my career so I wouldn't endanger our wedding, but you think nothing of running off to Nepal again."

"It's not…" she began but he held his hands up to hush her.

"Forget it. I'm canceling the wedding." He stood up and walked across the room and then turned. "I've been as accommodating as I can be, put up with your foolish wish to stay longer last time, but enough is enough. Go to Nepal. Do whatever it is you feel you must. And I'll go to Nam for the shoot that will cement my career forever."

"And then what?"

"I don't know. I'm not sure how I'm going to feel after this and refuse to make any promises. I'm too angry now and might say things I'll regret later."

As she watched him walk out the door, Beth wondered if she had just made the worst mistake of her life. "Eric," she called running after him. "I won't leave. I'll stay here and we'll get married as planned."

His back to her, Eric simply raised a hand. "Not now, Babe. The damage has already been done. Please just let me go without a scene and we'll talk when we get back."

But what if one of us doesn't return," she murmured to herself, feeling faint. *"What would the other one do or feel?*

CHAPTER TWENTY-FIVE

A jumble of emotions arrived with Beth when they landed in Nepal. She still felt guilty about choosing the trip over Eric, had no idea if Dorje had given up on her and married Shanti or fallen for another tourist, and wasn't even positive she'd view him the same way now. Although her passion for him seemed very real, what if the romance of an exotic setting and foreign culture had colored her vision?

Intruding in her thoughts, Marty asked, "Hey, My Lovely Lady, why such quiet-ness?"

She glanced at Marty who had shaved the hair growing down his neck and clipped the rest to a reasonable length. His socks now matched, albeit bright green, all in an attempt to win her over she presumed because he had been coming onto her.

"Just a few things on my mind."

"Missing your boyfriend?"

"What are you talking about?"

"The guy who put his arm around you at Lukla."

"Oh. He's doing a photo story in Nam right now and couldn't come."

Marty's voice rose and fell as if on a swing. "So how about cutting expenses by sharing a room in town. Separate beds, of course. No hanky-panky-ness."

"Thanks," she answered, trying to be gracious, "but my trip is paid for. They want a follow-up to the first successful story." With his Bassett Hound droopy eyes, it was impossible to not like the man.

After checking into the hotel, they met the other expedition members at dinner: two French men, three Brits, and two other Americans. Listening to their combined climbing experience, Beth felt confident they would make it. After a four-year ban on climbing by the Nepali government, Everest was once again under siege and so was her stomach when Marty announced to the others that they should hire this Sherpa he'd met last year. "He's strong, brighter than most, and speaks very good English." Marty then laid his hand on her arm as if they shared some special kinship. "Beth did this fantastic article on Sherpas last fall. I promised to help her finish the story and Dorje will be my liaison with the porters to get the inside scoop."

Hearing none of their conversation after that, Beth could think only of Dorje. Even if he was married, there was now a good chance she'd see him for an extended period. Marty had become her ally. "Have you been in touch with this Sherpa?" she asked out of nowhere, causing an abrupt halt to their climbing discussion.

"No," Marty answered, seeming somewhat surprised by her question. "There's no way to communicate with them, but he said I could find him through this teahouse in Namche."

Pemba, Beth thought and let them continue while she attempted to get food down a quivering, nervous stomach.

She and Marty shared the seat directly behind the pilot as they approached the airstrip at Lukla. She still marveled at how he calculated the angle of the short incline; however, the lump in her throat had nothing to do with landing but with the possibility of seeing Dorje when she disembarked. Going down the metal stairway, she searched a huge crowd of porters.

"Most of them are for us," Marty explained. "They carried our supplies fourteen days from Kathmandu."

"And now will go all the way up Everest?"

"No. I'm told they only go to Namche. There we hire porters for high altitude-ness."

Dismayed that Dorje wasn't there, she tried to focus on getting her gear loaded and heading out on the afternoon trek. Fortunately Marty and the other expedition members were too excited about their climb to interrupt her solitude on the trail, and she needed time both to adjust to being back and to sort out her feelings. She'd hurt two men: Eric by coming here and Dorje by not coming sooner. After five months, he had probably decided she never intended to return. If he was angry, she couldn't blame him but hoped he possessed a forgiving heart. All the way to Phakding, she fantasized about seeing him again: how their eyes would meet, the pounding in their hearts, the shortness of breath. It would be as if they had never parted. Keeping that image in mind, she wrapped up in her sleeping bag at night. Only then did visions of Eric shove Dorje aside. Guilt was a powerful force stealing her thoughts and reminding her that if anything happened in Nam it would be her fault. Instead of loving two men, she might have destroyed them both.

Climbing the interminable, 2,000-foot Namche hill the next day, Beth imagined Dorje standing at the entrance to the village, his black hair wet from having just washed in the spring. Would they still stir each other's emotions? Stopping to rest, she removed a brush from her shirt pocket and did her best with sweat-soaked hair and wiped the moisture from her face. After a series of long, deep breaths, she began the final ascent certain that he'd be waiting. But when she rounded the last mountain and saw only empty terraces where the Saturday market had been, tears welled in her throat.

Putting his arm around her shoulder, Marty asked, "What are you waiting for?"

"Nothing," she said blinking to hide the tears.

"Hey, you're crying."

"Don't be ridiculous. It's just sweat. I'm hot, tired, and covered with dirt. I'm going to wash in the spring."

"See you in camp then. I'm going to find Dorje and hire him before someone else does.

*   *   *   *   *   *   *   *   *

Pacing at the window, Dorje watched yet one more party of trekkers and porters arrive. For more than five months he had raced down to every foreign camp, but each time she wasn't there, disillusionment chipped away at his heart until he was convinced Pemba was right. Beth had liked the idea of being with a Sherpa more than the Sherpa himself. Having resolved not to suffer another disappointment, he swore not to go down there again. Sitting on the floor with his back to the window, he helped Droma Sunjo prepare buckwheat cakes for the next day's Dumje: the greatest of all Sherpa festivals that seeks to bring prosperity and health to the entire village by driving out hostile spirits.

"Why are you as nervous as a dog with a thousand fleas?" she asked. "You watch for her every day."

"Just more trekkers. It's useless. She won't be there." Agitated, he rose to check the barrels of fermenting *chang,* their lids plastered with dung to retain the heat.

In her self-imposed exile, his aunt had quietly studied the household and understood everyone better than they knew themselves. She gave the necessary nudge. "Go. And do it now."

One more piece of his heart eroded when Dorje observed an all-male camp. To mask his frustration, he casually asked a porter why they had set up so far from the center of the village.

"An expedition is coming and needs that area. I saw their porters in Lukla two days ago."

"And did you also see a woman with golden hair and eyes as blue as a morning sky?"

"No one like that. Only these trekkers and some expedition porters coming from Kathmandu. The climbers hadn't arrived yet."

Trudging back up to the house, Dorje pushed all thoughts of Beth from his head and heart to concentrate solely on helping his father who would bear the onerous task of providing food and drink for the entire village as one of the eight *lawas*. Responsible for the economic burden that rotated among families once very twelve years, *lawas* tried to show off and outdo each other. Unfortunately, Mingma had drawn the stone to serve the day after Pemba and couldn't begin to rival his ex partner's wealth, especially after spending all he had on prayers and the shaman at Tengboche plus Dorje's recent *dem-chang*.

That afternoon, Dorje felt like a traitor going to the temple, but it was an obligation he owed Pemba who had been a constant friend. The dispensing of abundant food and drink was not done solely to gain prestige but was an opportunity to earn religious merit through hospitality. Dorje arrived as a procession of lamas circled the *gompa* and then entered the courtyard surrounded by villagers. A drum, the moaning of long *dung-chen* horns, and the clash of cymbals signaled the beginning of the ceremony. The senior lama stabbed a dough *torma* shaped and decorated with colored butters in the form of an evil spirit and cast it into a pit. While several lamas added dirt and water and then covered the *torma* with stones, others chanted asking the gods for assistance in fending off demons.

Ready to party when the ritual ended, the villagers headed for the food. The fifth of an eight-day celebration where no one worked, everyone ate and drank as much as they desired in an atmosphere of relaxed sexual play. Lavish tables awaited them spread with vegetable and meat-stuffed *momos*, potato pancakes mixed with spices, fried breads, fresh fruit, yak cheese, and cooked rice balls to be taken home. Instead of the customary home-brewed *chang*, Pemba offered expensive bottles of Johnnie Walker afforded only by tourists. When the music began, men and women formed separate lines and shuffled forward and backward, laughing as they reeled and staggered. Singing bawdy songs, they pinched and tugged at each other in mock sexual encounters at the most elaborate party anyone had ever known.

Surprised to see his brother waiting outside when he arrived home, Dorje wanted to hold and protect him, but Nima had shunned him ever since the incident with Beth. There had been no words of recrimination or hostility, only a cold distance. Dorje was determined to end it now because his brother was as vital to him as his own limbs.

"How could you go to Pemba's party?" Nima demanded.

"I owed him that. He and Mingma put aside their difference to come for me just as you and I must do for Father tomorrow." He hooked his arm around Nima's neck and tired to touch their foreheads together, but his brother pulled away. "I love you, Nima, more than myself and want things the way they used to be." As much as Dorje ached for a great outpouring of emotion from his brother, he remembered needing to peel away layers of anger before letting Mingma back into his heart. So he must be patient and let Nima slowly strip his away too.

The next afternoon, Dorje watched two boys dressed as skeletons come out of the temple and whirl wildly about. In demon masks, other dancers joined their antics, greatly amusing the spectators. Then several lamas led a procession to a pit outside the village where they and the skeleton boys hurled rocks at a *torma* representing the universal enemy. With flames shooting up from the pit, a lama threw the broken *tomra* into the blaze. Shouting victory over evil forces, everyone marched back to the *gompa* ready for the party to begin. When they discovered only simple buckwheat cakes and *chang,* the festive mood quickly faded. Musicians played but no one danced. Instead, villagers stood about the yard in small groups gossiping. Quietly moving among them, Dorje listened to their hushed conversation.

"We had much better food last night," a woman whispered.

"And Johnnie Walker," said Chotari who had come often to Mingma's house and bragged about the high quality of his chang that left no grains floating on top.

Dorje was furious at him for complaining instead of accepting what his host offered because Chotari and all the others were denying Mingma his greatest opportunity to earn merit. About to throw them all out, he saw Droma Sunjo signaling him with palms down and shaking her wrists. She glanced sideways at Mingma standing beside his barrels of *chang*; head raised, shoulders back, eyes staring straight ahead. She approached Dorje wearing the scarf draped over her goiter and with Dawa in tow—a public show of support for Mingma. "Your father is proud," she whispered. "Don't let your anger rob him of that."

She was right. He had to find another way. Grabbing Nima's arm, he pushed a brass pot of *chang* into his arms and said, "Let's get this party moving."

Forcing a smile, Dorje asked Chotari, "Shall I fill your cup with the finest beer in the Khumbu?"

Startled, Chotari stared at him. "I suppose so."

"Good. And you?" Dorje asked the man beside him. "And you?" He continued around the courtyard with Nima trailing behind offering the same. After many of the guests had been served, the others took care of themselves and the grumbling gradually subsided.

Then to start the dancing, Dorje dragged Nima to the center of the courtyard and put his brother's arm around his waist, but Nima withdrew it. "Please," Dorje whispered. "Put away your feelings for now and let's show Father that we stand together for him." When Nima's arm slid around Dorje's waist and held onto his side, Dorje's insides rolled over and smiled pleased with the world again. Gradually twenty others formed a men's line with a steady swaying to get the song's rhythm. The line moved forward and backward, punctuating each stop and start with a stomp, increasing in speed to a frenzied climax before settling down to a more stately, hopping. Two new *madal* players sat down, rested their drums across their thighs, and began a song with an unusual beat. Whenever someone lost the rhythm, he suffered the jaunts and jeers of the onlookers. Mingma appeared in his long robe and full sleeves. He raised the hem and began to dance. Moving forwards and backwards, he touched his heels and toes, stomped left, right, and left again, each step punctuating the music so rapidly it was as if he knew where the music was heading before the drummers did. Struggling to keep up, the other dancers failed, including Pemba.

Watching his father, Dorje thought how magnificent he looked with his robe swirling—the center of the village attention and Dorje wanted to stand beside him. He studied Mingma's feet, trying to find a pattern. When one finally emerged, he closed his eyes to instill it in his head before stepping forward and putting his arm around his father's waist. With his gape-toothed grin, Nima joined on the other side of Mingma and linked his arm with Dorje's behind their father's back. His entire face burst into a smile as Dorje waited for the beat that started the sequence and jumped in with a right-foot stomp, left heel kick, left toe. But it was too fast. He and

Nima both stumbled about, always a beat or two behind. Staring proudly ahead, Mingma struck the ground harder and faster, challenging his sons to keep up. Dorje tried again and failed until he let his mind go and allowed his body to guide him. Finally keeping up beat for beat, he felt Mingma's arm tighten around his waist while father and son danced inches apart as if they'd always been bound together. Dorje's eyes clouded with tears as he experienced the love and wonder of a small boy again. Minutes later, Nima also got the beat and all three were in unison for the first time since childhood.

As Dorje walked back to the table for some *chang* afterwards, a strange voice sang out, "Buck buck. That was amazing stomping-ness."

Dorje spun around and recognized the American from last fall. "You're here with the expedition?" he gasped.

"Told you I'd be back." His arms out and feet mimicking Dorje's dance, the American sashayed toward him. "Ready to climb Everest with me?"

One of the field mice that had hibernated all winter and spring crept out of its burrow to see why Dorje's insides were suddenly alive. "You mean that?"

Marty stood before him, his tufted eyebrows and shaggy hair trimmed. "Just you and me to the top like we planned. Ready?"

Dorje couldn't believe the moment he'd waited for since they called him the Tenzing of the future had finally arrived. "Yes!" he shouted as the excited field mouse scampered up a wall and did a high dive off the top. "But I have no money, no gear. How...?"

"No problem, Buck buck. Expedition members have to pay huge fees for a climbing permit and we need porters. I'm hiring you just like I said I would."

Dorje's elation plummeted. "So I'm not going to the top."

Grabbing Dorje's shoulder, Marty wiggled it "No frown-ness. They're hiring Khumbu porters to carry half way up. Then experienced climbing Sherpas from Darjeeling will cut steps to the summit."

"But that's not me," Dorje said, feeling even more deflated.

"It will be once they see how strong and bright you are. Don't worry. We'll go up together."

Dorje watched his lips moving as Marty talked about crampons, ice axes, oxygen, and his companion who had come with him, but the words drowned in images of carrying repeated loads through the hazardous ice field, of his uncle's body lying lost somewhere on the mountain, of the many Sherpas who had died for nothing. His fate was to be Tenzing, not a lowly porter.

"You saw her at Lukla," Marty said.

Marty's words grabbed Dorje and yanked him back to the present. "What...who...?"

"You know. That gorgeous blond, the one I said I'd give up my wild ways for. Well, I think I've got a real chance with her because she already likes me. And with your help..."

"What are you talking about?"

Surprised, Marty's brows rose. "She wants to write about Sherpas climbing Everest and I promised to bring reports to her in Base Camp. I need you to give me the real story so I can impress her"

"Beth is here? Now?"

"Yes," answered Marty.

"Where is she?"

"Still washing up, I guess. But how do you know her name?" Marty shouted after him as Dorje frantically pushed through the drunken revelers and bolted from the courtyard.

Racing to the path overlooking the expedition camp, he watched her stroll up from the spring, head tilted, brushing her fingers through long, wet hair to separate and dry it. Having dreamt of this moment for months, he was suddenly scared and disappointed. She had come to write about Sherpas climbing Everest, not for him. Even the slightest hint of rejection in her eyes would rip his heart to shreds and he couldn't face that. He would send a note asking her to meet him in a private place. If she didn't show, he'd know he'd lost her and could mourn in solitude. Only problem was he could speak English but not write it, just like his father with the scriptures. Enamored with Beth, Marty certainly wouldn't be an ally in this affair, so Dorje went to the trekker's camp and asked if anyone spoke English and would write for him. A man in his twenties was delighted to aid a lover's tryst. The note read: *I want to see you. Meet me on the boulder with the prayer flags high above the gompa. I will be waiting after dark. Dorje.* After paying a young porter to deliver the note, Dorje strode back to the *gompa* courtyard, purposely-circumventing Marty, and quickly downed three cups of *chang* to give himself the courage to see her again.

CHAPTER TWENTY-SIX

Beth crawled from the tent as refreshed as a person could be who had just endured an icy sponge bath in public and then changed into wrinkled clothes. As soon as she stood up, a young Sherpa approached, bowed, and said, "Namaste, Memsahib." After handing her a piece of neatly folded paper, he quickly disappeared as if embarrassed. Beth just stared at it a moment, bewildered by having received a written correspondence in the middle of Namche. Having no idea what to expect, she carefully opened it and read that the man for whom she had traveled half way around the world wanted to see her that night. Her arms dropped to her side and her body sank. Why hadn't he simply come to her now, yearning to embrace her? Glancing around the camp and adjacent paths, Beth wondered if he was watching. With an uneasy tingling sensation, she read the note again. He wanted to meet her on a boulder on the hill above the gompa, probably because it was easier to let someone down in the privacy of darkness. If he told her he had waited too long and didn't love her anymore, she would have to understand and accept it.

At the sound of Marty's voice, Beth hid the letter behind her back. "Oh, such radiant-ness, my Everest queen. I shall erect a summit flag in honor of your beauty."

"Thank you," she said softly and touched his arm. "You're very sweet." *But I can never return your affection* she tried to communicate through her eyes but sensed he didn't get the message.

When the dinner conversation inevitably turned to logistics of the climb, Beth quietly slipped away. Normally as evening shadows infused the white walls with gray, a hush settled over the village. The noisy paths emptied of laughing children, women gossiping over their wash, and men smoking bidis and playing cards on stone stoops. The glow of hearth fires slowly seeped through shuttered windows like thousands of orange fireflies dancing in the dark. Walking through the village that night, Beth felt as if she were alone in one of those deserted cities in movies about a nuclear holocaust destroying all life forms. Everything was eerie, silent, and black until she neared the *gompa*. There, alerted to the music and the light of a hundred butter lamps, Beth discovered a courtyard filled with the entire village populous drinking, singing, and dancing with an unrestrained freedom. After watching them a few minutes, she spun each prayer wheel in the outer *gompa* wall clockwise before heading up the hill.

Half way to the top, Beth spotted a flashlight a hundred yards away in the center of a large, enclosed pasture. Slowly climbing over the rock wall, she strolled towards it, her stomach in knots, not knowing what to say or do. Dorje waited at the base of a large boulder painted in bright images of Buddha and local deities. Long strings of prayer flags radiating from the top stretch to the ground.

"I'm glad you came," he murmured.

"I am too." Immediately upon seeing him, Beth's heart boldly swept all reason away like dust motes on a windy morn. To hell with intellect. The promise of marrying a man who offered security and a lifetime of exotic travel had blinded her too long.

When Dorje said, "Come with me," and took her hand, she wanted nothing to have changed between them. Atop the boulder, they stood under a full moon ringed by an orange glow creating a pale haze around it. Reflecting moonlight, the jagged, snow-clad peaks stood like silent sentinels guarding the village accompanied only by the ruffling of prayer flags. His hand gentle against her cheek, Dorje caressed her lips with his until her passion pulled him deeper, insatiable for his kisses. No words spoken, no longing whispers, their bodies said it all in an unbroken embrace until the butter lamps dimmed and campfires turned to embers.

"You're shivering," he whispered, "and I have no bag to wrap around you now."

Feeling him hard against her and smelling his hair and skin, Beth felt it was as if the last few months had never existed. This was her reality. "Then make love to keep me warm."

Descending the dirt path with his arm around her, Dorje said, "We cannot go to Pemba's. His rooms are full of relatives from nearby villages who came for the Dumje."

"And your house?" Noticing a smile lurking behind his face, she asked, "What's so funny?"

"We all share the same room. You want to entertain my father, aunt, cousin, and Nima?"

"No," she shrieked and quickly covered her mouth. "So I guess it's my tent," she added in a whisper.

By the time they reached the expedition camp, everyone had gone to bed. With fingers flying, Beth and Dorje unzipped jeans and pulled shirts over their heads before snuggling in a one-person sleeping bag. Needing the full length of his naked body against hers, Beth pulled him on top the way they had lain on the mountain. "You kept me warm when I was dying," she whispered and felt tears lurking. "I love you so much."

"And I love you. I was afraid you would not come back."

"I'm sorry it took so long."

"And will you stay like Hamar?"

"Yes, always. But is he still here?"

"He and Lhamu work for Pemba and sleep in the room that was yours. Soon they will have a baby."

Dorje's news excited her more than he knew because it proved love was more powerful than reason. Her only mistake had been waiting too long to realize it, but it didn't matter now. She was here and had the rest of her life to listen to a heart telling her to give herself wholly to this man whose very presence allowed her to soar with wings unfurled.

Stroking her hair, Dorje whispered, "Why are you so quiet?"

"Just thinking about how I never want us to be apart again." His body slackened. "What's wrong?'

After a long silence, Dorje admitted, "Marty wants me to climb Everest with him."

"What?" she said stiffening under him. "How can you even think of doing such a thing?"

"Do not worry. They probably will not let me climb. So you are stuck with me until I die."

"That's not funny."

"I meant of old age."

"Then you will live a very long life with me taking care of you. And the first step is keeping you off that mountain."

He stopped her hand when she tried to reach between his legs and asked, "Tell me first. Are you going to stay at Base Camp waiting for news from Marty like he says?"

"Yes. But I want you with me while I finish the story about Sherpas on Everest."

"Will Marty not share your tent?"

"Good grief, no. Why would you think that?"

"He wants to be your lover and thinks that you like him."

"Well, I don't. So get that thought ridiculous thought out of your head. I only came with him because it gave me an excuse to see you."

"You did not need one," he said kissing the nape of her neck.

Raising her shoulders in defense, Beth said, "I was afraid you had given up and stopped loving me."

"Never."

"And what about Shanti?"

When he began his slow, sensual exploration with hand and tongue, she forgot the question and surrendered to the most passionate love making of her life. At the first misty rays of dawn, she felt him quietly trying to slip away without waking her. Yawning, Beth asked, "Where are you going?"

"I want to leave before Marty gets up. He will be jealous of us and I do not want to risk losing my best chance of getting hired as a porter and going to the top. it."

"But I still don't want you to go up there."

Pulling his jeans on and zipping them, Dorje said, "Tomorrow, I will tell you about meeting Hillary when I was five. They called me the Tenzing of the future and it has been my fate to climb ever since. This is my first chance since I returned to Namche. I must go. I hope you can understand." He leaned down to kiss her. "I will see you in Base Camp many nights and return from the top before you know I am gone."

After he exited the tent, she realized he had avoided the question of Shanti and never asked about Eric. They had much to discuss yet, but none of it seemed important as long as they were in love and together again.

* * * * * * * * *

Leaving Beth early, Dorje was confident no one had seen him. With his emotions reeling from everything that had happened in the past few hours and new decisions to be made, he knew two things were clear. He would fulfill his fate as Tenzing and nothing could shake his love for Beth that was rooted as deep as the strongest oak. Finding Nima at home shivering on the floor without a blanket, Dorje wrapped one around him and lay back to back with their bodies flush as they had slept since childhood. He chuckled, too much *chang* no doubt. Having finally made peace with his brother yesterday, he wondered how Nima was going to feel about Beth's arrival? And Mingma. After dancing in perfect unison with his father, Dorje was going to spring an Everest climb on him knowing his father considered it a sin to trespass on the abode of the gods. Months of good feelings could be wiped out in seconds.

Then there was Shanti, the most difficult of all, and almost six months pregnant with his baby after he made love to her the night he felt spurned by Beth. Even though Shanti's family had rushed the *dem-chang* to make their baby legitimate, he was still free to sleep with Beth. But Shanti would be hurt and she didn't deserve that. It was too much all at once. Not wanting to alienate everybody on the same day, Dorje decided to wait until after Everest to tell Shanti about Beth. Giving her and the baby all the rupees earned on the climb would help allay his conscience.

Feeling Nima restless behind him, Dorje decided to put off that confession too. While in Namche, he and Beth would simply have to appear aloof. Dorje rolled onto his back and stared at the ceiling. Of course, there was also Marty to deal with. Jealousy could hinder Dorje's chances of being hired for the expedition. Foolishly, he had let on that he knew Beth and reacted strongly to her being here, but perhaps the American didn't consider a lowly Sherpa competition for her affection and had passed it off. Too much to think about, Dorje pulled the blanket over his head and tried smothering his brain.

The next morning, Nima and Mingma teased Droma Sunjo about getting drunk, dancing, and flirting with all the men at yesterday's Dumje. Stooped over the hearth, she blushed and hid behind her hand giggling, which only made them more merciless. Grateful for the distraction, Dorje thought he was going to escape scrutiny until Mingma asked where he had disappeared to last night. His stomach soured like spoiled milk. Might as well get it over with because the climbers would be leaving soon.

"An American climber I worked for last fall is here with the expedition camped in the village. He wants to hire me again."

"But only as a porter carrying part way," Mingma said, his shoulders arching back and stiffening.

Although they were lined up in Dorje's head, the words were afraid to venture forth, so he gave them a swift kick out the door. "At first, yes, but he wants me to go to the top with him." His father leaned forward and rested his forearms on his thighs; hands clasped, and said nothing. "Like Hillary and Tenzing," Dorje threw out for support. "Remember how I met them at five?"

Mingma's unflinching stare cut through him like lightning splitting a tree. "You will not go," he uttered with a finality that would have daunted Dorje six months ago. "I have bad feelings about this."

"But I must." Empowered by Beth's love, Dorje felt invincible even in the face of his father's edict. "They called me the Tenzing of the future."

Mingma rose and started that infuriating pacing that still unnerved him. "You were a silly boy begging for candy. They were only playing with you. It meant nothing."

"It did to me. I want to do something important in my life."

"And what is so important about climbing a mountain that you risk angering the goddess Miyolangsangma who protects it?"

Dorje didn't have an answer except that people came from all over the world to do it.

Fortunately, Droma Sunjo intervened and he didn't have to respond. "So you will die like my Lhakpa," she said with eyes downcast and the blush of a few moments ago having paled. Never in five years had she entered into a family discussion—she who usually understood him better than anyone.

Lhakpa had been reckless carrying a double load and traveling at night, but Dorje wouldn't remind her of that. "I promise to be very careful and return quickly to you, the woman with the prettiest smile in Namche."

Now Nima took at turn at him. "Oh yes, my careful brother who has never done anything insane like standing in the middle of a river at the top of a 300-foot waterfall."

"I have good balance and knew what I was doing. I was never in danger."

"Or when you dangled from a single cord on a 400-foot cliff digging in a bee's nest."

"I was with a band of honey-hunters who do it all the time." Now he got up and started pacing. Maybe it was genetic. "I don't want to argue. I haven't even been hired as a porter yet and will have to prove myself as good as the climbing Sherpas from Darjeeling if I want to go to the top." That news appearing to ease the tension since no one seemed to think he could do it, Dorje felt a little insulted but decided to let it go.

Looking for Marty in the expedition camp, he purposely ignored Beth to avoid arousing jealousy. "Hey, Buck buck," the American yelled and jumped up to introduce him to the other members and the sirdar who spoke some English. "This is Dorje, the Sherpa I told you about."

Dorje bowed and welcomed them to his village; then he spoke of the many trips he'd made to Everest. Seemingly impressed by his fluency and Marty's recommendation, the sirdar hired him to carry from Base Camp to the Western Cwm and also asked him to locate some local yaks to carry from Namche to Base Camp.

"Hurray! Give me five," Marty whooped and slapped Dorje's hand. Obviously he didn't consider this Sherpa porter a threat in his pursuit of Beth.

Insulted for the second time that morning, Dorje challenged him to a hand jive contest. Starting slowly, he slapped his knees on one and two, clapped both hands on three and four, and quickly completed the entire sixteen-count routine without missing a beat.

"You've been practicing," Marty said, his voice rising and tufted eyebrows twitching.

"And can do it faster than you."

Amused by their competition, the other climbers joined in along with a few daring porters. Dorje slapped his knees, thumped his fists, bumped his elbows, hands flying, body wiggling, giggling out of control, faster and faster, too quick for anyone to keep up—not even Marty. "Aha!" he shouted gleefully when they were all a beat or two behind, slapping when they should have been clapping. Knowing Beth was watching, he gave Marty a final high five, turned, and walked away. *No threat, no competition? We'll see.*

He waited for the cover of darkness to steal into Beth's tent that night. "You were incredible at hand jive," she whispered, "just like the first time I saw you. But where were you? I thought you'd never get here."

After a hard emotional day, Dorje leaned back on his elbows with his legs stretched out in front to relax. "I had many things to do. The sirdar hired me to carry from Base Camp to the Western Cwm. My father, my aunt, and brother were all angry when I told them."

Releasing his hand, Beth sat up and locked her arms around her knees, staring straight ahead. "They're not angry…just scared like I am."

"Do not be. I am strong."

"So is the mountain."

"I do not want to waste time talking." He grabbed her around the waist from behind and pulled her down on top of him.

"So what else do you have in mind?" she asked playfully.

"I cannot get enough of your kisses."

"Then I shall bury you in them."

Making love to her was like communing with the gods and left him numb all over. Transported to a different realm, he wasn't aware until he awoke an hour later that she had covered him with her bag and crawled inside. "Look what you did to me," he whispered. "Now I am too weak to climb a mountain."

"Then we'll make love every night until you're like an old grandpa waving your walking stick over your head and can't leave me."

Once again, Dorje departed just before dawn and slowly strolled north to Khumjung, not wanting to arrive too early. Finding Shanti bathing at the village spring, he remained out of sight watching her discreetly remove one arm at a time to wash her torso. Her traditional wrap-around tunic and blouse were designed for expansion. To accommodate her growing belly, she needed only to loosen it. When Shanti leaned down to wash her long, black hair, Dorje rushed to help. Her eyes closed, she wasn't aware of him until he slowly poured water over her head and gently rubbed her scalp. Such affection he felt for her and their child. His stomach tightened at the thought of telling her; he couldn't do it now. Later. After he had climbed Everest and could offer her something.

"Why are you here so early," she asked as he combed his fingers through her tangled hair.

"To see you and make sure everything is all right."

Questioning him with her huge, brown eyes, Shanti asked, "But aren't you coming to my bed tonight? It's been days."

He drew the wet strands back from her face and kissed both of her high round cheeks. "I've been helping my father with the Dumje."

"And now?"

Dorje touched his forehead to hers to avoid the inevitable, disappointment in her eyes. "I can't tonight. I have to get ready to leave early in the morning."

"For what?"

Even this much of it was harder than he thought. Stealing himself emotionally, he said, "I hired on as an expedition porter and will be gone many weeks."

When she tried to pull away, he cupped his hand behind her head and held her, whispering, "Don't worry. I'll be back long before our child is born and bringing you many rupees."

"I don't want rupees. I want you here with me." Shanti arched back and peered into his eyes. "Why didn't you say something before?"

"I did. You know about meeting Hillary and Tenzing and wanting to climb. I just found out yesterday that an American I worked for last fall came back. He hired me to go with him."

"And what if you never return? What if something happens?"

With his warmest smile and most confident tone, he answered, "But nothing will and I'll be back before the monsoon. Remember making love on the hill at summer pasture?" he added to distract her.

"Yes. You were the most handsome boy there." Placing his hand on her belly, she said, "See how our baby moves."

Feeling a flutter of life beneath his fingers, Dorje's heart warmed. "I'm certain she will be as beautiful as her mother."

"Or as willful as his father."

They spent the morning talking about names and how their child would go to Hillary's school in Khumjung to become a great teacher. All the while, Dorje sensed she knew something wasn't right, but he still couldn't tell her.

Nor did he speak of being with the beautiful Sherpani when lying with Beth that night. Nothing could interfere with making love to her. Responding to every movement and sound, he wanted to give her the greatest pleasure possible. Discussion of Shanti and the baby would come later, perhaps when he got the courage to ask about Eric.

CHAPTER TWENTY-SEVEN

To reach the summit, Dorje would have to move up the hierarchy of porters: those who carry only to Base Camp, those who shuttle loads through the icefall and Western Cum, and the climbing Sherpas who save their strength for the final ascent by not carrying until they are on the mountain itself. From this group, two or more would be selected to accompany assault teams to the top. And for this, he would need Marty's help, so he wanted to delay the American's discovery of his relationship with Beth as long as possible.

When he returned from Shanti's, Dorje talked to his father about hiring their animals out to the expedition. "I want nothing to do with these strangers. Don't speak of this again," Mingma snapped with his usual tone of finality.

A man worthy of a beautiful woman's love, Dorje was no longer easily held down. "You were once the wealthiest trader in Namche," he reminded his father. "But now borrow from your cousin in Phakding. How will you repay Kancha? By selling dung when you can get ten times that amount without even working."

"It's better than selling my soul like you and Pemba. I thought you understood me now," Mingma said with sadness in his eyes.

"Yes, but I don't like watching you suffer. They will pay well, enough to return your rupees and still have enough to buy grain for the finest *chang* in Namche."

After an hour of such discussion, Mingma finally relented. As Dorje was explaining to the sirdar and expedition leader that he could provide fifteen yaks, Marty approached wagging a finger through a hole in his shirt. "Hey, Buck buck, need to talk to you when you're done." Dorje put him off as long as he could, assuming the man had heard them in the tent last night. In a confidential voice, Marty said, "If you'll do me this big favor, I promise to get you to the top. I think Beth really likes me. We played cards all morning and talked about how much we both love Colorado. When we get back to the States, I'm going in for some serious dateness." With one brow raised, he whispered, "And if I'm lucky, I'll get into her tent at Base Camp."

Eyeing him, Dorje tried to assess if there was a remote possibility he was right and finally concluded the man was hallucinating the way *mikarus* do at high altitude, even though they were only at 11,300 feet. "What favor?"

"I planned on hiking all the way to Base Camp with her. You know, getting a little friendlier each night. But instead, we're going to practice on your 20,000-foot hills for about ten days before tackling serious altitudeness on Everest." He draped an arm over Dorje's shoulder and hung on him. "So, Geronimo, I want you to take care of her for me until then. The sirdar speaks a little English, but he'll be with us, That leaves only you and I know I can trust you to make sure she's all right and answer any questions about Sherpas. Deal?"

"Deal," Dorje answered, suppressing the huge grin eager to sprint across his face. The problem of acclimatizing that had caused so much grief when working with trekkers had just given him a ten-day reprieve by getting rid of Marty. "I will go tell her we leave tomorrow after the yaks are loaded." He would also explain he didn't want to risk Marty seeing him come to her tent that night and they would soon have much time alone.

The following morning, Dorje said good-bye to the expedition members and then sent Beth ahead to Tengboche with the porters so no one would see them leaving Namche together. Single-handedly driving fifteen heavily laden yaks up rocks taller than their short legs proved more grueling than Dorje anticipated. And keeping the recalcitrant beasts from tossing their loads 500 feet down to the Dudh Kosi sent him running back and forth always on the uphill side so an angry horn didn't shove him off. He was exhausted by the time he turned them loose to graze in Tengboche.

After finally removing most of the day's dust and sweat, Dorje crawled into Beth's tent to make love in the afternoon. As they lay together afterwards, she asked the question he was dreading but knew had to be answered sometime. "I had a lot of time to think while trekking today and wonder if you're still engaged to Shanti?"

Nervous about admitting the truth, he was more afraid of lying and having her find out. His voice faltered and then rose as if the muscles in his throat had stretched too thin. "Yes, because she is large with my child."

"She's pregnant?"

As she shrank from him, Dorje tried to explain. "I went to her because I thought I was not important to you. I was just another Sherpa."

"You've never been that."

"I did not know. And my father had gone to her father to arrange our marriage."

"This changes everything," Beth said removing her hand from his thigh.

"No, it is all right. Our families rushed the *dem-chang* so our child will not be born in shame."

"So you're even closer to marriage."

"But Shanti and I do not live together and we are still free to be with other lovers."

"It's a strange set up, if you ask me, but what do I know. I'm sure our customs will seem strange to you too. What's this *dem-chang* like anyway?"

"My family and friends wore their best clothes and walked to Shanti's home in Khumjung. Her family served them beer and tea followed by rice and vegetables. Then my family gave *katas* to hers and her father talked about how the two families are now joined. When all of that was done, everyone drank *chang* and danced all the night. Mingma and Nima stayed at her uncle's house partying until the next morning."

"And you and Shanti?"

"We were not there. The man and woman who will be married a year or two later are never part of the *dem-chang*."

After an interminable silence, Beth asked, "And does she know about us?"

Wanting to savor the after-glow of lovemaking, Dorje wished Beth would stop asking these awful questions. Moving closer to bury his face in her hair, he said, "No. I went to her yesterday and spoke of the climb. I said I would be gone for weeks but nothing more."

Beth's voice seemed detached from the woman lying beside him. "Why didn't you tell her?"

He forced Beth to look at him. "It has nothing to do with not loving you. I did not want to hurt her now. I will tell her when I return from Everest and can give her and the baby all the rupees I earn. Now I ask the same question. Does Eric know about me?"

"No," she admitted. "He doesn't even suspect you, but he does sense that things aren't right between us. We've put off the wedding until I get back and we see how things are."

Now Dorje rolled over and turned away with a long, exasperated exhale. "And just how *are* things?"

"Perfect with you. Never in my life did I imagine I could love someone so much or be so completely happy."

"So why did you not tell Eric?"

She grabbed his hair and gave it a playful tug. "Because, silly, I didn't know if you were married or if you'd even remember me."

He clasped both hands around her buttocks and murmured, "Come here. I will show you how much I remember." He made love to her again with more passion that he thought possible. No more secrets, no more uncertainty; he was ecstatic beyond anything he'd ever dreamt.

* * * * * * * * *

Beth woke to the deep, sustained tones of the long *dung-chen* horns coming from the monastery. It seemed an eternity ago that the lamas had prayed for her, almost as if the storm and all that followed weren't real. But the man lying beside her was. Propped on her elbows watching him sleep, she was suddenly overcome and began weeping. Afraid of loving, her mind had tried to resist Dorje by continually injecting doubts and shoving temptations in her path like the trip to Mt. Roraima. But it had failed and nothing mattered now except lying here in a frigid tent at 12,680 feet with an unschooled man who had taught her how to feel. She would never give that up no matter what the cost. "Promise you'll never leave me," she said when he finally gazed at her through sleepy eyes.

"Never." He gently pulled the hair back from her face and lightly traced her cheek. "And how long have you been waiting for me to wake?"

"Forever." She grinned and gave him a big kiss. "So get used to it because you're stuck with me until I die." As they dressed, Beth said, I want to hike with you and the yaks. Might as well get used to them, hadn't I?"

Dorje chuckled. "You will not like it."

"But I'll like being with you," she said, lying on her back with her hips in the air to pull on her long pants and zip them.

He was right about the yaks. They grunted and balked on steep sections, kicked a constant flurry of irritating dust up her nose, and generally made life miserable. But she loved giggling with Dorje, giving him spontaneous kisses, holding his hand when the trail was wide enough, walking single-file to tickle his butt when it wasn't. To give her plenty of time to acclimate, he said they'd only travel about four hours a day and sleep at each new altitude before moving higher again.

On the way, he took her to the monastery in Pangboche to see a yeti scalp and hand. An old man with skin seamed by wrinkles and darkened by wind and smoke carefully guarded the relics. Holding the iron-hard scalp with red bristles, Beth didn't know what to believe. The Sherpas were adamant about the creature's existence and many reputable climbers had found tracks, including Hillary and Tenzing in 1953. However, Hillary's yearlong search in 1960 had been fruitless. Beth smiled and returned it to the old man. Real or not, the possibility of a yeti pursuit above Namche had been the most thrilling and romantic evening of her life.

They camped at 14,031 feet in Periche and from there continued up the valley past the *yersa* hut where Mingma had first brought them after the storm. "I was so cold and sick all I can remember is lying with my head in your lap and hearing you and your father going on for hours."

"Oh yes. A most surprising story that explains why he didn't come for me."

Listening to Dorje talk about Mingma and his Tibetan wife, Beth felt even closer to him and knew this was the man who would share the rest of her life. "They were lovers from different worlds like us," she said, "but we don't have a Chinese invasion to tear us apart." *Only a mountain*, she thought but crushed the words into pieces fine as sand and swept them away.

They camped at 16, 269 feet in Lobuche and after climbing a tributary moraine early the next morning, they stood looking at the great Khumbu Glacier stretching all the way to the base of Everest. What possessed men to come here and trudge through ice and snow just to go up a mountain? It was beyond her. Perhaps she should be writing about the insanity of foreign climbers instead of the Sherpas who work for them. At least they had an economic incentive. By noon she and Dorje reached the highest *yersa* in the valley, Gorak Shep, land of the crows. It was a desolate land of sand and rock where only the sharp tongue of a yak could forage. After resting an hour for lunch and letting the animals graze, they continued on to Base Camp at 17, 519 feet. Having dreamed of seeing the summit of Everest up close with its trademark plume of condensation trailing off into the jet stream, Beth was disappointed. "Where's the top?"

"You cannot see it from here. Only from Gokyo or a black hill on the other side of Gorak Shep called Kala Pattar."

She sank onto a boulder, exhausted, short of breath, and disappointed in this wasteland of rock and ice: not the exotic gateway to the highest point on earth that she had envisioned. Watching the yaks snort past with hoarfrost clinging to the hair on their flanks making their legs look even ridiculously shorter, Beth wasn't sure she could do this forever. For three days and three nights when the temperature dropped below zero and her breath froze, she'd been considering talking to Dorje about their future and where they would live. Namche didn't hold the same long-term allure for her it apparently did for Hamar

That evening as the mountains smothered them in deep shadows, she and Dorje lay buried under a mound of blankets in their sleeping bags zipped together, their feet pointing away from Everest so as not to offend the goddess Miyolangsangma. Beth listened to the groan and creak of the glacier shifting and the quiet murmur of porters in nearby tents chanting mantras to the gods for their tolerance and protection. When a faint crash sounded in the distance, she shot straight up. "What's that?"

"Only an avalanche," he reassured her.

"Only?"

"It is far away. Do not be afraid."

"Sorry," she said, lying back down. "Can't help it."

Rummaging through his jacket, Dorje withdrew a piece of braided red string. "Here," he said tying it around her neck. "I brought this *sungdi* blessed by the monk at Tengboche. It will protect you."

Fingering it, Beth felt an unexpected calm settling over her and realized this is what she had come to write about: mountaineering from the Sherpa point of view, and she was beginning to think like one. The ice and snow reflecting off the mountain walls in the moonlight filled the tent with a strange whiteness. Dorje was gazing at her while gently running his finger over her lips as if he knew she wanted to talk. It seemed the right time.

"I've been thinking about our life together," she began. His finger paused on her lips as if to hush her, but she removed it. "I wonder where we'll spend it." She waited, a bit quivery inside, uncertain of his thoughts.

He playfully tugged her earlobe and whispered, "Wherever you want."

"Really? You'd consider coming to the States with me?"

"Yes. I know you will bored here and I want to see outside of Nepal."

She grabbed him and pulled him on top with her hands on his cheeks so she could look at him. "I'm so excited. You can travel all over the world with me."

"And what will I do there, be your Sherpa porter? You know I did not go to school and cannot read or write.

"I'll teach you and soon you'll be writing the stories instead of me and I'll be out of a job."

"Then you can be my porter," he said with a nervous laugh.

"Hmmm," she purred and reached between his legs, determined to make wild passionate love again. "But only if you don't take too many clothes along."

The next morning, the lowland porters started their long journey home to Kathmandu, leaving only the cook and kitchen boys to set up camp. "I want to help," Beth said, arms akimbo, surveying dozens of food containers, kitchen utensils, medical supplies, tents, ladders, and climbing gear. "I want to participate, not just write about it."

Dorje chuckled. "You do not know what to do and will have to wait until I get back from Gorak Shep. A Sherpani down there is going to return the yaks to Namche for me."

Beth swaggered towards him "I'm going with you. You're not getting rid of me that easily."

But by the time they returned that afternoon, the altitude had zapped her. "Tomorrow," she yawned. "We have five more days before the climbers and their porters arrive." Leaning over as if to tie her boots, she rolled a snowball and flung it at Dorje, catching him completely off guard.

"You demon," he yelled and scooped up a handful to hurl back. Giggling and tossing snow, they chased each other over the glacier and bombarded the other Sherpas who gleefully joined in the fight.

Panting and doubled over with her hands on her knees, Beth finally pleaded, "I give up. No more. Have mercy on me."

"Like you did on me last night?" Dorje asked with a fistful of snow hovering above her. "Promise that you will be good?"

"I promise," she answered with an impish grin.

Their chase had brought them to the 2,000-foot icefall at the head of the glacier. From a distance, it looked like a frozen waterfall, but Beth now realized the groaning and cracking she'd heard in the night was ice breaking into immense blocks. The turquoise pinnacles towering 100 feet overhead created an eerie maze of shifting, unstable ice. And she was afraid. "You're not going up there?"

He eyed the icefall as if searching for a route. "Yes, many times, I think."

Sadness resonated in her voice as she huddled against him for warmth. "I don't want you to go. It's too dangerous. Stay here and we'll do the story together by talking to porters as they return."

"I have to."

"No, you don't," Beth tossed back angrily.

"Since I was five, I have been the Tenzing of the future and the future is now."

That made no sense at all, but she gritted her teeth and kept her mouth shut to keep from alienating him. Then he surprised her by revealing he'd been thinking of their future too and had real insight into himself. Arm in arm, they started walking back to camp. "In Namche, I am an important man and earn many rupees because I am strong, know the mountains, and speak good English for big tips."

"And are also extremely sexy."

He gave her a quick squeeze and smiled. "But in American, I will be nobody."

She hip jostled him and grinned. "Not after tomorrow. Remember, I'm going to teach you to read and write. Besides, you understand things better than anybody I know. We can travel around the world with you providing the brains and me the grammar. Or you can learn photography and take Eric's place."

"I do not want to depend on you. I must do something that will make me feel important on my own. Even in your country, people will respect a Sherpa who reached the top of Everest. Will they not?"

She wanted to say no one would care but that would be lying. "Of course," she admitted reluctantly. "People all over the world will respect that."

The next three days, Beth took her mind off Everest by focusing on setting up tents, unpacking crates, and helping organize the kitchen with the cook's consent. Easily winded at that altitude, she took frequent rests to teach Dorje who devoured everything she offered. Never had she seen such a quick and eager mind. The day before the climbers were due, the two retreated to her tent to make love. Lying cradled in Dorje's arms afterwards, Beth lazily watched the sun and clouds playing peek-a-boo on the roof. Life was good now but how long would it last?

Suddenly the words, "Hey, Buck buck, where are you?" bounced into camp like a ball hit out of the court. Having heard no English other than Dorje's for nine days, she decided the altitude had finally gotten to her and she was delirious. But other voices followed, French and British.

"What is happening?" Dorje asked, roused from a deep, orgasmic sleep.

"They're here," she whispered.

"Who?"

"The climbers." She quickly pulled on her pants and shirt and then reached for her jacket and boots. "Wait here until it's clear." As she exited the tent, Dorje was swearing at himself. "I'm here, Marty," Beth called, almost hoping he'd spot Dorje and the whole expedition nightmare would be over.

"Hi, radiant-ness," Marty chirped and threw his arms around her for a tight hug that lasted much too long for comfort.

"How were your climbs?" she asked, gracefully releasing herself.

"Fantastic-ness. We did two 20,000-foot peaks, no problem. How about you, Darling? Did Dorje take care of you okay?"

Darling? How dare he? She mumbled to herself. *And yes, more than you'll ever imagine.* "We hiked slowly so I wouldn't get sick and he taught me how to set up camp. I have many good notes."

"Great. I knew he would," Marty said, looking around. "Where is he anyway?"

"I'm not sure. I was napping." Glancing over her shoulder, she saw the tent flap move and decided to distract the climbers by walking them up to the icefall. Dorje crept from her tent and joined them. As they all chatted excitedly about the days to come, Beth tried to summon enthusiasm, but inside her an ominous dread flowered and sank its gnarled roots deep.

CHAPTER TWENTY-EIGHT

While some of the expedition members scouted the icefall, the sirdar put Paul—a tall, lanky Frenchman—in charge of working with the Sherpas the next two days. He issued winter gear to every porter: a down bag and pad, waterproof leather boots with fur lining, wool socks and hat, double-layered gloves, goggles, an inner and outer pair of pants, wool shirt and sweater, plus a heavy jacket. Having never worn anything more substantial than cheap canvas shoes from China, the porters now had to get used to stiff leather boots with crampons. Finding them awkward, Dorje wondered how he'd ever climb a mountain in such things. They practiced crawling across an aluminum ladder suspended on blocks of ice, cutting stairs with an ice axe, and using an ascender on fixed ropes to keep from sliding backwards. It was all so new and thrilling that Dorje sneaked into Beth's tent each night full of confidence and chattering in rambling, excited bursts about reaching the summit. For fifteen years, the mountain had been silently trying to seduce him with its mysterious folds of rock and ice. And now his long, love affair with Everest was about to be consummated.

Snuggled in their bags, Beth said in a voice lacking his enthusiasm, "They haven't asked you to go to the top, have they?"

"No," he answered disappointed. "But Marty promised to get me there. And when we start through the icefall tomorrow, the others will see how strong I am."

"And when will I see you again?"

"The day after tomorrow I think. We have to move all the gear from here to Camp I and it will take many trips." Her subdued manner perplexed Dorje. He wanted her to be proud and eager for him. Lightly running his finger along her cheek, he whispered, "What is wrong?"

"I'm scared and don't want you to go. I've heard the ground can yawn and swallow a man whole."

"I promise to turn back if things look bad and spend every night making love to you." For now he wanted to take her all in—the aroma of her hair, the sound of her beating heart, the feel of her breath on his cheek—and carry them tucked inside for courage and strength when he needed them. Knowing that having sex on the mountain was a sin, he would offer many prayers on his journey.

The next morning, the porters refused to depart for the icefall until they had conducted an elaborate *puja* ceremony honoring the goddess residing in Chomolungma. She did not like to be trod upon and any misstep could invoke serious retribution. Spirits, evil forces, and ghosts of those who died on the mountain dwelled in her heights. One of the most grievous offenses was having sex or what the Sherpas called *making sauce.* Being guilty of this transgression, Dorje erected an eight-foot, rectangular stone *chorten* supporting a tall pole crowned in a juniper bough. Strings of the five-colored prayer flags representing the five elements radiated from the top to stone anchors on the ground. After placing smaller juniper boughs around the stones, Dorje lit them sending smoke circling toward the summits above. While playing a drum and brass cymbals, a lama read from an ancient Tibetan script asking the goddess for fair weather, permission to climb, and for protection from accidents. He then blessed the offerings of rice, bread, *tsampa,* and *chang.* After large plates of food were given to the goddess, the Sherpas took small amounts of rice between their fingers and tossed them to the sky to draw attention to themselves and ask her assistance. The remainder of the food was shared by all as part of a ritual meal. At the end of the ceremony, a bowl of *tsampa* was passed around and the porters smeared the barley paste on each other's faces.

Beth accompanied them to the icefall. Having said farewell in the tent when he left before dawn, Dorje ached to hold her in his arms again, but he could only convey love through his eyes as he promised, "I will return soon and tell you how it is for a Sherpa porter traveling in the icefall so you can write your story."

"I'll be waiting."

"Time to go," Marty interrupted. "Give me a hug for good luck?" Not offering her a chance to refuse, he grabbed Beth for a tight squeeze and sashayed in front of the expedition members wiping his brow. "Whew. What hot-ness." Such arrogance. Dorje wanted to shove his face in the snow but a tiny shake of Beth's head said to let it go.

With a long breath, he arched his back to rid the tension and took his first steps toward Everest. The icefall was a maze of enormous ice blocks resting on a ground riddled with innumerable crevasses. Staring at the towering pinnacles, Dorje remembered Marty's defiance of the gods last fall when he yelled *Geronimo* and strutted beneath the overhanging ice. Was it wise to trust his life and future to a self-proclaimed wacko who took risks simply to prove something to a father half way around the world? Roped to him with Paul in the lead and 30 other porters behind, Dorje vowed to be ever mindful and not fall prey to Marty's precarious and erratic nature.

Two hours earlier, the other Americans, Mark and Sean, had gone ahead to make sure the route prepared the day before hadn't altered due to new avalanches or toppling séracs. Constantly probing the ground in search of hidden crevasses, Paul and Marty told Dorje to warn the other porters not stray from their tracks. As they wound through a forest of séracs tilting in all directions, the blue-ice pinnacles loomed forebodingly in their cold silence. The porters walked without speaking, not wanting to disturb the spirits inhabiting the towers. Suddenly, as if the mountain had decided to stretch, the ground moved slightly, and a narrow tongue peeled off one of the séracs plunging downward in a mass of shattering ice. A sickening horror swept over Dorje. Was this a terrible mistake that would take him from the woman he loved? He clamped his jaw shut to keep from trembling and exposing his fear to Mary and Paul.

"How can we carry in a land where men are not meant to walk," bemoaned Rinji, the weakest of the porters. Shaken by the uncertainly of each step, the Sherpas began quietly murmuring, *"Om mani padme hum."*

With sheer walls or deep crevasses surrounding some blocks, they were impossible to go around and had to be climbed. Going in advance, the Americans Mark and Sean had used ice axes to carve stairs over a two-story pinnacle. Many of the Sherpas had never worn shoes before. The cumbersome boots and crampons caused frequent misplaced steps and slips, leaving several porters dangling helplessly until someone could haul them up. When they reached a crevasse too long to detour and too deep to descend, Paul and Marty stopped to confer. The walls had been undercut, leaving lips of unsupported snow suspended above a chasm widening into blackness. The Americans had lashed together eight-foot sections of aluminum ladder and lowered it across, but it lay at an upward pitch on the uneven sides of the fissure. Rinji kicked a block of ice over the edge and the porters listened to it explode in the depths. Muttering nervously among themselves, no one wanted to proceed. Taking a few steps and then quickly returning, Paul declared it too dangerous for them to walk across with heavy packs and slippery crampons.

Marty grimaced with his eyes stretched wide. "A little scared-ness here," he whispered even though Dorje was the only Sherpa who could understand him anyway. "And I don't want to go first." Thinking how Marty had been coerced into going first in the cave, Dorje empathized with him. The American's mouth and body were speaking simultaneously but communicating different emotions. In a voice so low it could have belonged to someone else, Marty uttered, "Remember what I said about life being like a stubborn old mule. You have to smack it across the head every once in a while to keep it in line. Well, it's time for some head smacking." Crouched in a half crawl with all fours in contact with the ladder and seat in the air, he kept a low center of gravity. One knee dropped to the rung for balance each time he alternated his arms and legs. Reaching the other side, Marty drove the axe shaft into the snow and anchored the rope around its head.

Dorje was next. As he stared at the ladder hovering over a bottomless abyss, an ice-cold fear gripped him, but he immediately dismissed it, unwilling to tolerate any doubts about himself. He was young and in love; he was indomitable. However, as a precaution, he opened a small pouch at his waist and sprinkled *chaane* into the crevasse before lowering himself to the ground. "Geronimo," he whispered and started across with a stuttering heart. Moving hand over hand, he peered between the rungs at jagged blocks of green ice below threatening to shatter him if he fell. At mid point, the ladder suddenly sagged and swayed, shifting his load to the right. He felt the cold hand of a *shrindi* ghost trying to wrench him from the ladder and hurl him into oblivion. Seat still in the air and one knee to the rung, he froze afraid to let go and move forward.

"Come on, Buck buck, you're doing great," Marty shouted from the other side. "Just inch your hand along."

His arms quivering under the weight of the pack, Dorje's body that had never failed him was shaking like an old lady's and he could not accept that. Slowly lowering his knee to take the pressure off his arms, he didn't dare look down again as he slid his right hand forward an inch. He brought the other foot up and straddled the rung with his crampon, moved the left hand, and then the right knee, thus gradually making his way across.

"Give me a high five!" Marty shouted as Dorje threw himself onto the snow and crawled up the bank. Glancing back at the porters, he expected to hear gales of ridiculing laughter, but they were just as frightened as he. He dumped his load and calmed himself a moment.

"You just made it possible for them to cross. Seeing me do it wasn't the same," Marty said, bolstering Dorje's self esteem. "Now help me with the rope. This is serious bridge-ness"

Dorje talked the other porters across in Sherpa, one inch at a time. Coming last, Rinji's face was terror-stricken. When the ladder sagged at center point, he lurched and dropped over the side.

Dorje grabbed the rope tighter and slammed his heels into the snow, but Rinji and his load were dragging him toward the unstable lip. Dorje's entire insides went on hold as he prepared to disappear into the void and never see Beth again.

A rope jerked him from behind as Marty ordered, "Push with your feet!"

Shocked back to his senses, Dorje dug his crampons in and quickly shoveled backwards as Marty held the rope. Working together, they got him onto solid snow again, but Rinji still dangled helplessly.

"Now let's reel him in like a large fish," Marty said calmly.

Getting his body operational again, Dorje gripped the rope and reached hand over hand, pulling with all his strength until Rinji was safely across. Everyone looked shaken by the experience. As the porters murmured among themselves, Dorje wondered if they would turn back. They were only here to do a job, get paid, and leave the mountain as soon as possible. Before expeditions arrived, Sherpas had no notion of climbing and saw no reason to expose themselves to unnecessary risks when life was so full of them anyway. Since they resented those who climbed to prove something or gain recognition, he kept his own desire to reach the summit a secret.

After Paul roped Rinji between the two strongest porters, everyone headed out again. Hoping they had passed through the worst of it, Dorje's heart sank when they reached a maze of enormous crevasses threatened on all sides by crumbling séracs. Walking became almost impossible as the porters stumbled over recent avalanche debris and shattered ice. They hadn't gone far when the mountain shrugged with a strange creak and tremor that split a pinnacle in half and swept it past them in a merciless jumble of ice that rocked the ground before shooting into a gaping crevasse. A deathly silence fell over the group. No one wanted to cross the ice-strewn slope under the tilting remains of the tower. Dorje hated being in the middle of something he couldn't control, hated being this afraid. Suddenly doubting himself, he wondered if he had the courage to be the Tenzing of the future. The other porters chanted mantras as they scattered *chaane* across the ice and on the séracs. They too were frightened but he expected more of himself.

"We have to get through there," Marty said, zipping his jacket. "The sun's already setting and it's only two o'clock. It will be freezing soon."

Reluctantly the porters followed him, threading their way directly up a steep gully formed by great blocks stacked carelessly on top of each other. With overhanging ice perched high above on every side, they crept through the narrow passage, sometimes squeezing between the pinnacles, always listening to creaking and groaning ice. Holding his breath, Dorje tried to still the heart echoing loudly in his head, certain that any noise or movement would send the unstable masses tumbling about them.

They reached Camp I in the icefall at 19,500 feet just before four o'clock. Exhausted and cold but mostly frightened, the Sherpas huddled around communal stoves to warm themselves. Marty came to Dorje's fire and crouched beside him. "You did well today. It took courage to go first."

His words struck the cold air with a hollow sound because Dorje knew it wasn't true. Hands tucked under his armpits, he pulled himself tighter and stared at the flames. "I was not brave," he muttered, shivering. "I was scared."

"Scared? Well, we all were. Scared shitless," Marty said with a laugh that ruffled through him like a dog shaking after a bath.

An involuntary snort of laughter escaped Dorje. "Scared shitless?"

"Hey. That was the most difficult piece of mountain I've ever been through and it was your first time. You've got nothing to be ashamed of."

After dinner, Dorje crawled into his bag, too exhausted to sleep. He had seen dead bodies brought down from the mountain, how rigid and pale they were. But never had he imagined himself that way until today when he peered into the depths. It could end so quickly and without warning: a sag in the ladder, a misplaced step, loose crampon, or a frayed rope. Listening to the crack of a sérac breaking free, he felt adrift on a river of ice that was moving, crumbling, and toppling all around. And it terrified him. Tomorrow he would start back through the icefall for three more carries from Base Camp. Having promised Beth to turn around if things looked bad, how could he determine that moment when things were constantly in flux? He listened to the groan of glaciers settling for the night and the occasional rattle of falling stone. The crack of ice and snow breaking loose sounded not far away followed by the roar of an avalanche tumbling down the mountain ready to engulf their camp. Shuddering, he pulled the bag over his head and pretended not to hear.

CHAPTER TWENTY-NINE

The next morning, the climbers planned on remaining in Camp I to acclimatize and explore Camp II while the sirdar and porters returned to Base Camp for another load. There had been no singing or joking at the porters' fire the night before. Having an accident that early on the first day was a bad omen and had shaken everyone. Most wanted to quit, turn around, and go home.

Determined not to shave until he returned from the summit, Paul scratched the black stubble on his face as he took Dorje aside. "Explain that without their help supplying the camps, the expedition can't go on. We've waited four long years and traveled great distances for this opportunity."

"But why do they come?" Rinji asked when Dorje spoke to them. "What's the point? Mountains are for grazing."

"It doesn't matter why. You will earn more rupees for your wife and three children than you can in many months of farming."

Arms folded over their chests, the porters agreed this was their greatest hope of fending off starvation through the winter. Otherwise, they'd have to leave their families for six months to work in India. But that didn't keep them from grousing all the way down the icefall about how they faced greater risk than the lazy *mikarus* who were experienced climbers, had better equipment, weren't burdened with awkward loads, and didn't make repeated trips. A new fissure had opened during the night and a crumbling sérac had buried a portion of the trail, requiring a new one be cut. Realizing the mountain was alive and moving made the giant ice pinnacles, yawning crevasses, and masses of overhanging snow loom more menacingly.

While the porters fretted and complained, Dorje tried to figure out what to say to Beth. Marty wanted him to brag about his heroic exploits in saving Rinji, but Dorje wasn't about to bolster his chances with her. If he described how dangerous it was to crawl across a crevasse heavily loaded and wearing slippery crampons, she would rightfully argue against his going back. But if he quit now, he'd forever be a boy frozen on a ladder staring into the abyss instead of the man she deserved. He must arrive in America as a respected Sherpa who had climbed Everest, not an uneducated yak herder and porter.

Beth was standing several hundred yards away with her back to them when Dorje and the porters reached the end of the icefall. He released the safety rope and began slowly walking toward her, remembering the first moment he had gazed upon her at Lukla. How his spirit had soared that day. She must have sensed his presence because Beth suddenly turned and stared as if she couldn't believe he had really come back to her. "Dorje!" she cried with a voice as fresh as mountain air.

The thought of holding her again had guided him through the treacherous icefall. Now unable to wait a minute longer, he ran across the rock-strewn glacier and swooped her into his arms. "Did you miss me?"

"And why would I when I have all those handsome yaks for companions?"

"Ahhh, but can they satisfy you like I do?" he said carrying her to the tent with an impish grin.

Grabbing his jacket, she peered around him at the porter audience. "And what about them? You should be ashamed of yourself."

"Let them stare. They are only jealous," he answered and lowered her into the tent for an afternoon of lovemaking.

Afterwards with Beth lying comfortably in his arms, Dorje stared out the door at the massive peaks in this land of gleaming ice, their razor-sharp ridges climbing to impossible heights. Was Everest beyond his reach? And did he dare risk losing a single moment like this to chase the dream of a five year old? Right now, loving her seemed all that mattered but he knew he had to do more. He watched the last rays of sun burn on the highest rocks, turning them from scarlet to a deepening blue. The crystals of their mighty ice-fluted walls glistened as the peaks slowly vanished and the landscape crept into darkness.

The next morning, three porters demanded their pay for carrying to Camp I. Rinji's accident was a bad omen and they were returning to their families. With Dorje as a translator, blond-haired Mark tried praising their superiority over *mikarus,* appealing to their sense of loyalty, commending their bravery. But nothing worked. They were convinced something had angered the gods such as Dorje making sauce. It was not an auspicious time to be on the mountain and they were going home. All the others, including Rinji, remained for one reason only—money.

"I will be back in two days," Dorje promised Beth when she accompanied him to the end of the glacier. "I am glad a doctor and reporter have come to camp. Now you have someone to talk to while I am gone." Holding her as long as he could, Dorje whispered how much he loved her and would carry the sweet taste of her kisses with him through the icefall. Finally the other American, Sean, was growing impatient. Donning his most engaging smile, Dorje said, "Write all that I described and I will be back before you miss me."

Her lips were pressed tightly in a straight line as Beth bit them trying to hold back the tears already trickling down her cheeks. "Be careful."

"I promise. And I love you," he whispered wanting to feel the warmth of her skin to the last second.

Mark led them back into the icefall this time with Dorje roped behind him followed by the other porters. Plodding around a crevasse that had opened since yesterday, Dorje wondered how to approach the subject of his relationship. When they finally stopped to rest 40 minutes later, he summoned the courage. "I ask that you do not speak of Beth and me," he told Mark.

"Your affair is your business," Mark answered with a kindness Dorje had come to expect from him. "I will say nothing." It was as short and simple as that. Dorje trusted and liked this American with a square jaw, hair the color of Beth's, and eyes that changed from blue to green depending on the day. Tall, strong, and intelligent, he appeared to be the most capable climber on the expedition.

When they entered a maze of ice pinnacles, Rinji nervously scattered thorns to keep evil spirits from following them. By mid afternoon, they reached Camp I again, exhausted but without incident. Over the next eight days, the porters shuttled more than two tons of gear and provisions up the mountain. Each time Dorje said good-bye to Beth, it became more difficult because he knew the greater challenge still lay ahead. During the nights he crawled into his bag alone, he could feel her lying beside him and remembered how she tasted and smelled, the softness of her skin.

Everything about her pleased him. Did she know how very much he loved her? With Camp I supplied, they would begin moving to Camp II and he might not see her for many days.

The next phase was a disastrous combination from the beginning. Marty and a thin-lipped Brit named Jarvis were in charge of leading the porters up the next portion. Put off by the aloof, humorless demeanor of the Brit, Marty had switched the salt and sugar for the man's beloved tea their first night in Base Camp. When Jarvis spewed it out in disgust, Marty accused him of wearing his shorts too tight, and they had been at each other ever since.

"Such uptight-ness," Marty commented to Dorje as they started out. "With that beak-like nose and beady eyes, it's a wonder he doesn't fly."

Laughing, Dorje said, I do no think he likes you either."

"Well, I hope not. Ugh, imagine the likes of him with me." Marty stopped and leaned on his ice pick. "I'd rather talk about my beautiful Beth," he said with a pause between words as if short of breath. "I haven't seen her since we left Base Camp. Has she asked about me?"

My beautiful Beth? His stomach roiling at the thought of Marty being with her, Dorje didn't dare jeopardize his chances by speaking the truth. "Yes, and I told her about you saving Rinji just as you asked."

"Was she impressed?"

"She thinks you are a very brave man."

With a silky murmured, Marty asked, "Is she waiting anxiously for me in Base Camp?"

Wanting to tell him to just forget it, Dorje again shoved the eager, vengeful words back into their holes with severe warnings against trying to sneak out. "She was there when I left."

"Not too cold or sick?"

"No, she was well," he answered. "We are behind now and must catch Jarvis."

"Ah, yes. Go with the bird."

After roping up with the Brit and the porters, they climbed upwards to the Western Cwm—a deep, snow-filled valley spilling over the icefall. So close now with Everest on their left, Dorje stared at the black rock face below the summit, denuded of snow by an ever-present wind. After slogging though ice and snow for weeks and being filled with doubt, he finally experienced an emotional rush.

Flanking the valley on the right, were the granite walls of Nuptse with its dazzling fluted ice and hanging glaciers. Four miles straight ahead stood the 4,000-foot lower wall of Lhotse, which had to be climbed. With ice pinnacles no longer cracking and toppling around them, the valley was strangely silent. It was a stillness so deep that Dorje heard only the crunch of his boot and his sleeve brushing against his jacket as he swung the ice axe forward. Even though the stretch ahead appeared a vast, flat area of endless snow, it too was riddled with innumerable crevasses, some narrow enough that Marty seemed compelled to jump across them. In the lead now, he spotted one, yelled, "Geronimo!" and took a flying leap but fell short by a crucial inch. Frantically scrambling to stay on top, he jammed his axe in and clawed the snow with his free hand, but the unstable lip ripped loose and plummeted into the depths, leaving Marty dangling over turquoise ice like a yoyo at the bottom of its string. The initial thrust had yanked Jarvis skidding to the brim. Having gone over the Rinji incident a hundred times in his head, Dorje responded by pure instinct now and quickly dug in to halt the slide. With the weight of the porters behind him, they first pulled Jarvis back to safety before hauling Marty out of the crevasse.

The Brit was furious. "You fucking American! What in the hell were you doing?"

"Hey, loosen up, Jarv. You just gotta smack heads now and then."

Jarvis paced as far as the rope would allow, waving his arms and swearing. "I don't know what in the hell you're talking about, but I'm not trusting my life to an idiot like you. And anybody with half a brain won't either."

"Good," Marty grumbled to Dorje after they set out to walk around the crevasse. "I don't want to climb with him anyway."

While agreeing with Jarvis, Dorje kept his mouth shut, unwilling to gamble with his chances of going to the top. Instead he chuckled to himself wondering if Marty wanted him to brag about this incident to Beth.

Reaching a crevasse too long to circumvent, they discovered Mark and Sean had left another ladder. After repeated trips through the icefall, Dorje was amazed at how quickly the mind adapts. He'd been so scared crawling on the first one and never wanted to face such fear again. Since then he'd crossed dozens of times and now simply walked on the aluminum rungs in the same slippery crampons while holding onto a fixed rope.

They unloaded at Camp II in the Cwm where the Americans were waiting to set up tents and supplies. As Jarvis, Marty, Dorje, and the porters headed back down to Camp I, the clouds thickened and turned everything pale gray. An hour later, large flakes drifted lazily and settled on the everlasting snow creating a featureless landscape.

Sharing a tent for the first time, Marty wanted to talk about Beth. "I usually date a woman six or eight months and then move on when another one comes along. And somebody always does who seems more interesting or more attractive, at least in the beginning."

"There must be many women in America," said Dorje.

"Thousands. And if you can dance well, they come running to you. My father thought I'd grow up liking boys better than girls because I loved dancing. How wrong could he be? While the so-called tough guys were patting each other's seats playing football, I was holding onto beautiful women, but he just couldn't grasp that."

"With so many, you do not need Beth."

Marty rolled onto his stomach and leaned on his elbows, staring at Dorje. "Oh, she's not like any other woman. Beth is pure luscious-ness like deep, dark chocolate that you want to wrap up in your pocket and keep forever." A wiggle rippled from his shoulders all the way down to his toes. "For a woman like her I'd wear matching socks every day." He leaned down and whispered as if in great confidence. "And I've never said that about anybody. I will do anything to keep her."

You can't keep something you don't have, Dorje told himself

Heading back up the Cwm the next morning, the party encountered a deep layer of fresh snow that made walking an ordeal of sinking in knee-deep, dragging the back leg out and planting it, and then sinking again. The heat stored in the black, rock faces of Everest and Nuptse turned the valley below into an oven, wilting porters under their heavy loads. Stopping often, they huddled over their axes, mouths agape struggling for breath. Almost as if taking turns, one of them would crumple to his knees, clutching his axe, and crawl out again to continue the monotonous plodding upward. Dorje warned them against eating lumps of snow because it would only flay their dry throats more. They paced themselves by the slowest man, Rinji, who had been taking two steps, stopping, breathing heavily, and then taking two more. All of a sudden with a frightening moan, he collapsed. The ragged string of porters halted and stooped over their axes, panting. Trudging back to him, Marty tried to stand Rinji up, but the small, wiry man sprawled helplessly in the snow. Seeing the opportunity to prove himself, Dorje told two other porters to tie Rinji's load onto his.

"Are you crazy?" Marty asked. "Don't be a wacko like me."

"I have carried two loads before."

"Not up here. Haven't you noticed it's damn hard to breathe?"

Stubbornly, Dorje pushed his hand out, palm down, and wiggled it back and forth, warning Marty to back off. But when he began walking, the extra load pushed him even deeper. Ten minutes of unrelenting heat and thigh-deep snow staggered him. Having never been this high before, his head was throbbing with the pain everyone had complained about for days. On straw legs, he fell face forward.

"Get rid of Rinji's load," Marty ordered.

Pulling back onto his feet, Dorje insisted, "No. I can do it."

"Not up here. Every hour you're above 19,000 feet your body dies a little. Then one day you can't do it anymore and have to go down. That comes at a different time for everyone."

"That is why you went down on Kangchenjunga," Dorje said.

"Yeah," Marty answered with a wheezy quality to his voice. "Wasn't a storm that turned me back. I just got too damn sick. I coughed so hard I broke a couple of ribs and was throwing up all the time." Not allowing Dorje to resist, he untied Rinji's load. "Promise me we'll go to the top together, no turning back for any reason. If I don't make the summit, it will be because I died here."

"I will not turn back."

"But you must swear that we'll go together like Tenzing and Hillary."

"I promise," Dorje said as Marty pulled Rinji's load off. "Both of us no matter what happens."

"The first thing you have to learn is to save your strength for the mountain like those climbing Sherpas from Darjeeling. Conserve-ness"

"I want to show them I am strong enough to make it."

"Worry about that later. Right now, just make it to camp."

Dorje left Rinji's load in the snow and went on with a grateful body but angry heart. Having never given up on anything before, he didn't like the feeling. When he reached Camp II at 21,300 feet in the middle of the Western Cwm, he dropped his load and immediately waded back through his own tracks to retrieve Rinji's. By the time he returned after sunset, the temperature had dropped far below zero and another storm was approaching. Too tired and sick to eat, he crawled into the tent with nine other porters.

During the night, thin drifts of snow seeped through the roof, and condensation from everyone's breath froze on the ceiling. Any brush against the fabric caused an immediate storm inside. When Dorje woke in the morning, his bag and clothes were wet. His pad had deflated, leaving his bottom pressed against nearly bare ice. Numb with cold, he fumbled with the zipper but his swollen fingers weren't cooperating. Knocking his hands together and blowing on them, he tried warming them enough to pick up the frozen boots. Fortunately, another porter had lit the stove, so he and Dorje sat thawing their boots and complaining about how miserable they felt. The smell of roasting leather slowly roused the others.

When Rinji stirred, they realized that in his stupor the night before he hadn't taken off his crampons and had merely pulled his bag over himself rather than climb inside. Dorje removed the metal spikes so they wouldn't tear the tent. Rinji was trembling. "I can't feel my feet," he gasped so faintly that Dorje barely heard him. As a young child, he'd seen a climber coming down with black, frostbitten hands and face and later heard they had cut off the man's fingers and toes. Dorje leaned out the door and yelled for help. Mark and Jarvis came running. "I think his toes are frozen," Dorje explained.

Mark quickly unlaced Rinji's boots and carefully pulled them off. "Tell him to try wiggling them."

"I can't," Rinji explained in Nepali, his voice growing more urgent. "Can't feel anything at all."

Removing Rinji's socks, Mark said his feet were hard and icy to the touch with the blue-white tinge of frostbite. "We'll warm them slowly, but I think it's already too late," he whispered to Jarvis, seeming to forget that Dorje could understand.

"He wore his crampons all night," Dorje added, "and slept out of his bag."

Mark cupped his hands around Rinji's toes. "The metal probably drew more cold into his feet."

"I carried his load most of the way," said Dorje.

Jarvis nodded. "Yes, we all heard about that."

Lowering the porter's legs to the floor, Mark set them closer to the fire while he told Dorje, "Explain that he must return to Base Camp immediately and someone will carry him."

"I'll go," said a porter from the rear of the tent when Dorje translated. "I don't want to work anymore."

"Me neither," said another, and then a third and fourth.

Soon they all told of knowing someone who had lost fingers and toes with frostbite. The mountain gods were angry because their abode had been polluted by sex and excrement. Dorje translated their desire to leave but said nothing about angry gods, knowing the climbers wouldn't understand. Once again he voiced Mark's appeal to their pride and natural desire to help. The porters finally bargained for a full day's rest at Camp II if they stayed.

"I will take him," Dorje said, his heart aching to see Beth. "I am the strongest and fastest porter you have. Plus, I can translate between him and the doctor."

While they were preparing a *doko* to transport Rinji, Marty sauntered over to the tent with a cup of the hot lemon drink they used to fortify themselves. "What's up, Buck buck?"

"Rinji cannot walk. I will carry him to the doctor in Base Camp."

"Base Camp? I'm going too." Marty told Mark and Jarvis, "The snow covered our trail. I'll need to guide them down." When the men still expressed doubt, he added, "Dorje and I need to practice working as a team if we're going to the top together."

"We've already picked the assault teams and you're climbing with Jarvis," said Mark.

The Brit threw his hands in the air, walked away a few steps, and strode back, his face as hard as the black face of Everest. "I wouldn't trust my life ten feet with Marty. He's an irresponsible madman and I won't climb with him."

"Then who?" asked Mark. "Everyone is paired up."

"I don't know. We'll decide later. Anybody but him."

A mantle of new, unstable snow concealed the hundreds of crevasses that crisscrossed the landscape where they had passed only the day before. Marty probed endlessly, searching for deadly fissures with Dorje cautiously following in his tracks. Once again, he sank knee deep but his spirit rose with visions of standing on the summit, higher than birds can fly. The promise of accomplishing something that grand made all else bearable. But his mood suddenly plunged back to earth when Marty announced, "I'm really going to Base Camp to see Beth again because wacky Marty is crazy in love for the first time ever in his life." His words leapt into the air and chased each other around like giggling children. Dorje wanted to scold them and drive them home without supper. They had no right to be joyous. Beth was his love, his life, and his future. Not Marty's.

CHAPTER THIRTY

Beth was going crazy at Base Camp. Every time an avalanche thundered down a mountain or a sérac toppled in the icefall, she wanted to scream. It was worse than waiting for a soldier to return from war because she was at the battlefront hearing the artillery. And this enemy was powerful, unpredictable, unwilling to negotiate. All she could do was light a juniper bough every morning and pace around chanting, *"Om mani padme hum,"* to Dorje's gods. Her only respite was conversing and playing cards with the British doctor and French reporter who shared this god-forsaken, groaning glacier with her. Assuming she was here simply to write a story, they had no idea the hell she was enduring. To make things worse, those damn guilt gnats kept flapping their wings to remind her that Eric was probably getting his head blown off somewhere in Nam because of her.

Nights were the worst. Even wearing her parka in the sleeping bag, she could not get warm without Dorje's body heat. She lay shivering and wondering where he was and if he longed for her half as much as she did for him. Every afternoon, she hiked to the base of the icefall and stood for hours searching between the pinnacles for him to travel down the ice river and throw himself in her arms. As the days blurred together in this frozen nightmare, her stomach gnawed at itself.

The only other denizens were a cook and two kitchen boys, a Sherpa who periodically dug a new *charpi* and took care of the camp in general, numerous porters who shuttled fresh eggs and fruit from the lower Khumbu villages, plus curious village eyes coming to observe an expedition after the four-year hiatus. Late one afternoon, Beth and her two western companions were playing a three-handed game of hearts in the dining tent. Just as she was about to slap the queen of spades on the doctor's trick, loud shouts and commotion from outside the tent panicked her. Had the awful moment she'd been dreading finally arrived with news of something happening to Dorje? Dropping their cards, they all raced to the icefall and watched two dark figures slowly making their way through the maze of séracs and crevasses. Waiting was interminable.

As the figures neared the end, one of them yelled and started schussing down a narrow valley. Remembering Dorje skiing the first day they met, Beth's entire being melted in relief until, "Hey, Sweet-ness, I'm back," careened off the ice with a chilling blow. Marty strutted onto the glacier, dropped his axe, grabbed her face between his gloves, and kissed her. "Glad to see me?"

"Yes, of course," she answered, dazed. Beth politely stepped back. "What's happened?"

"One of the Sherpas has severe frostbite in his toes and might lose them. I volunteered to bring him down just so I could look on your radiantness again."

"Which Sherpa?" she asked, her voice growing thin.

"Rinji, the little one who should have never gone up there. But I guess he has three kids and needed the money."

"A family that needs its father whole. And the others?"

"Everyone is tired, cold, and sick," he said walking her back to camp.

His face was gaunt and had a faint blue cast. "You look thinner," she observed.

"Yeah. We all have headaches as big as a house, coughs that break your ribs and shred your throat, dizziness. Nobody feels like eating and when you do, it makes you sick. The trail is spotted with colorful vomit stains. One of the French cut his hand and it still hasn't healed. It's hell up there and we haven't even reached the death zone yet."

"So why do you do this?" she asked, seeking some kind of logic.

Marty perked up and wiggled his eyebrows. Grinning and in his usual sing-song voice, he answered, "Because I have to."

Before she and Marty reached camp, something tugged at her—a feeling, an unheard voice. She turned and gazed at a shadowy image in the distance, bathed in the strange glow of sunset. Dorje had come back to her. On legs trembling like the quaking aspen leaves at home, Beth tried to appear casual as she strolled towards him, her heart racing. They met without an embrace because of Marty and Rinji.

"I was so scared," she whispered. "Don't ever leave me here like this again." He removed his goggles and stared at her with all the love a man can communicate through his eyes. "Do not worry. I am the smartest and strongest on the mountain. Nothing will happen to me. Soon I will reach the top and return to spend the rest of my life with you."

Beth swallowed the tears flooding into her throat. "Are you coming to my tent tonight?"

"The largest yeti could not keep me away."

She brought her notepad to dinner and tried to distract her yearning by asking every possible question about a porter's life on Everest. Sitting across from her, Dorje locked his feet around hers under the table with a knowing smile as Marty bragged about keeping his promise to give her the inside scoop. When all the lanterns, stoves, and flashlights dimmed, Dorje slipped through her tent flaps and zipped the door behind him. Naked in a minute, they pulled the sleeping bags over their heads to muffle sounds as they explored every inch, skin on skin. Beth held him tightly as Dorje came in waves of shudders that seemed to never end.

"You killed me," he said laughing and then rolled onto his back and collapsed. "I have never felt anything like that. I love you so much."

"Me too," Beth whispered. "Me too."

Dorje dressed shortly before dawn. "I have to go now," he said, pulling a wool shirt over his head. "But you stay warm here. We will meet again at breakfast."

With the heat of his body still lingering in her bag, Beth watched him through the door as he started for the porter's tent. Suddenly a figure confronted him spitting angry words. "I heard voices in her tent when I got up to piss, but I thought it was the Frenchman or doctor." He shoved Dorje with both hands, knocking him backwards. "Not you, an ignorant, ungrateful Sherpa." He shoved him again. "I got you this job and how do you thank me? By fucking the only woman I've ever loved. I meant it when I said I'd do anything to keep her." He charged at Dorje with swinging fists but missed.

"You can't keep what you never had," Dorje muttered as they prowled around each other like two angry bulls, steam pouring from their mouths.

"Beth's mine. You don't understand western women."

"But I know her," Dorje said. "And you will never have her."

"You bastard," Marty growled and punched him square in the face.

Dorje checked the blood streaming from his nose and returned a blow to Marty's cheek that sent him reeling onto the ice. He lunged on top of the American and they rolled across the glacier with flailing fists.

"Stop it," Beth ordered, shivering in her bag outside the tent. "Stop it." Dorje released Marty's jacket with a final push to the chest and then got back to his feet and stood beside her.

"Marty, I'm sorry," she said as he slowly rose.

Wiping blood across the back of his sleeve, Marty asked, "How could you let a porter into your tent instead of me? I thought you had more class."

Feeling Dorje about to explode, Beth grabbed his arm. "Marty, I'm sorry if I hurt you, but I've never led you on."

"When you came here with me, I felt it wasn't just to write a story."

"You were right. I've been in love with Dorje since last fall and returned to tell him so."

His face wrinkled in confusion. "Why didn't anyone bother to tell me?" With a cold, menacing stare, he addressed Dorje with bitterness. "You let me talk about how much I wanted her and how I thought she liked me. But you never said anything. Why?"

"Because you are my friend and I wanted to climb Everest with you," Dorje answered.

"Well, that's not going to happen." Marty snarled. Starting to walk away, he turned and marched back. "And I'll see that nobody does either."

Beth felt Dorje's body slacken as a sixteen-year dream vanished. "Come back inside. You're wet and shivering." As they lay together waiting for the first glow of dawn to crawl across the roof, she didn't know how to comfort him. Making it to the top was important for his self-esteem, but at the same time she was relieved he would no longer be risking his life. "I have enough for a great story already. We can go back now and arrange for your passport." Tickling him where he was most vulnerable, she got no response. "I can hardly wait to show you all the things in America. Lights and heat that turn on by pushing a button, warm water that comes out of the wall, indoor toilets that flush everything out of the house, machines that wash and dry your clothes, giant stores with everything imaginable to buy, cars to drive instead of walking. Hundreds and thousands of exciting things."

"I will be like a child in your world."

"Hmmm," she purred and slid her leg between his. "But I desire the man in you."

Thinking she had surely convinced him to return to Namche, Beth was shocked and upset when he prepared to head back up the icefall with Marty after breakfast. "What are you doing? I thought we were going down."

"We will and soon, but first I must finish my porter job to earn enough rupees for Shanti and the baby."

"But I have much more than you can make and will gladly give it."

"I must do this myself. Not take money from you."

Anguish enveloped her as Beth said, "I understand. Of course you must go. I'll wait here and keep our bed warm until you return."

Striding twenty feet ahead, Marty entered the icefall without looking back as Beth and Dorje held each other in a long embrace. "You are my one true love," she whispered, struggling to contain the tears. "You're everything I want in this world. So please hurry back to me."

"I will. Do not worry," he said and kissed each tear one by one. "Now I must go with Marty. He is angry but knows that it is not safe to travel alone."

Feeling as though a piece of ice had lodged in her stomach, Beth waited until they disappeared in the turquoise sérac forest. Then she returned to camp trying to ignore the distant boom of an avalanche.

CHAPTER THIRTY-ONE

Catching up to Marty, Dorje roped together for safety without speaking or making eye contact. Knowing tempers were as thin as the air and could last as long as ice on the mountain, he murmured, *"Om mani padme hum,"* through the icefall to appease the goddess Miyolangsangma who resided in the mountain. When men polluted it with any conduct that generated emotions such as anger or jealousy, offensive smells such as roasting meat or burning garbage, or engaged in sexual activity, the goddess became ill, and when she was ill, all those near her became infected too. He'd heard many stories of people around Everest suffering because they failed to give her the proper attention she required. None of this did he communicate to Marty because he knew westerners didn't share his beliefs, and he was in no mood for a debate.

Without the burden of a heavy load, they reached Camp II in the Western Cwm by mid afternoon. Not a word had passed between them, but Marty's scathing remark in Base Camp repeated itself 100 times in Dorje's head. *Not you, an ignorant, ungrateful Sherpa.* Any kinship Dorje had felt for the man now lay buried in a pile of steaming shit. He was glad to be rid of him when the expedition members and climbing Sherpas left to explore, mark, and prepare the route to Camps III and IV. Meanwhile with continuous movement in both directions through the Cwm, the camps constantly expanded and contracted as porters carried provisions in from lower ones and then out to higher ones.

Soon the Khumbu porters would be sent back home while the climbing Sherpas finished setting the route and moving provisions to Camp IV on the South Col. The morning Dorje was due to return, he overheard two of them telling the sirdar they were quitting. They were worn out and sick after spending more than a week on the Lhotse Wall cutting ice steps and setting fixed ropes to transform the technical route into one a heavily laden porter could follow. More importantly, they were scared of the poison gases on high passes that dulled one's mind. Rinji's carelessness in the tent was a bad omen. Insisting there were no poison gases and the climbers couldn't go on without supplies, the sirdar still failed to alter their decision. "*Toi ye!*" he yelled with a large spit as they started down the Cwm. The window for making the ascent before the monsoon was rapidly closing. With only three climbing Sherpas left to haul loads and fix the route to the South Col, it would be impossible to be ready in time.

Dorje stepped forward. "I will carry but only if I'm paid the same as the Darjeeling Sherpas."

The three remaining Sherpas argued against him for over an hour saying he lacked experience, had never worked at such high altitude, and had already spent his strength and energy carrying from Base Camp. He would never make it. Dorje wanted this too much: extra rupees for Shanti and the baby plus an outside chance of going to the top. So he fought fervently and eventually gained Paul's assent only because the man was desperate to proceed as quickly as possible. He and Henri, the other Frenchman, plus a Brit named Roger were going to acclimate at Camp III while Jarvis stayed in the Cwm with a debilitating headache and the Americans moved down to Camp I to rest a few days at a lower altitude. Claiming it was too dangerous to sleep on the Lhotse wall, the Sherpas would remain here in the Cwm and move supplies straight through to Camp IV the following day. Dorje had never been higher than where he stood now at 21,3000 feet and wasn't sure how well he'd perform higher. But Paul had tossed out a challenge and he had to accept. To prove himself, he would carry the two tents for the South Col.

"I'm going up too," Marty announced out of nowhere. "I want to acclimate and be ready for the first or second assault team."

"The three of us and Jarvis are making up those teams," said Paul whose black stubble had grown into a rough beard.

"Then I'll go third."

His beaky nose rising and falling with each word, Jarvis said, "No one is crazy enough to climb with you. I sure as hell won't."

Listening to them, Dorje saw his outside chance of going to the top topple like a broken sérac. Everyone was paired up except Marty and going with him was unthinkable.

The party of five roped together and plodded through knee-deep snow for two hours to the base of the 5,000-foot Lhotse wall. As Dorje stared at the near-vertical rise, a sickening dread coursed through him, but he shrugged it off because fear caused mistakes. As a precaution, he silently chanted his mantra during the four-hour climb using fixed ropes set earlier by the climbing Sherpas. Seeing Camp III perched precariously on a narrow ledge and exposed to the whims of nature and avalanches, he understood why they refused to sleep here. With no level ground to stand on, they had notched two tent-size terraces into a wall of blue ice at 23,600 feet.

The two Frenchmen and Roger took the larger tent leaving Marty and Dorje in the smaller one. Neither of them spoke as they prepared their sleeping areas. Finally breaking the long silence, Marty asked, "What are you doing up here?"

"Earning extra rupees," Dorje answered defiantly, unwilling to give details about Shanti.

"Why bother?" Marty grumbled as he beat extra clothing into a pillow. "Beth will take you home like a souvenir."

Souvenir was not in Dorje's vocabulary, but he got the negative implication. "I will go to the top and make her proud of me."

"You'll never get on a team and even if you do manage somehow, she'll have fun at first showing off a real live Sherpa from Nepal but will soon become bored and wonder how to get rid of you."

"We are going to travel many places and write together."

"Hah!" Marty tossed his head back and howled. "You can't even read or write your own name. How are you going to keep a woman like Beth interested?" He was digging up all the doubts Dorje had buried under a rock and hurling them like wet dung.

Dorje wanted to hurt him back. "She loves me. We will stay together forever."

"Don't kid yourself," Marty said, crawling into his bag. "She's in lust, not love." He zipped it over his chin. "I may end up with her yet."

"She will never love you," Dorje muttered.

Before extinguishing the lantern, he checked the inside thermometer—ten degrees below zero. Due to the constant threat of avalanches sweeping down Lhotse, their tent was securely anchored to the ice wall. Dorje rolled over with his back to Marty and tried to sleep, knowing tomorrow he faced the long and laborious task of cutting the final steps and setting fixed ropes to Camp IV. All night the wind roared and shook the tent in violent gusts, forcing its icy breath through the fabric and into his bones. The wind buffeting the walls next to his head and Marty's incessant coughing spells allowed only fitful moments of sleep. He had finally drifted into a sweet dream of Beth when hurried movement yanked him back.

"What are you doing?" he asked Marty who was trying to pull on his cold, stiff boots.

"Going outside to take a piss."

"It is too dangerous. Just lean out the door."

"Why don't you just worry about yourself," Marty grumbled as he stuffed the laces in the sides.

"You stupid *mikaru*. Put on your crampons. One wrong step and you will slide 2000 feet off the mountain."

"Leave me alone. I know what I'm doing."

"You make a problem for everybody. That is why no man wants to climb with you."

"I'll get to the top even if I have to go by myself."

In the bright moonlight reflecting off the snow, Marty roped himself to the wall and sought a place to stand on the narrow platform. He unzipped his pants and then without warning doubled over with his hands on his knees and vomited. His body rose and fell in waves with each gasp until the last heave threw him off balance and he started sliding. Dorje held his breath hoping the piton and rope would hold when Marty bounced at the end. After being sick in the Cwm, why had this idiotic man even come up here? It was a Sherpa's job to take care of *mikarus* and Marty's carelessness would make Dorje look bad, jeopardizing his already-slim chances of going to the top. Scrambling onto the shelf above him, Dorje planted his axe to secure the rope and anchored himself to the wall. His hands so cold he could barely grip the rope, Dorje pulled the American up inch by inch, unhooked him, and dragged him back into the tent.

"Why did you do it?" Marty asked. "You had a perfect opportunity to get rid of me."

"It is my job."

"Well, I probably wouldn't have saved you," he muttered and crawled back into his bag. "Remember that." When daylight filled the tent, Marty asked him not to speak of last night. "It will keep me from making an assault team."

"I saw you throw up in the Cwm. You will get sick like you did on Kangchenjunga."

With the dry, hacking cough Dorje heard all through the night, Marty answered, "I already told you I'm not turning back this time."

"Then you will die here."

Stuffing clothes in his pack, Marty answered, "Perhaps, but at least he'll know I wasn't a coward."

"That father of yours who is not here? I do not understand you *mikarus*."

"You don't have to," Marty answered as he fastened the clasp. "Just get us up there." That said, he exited the tent and joined the others.

Paul suggested they all use oxygen above Camp III. Dorje wanted to prove he could climb without it but decided he'd better get used to wearing a mask. It was big, covering everything from his nose down over his mouth, and made of thick, heavy rubber that smelled. He quickly discovered that goggles and a mask were incompatible with straps competing for the back of his head. Also if he pressed down on the goggles to make them fit, the mask pushed off his face. If he pushed up on the mask, the goggles rode too high and created a gap that fogged up when he exhaled. Plus the continual hissing sound as he breathed made it impossible to hear anything outside himself. He was as deaf as Droma Sunjo's son Dawa.

Roped together, the party continued up the Lhotse face. More conscious of the dangers now, Dorje focused on each movement. After knocking his hands together to get the circulation going, he grabbed the fixed rope, kicked the crampon toe spike into the ice, and shifted his weight onto the step. Then he moved the ascender up the rope and let the teeth lock into place. Slowly repeating the process, he climbed the wall with Paul in the lead followed by Henri and Marty, with himself and Roger last. Having never been part of a group setting new ropes, Dorje didn't realize how tedious it was. As he stood waiting for Paul to hammer the next anchor, Marty's comment that Beth would quickly lose interest gnawed at him again. It was even more imperative now that he reach the summit while he imagined her beaming face as he paraded triumphantly into Base Camp, waving his ice axe over his head like the old ladies with their walking sticks. Lost in his reverie and isolated from outside sounds, Dorje didn't know what made him look up at the very instant an ice block came tumbling towards him. Yelling at Roger immediately below, he clung to the wall as it flew past and struck the Brit who fell backwards, losing his grip on the fixed rope. Jamming his axe into the wall, Dorje braced for the inevitable jolt and held tight. Then quickly removing his goggles for a clearer view, he saw Roger hanging limp and blood-splattered. Dorje tugged on the harness rope to alert those above him because he didn't know what to do next. The Darjeeling Sherpas were right about his inexperience being a hindrance. The harness rope slackened as the Frenchmen and Marty descended. Moving lower in advance of them, Dorje reached Roger who was dazed but conscious. After securing him to the wall, Paul checked for injuries and elicited a shrill cry when he probed the Brit's ribs. Roger would have to return to Base Camp and relinquish all plans for making the summit.

As they were discussing who should take him down, Dorje spotted the climbing Sherpas about forty-five minutes below, having apparently left Camp II before sunrise to carry straight through to the South Col. Seizing the opportunity to prove himself, he said, "One of them can take Roger down, and I will move his supplies on to Camp IV."

"I'll help Roger too," Henri added. "I've been trying to hide it, but I'm not doing well at this altitude. I'm sick, can't sleep, have bizarre visions. It's just not safe. I'm sorry, Paul, but I don't think I'm going to make it. You need to choose a new partner."

"No need to apologize. We knew coming over here that only half of the members were likely to summit. I'm just sad to lose you."

As they prepared Roger for the descent, the discussion turned to the cause of the flying ice and everything pointed at Marty. Under pressure, he finally admitted to having accidentally dislodged it with his axe in his eagerness to set more pitons and move up the wall faster.

Disgusted, Paul made no attempt to hide his feelings. "That impatience of yours could be fatal. So curb it."

Without supplemental oxygen, the Darjeeling Sherpas arrived giving out short staccato whistles through their teeth to keep their spirits up. The oldest seemed relieved to hand over his porter's duties and take Roger down. Marty and Paul each took one of the tents so Dorje could take on the old man's share of the supplies. Feeling a bit cocky, Dorje removed his mask but was soon humbled as he tried keeping up with the other two Sherpas who had come all the way from the Cwm while he was only carrying the load of a man twenty years his senior. After an additional short climb up the face, the route veered left and traversed the Yellow Band: a series of steep, broad ledges of brittle sedimentary shale, limestone, and sandstone. The crampons that had provided secure footing on ice and snow skittered on the rocks and Dorje lost his balance twice. Finally reaching the Geneva Spur, the party climbed directly upwards on the huge, strenuous rock ridge. Once on top, they followed a long but gentle traverse across rocky terrain to Camp IV on the South Col at 26,300 feet.

Sinking onto the bare surface, Dorje shrugged off the load and slapped on his oxygen mask. Listening to the now-comforting hiss, he surveyed

Camp IV, the final staging area for the assault. It was a desolate, inhospitable plateau of wind-swept black rocks and bluish ice. Its flatness with a 7,000-foot drop off into Tibet on the east and a 4,000-drop to the Western Cwm on the west was how Dorje had imagined the edges of the world before a westerner convinced him the earth was round. The heat reflecting of the black rocks surrounding the Cwm now seemed inviting with freezing temperatures and a gale-force wind tearing across the exposed col. Deep snow covered the adjacent slopes but everything not frozen into place appeared to have been blown off into Tibet.

Removing his mask, Paul spoke within inches of Dorje's ear, "This is the windiest spot on the earth. It never stops blowing here. It's also the world's highest garbage dump," he added, referring to the hundreds of empty oxygen canisters, shreds of frozen canvas, bent metal poles, and empty food tins. "We have to get the tents up so the Sherpas can sleep here tonight and then set fixed ropes towards the summit tomorrow."

"I will tell them" Dorje shouted back. Although completely spent, he couldn't lose face in front of two who had carried all the way from Camp II in one day. Offering to help, he had no idea how daunting the task was. Gripping the edges with gloved hands, they wrestled flapping canvas that knocked them off their feet and bent the poles. In desperation, Dorje threw himself on top to hold a tent down while the Sherpas anchored it with rocks, poles, and climbing ropes. Marty and Paul took refuge in the first one while the Sherpas erected the second with an even greater struggle. Exhausted, the Darjeeling Sherpas and Dorje crawled inside and collapsed with the tent walls slapping and whipping about them.

When he could finally breathe without thinking he'd faint, Dorje spoke to the Sherpas for whom he now had the greatest respect. "How could you come all that way in one day and without oxygen?"

Zopa, whose name meant patience, answered, "We didn't tire ourselves carrying from Base Camp like you, Foolish Boy. But you are much stronger than I thought."

"And have proven yourself worthy," added Namkha whose face was worn by wind and sun. "But be careful. I have seen accidents when decisions are made in haste."

"Then you've been here before?" Dorje asked.

"Many times," said Zopa. "We came with the large American expedition in 1963. Nine hundred porters carried 27 tons of supplies to the Base Camp. We set the ropes but only six Americans reached the summit."

"Are you going up this time?"

"Only if they ask us too," Namkha answered.

"I want to go too," Dorje said, feeling a rush of excitement.

"Perhaps you will. But choose your companions carefully."

The three talked for half an hour while Paul and Marty rested for the return trip. Dorje learned Zopa and Namkha were from Phakding and had carried and set lines for several expeditions. They and other Sherpas had moved to Darjeeling many years earlier seeking work and had been on the mountain from the Tibetan side as well. Now that the climbing ban had been lifted, they were home again. Dorje wanted to spend the entire night learning from them but Paul raised the tent flap to say it was time to descend in order to reach Camp II before dark. Giddy with the prospect of the Sherpas' support of his ascent, Dorje emulated them by making it all the way down to the Cwm without oxygen and felt stronger with every step.

CHAPTER THIRTY-TWO

Dorje, Marty, and Paul slogged into a nearly deserted camp after dark. Jarvis joined them in the dining tent for hot tea, soup, and noodles. He explained that Henri, Roger, and the Sherpa pushed on down to Camp I, and he'd heard the Americans had descended to Base Camp to rest for a few days because Sean was sick.

"That leaves just the three of us for the first assault," Marty said.

Paul peered at him over a cup of tea with the steam rising in his face. "You should join your American friends who have enough sense to go down when they're not well." When Marty shot an accusing look at Dorje, Paul added, "He didn't have to say anything. I heard you last night and we've all been listening to you cough for weeks. Plus you look like a walking cadaver with bones showing through your clothes."

"I always lose weight at altitude," Marty announced with an impatient edge in his voice. "We all do. It doesn't mean a thing. I've never been more ready."

"Well, you're not climbing with me," Jarvis said reaching for more tea. "I don't trust you."

"Nor do I," added Paul. "Try your countrymen. Maybe they're used to the likes of you."

Marty slumped in the chair, staring at his fidgeting hands. "They've been climbing buddies since high school and already said they're going alone."

Seizing the opportunity, Dorje quickly put himself before Paul and Jarvis. "I want to go with you."

"Have you been up Everest before?"

"No. But I am very strong and can carry much."

Paul pushed away from the table to leave. "Sorry, but can't risk it. Not with you or Marty. I'll take my chances with Jarvis here. Right now, I'm exhausted and need to grab some sleep. Suggest you do too."

When the others left, Dorje stayed behind to ponder his choices. He had promised Beth to only carry, but he was so close to turning his dream of standing on Everest into a reality. And it might be his last chance if he leaves with her. How could he not try even if it meant climbing with the only man left—Marty? Once again they were forced to share a tent. Dorje tossed his bag inside. "We must talk."

"No tonight. I'm too tired."

"Now," Dorje demanded, bent on getting the answer he needed. "We were Hillary and Tenzing going to the top."

"Until Tenzing stole Hillary's woman."

"She was never yours," Dorje snarled back, tired of having to repeat this.

"She would have been if you'd kept your pants zipped while I was gone."

"She was only being nice to you. We were lovers last fall and she came back to me."

"Bull shit. She had no plans to come until I asked her."

"That is not true."

"Oh yeah? Ask her."

"I do not have to." Dorje crawled into his bag and zipped it up. "I want to talk about Everest. No one will go with you."

"And they don't want you along either because you don't know what you're doing." Marty pulled his bag over his chin and his hat down over his ears. "Since neither of us can go alone, I figure we're stuck with each other. When we come down, Beth can choose the better man and it will be me." Trying not to explode, Dorje rustled in his bag to get comfortable. "Then it is decided?" Marty asked

"I have no other choice." Freezing, Dorje curled in on himself and imagined Beth was lying in his arms. He could feel her warmth and smell her skin and hair. In only a few days, he would see the love in her eyes and taste her lips again. Taking a long, deep breath, he was at ease with himself once more and confident of their future.

The next day Dorje began his new role as climbing member and no longer had to carry. He, Jarvis, Paul, and Marty rested in the Cwm while the Darjeeling Sherpas moved food and oxygen to the South Col and finished setting the fixed ropes above it. Fresh from Base Camp, the Americans chose to acclimate and be the third assault team. When the weather looked promising four days later, the first team of Jarvis and Paul prepared to leave for Camp III the following morning.

At sunrise, clouds with a crisp, red glow outlining their frayed edges hung over the camp as Sherpas conducted a *puja*. Having returned to the Cwm, Zopa and Namkha tied blessed *sungdis* around every piece of equipment and passed them through juniper smoke to bathe them in protective incense. Sitting cross-legged before prayer flags fluttering in the breeze, Zopa asked the gods for understanding and tolerance of their actions. Eyes closed, Dorje chanted a mantra to bring himself into a meditative state with a clear mind able to receive the wisdom of the deities in complete awareness. Once again, he sought forgiveness for his sins of quarreling and being guilty of too much desire. At the conclusion, everyone chanted in unison in a long rising tone while tossing handfuls of *tsampa* skyward. Then they rubbed the remainder into each other's hair and faces to incorporate the blessing.

After Jarvis and Paul departed for Camp III, Dorje discreetly asked Mark for help in composing a letter to Beth. "If I do not come back, promise you will give it to her." Mark's smile reached all the way to his compassionate green eyes as he printed words dictated from Dorje's heart for him to copy in his own awkward handwriting.

To my beautiful Beth. Tomorrow I will leave for the top of Everest. Please understand why I must do this. It is my fate and I want to make you proud of me so you will never be ashamed. If I do not return, know that our spirits will always be together in this life and all those that follow. You are my sunrise and my sunset. You will always feel my arms around you and my lips on yours. I will never stop loving you. This I promise with my entire heart. From the man who loves you more than his own life. Dorje.

He wished he spoke better English so the words could express the true depth of his love, but it didn't matter because the letter was needed only if some freak accident occurred.

Waiting for Marty the next morning, Dorje stared at the stunning 360-degree scenery around him: a series of icefalls on one side, the southwest face of Everest on the other, the Lhotse face, and the Nuptse wall with its contorted wavy lines of sedimentary rock. The mountains seemed less ominous in the early light with their forbidding faces lost in deep shadows and the sun catching their delicate snow flutings glimmering above the blue ice. Dorje felt healthy and strong again, ready to take on the mountain.

When they arrived at Camp III on the Lhotse face six hours later, Marty crawled into the tent in a convulsive fit of coughing and waved at Dorje to give him the oxygen they had agreed to conserve for sleeping. After regulating it for a low flow, the American rested while Dorje melted ice for cooking. Neither felt like consuming much.

"We're almost there," Marty said, breathing easier now without the mask and sipping hot lemon drink. "There's no turning back this time...for any reason. I can't fail him again."

Dorje knew he meant the father he'd talked about months ago, and he remembered thinking what an awful person to force his son into things against his nature. Generally not caring what anyone else thought, Marty desperately sought the man's approval and that need cast a dangerous pall over him. Nervously ruffling his hands through hair grown long and shaggy again, Marty said, "In spite of our differences over Beth, you must keep your promise to go to the top. No turning back for any reason." Dorje was still too angry to give Marty the reassurance he wanted even though he intended to go because he wanted it for himself.

Unlike his first sick night at Camp III, Marty used a low flow of oxygen and made it through seemingly without incident. But when daylight filled the tent, Dorje spotted a pinkish froth on the floor. Alarmed, he demanded, "What is this?"

Shivering violently with the bag tied over his head and only his face exposed, Marty answered, "Just a little cold. I'll be okay once I start moving. Fix me something to drink." After hot lemon juice and soup, the American warmed up enough to pack his gear and head out wearing the oxygen mask Dorje found so awkward and annoying that he chose not to use it. If the Darjeeling Sherpas could climb to the South Col without one, so could he. Preoccupied with visions of Beth's shining eyes when he strides triumphantly into Base Camp, Dorje failed to notice Marty's languid pace until the American reeled from side to side as if drunk and crumpled.

Infuriated that he was stuck with Marty's irrational, reckless behavior rather than someone like Mark, Dorje yelled, "Get up or you will freeze."

Drawing his arms in under himself, Marty pushed onto his elbows. His head still to the ground, his shoulders rose and fell as he gasped for breath.

"Move," Dorje shouted, knowing that they'd freeze if they didn't keep going.

Lifting himself onto his knees and slowly tottering to his feet, Marty nodded at him and began dragging one foot after another. They traversed the brittle Yellow Band with their short-pointed crampons scraping and sliding on the rocks and then climbed the Geneva Spur to its highest point before dropping 200 feet to the South Col. As before, it was cold, windy, and desolate—a land of black rocks and blue ice. Staggering on soft, noodle legs, Marty made it to the tent, pushed through the door, and collapsed. Dorje checked his tank. Almost empty. He found another and hooked it up. In a short while, the American was breathing easier and accepted a few pieces of cheese and biscuits while Dorje thawed a frozen fruit tin over the stove. Watching him, Dorje knew that without Marty he wouldn't even be here, but with him he could fail. Jarvis and Paul had more sense.

Stepping out into the wind with binoculars, Dorje searched for team I above the Col. They were one day ahead, planning to sleep in the Camp V at 27,900 feet which had been left by the 1965 Indian expedition. Feeling it was too dangerous to go directly from the south Col, Hillary and Tenzing had used a high camp as had the large American expedition in 1963. In the morning, Jarvis and Paul would push from there toward the summit.

Holding the binoculars to his eyes, Dorje chuckled remembering the first time a *mikaru* had shown him these strange black cylinders that made mountains move closer. Now he was going to the greatest of them all. And tomorrow, Mark and Sean would be watching for him. Seeing no sign of Jarvis and Paul, Dorje decided they were already in their tent preparing for the morning and he should do the same. No longer needing to prove himself to make an assault team, he needed only to focus on getting to the top.

His thoughts had moved in slow motion all day and Dorje knew the lethargy of high altitude could cause fatal errors. If using oxygen would forestall that, he would put up with the fogging and hissing a few days and nights. The wind howled and bombarded the tent wall near his head and drove the cold into his bones again. Marty was shaking like Nima's skinny body when they were young. Soon the flapping canvas became background noise and the only sound heard was his own breathing as he dreamed of sleeping wrapped around his little brother again. Nima, two legs of the same frog, hopping and laughing. How would they survive an ocean apart? Dorje couldn't leave without him and Beth would understand his wanting to take him to America. She liked Nima and he adored her. Picturing his brother running down to Lukla with his funny little freckles and arms waving, Dorje smiled as he drifted into sleep. Life was good and in two days he'd finally be standing on the highest point on earth.

Marty's hair stuck out at the sides and crawled down his neck as it had when they first met. Watching him eat hot cereal the next morning, Dorje wondered how the man thought Beth could ever love him or why all those legendary other women had been attracted to him. It must have been his wacko personality and crazy dancing. The two men strapped on their masks and regulated the flow, fastened the crampons with swollen, stiff fingers, and donned a double pair of gloves. The sky was clear when they exited and miraculously the wind had slowed to 30 miles per hour. From the South Col they plodded 1,000 feet up a 50-degree slope along a couloir where the Darjeeling porters had cut steps. Traveling slower than a baby can crawl, they moved only two to three body lengths at a time before stopping to rest. Experiencing waves of dizziness and exhaustion and sapped by cold, Dorje feared at times he was losing his own grasp on reality. Watching Marty's lethargy and confusion sent an even greater fear through him. Using hand signals, Dorje kept asking if he was all right. The American nodded and waved him on, but his body spoke something else. Not knowing the signs of serious illness at this altitude, Dorje wished Zopa and Namkha were here.

Reaching a short section of smooth, loose rock not compatible with slippery crampons, he was grateful the two Sherpas had set fixed ropes. Immediately above it, Dorje and Marty stepped onto a flat spot at the beginning of the southeast ridge. Marty sank in the snow with his upper body draped over bent knees and breathing hard. A frosty white layer covered the hair protruding from under his goggles and hat. He mumbled something Dorje couldn't understand wearing a mask. Removing it, he yelled, "What?"

With two lethargic slaps on the ground beside him, Marty shouted, "I think this is the Balcony. We're almost there."

With only one more day to the top, Dorje sighed in relief, feeling slightly more confident now. Another 100 feet of climbing and they discovered a partly-level camp on a small shelf chipped away with an ice axe and sheltered by a rocky cliff—elevation 27,600 feet. Only Kangchenjunga far to the east was visible higher at 28,169 feet. Altitude sickness had turned Marty back on that mountain, so why did he think he could make this one? Dorje would ask later but for now was too anxious for Jarvis and Paul to return saying they'd reached the summit. If their experience and strength failed them, what chance did an untried yak herder and ailing, mad man have? After settling Marty in the tent, melting some ice, and forcing down some tea and biscuits, Dorje stood outside with the binoculars. With the summit four hours away, it was still too early but he didn't want to miss one second because their victory could be the only one he'd savor. The prospect of failure turned the air stale and heavy, weighing down on him. Everest the only gift he had to offer Beth, he couldn't return without it.

Two hours later, Team I came into view. Never shifting his gaze from them, Dorje waited for some kind of signal. When an arm went up and slashed through the air, his insides bounded with excitement and he had to grab his voice to keep it from doing somersaults. "There they are! And they made it!"

Marty emerged, cramped and shivering, looking puzzled by all the noise. Dorje handed him the binoculars and pointed. Spotting the climbers, Marty gave him an awkward, lethargic high five before returning to bed. Watching the men descend with stiff, clumsy movements, Dorje wondered if he looked like that. When they were within 40 minutes of camp, he lit the stove and heated water for soup and tea.

Jarvis and Paul removed their masks long enough to eat and drink. "The South Summit is about 1200 feet above here," Paul said in a raspy voice barely above a whisper. When Jarvis tried to interrupt with hand signals, his partner explained the Brit had temporarily lost his voice due to deeply inhaling the cold oxygen with no moisture in it. "He wants me to warn you about the rocks about 400 feet below the South Summit. One slip of your crampons and you're dead, so go around to the east." Acknowledging Jarvis again, he added, "But that's dangerous too because you'll be in waist-deep snow and avalanches are a threat. Try to stay in the path we cut."

"And how far from there?" Dorje asked, still reeling with excitement.

"The South Summit is about half way up. Another 300 feet or so and you're on top. But first you have to traverse a very thin ridge with a cornice of overhanging snow and ice on the right. It forces you off the crest and onto the steep left-hand side where snow is plastered to the rocks. It's the most exposed section and one wrong step sends you 10,000 feet down to a glacier on one side and 8,000 feet into the Cwm on the other. Jarvis was motioning with his hands again. He seemed fixated on rocks as Paul nodded and then described the famous Hillary Step—a 40-foot rocky pitch that had to be climbed before reaching a gentle slope to the summit. As soon as they had consumed enough liquids and a had few pieces of cheese, the two headed down to the South Col for the night, explaining that most serious accidents occurred on the descent when climbers were tired.

Their success was exhilarating news. Not wanting to do anything that would jeopardize his chances, Dorje used oxygen and slept with his bag pressed against Marty's so they could share each other's warmth. When his partner mumbled something, Dorje rolled over and put his ear to his mask, but the words were muted and garbled. Perhaps Marty was only dreaming. The Darjeeling Sherpas had told Dorje of oxygen-starved *mikarus* hearing and seeing strange things. At high altitude, they themselves had experienced visions of gods standing before them and speaking. Dorje lay back down with his own visions of a goddess. Would she know the moment he first set foot on top of the world tomorrow? Dorje forged all his emotions into one single dream of returning as her hero.

CHAPTER THIRTY-THREE

Waking shortly after 3:30 in the morning, Dorje lit a small lantern and discovered Marty huddled in the corner, without oxygen, swatting wildly at the air. "Get them out of here!"

"Get what out? Dorje asked, alarmed if he had slept through some invasion.

"The bats. I don't want to go first."

Now Dorje understood what Mark had called hypoxia: an oxygen-starved hallucination. He quickly searched for a fresh bottle. "Go where?"

"Into the cave. I don't want to go. I'm afraid."

"You do not have to. Stay here."

"I can't. You'll get mad and call me a coward."

Dorje wondered if his strange companion who loved fun-ness and games was teasing him with this ridiculous talk to ease the tension before they set out. All such thoughts vanished when Dorje moved the lantern closer and saw Marty's vacant eyes and bluish-white skin—the way Dorje envisioned a *shrindi* would look. *Where was the damn oxygen?* Frantically throwing things about the small tent, he realized his brain wasn't functioning either when he discovered the bottles sitting by the door, exactly where he'd left them last night. It was time to make the summit and get off this mind-numbing mountain.

He strapped a mask attached to a full cylinder over Marty's face and regulated a higher flow and then melted snow for hot lemon juice and cereal. After forcing both down the American, he ate and drank a small amount himself even though he had no appetite. No one did up here. Now what should he do with Marty? While talking to him last night, Dorje learned his companion had made it to within 500 feet of the summit of Kangchenjunga, crawling up the last 100 in a foolhardy attempt and would have slithered the rest on his belly if he had to. "But I passed out," Marty confessed, "and a couple of well-meaning, goddamn Sherpas interfered and carried me out. Promise you won't do that," he added in a somber tone. "I might as well be dead."

"I won't," Dorje had said but what good were promises to a dead man?

Watching Marty languish, he knew the American couldn't make it, but Dorje had already decided to go on. How could he not after being this close and Beth waiting for him? He'd be her hero—the first man to summit alone. The trail was cut; the ropes, fixed. Using oxygen and with a strong Sherpa pace, he could be up and back in record time. Babbling incoherently, Marty seemed oblivious to his surroundings.

"Go back to sleep," Dorje said in his most fatherly tone. "We are not going in the cave. I am afraid of the bats too." After wrapping Marty tightly in both bags, Dorje adjusted his oxygen, and set another bottle beside him.

Dorje had slept in his boots, wary of their freezing and being too stiff to put on before sunrise. Layered in every possible piece of clothing, he next crouched beside Marty to tell the lie of his life, but it was the only way to keep him from following and jeopardizing the climb. Not sure which world Marty was inhabiting at the moment, Dorje said simply, "It is too cold and windy to travel today. I am sick and need to go outside for a short while. Sleep and get strong enough for tomorrow." Mumbling something unintelligible, Marty made no attempt to get up.

Dorje crawled outside and zipped the door securely behind him. Flat, gray clouds with ragged edges sprawled across the sky blowing from the south—a sign of moisture coming up from India. He must hurry. After scattering *chaane* and praying to the goddess Miyolangsangma to protect him, Dorje put on his crampons and headlamp, adjusted the regulator to a climbing flow, and started up the Southeast Ridge. He hated the oxygen's metallic breath but needed the edge it gave because he couldn't afford to react lazily or with poor judgment. Any wrong decision could be fatal. With every step demanding intense physical effort and concentration, he moved with a slow, laborious pace attempting to find a rhythm. Taking four steps and stopping for a few gasps worked better than rushing up eight or nine before resting. He felt the energy draining from his body and focused solely on breathing. Holding onto one thought long enough to decide where to put his foot next became a monumental task. Alone in a vast world of snow and ice, the only sounds were the crunch of his boots and the deep breathing echoing inside his mask.

The steep snow ridge plummeted thousands of feet to his left and cornices hung over an immense, empty space to the right. As he climbed endlessly, Lhotse slowly dropped away. Following the tracks left by Paul and Jarvis, Dorje plunged his axe in, took a step, breathed, took another, breathed again. *Place one foot, take five breaths, lift and place the next, take five breaths* became his mantra. He was alone on the great white shelf, higher than any being on earth at the moment, and felt very much alive knowing that every move could be his last. He wished Beth, Nima, and his father could see him now, plodding steadily upward to become one of the elite few who had made it and the first to do it solo.

Dorje stopped to give his quivering legs a rest and watched the sun rise behind Kangchenjunga, its ice crystals shimmering in a dazzling array. Thousands of feet below him, the Western Cwm looked like a calm, milky river with granite banks. And perched atop a spur in the distant Imja Valley, stood the eloquent silhouette of the Tengboche monastery. The monks would be at morning prayer by now, and in his mind he heard the low hum of their chanting, the haunting drumbeats, and the eerie moan of the long *dung-chens*. Reaching for the *sungdi* blessed by the Tengboche lama to protect him, he remembered giving it to Beth at Base Camp.

Four hundred feet below the South Summit, he encountered the treacherous rocks Jarvis had warned of and took the path around them in waist-deep, unstable snow that felt about to collapse under him with every step. By 9:00 a.m. he arrived on the snowy dome of the South Summit at 28,700 feet and sat down to change his cylinder. Seeing an oxygen bottle with the mark of Union Jack on it, Dorje imagined it being left by Hillary and Tenzing in 1953—the year he was proclaimed the Tenzing of the future. And the future was now. He could see the Cornice Traverse, the Hillary Step, and the final slopes to the summit. Only 300 more feet to fulfill his fate and return to Beth a hero. His eyes passed over the Cwm dotted with the tents of Camp II 8000 feet below and the High Camp where Marty was sleeping wrapped in two bags with plenty of oxygen and water. He'd be all right for a few more hours.

After adjusting the regulator for a higher flow, Dorje set out for the most intimidating section of the climb along the narrow ridge where a misplaced step would send him tumbling 10,000 feet. As he headed up, an image appeared in his mind—something he hadn't noticed but had seen. Perhaps it was the altitude playing with his brain. To make sure he wasn't hallucinating, Dorje looked back and there it was: a dark spot 200 hundred feet below him, something he hadn't passed on the way up. His heart lurched. It couldn't be. Removing the binoculars from his pocket, he focused on a bright green parka lying on the Southeast Ridge. Not moving. "Damn! Damn! Damn! Why did you leave the tent?" Looking again, he hoped he was wrong, but it was Marty with his face buried in the snow. An image that had lingered in him since childhood crawled from its dusty corner again: the face of a climber on a stretcher, skin blackened as if charred, fingers and toes that would be cut off. He too had lain in the snow.

"I will not stop now," Dorje yelled. "We agreed. No turning back for any reason." He shoved the binoculars back into his pocket and continued up. "You cannot expect me to come down now. I am almost to the top of the world." His legs were too heavy to move and every breath seared his throat. With black, angry thoughts roiling in his head, Dorje drove his axe in the snow and slumped over it. "I should just leave you there, you wacko *mikaru*. You want to die anyway because of your stupid father. So why should I give up my mountain for you?" He rose again, dragged his left foot forward and planted it, and then his right. Two deep breaths and he was moving again. Nothing could stop him now, not a cornice, not the Hillary Step, and certainly not a jealous idiot who had called him a bastard and punched him in the face. Dorje had endured headaches, nausea, extreme physical and mental exhaustion to get here. The summit was in sight and the ropes were set. One hour to the top and two down. He had waited 16 years for this moment; Marty could wait a while longer. Cursing each delay, Dorje took the binoculars out again. On his hands and knees now, Marty was crawling up the ridge as he'd done on Kangchenjunga. Dorje turned back to the mountain. It wasn't his problem. He didn't tell him to leave the tent and come up here. The man wouldn't turn around for him, so why should he give up everything? A promise made.

"Aggghhh!" Dorje yelled so loud his throat burned. "No, no, no!" His cry pierced the thin, cold air and shook free a fragile lip of snow. A tiny avalanche toppled toward him, the snow bouncing and flying in the air as it gained momentum. Standing there, he let the powder strike his face. And it was cold, deadly cold. With almost three more hours of climbing and descent plus a rapidly approaching storm, Marty would be dead by the time he got there. Probably was close to it already.

He whipped his body around and slammed one foot in the track he'd just made. Staring at the dark spot on the slope, Dorje was unable to take the next step. The summit with its wind-blown plume was beckoning to him and he was turning his back on it. "Toi ye!" he yelled and spit. Then he planted his axe and stepped forward, took a couple of remorseful breaths—and started down.

With frozen hair, eyebrows, and lashes and with icicles hanging from his nostrils, Marty was floundering in the snow. When Dorje reached him and found the cylinder not empty yet and a fresh one in his pack, he ordered, "Go back to the tent. You are sick."

Marty's words came out in disconnected bits and pieces wandering in every direction, but Dorje got the message. His climbing partner was going to the top and he couldn't stop him. If he tried to take him down like the Sherpas on Kangchenjunga, Marty would fight him all the way. "Now help me up," Marty shouted.

What should have been a simple maneuver was almost impossible. As the Darjeeling Sherpas had warned, weeks of carrying had sapped Dorje's strength. He hated feeling like a frail grandpa. Using the binoculars, he frantically searched for Zopa and Namkha who planned to come up with the Americans. They should be at Camp V or at least the South Col by now. No sign of anyone. Perhaps the storm threat had turned them back.

Marty's lids closed and rolled open again like the slow blink of a frog. Removing his mask momentarily, he yelled, "Just get me to my feet and rope up. Hillary or Tenzing couldn't have made it alone and neither can you."

Confused and no longer trusting his instincts, Dorje didn't know if he should tie up with Marty or not. Mark had warned him about being in the Death Zone where there's not enough oxygen to sustain life. The brain loses its capacity for reason and decision making and lassitude diminishes bodily responses.

Remembering Paul's warning about the most exposed section of the climb, Dorje finally concluded it was best to have someone belay him, but he still didn't feel good about it. Dorje exaggerated his lips around the words to make sure Marty understood. "You will walk not crawl like a baby." He resented having to make the arduous climb back up to the South Summit and around the treacherous rocks just below it where every step plunged him into unstable snow almost to his waist. Roped behind him, Marty used Dorje's tracks but still stumbled and too often lay in physical collapse until Dorje went back and pulled him onto his feet. "Get up. I cannot carry you," he shouted. When both were upright and moving, Dorje calculated they gained about twelve feet per minute.

From the South Summit, they stared at a 400-foot ridge of snow plastered to intermittent rocks—the exposed section Paul had spoken of. The only route was along a knife-edge, twisting line between a cornice on the right and a sheer drop on the left. Venturing too far onto the cornice, they risked it breaking away and sending them tumbling 10,000 feet down the Kangshun Face into Tibet. A misstep to the left would send them careening 8,000 feet down the Southwest Face into the Western Cwm. Thin, wispy clouds were drifting up from the valley and the sky was ablaze with purple and crimson, both possible signs of unstable weather and moisture coming from India.

"We must hurry," Dorje said. "I will go first and you wrap…"

"Don't tell me what to do," Marty growled as he planted his axe and wound the rope around the head. "I know more about this than you."

"Then you should know to go home."

Uncomfortable trusting his life to him but afraid to cross without a belay, Dorje traveled 100 feet along the Cornice Traverse. Feeling groggy as if he'd had too much *chang,* he now took seven breaths for every step, his ragged lungs sucking wildly at the air. Bone weary, he turned to anchor Marty and waited for him to follow. When his erratic, unsteady gait veered too far to the right, Dorje shouted, "Careful," but doubted his voice carried far through the mask. A second later, the American was on his stomach sliding toward the 8,000-foot drop into the Cwm, If the anchor tore free, Dorje would go with him. His heart slamming in his throat, he watched Marty drive the axe head and arrest the fall with snow flying back in his face. He hadn't thought the man capable in his condition but apparently terror worked miracles. The entire incident lasting only a few seconds seemed an eternity between life and death.

Forty minutes and thousands of gasping breaths after leaving the South Summit, they reached a rock cliff rising 40 feet straight out of the ridge and blocking it off. It appeared impossible to climb, smooth with almost no handholds. "The Hillary Step," Marty mumbled, his speech almost incoherent after depleting his last strength in the fall.

"Where are the ropes?" Dorje asked frantically looking around. "We're supposed to have ropes."

Reaching into the heavens, Everest created its own weather with a constant wind flapping furiously about them. "There," Marty said pointing to a rope blown over the cornice and lying in a dangerously exposed area 50 feet below.

"But how will we get past without it?"

Marty pointed to a steep, narrow gap between one side of the rock and the adjoining cornice, an impossible place without a fixed rope. Dorje had promised Beth to turn around if it looked bad and this did. He was considering giving up when he thought about Hillary and Tenzing going where no man had gone before. Tenzing wasn't afraid and Dorje had to be like him. "Belay me," he yelled at Marty using hand signals. "I'm going up." Wedged in the gap, he pressed backwards with his feet against the hard snow and inched upwards. Since going back for Marty, he had tried to ignore his frozen toes, but exerting pressure on them now engulfed him in pain. To cry out would waste precious oxygen and his tank was already reading low, so he tried to lessen his distress by mentally diffusing the pain over his entire body.

Once Dorje was over the Hillary Step, Marty sagged against the rock. "I'm too tired and sick to go on," he shouted.

The route had flattened into an easy, half hour walk in Namche, but here in the Death Zone Dorje wondered if he could make it. His back to Marty, he told himself he had already done more for him than was expected and the American would have to be satisfied with making it to here. It was farther than he'd go to on Kangchenjunga, and Dorje wasn't about to risk losing his own dream. Silently chanting his new, seven-breath mantra *Place one foot, but take seven breaths now, lift and place the next, take seven more breaths,* Dorje continued toward the summit until he was curiously straining against a rope. Damn. In his muddled thinking, he'd forgotten to release himself from Marty's belay.

As his clumsy fingers tried to open the clip, Dorje looked back at Marty wedged between the rock and cornice, the man's earlier laments, *If I don't make it to the top it's because I died here,* and *I might as well be dead* resonated in Dorje's head. Marty wanted it as badly as he did, but there wasn't enough time with more wispy clouds rising from the Cwm and Dorje's oxygen running low. Besides, Marty said he was too tired and sick to go on. Finally getting the clip open, Dorje simply stared at it in confusion. His thoughts having exploded into a thousand little pieces, he couldn't assemble them to make sense out of anything and was afraid of the wrong decision. Helping Marty, he would risk crippling his own chances of making the summit, but how could he be anyone's hero, especially his own, if he left him behind? Questioning whether his shaky legs could bear even his own weight, Dorje snapped the clip shut and trudged back to the Hillary Step. After sinking his axe and digging his heels in next to the rock, he pulled the rope taut and signaled Marty to walk up the inside of the cornice while he pulled. Dorje's arms and legs quivered and spots floated in front of his eyes. Afraid of blacking out, he wrapped the rope around his wrist so he wouldn't lose Marty in case he did. After an interminable struggle to haul him up, Dorje collapsed with his mind in a fog and body screaming it could go no further.

Lying beside him, Marty raised his arm in slow motion and gave Dorje two grateful, light pats. With the summit in sight and only 30 or 40 minutes away, Dorje rolled onto his hands and knees, and then pushed to his feet. So dizzy he almost keeled over, he waited for the waves of nausea to pass before reaching for Marty's hand. Shortening the rope and tying it to both harnesses, he could drag his companion up the mountain if he had to. Even though the slope had flattened, a precipitous drop on either side still posed a constant threat.

Stopping and taking seven breaths for every step, Dorje ignored the pain, nausea, and cold and continued upwards. As he stepped onto the table-sized summit, sixteen years of emotions overwhelmed him and clouded his eyes. Wishing his father, Beth, and Nima could see him standing on top of the world; Dorje motioned for Marty to take his picture as proof. Next to strings of prayer flags flapping furiously in the wind, he held the axe over his head in victory. After taking Marty's picture, he stood relishing the moment when he was higher than anything on earth and had an unobstructed view in every direction. To the north were the rolling, brown hills of the Tibetan plateau, Kangchenjunga to the east, Makalu to the southeast, and Cho Oyu to the west. After tying a red ribbon from his father's hair around a rock to anchor it and placing it with the pile of offerings, Dorje signaled Marty that they must start down. The first flakes had begun to fall.

CHAPTER THIRTY-FOUR

The air hung heavy and foreboding around Dorje. Anxious to get off the mountain, he drove himself and Marty staggering down the summit ridge. They reached the Hillary Step in only twenty-five minutes where Dorje lowered Marty down the gap and then wedged himself between the rock and cornice as before. Fast-moving storm clouds darkened the sky making the knife-edge Cornice Traverse even more perilous. At risk of blundering off the edge in the flat, dimming light, they went one at a time belaying each other. Terror gripped Dorje every time Marty pitched left or right in a hypoxic stupor.

By the time they reached the South Summit, the American was reeling and falling every few feet. Resting a moment to check their tanks, Dorje guessed about two hour's worth—enough to make High Camp where the Mark, Sean, and the climbing Sherpas would be waiting with fresh supplies. Short-roped again, Dorje led Marty around the rocks below the South Summit in waist deep snow, never knowing when it would give way and swallow them whole. Progress was slow with Dorje having to pull his partner out of every snow pocket and hold him upright. By the time they stood at the top of the Southeast Ridge, his strength had deserted him. The Darjeeling Sherpas were right. Ferrying loads to and from the lower camps had taken too much out of him and ill prepared him for this. Barely able to concentrate on where to place his foot next, Dorje couldn't carry Marty another step. His thoughts had climbed in and out of so many places; he no longer knew what was safe. Both of them on the verge of collapse, Dorje knew they couldn't walk the long descent to Camp V. Choosing to glissade down the ridge in twenty-foot visibility augured sudden death, but it seemed the only way. Wind-whipped ice and snow lashed their faces with such violent force Dorje couldn't see his own feet through the goggles. After dragging Marty by the harness to get him started, Dorje sailed down the slope, experiencing a strange detachment from his body.

When the slope leveled out, Dorje looked at Marty who was frantically trying to unhook himself from this madman, but his fingers were too cold and stiff. Dorje pulled him to his feet and towed his stumbling companion down to the High Camp. As if a cornice had caved in under him, Dorje's spirit plunged when he opened the door of an empty tent. No climbers or Sherpas to help him, no fresh supplies, and a storm about to engulf them. His mind was clear enough to understand that being stranded here meant certain death. Using the two remaining oxygen bottles to replace their empty ones, he prayed more were waiting at the South Col.

"We will go lower tonight and wait for the storm to pass," he said, trying to hide the fear overcoming him.

Raging with a new ferocity, the storm had covered yesterday's tracks and dropped visibility to fifteen feet. With no hope of getting his bearings from a distinctive rock or ice feature and the driving snow pummeling his face, Dorje set out blindly with only memory to guide him. The sky and ground had merged in a uniform, blank whiteness. With each step, they risked falling through an unseen hole and disappearing into the void or taking a wrong turn and walking off the ridge. The Balcony, poised at the top of the Southeast Ridge, had provided a welcome rest on the way up but now whispered threats of the rocks lying immediately below. Worming his way across, Dorje probed the snow searching for the fixed ropes.

"Do not move," he shouted to Marty. Knowing that without them a blind descent would be suicidal, Dorje brushed through the snow with hands so frozen he couldn't curl them into a fist. Had the storm devoured the ropes or had he only imagined them yesterday? Confused, he froze and was incapable of moving in either direction.

Marty robbed him of choice. Mumbling something that sounded too much like *Geronimo*, he stepped onto the rocks. In sickening disbelief, Dorje heard the crampons strike the stone and skid. Marty pitched forward and tumbled past while Dorje stood there transfixed, lassitude having robbed him of instinctive action. Seconds later, the rope plucked him from the ridge and hurtled him after his partner. Axes and crampons were useless on granite as arms, legs, and backs bounced off the boulders.

Then suddenly Dorje was airborne in a deadly free fall until the rope's springy recoil jerked him back up and slammed him into the mountain. Shocked back to reality with excruciating pain searing through his left leg, he closed his eyes and screamed before attempting to coordinate his scattered thoughts into action.

Then he anchored himself with the axe and toe pick of his right foot before looking for Marty. What had halted their descent? Blinking and gazing upward, he saw only heavy snow falling from a gray mist. He tugged the rope that appeared to have caught on something, perhaps a rock. When it slackened, Dorje's stomach crawled up into his throat. What was happening? This time instinct immediately took hold and he flattened against the wall when a boulder thundered past and disappeared as if consumed by an immense, insatiable beast. Sailing after it, the rope dropped and then hung limp from his harness. Where was Marty? Clinging to life as he was, or had he cut the rope deciding to die here rather than fail his father? Dorje slowly drew the cord through his gloves, hoping for resistance. Within fifteen feet of the end, he finally got it. Marty was not far below. Dorje removed his mask and yelled repeatedly. When he had called to Beth in the storm, the wind snatched his voice and buried it. Would the American hear him now? He whipped the rope and it rippled a response. Ten minutes later, Marty swung his axe into the wall beside him and mumbled, "What now. I'm scared shitless."

The storm had escalated into a full-scale blizzard. Disoriented and in the midst of a whiteout, Dorje guessed they were on the steep slope below the ridge with heavy cornices looming above them. He signaled Marty to remove his mask so they could confer, but even then it was hard to communicate with snow pelting their faces. He motioned above them. "It is not safe to go up." Then he tugged on the rope and pointed at the traverse ahead. "We must cross one at a time again. I will go first. Belay me." Marty nodded lethargically.

The sky and ground were indistinguishable, a grayish white. Probing with his axe Dorje inched along, holding his injured leg slightly back as he pushed off on the good leg and then dragged the other forward. The foot caught each time, sending a flare all the way through his groin until pain filled every conscious thought. When the rope was taut, he stopped and rammed his axe into the snow to belay Marty while he crossed. Then the American anchored Dorje while he continued to break trail, praying each time that the crampons would hold in soft, fresh snow. With this tedious, difficult work, Dorje's admiration of the Sherpas' trail preparation steadily increased. Gusting with menacing winds, the storm tried to sweep them off the mountain. Every sound that threatened a cornice collapse burgeoning into an avalanche echoed louder in his head.

Hampered by frozen hands, Dorje was slow in setting the next belay. Glancing back to warn Marty, he saw him remove his anchor and start across too soon. Before Dorje could sink the shaft, his partner slipped and plunged down the hill, arms and legs flying. And seconds later, Dorje was jerked into a tumbling dive, striking his head on a boulder on the first roll. In a state of mental confusion, he frantically tried to sink his axe, but the slope was too steep; the snow, too loose and slippery. Sliding on his stomach feet first, he made a final desperate attempt and drove the pick so hard it almost ripped out of his hand. The axe gouged a jagged scar, deeper and deeper, spraying snow in his face. He yelled and pushed harder with all that was in him until the axe finally arrested his fall. With his hands cold and stiff, unable to hold on much longer, he kicked the crampon of his good leg to brace himself for the inevitable jolt when the rope reached full length.

"Agghhh!" He bounced and held as Marty's weight tried to yank him free. His arms quivering and his injured leg on fire, Dorje couldn't hang on much longer waiting for Marty to find a hand or foothold. The American's weight threatening to wrench him from the hill, Dorje closed his eyes and summoned all his strength into those few seconds that meant the difference between life and death. *Just one more second, just one more. Hurry, Marty.* Suddenly the taut cord slackened. Had Marty finally dug his crampons in? Dorje yelled and shook the rope, begging for it to ripple back as before, but it remained limp as a windless flag. With mounting dread, he whipped it harder three, four, and five times before getting a response.

Cold, terrifying images of their plight surged into his aching head, but Dorje refused to look. Instead, he busied himself kicking to create a step where he could rest his weight fully on his right leg and reduce the strain. Feeling a bit more comfortable now, he was confident that Marty had done the same. Gripping the axe shaft in one hand, he pulled the cord shoulder high and snapped it like a whip. The rope coiled towards him before lashing back into the gray, enveloping mist where it met resistance reassuring him that Marty was still there.

Clinging to the axe with both hands and his forehead against the wall, Dorje was comforted by his only companion—the hissing inside his mask. How much longer would they have together? He checked the pressure gauge. Almost empty. Now what? Feeling his life slipping away, Dorje tried to pull things together and formulate a plan, but exhaustion and confusion reigned. His right hand, succumbing to the cold, had already lost its feeling and could no longer grip the axe. Afraid of falling, he grasped the shaft with the left and used his right arm to drape the rope over the shaft to anchor himself in case he lost consciousness. With the slope too steep to traverse, no more pitons, and a leg that couldn't support him, his only hope of survival was a Sherpa rescue. Fierce winds battered and whipped him as if he were a tent canvas. Turning from the tiny ice splinters lacerating his face, Dorje listened for the comforting hiss but it too had abandoned him. The air tasted bad now so he ripped the mask and tank off and watched them disappear in the gaping jaws of the gray beast below.

In a limbo state, he felt his spirit leave his body again and stand apart, viewing him in a detached manner. When it turned to walk away, Dorje grabbed it by the shoulder and forced it back. He wasn't ready to die and would never give up. With his jacket and hood zipped over his face, he breathed his own warm air and fought sleep, afraid that he might not wake. With the mask gone, the taste of his own blood trickling down his face sickened him.

His mind wandered from this cold, alien world to the warm Solu hills of his youth where marigolds mingled with wildflowers and begonias had just begun to bloom. He heard Beth laughing as she ran barefoot over the hills. "You can kiss me if you catch me" she tossed over her shoulder with her hair flying like shafts of wheat in the wind.

"Kiss you I will," he murmured and raced after her, willing to surrender his soul for the taste of her sweet lips. Catching her in the meadow, he gently lowered her to a carpet of primrose and iris. Brightly hued rhododendrons and orchids splashed the surrounding hills with color as Dorje enfolded her in his arms and made love on a lazy afternoon. "I will love you forever," he whispered. "As long as snow falls on the mountains and rivers run wild."

She gazed at him with her poppy-blue eyes. "And I will love you as long as my heart beats here," she purred and pressed his hand to her breast. Inhaling the delicate aroma of her hair and skin, he drifted off to sleep.

"Dorje," someone shouted. He shook himself awake and saw ten-year-old Nima reclining on his elbows beside him, his legs stretched out in front. Chewing on a long piece of grass like an old yak, Nima grinned. "I saw you kissing Pasi behind the banana trees."

Dorje pulled his brother's long hair down over his eyes. "You are as blind as an old man out in the snow too much. We were only picking fruit."

"No, you were kissing," he said with that intuitive, knowing look that had arrived in the world with him. "She's the most beautiful girl in the Solu."

"You're too young to notice such things."

"But she is." Nima touched the flower to his lips. "And I want to kiss her too."

"Well, you can't." Grabbing his brother's arms, Dorje held them over his head with one hand while tickling the funny spot that only he knew. Nima squirmed, kicked, and giggled making the freckles bunch up on his nose. He squealed for mercy but got none as they wrestled and rolled among the flowers until exhausted. Flopping onto his back with his arms thrown out to the sides, Dorje pretended to be exhausted. When Nima wasn't looking, he plucked a handful of grass and tossed it at him playfully.

"Dorje," their mother called from the small stone house below. "I have sweet rice pudding for my boys."

"Come, my little brother," Dorje said, pulling him onto his back for a ride. "Let's go home."

With Nima's skinny legs locked around his waist and his arms clutching his chest, Dorje knew they were inseparable forever. His brother's breath warm against his neck, he looked over his shoulder and whispered, "I love you."

"Dorje," someone called again, but lassitude, resignation, and hypothermia battled for possession of his thoughts. All he wanted to do was sleep, but a tall figure appeared shimmering in the mist. His long robe billowed in the wind as he approached. The striking features seemed gentler now like the softened edges of a sucked hard candy. The penetrating eyes that had always frightened Dorje were comforting when his father said, "Let's dance together." Putting his arm around his son's waist, Mingma shuffled forward and backward, touching his heel here and stomping there at an ever-quickening pace. Clutching his father's robe, Dorje matched him step for step, their spirits in harmony as they danced the rhythm of life.

"I'm so very cold and tired," Dorje finally whispered.

"Yes, sleep now, my son, and don't be afraid. I'll take care of you." Mingma lifted him into his arms and Dorje was a boy of five again. Nestling his weary head against his father's shoulder, he closed his eyes, feeling safe and loved, knowing he'd never had to watch and wait again. Swaddled in a snow blanket, his bloodied face whitened with hoarfrost, Dorje smiled as he drifted into a deep hypoxic reverie.

CHAPTER THIRTY-FIVE

As Beth watched Dorje and Marty disappear behind a tilting sérac, an ominous specter moved into her and settled down with hands clasped behind his head and legs outstretched, intending to remain until Dorje's safe return. She tried evicting this unwelcome guest by telling herself the morning's fight eliminated Dorje's chances of going to the summit, and he'd already been through the icefall and Cwm, so no danger there. But her heart knew any logic professor would fail her on that bit of spurious reasoning. Slamming the door on fear, Beth strode back to camp determined to concentrate solely on how beautiful the clouds were this morning hanging above the peaks in layers of purple and pale pink.

That strategy worked until she witnessed the doctor treating Rinji's frostbitten feet and learned most of his toes would be amputated. Then how would this sweet, little man support his family? Was there some kind of Sherpa insurance to protect them from the dangers imposed by inane westerners who felt compelled to prove themselves? Dorje had told her none of his people cared about climbing before the *mikarus* came. Even now, most did it only for the money, but at what cost she wondered. Relying on these thoughts to occupy her mind, Beth added them to her journal. During the afternoon, she chatted and played cards with the doctor and reporter—anything to fill the space nightmares tried to invade.

Shortly after lunch one day, she heard a horrendous boom and watched the very sérac that had swallowed Dorje from view crumble in a white explosion shooting powder hundreds of feet in the air. Knowing that melting in the afternoons created instability in a land already in flux, she whispered, *Don't travel then* in her private conversation with Dorje having convinced herself he heard her thoughts, Beth was confident she'd know if something happened. Otherwise, the waiting would be intolerable.

When Mark and Sean returned to Base Camp to recoup before the final assault, she learned that Dorje and the others were all right. Beth gave fear a shove toward the door but it braced its feet against the jambs. Unable to oust it, she consoled herself with visions of Dorje simply carrying a few more loads through the Cwm to earn rupees for Shanti and the baby and then coming back to her. However, the arrival of Henri, a climbing Sherpa, and Roger with bandaged head and ribs the following day buried all such illusions. Beth did the maths. Two Sherpas had quit earlier and now this one had come down. That left only Dorje and two others to supply the upper camps. Not feeling much like eating, she joined Henri and Roger in the dining tent for details.

"Your Sherpa's in better health than the American," said Roger.

"And might end up having to be his partner," added Henri. "Rumor is Paul and Jarvis don't trust Marty and won't climb with him."

Unprepared for this, Beth choked on the words. "But Dorje and Marty had a terrible fight the morning they left. How could they go up a mountain together?"

"I don't know that they will." Henri shrugged. "It's just my guess."

Beth turned back to Roger but he opened his hands in a show of equal uncertainty. Her bouncing leg unsettled her stomach even more. "When would they go?"

Henri leaned forward and rested his arms on the table while stirring his tea. "The first team in a few days, I suppose, or whenever the weather looks promising. There aren't many climbing windows before the monsoon."

"Surely Marty and Dorje wouldn't be first."

Henri shook his head. "Probably not."

"But when will we know?"

"Not until the first team comes down," Roger answered and rose from the table. "I'm still dizzy and have a horrific headache. I need to go to bed so we can leave for the hospital early tomorrow."

Shivering alone in her tent, Beth pulled the bag over her ears to drown out the endless groaning and cracking of shifting ice. Tomorrow, she would write of Sherpa families forced to endure every trekking and climbing season knowing that a father, son, husband, or brother might not return. She didn't know how they stood it year after year.

Mingma stood on the spot where he had carried his five-year-old son on his shoulders for his first view of the highest point on earth. His breath rising in a mist, Mingma looked at the snowy summits of Everest, Lhotse, Nuptse, and Ama Dablam etched sharply in the crystal air. "What drives my son to go where you forbid?" he cried to the mountain gods. "Why does he risk a most precious incarnation by defying you? Help me to understand." In the high mountain air, the gods were silent because only Dorje knew the answer.

A familiar voice rose behind him. "Droma Sunjo said I'd find you here. I have news from Everest."

His heart trembling, he turned to Pemba. "What do you know of my son?"

"Only that he is alive and twice saved a porter named Rinji who arrived at the hospital two days ago. They have to cut off his toes."

"I'm sorry for the porter. But the goddess will keep punishing us as long as we trespass and pollute her. This has to stop."

With a western hat resting atop his large ears, Pemba said, "You are blind in one eye, my old friend. She has also rewarded us with great wealth to build finer temples and train more monks."

"Who must now pray for the souls of those who died on the mountain. All your rupees can't buy them back."

"We'll never agree on this and I'm tired of arguing," Pemba said. Turning back toward Namche, he tossed words over his shoulder. "I just came to tell you about Dorje."

Proud of his own inner strength and how he had survival great sorrow, Mingma found it difficult to seek help from someone he had recently considered his enemy. "You're the only one I can turn to." Pemba paused and looked back. "Please come to Everest with me. I have a heavy feeling that danger awaits my son."

"As do I," Pemba said, his shoulders slumping. "You know I care for him too. We'll take five yaks loaded with tents, blankets, food, and water, plus have room to bring things in return."

Mingma found Nima on a hill north of the village. Instead of lying blissfully among the wildflowers, his peaceful, younger son was at great unrest, pacing and yelling at the animals.

"Why so troubled?" Mingma asked.

"The sky is not right."

"But it's clear. I see no clouds."

"But they'll come soon and I don't like how it feels."

Learning long ago that Nima sensed things the way his mother had, Mingma trusted him. "That's why Pemba and I are going after your brother to bring him home."

"I'll come too," Nima added in a gray voice that made the journey seem even more ominous.

Leaving at dawn the next morning, they reached Base Camp four days later a few hours after it had begun to snow. Having had no reason to come here previously, Mingma didn't know what to expect. The debris left by earlier expeditions appalled him and confirmed his belief that foreigners polluted the mountain and angered the gods.

"Follow me," said Pemba. "I've been here many times in the past buying what's left from expeditions to sell in my teahouse. I got chocolate from the Swiss, caviar from the Russians, tea from the British, cheese from the Dutch, and made a huge profit from American goods in 1963." He led Mingma and Nima to the supply tent where the cook and kitchen boys were selecting items for dinner. "We're looking for Mingma's son Dorje."

"He's on the mountain with the others," said the cook.

"But what do you know of him? Is he well?" asked Mingma.

"He was strong and healthy when he left here about a week ago, but you can ask his woman. She stands every day at the bottom of the icefall waiting for him."

"Shanti here?" Nima exclaimed. "How could Dorje let her come? It's not good for the baby. Father, you must make her go back to her family."

When Mingma hesitated, Pemba said, "Go to your future daughter-in-law. She needs you. Nima and I will put up the tents and prepare our beds."

The cook pointed the way and Mingma left walking blindly in the heavy snow, the uneven surface of the glacier cold and threatening under his soft leather boots. He finally spotted a dark figure standing at the base of a frozen waterfall. When she heard his approach and turned, Mingma met not the square face and long black hair of the Sherpani bearing his grandchild but the woman who had made his son's heart cry with longing through all of winter and spring. Part of him was angry at her for intruding in Dorje's life, but the other part was grateful his son had experienced the passion he might not ever feel with Shanti. This blue-eyed woman was Mingma's Nimputi, and a man finds that kind of love only once in his lifetime. So when she looked at him, her eyes brimming with tears, he couldn't turn away. Opening the wings of his robe, he enfolded her in his arms for she was also his lost daughter. Her body shivered as she laid her head against his chest. He quietly stroked her snow-matted hair and whispered all was well. Tomorrow Dorje would come bounding through the icefall. Knowing she didn't understand his words, Mingma hoped she recognized the tenderness and love in his voice.

With his protective arms around her, they walked in silence toward a glow emanating from the kitchen tent. When they reached the dining tent where two *mikarus* were waiting, she surprised him with a large hug that reminded him how soft a woman feels and how sweet the aroma of her hair. Tonight he would weep for Dorje, Nimputi, his two daughters, and also this woman whose eyes were plucked from the sky on a spring morn.

"Where's Shanti?" Nima asked when Mingma returned to the dining tent. "You didn't leave her?"

"I'm sure she's fine and with her family."

"Then who?"

Knowing the American had also entranced his younger son, Mingma waited for him to make the conclusion. It seemed easier than trying to explain.

Nima searched everyone's face, his eyes begging for an explanation. Then it hit him. "When did the American woman get here?" he asked the cook.

"She arrived in Lukla with the other *mikarus*. I first saw her there. She and Dorje have been making sauce and offended the goddess. That is why we have bad weather."

"She's possessed my brother just like she did me," Nima said, starting for the door. "And turned him from his baby and the beautiful woman he's to marry."

Mingma's outstretched arm barred him. "I will not have this family torn apart by anger and jealousy any longer. Your brother's only sin is falling in love. And you will not rob him of that as I was robbed. So leave her be and go to bed." Nima faltered. "Do as I say," his father ordered. "And treat her as a sister."

Mingma followed his son to their tent and then sat wrapped in yak wool blankets praying to the goddess to forgive Dorje's actions. "The boy is young and meant no dishonor," he whispered to himself. Throughout the night, he chanted the Tibetan scriptures memorized over many years of recitation and prayed the sun would shine again on the morrow.

CHAPTER THIRTY-SIX

Fear a permanent resident now; nights were the hardest for Beth as she struggled with not knowing where Dorje was or if he was dead or alive. The comforting intonations from Mingma's tent gave her some strength against the creaks and groans that made sleep sporadic. When she woke in the morning, sunlight was dancing on the roof, an auspicious sign. She dressed quickly and went outside, confident that Dorje would ski through the icefall today. Hearing Nima's voice, she walked toward two tents pitched 100 feet from camp. "*Namaste,*" she said bowing.

"*Namaste,*" replied Mingma with a warm smile, but his younger son wouldn't acknowledge her.

"*Namaste,* Nima," she repeated.

When he looked up with those freckles and sweet, boyish eyes, she said, "Please be my friend," and hoped he remembered some of the English lessons. "You and I wait for Dorje together."

His rigid lips softened at the corners and turned up in a subtle smile. "No clouds," he said pointing to the sky.

She grinned. "Yes, no clouds for us to play with, my brother." Buoyed by his smile and the clear sky, she asked the cook to prepare enough breakfast for Dorje's family and invited them to the dining tent.

Pemba spent the rest of the morning bargaining for goods while Beth, Mingma, and Nima took turns waiting at the base of the icefall. First to spot Jarvis and Paul in the sérac forest, Nima ran to camp, screaming and waving his arms. Beth's spirit soared thinking Dorje had finally returned but quickly plummeted as she watched two *mikarus* struggling down the glacier, their bodies stooped, barely able to lift one foot after the other. After ordering hot tea and soup, she set a place for them in the dining tent.

"What happened? Where are the others?" she pleaded once they were settled. As their story unfolded, Beth tried to explain to Mingma and Nima using gestures and the few words Nima had learned from her. Jarvis and Paul had made it to the top and stopped briefly at High Camp on their way down where they visited with Dorje and Marty who were preparing to summit the following morning.

"How were they?" Beth asked anxiously.

"The American was sick but the Sherpa appeared strong and eager," said Paul. "We stayed only a short while because we were done in and wanted to reach the South Col before dark." He explained they were headed back toward Camp II the next morning when it began to snow. They met the Darjeeling Sherpas and the Americans trying to find the fixed ropes on the Lhotse Face, but all was obscured in the flat, white light.

Jarvis continued. "Agreeing it was ill advised to climb in such weather, the four of us turned back toward the Cwm while the Sherpas went ahead to search for Dorje and Marty."

Told you so, fear whispered in her ear.

Shut up. It doesn't mean he's hurt, she yelled back in her head. But watching Paul's gaunt face and his eyes sunken in deep, gray hollows, she couldn't hush fear's incessant voice.

"We watched them with binoculars," the Frenchman continued. "Both made the summit with Dorje dragging the American up, but it was snowing on their way down and we lost sight of them just below the Balcony."

"But you saw them again right away," Beth said, giving fear a shove.

"Sorry," Jarvis answered, turning the teacup in his hands. "The snow was too thick to see."

"Why aren't all of you searching for them?" she shouted.

"Zopa and Namkha insisted on going on alone. We would get lost too and only make things worse," answered Paul. "The Americans and sirdar spent the night in Camp II with us. Jarvis and I came down because we're too sick, but the others are waiting in the Cwm. Don't worry. Zopa and Namkha are strong and will find them."

Beth curled in on herself like a wilted flower that had shriveled and lost its bloom. "Dorje up there," she told Mingma and Nima trying to mask her tears. "We wait for him."

While she and Nima stood shivering at the base of the icefall until after dark, Mingma and Pemba burned juniper incense and made rice offerings

to the goddess Miyolangsangma. They chanted prayers in a low monotonous intonation that droned through the silence of the camp until dawn.
Alone in her tent, Beth refused to listen to fear's mockery and convinced
herself that last night's prayers had ended the storm and brought sunlight. Tonight's would bring Dorje back to her.

As the sun rose, color flooded the earth's highest peaks with pink and
gold pouring down the fluted walls and spilling over the glacier. Beth
stretched her arms with her face to the sun bathing in its warmth. Surely
such a resplendent beginning could only herald good news. For the first
time in two days, she was able to converse dry eyed. To pass the time until
Dorje arrived, she played cards with the cook, kitchen boys, and Nima,
drank hot tea, and savored Dorje's favorite dish of *rigi kur:* crispy potato
pancakes served with a big lump of yak butter. The world felt good this
morning.

Pemba was the first to see them. Hearing his shouts, Beth and Nima
dropped their cards and raced each other giggling to the end of the glacier.
They teased and played as they had last fall while pointing to shapes in
the clouds, but now, they were trying to make out individuals in an icefall.
Too far away yet, the climbers appeared only as dark specks against glistening white, but she was certain Dorje would emerge triumphant. When
the roped figures traversed the rim of a crevasse to detour around it, she
counted only five. Had Zopa and Namkha remained behind or had the
Americans gone for an assault in clear weather? Awaiting Dorje's arms,
she quashed all other possibilities.

Standing beside her in his blood-red robe and bold features, Mingma's
presence had struck her the first day in the market place. There was an
undeniable pride that set him apart. Dorje had told her of Nimputi and his
daughters and why his father didn't come for them in the Solu. She was
glad they'd made peace and Dorje could return to him with a forgiving
heart. On her other side, was Nima. How different from his father and
brother, a gentle, intuitive soul who couldn't hold onto anger.

Beth held her breath as the figures drew near enough to identify. First
came Mark followed by Sean and the *sirdar*. Her confidence eroding, Beth
clutched Mingma's sleeve to steady herself. When the last two climbers
disappeared in the shadow of a sérac, fear cried out. *I won.* but she refused to
listen. Stooped over their axes as if consumed by fatigue, the Sherpas emerged
each dragging something over the ice. She grabbed Nima as her legs buckled.
Mingma caught her other arm and held her as they desperately searched for
two more figures. Perhaps Dorje and Marty were waiting for the others to pass
so they could ski down with bravura yelling *Geronimo.*

Forty-five minutes later, Mark, Sean, and the *sirdar* exited the icefall and approached Beth. She was so apprehensive she could barely comprehend what Mark was saying. In limited English, the sirdar had recounted the experience of the Darjeeling Sherpas to him. After losing sight of Dorje and Marty just below the Balcony, Zopa and Namkha had gone up immediately looking for them and searched all night using headlamps and repeatedly calling Dorje's name. But it was impossible to see anything.

Beth started shivering uncontrollably as if her blood had turned to ice. Teeth chattering and feeling faint, she clung to Mingma while the sirdar talked to him in Nepali.

"Beth," Mark whispered. "Do you want to hear more?"

"Nooo," she cried, shaking her head with tears streaming down her face and then, "Yes, I have to know."

Gazing at her with much tenderness in his eyes, he continued. "In sunlight the next morning, they probed everywhere below the Balcony, looking for footprints, but all had been buried or blown away. They had almost given up when Zopa spotted something on a steep slope 100 feet below them. Namkha belayed him while he rappelled down to Dorje and then to Marty 40 feet further below."

Beth inhaled so quickly the cold burned her throat. "Nooo, nooo," she sobbed. "He's not dead. Don't tell me that."

"I'm so sorry. No one could have survived the night with his head injury. They're bringing him and Marty down now. The American has severe frostbite but will survive." His eyes moist, Mark withdrew a paper from his pocket. "He loved you very much and wrote this in case he didn't return."

Gratefully taking it, she was much too absorbed in the Sherpas bringing down the one being who had taught her that she could love. Dorje was wrapped completely in a sleeping bag. Needing to see him once more, she dropped to her knees and tried untying it with trembling fingers.

The sirdar wiggled his hand side to side. "No. Lama must come first."

Sobbing convulsively, Beth lay beside Dorje with her head over his heart, wishing her love could make it start beating again.

"He saved my life," said a familiar voice. Marty was sitting on a makeshift stretcher with his hands and feet wrapped, a bluish cast to his face. "I may lose a few fingers and perhaps even toes, but I'm here and only because of him."

"What happened?"

"You couldn't see anything and your mind plays cruel tricks on you up there." His voice thick with emotion, Marty said, "It was an accident. Nobody's fault. We fell."

The doctor had joined them and instructed the Sherpas to take Dorje and Marty on down to camp. "I swear it was an accident," Marty called back to her.

Mingma lifted Beth to her feet with a protective arm around her. She buried her face in his robe, sobbing, as pain and desolation wrapped their tendrils around her heart leaving her so heavy with them she thought she would drown. Nima was crying too. As Mingma gripped them both, Beth couldn't imagine the depth of his sorrow after finding his oldest son only to lose him again.

Despite Beth's pleading, Mingma, Nima, and Pemba wouldn't join the expedition members for dinner that night, preferring to build a dung fire outside their tents and mourn in private. Knowing Mingma blamed foreigners for the many deaths among his people, she couldn't argue because he was right. None of them would have gone on the mountain otherwise. Her eyes still swollen with tears, she looked around the table at the gaunt, sun-baked faces and wondered why they did it. To prove something to themselves and the world? Power? Glory? Were any of those worth the loss of life? Opposite her, sat a different Marty from the presumptuous, wild-talking man who had left camp many days earlier.

"You were smart to choose Dorje over me," he said in a thin, dry voice when the others seemed engrossed in their conversations. "He was a much better man than I am or ever will be."

Tears started welling up again at the mere mention of Dorje's name, but Beth wanted to know everything that happened the last hours of his life to help her feel closer to him. Marty explained how Dorje saved him on the Lhotse Wall. "I'm not certain I would have done the same."

"Surely you would have."

Shaking his head, he said, "I don't know. I honestly don't. We were both still so angry then."

Seeing the pain in Marty's face, Beth knew such doubts would haunt him forever. "It's all right," she said softly. "Tell me more."

"Dorje wanted to reach the summit so bad and knew I was too sick to go on." Pausing, Marty wiped his hands across his eyes and sucked tears back inside as he continued. "I was delirious and hallucinating so he wrapped me in two bags and left plenty of oxygen before setting out."

"By himself?"

"Yes. And he would have made it easily, up and back, if it weren't for me. Like an idiot, I left the tent and followed his tracks until I couldn't walk. He was already on the South Summit before he discovered me crawling up behind him."

"So what did he do?"

"Probably yelled every expletive in the world before turning back for me and greatly jeopardizing his chances of getting to the top and his very life." His bandaged hands trembling, Marty said, "By the time we reached the Hillary Step, I was so wasted I couldn't move and sincerely wanted him to go on alone. He was within 30 minutes of the summit and didn't deserve to fail because of me."

"But Jarvis and Paul said you both made it."

"He did," Marty answered, his words now heavy and wet with emotion. "I only made it because he hauled my ass up there. I don't know where he found the strength to do it, but I'm convinced it took too much out of him and contributed to all that occurred later. At least I have photos to prove we stood on top of the world."

Tears rushed into her throat. "I want copies," she said trying to swallow them.

"Of course. When we get back to Colorado if you're still speaking to me. I know now that you never had an interest in me. I'm sorry for how I acted."

"It's okay," she said laying her hand on his arm. "Now tell me the rest. I have to know it all."

"A storm hit us and we couldn't see anything trying to traverse a very steep slope. He went ahead to belay me and then I'm not sure what happened." As if trying to reconcile events in his own mind, Marty said, "You can't think straight up there. I guess I was hallucinating again because I was sure I saw the two climbing Sherpas standing beside Dorje, smiling and waving me on. So I removed the anchor and started toward them." His voice wavered. "Then suddenly I was falling and dragging him with me, certain that we were both going to die. But miraculously he stopped the fall and held as the rope slammed me against the snow. For what seemed like an eternity, I struggled to kick my toe pick in and take the weight off him. He whipped the rope and I lashed it back to let him know I was all right. Then I must have passed out because I don't remember a thing until a Sherpa rescued me." Elbows on the table, face buried in his hands, Marty shook his head. "Believe me, Beth, I'd give anything to have died instead of him. When I saw him, his face was covered with blood from a head wound. Why couldn't that have been me?"

After trying to reassure Marty that it wasn't his fault, Beth excused herself saying her stomach was too upset to eat. She yearned for the solitude of her tent where she could cry as long and hard as she wanted without everyone trying to comfort her. There was no consolation. Dorje was dead and her life would never be the same. Feeling empty and alone, she questioned whether she would allow herself to ever love again because the pain of loss was too great to bear more than once. When there were no more tears left, she lay with her head pounding, unable to breathe through her nose, eyes swollen. She remembered the note Mark had given her. Where did she put it? Searching everywhere, she found it in her shirt pocket, next to her heart.

To my beautiful Beth. Tomorrow I will leave for the top of Everest. Please understand why I must do this. It is my fate and I want to make you proud of me so you will never be ashamed. If I do not return, know that our spirits will always be together in this life and all those that follow. You are my sunrise and my sunset. You will always feel my arms around you and my lips on yours. I will never stop loving you. This I promise with my entire heart. From the man who loves you more than his own life. Dorje.

She read it over and over, memorizing every word and knew that it was true. Dorje would always be a part of her in this life and any that followed.

CHAPTER THIRTY-SEVEN

His older son lying wrapped in a bag on the ground, Mingma gently lifted Beth to her feet and held her in one arm and Nima in the other, both children crying. He had lost his wife and watched two small boys go away, lost Nimputi and his daughters, and lost his livelihood. Through it all, he had tried to remain strong, but this was more than he could endure. While knowing death was a critical part of the cycle of birth, death, and rebirth, Mingma didn't want to let go of the son he had just found again. Beth seemed so fragile as if the life had poured out of her. After walking her to the dining tent, he joined Nima and Pemba to grieve in private. Worried about his son's untimely death, Mingma feared Dorje's ghost would become a *shrindi* wandering and waiting to be dispatched to heaven or one several hells. Some ghosts were simply lost and roamed about unaware that they were dead, but others became malignant spirits causing much trouble.

"We must do everything we can to help your brother reach a favorable rebirth," he told Nima. Pemba and I will leave at sunrise with Dorje to prepare his funeral before it is too late. Follow soon with Beth and the Americans who treat her so kindly." As Nima agreed, his mournful face reminded Mingma that his younger son was also grieving. In a softer voice he added, "And sleep in warm houses. You know Sherpa doors are always open."

At sunrise, Pemba loaded all the expedition supplies he had bargained for, the tents, and bedding. The fourth yak bore Dorje's wrapped corpse and the fifth would carry the personal gear of Beth, Nima, and the three Americans. The sirdar had already left to hire additional porters to break camp. Mingma knew he must put away his sorrow for now and direct all efforts toward helping Dorje's spirit. Immediately upon reaching Namche, he sent for a lama to properly dispatch Dorje to his next life. The lama arrived in a sleeveless, magenta cassock wrapped over a gold, high-collared brocade shirt and tied with a sash at the waist. While pulling a few hairs from Dorje's head to create an opening for his spirit (*sem*) to depart, he recited prayers to help send it to the heaven of boundless light. Consulting his astrological charts, the lama announced that the most auspicious time for disposing of the body was three days hence and it should be cremated facing east.

The initial ceremony concluded, a man from the village prepared Dorje by wrapping him completely in a white cloth and then tying him in a seated position in front of a temporary altar. Behind him stood six *torma* dough cakes coated with colored, melted butter and decorated to represent deities to whom the lama prayed to relieve Dorje of the burden of sin. While reciting from the *Tibetan Book of the Dead,* the lama prepared the *sem* to travel through the after-death state that lasted 49 days. Speaking directly to Dorje, he instructed him not to be afraid of the startling, horrific deities he will encounter but to know they have come to protect and lead him to one of the six spheres of the wheel of life.

When Beth and Nima arrived the following afternoon, Mingma sent for the Khunde doctor to explain Sherpa rituals to her. While lamas chanted solemn recitations accompanied by drums, the clash of cymbals, and blowing of a thighbone trumpet, friends and family came to express sympathy and make offerings to Dorje. They placed flasks of *chang* on a table before him to be consumed later by all present.

Watching Beth sitting stone faced and silent, an object of great curiosity to all, Mingma wondered what she was thinking. How did she feel? He had no way of communicating with her other than the tone of his voice and softness in his eyes. Rarely moving from the window bench, she remained the full two days and nights with Nima ever at her side. On the final day, Shanti arrived swollen with Mingma's grandchild. When she dropped to her knees crying before Dorje, he glanced at Beth wondering if she knew and decided that she must. But instead of anger or jealousy, Beth's face expressed sympathy.

Nima interrupted his thoughts. "Father, I've decided to use my rights as the younger brother. I will marry Shanti and take care of Dorje's child so I can always feel him with me."

While relieved because the marriage could take place without the necessity of another expensive *sodene* or *dem-chang,* Mingma worried that his younger son might not experience the passion he and Dorje had felt in their love. "Is there no one else, someone you love?"

"No one I can have," Nima murmured with downcast eyes.

When Shanti rose and saw Beth, her face changed from grief to bewilderment. Mingma quickly asked Nima, "Have you spoken to her of this?"

"No, but I will do so now," he said and strode across the room, a boy about to become a man.

At sunrise the morning of Dorje's cremation, a thighbone trumpet announced the funeral procession leaving Mingma's house that was led by a young lama carrying a prayer flag. Following him were other lamas and a man carrying the corpse still wrapped in white cloth for the journey. Long, telescoping *dung-chens* droned a death dirge reverberating through the hills as the procession climbed the highest ridge to place Dorje on a pyre close to the sky. Walking slowly, lamas recited from a book showing the path to Devachen, the heaven of Sherpa belief. Only Mingma and a few helpers who would prepare the fire and tend to the lamas' needs accompanied them. This was all that custom required. Hoping Beth would understand, Mingma asked the Khunde doctor to explain she must remain behind because women never attended cremations.

Setting Dorje aside for a moment, the lamas prepared a temporary altar made of stones arranged in two tiers and covered with a yak wool blanket. They placed the six *tormas* from inside the house on the upper row and ritual items on the lower one. Playing cymbals, trumpets, and drums, they began more recitations while helpers carried Dorje to the pyre and undressed him. After attaching pieces of paper containing prayers to seven parts of his body and placing an imprint of the wheel of life above his head, they built him into the pyre in a seated position surrounded by logs covered with juniper branches. The senior lama gave Dorje's *sem* the necessary direction and motivation to move to the next stage by saying he must give up all thought and attachments to this life because he no longer belonged to this earth. He must go happily to the next world and not trouble the living as a restless *shrindi.* As the lamas resumed their chanting, helpers lit the funeral pyre from the four cardinal corners. While the fire burned, they fed the flames with offerings of grain, grass, butter, honey, and small sticks.

Watching the fire slowly consume his son's body, Mingma prayed that Dorje would have a favorable rebirth. Much depended on the merit and karma accumulated in his lifetime, but friends and family could assist in earning more during the 49-day transitional period between death and reincarnation, the *bardo*. For this, Mingma would go in debt for many years paying lamas to repeat a sacred text at least 1,000 times and financing the final distribution of food and money to all the surrounding villagers. Fortunately, Pemba had offered to donate the supplies he purchased at Base Camp and Droma Sunjo would prepare rice balls, butter, and *chang*. Each item accepted by a villager or any stranger passing through earned *sönam* for Dorje's reincarnation occurring on the 49th day

When the pyre burned down, Mingma returned home for the final *narpa* rites where a lama called upon Dorje to present himself on a name card and remain there until directed where to go. At the conclusion of the long ritual, the lama sent him to Devachen and then dipped the name card in melted butter and lit it. From then on, Dorje's name would never be mentioned again lest his *sem* be confused and believe he was still alive, thus hindering his transition to the next life. Even though Mingma would never utter the word *Dorje* again, his son would remain in his heart and thoughts. With Nima married to Shanti, Mingma could smother his grandchild with the love circumstances had denied his own children

Two days after the cremation, Beth said she must return home. Having grown to love her like a daughter, Mingma didn't want her to leave, but he understood there was no place for her here. Needing to remain in Namche until the end of the *bardo,* he couldn't accompany her to Lukla but the Americans had waited to make the two-day trek with her. With Marty already in Kathmandu for frostbite treatment, Mingma and Nima walked to the village edge with Beth, Mark, and Sean. His fingers trembling and his insides weeping, Mingma placed a silk *kata* around her neck, bowed with his hands together, and whispered, "Namaste."

"Namaste," she replied with moisture forming at the corners of her eyes like drops of morning dew. When she grabbed him in a long, tight hug, he stroked her beautiful, silky hair and kissed her forehead, fighting desperately to reign in his own tears. After hugging Nima who couldn't contain his sorrow, Beth turned and headed out of their lives forever.

*** *** ***

The trip back to Lukla was worse than Beth feared. Memories of Dorje ambushed her at every turn in the trail. She saw him helping the old ladies over the bridge, skiing down a muddy hill, explaining the meaning of the prayer flags, advising them to walk to the left of mani stones. His presence was so strong, she kept hearing him whisper, "I love you," and feeling his breath on her cheek. Too often she took her eyes from the trail to search for him and lost her footing. Only Mark kept her from falling over the edge emotionally and physically. Every moment alone, she re-read Dorje's letter promising they would be together in this life and all those that follow. Accepting his faith, she would hold onto it forever.

Sitting in the STOL at Lukla, Beth remembered a Sherpa in a green hat that said SKI VAIL competing in a hand jive with an American wearing socks that didn't match. And something stirred deep inside her. As the small plane sped down the runway to lift off just before reaching the cliff, she pressed her face to the window, looking behind her, certain that Dorje was calling her back. Tears filmed the glass as they rose over giant ridge systems stretching in all directions and steep hills scored by deep gullies. As the ice-clad mountains filling the horizon to the north slowly disappeared, the finality of Dorje's death cut an immense hole inside, leaving her raw and bleeding.

"Are you all right?" Mark asked when she threw her head back and closed her eyes, biting her lips.

"No," she whispered, trembling.

"I understand but you will be in time," he said touching her arm. "You're a beautiful, intelligent, desirable woman with your whole life ahead."

While she and the Americans waited two days in Kathmandu for the next flight out, Beth strolled the streets she had visited the first time here with Eric. Poor man. She hadn't thought of him in weeks. Where was he now, still in Nam, still alive? Or had she sent him off to die too? Unable to deal with such thoughts now, she shoved them from her mind. Perhaps when she was back home, they would talk and discover each other again.

Entering Freak Street where flower children existed on pies and hash, she looked for the woman with pale green eyes and delicate mouth. "The cause of all human suffering is desiring what we can't have," the woman had told her. "To become truly awake like Buddha, we must be unflappable and accept whatever comes along as part of a divine and perfect universe." Beth had fought all morning to keep from crying but grief was a powerful force. Sinking to the curb, she wept trying to understand how Dorje's death was part of a divine and perfect universe. It didn't make sense. None of it did right now. Maybe when she got back home, things would become clearer, but the pain would never disappear. It had crept into every pore.

On board the plane, Mark and Sean were seated across the aisle. Beth was next to the window with an elderly woman beside her, the veins in her aging arms as fine as the tracery in a leaf. Twenty minutes into the air, the captain announced, "Ladies and Gentlemen, those of you seated on the left now have your last view of the majestic Himalayas and their crown jewel, Mount Everest."

"Which one is it?" the woman asked leaning across her.

"There, the one with the black triangular face constantly swept clean by the wind," Beth answered.

"It doesn't look taller than the others. Why would anyone want to climb it?"

"I don't know. I honestly don't know."

When the mountains were out of sight, the woman leaned back against her seat. "You're a long way from home, Dear. Are you here all alone?"

Wet eyes averted from the woman, Beth nodded.

"Why? Doesn't a pretty girl like you have a boyfriend?"

Fingers pressed together, she tapped her lips and whispered, "I did once."

"Well, many more will fall in love with you. You'll see," the woman added, giving her a grandmotherly pat on the leg.

Turning to her, Beth said, "Perhaps, but I've learned it's not important how many people love you. What matters is whether you can love them."

Closing her eyes to discourage further conversation, Beth wanted to be alone with Dorje these last minutes over Nepal. He had taught her how to feel and soar with wings unfurled, but never again would she experience the heights they had flown.

GLOSSARY

Aalu	Potato
Baabu	Father
Bajai	Grandmother
Bardo	A transitional after-death state during which the next reincarnation is determined
Bidi	Cigarette made of a pinch of tobacco, rolled in a leaf, tied together with a string
Bistarai	Slowly
Chaane	Protective mixture of blessed grains of rice and sand from a mandala
Chang	Powerful, locally brewed beer made from fermented barley, rice, millet, or maize
Chapatti	Flat, round, unleavened bread cooked over an open fire
Charpi	Toilet
Chorten	Buddhist conical structure, conical in shape, made of plastered rocks
Chomolungma	Tibetan word for Everest, Mother Goddess of the world
Damaru	Hour-glass shaped drum made from human half skulls
Dem-chang	Beer typing ceremony that confirms a proposal. One step before marriage
Dhal bhaat	Rice with lentil broth. A staple food
Dhyangro	A two-headed drum
Doko	Basket used by porters, supported by a tumpline over the head
Dumje	Major Buddhist festival held at the village for the benefit of all
Dung-chen	Long telescoping horn
Gompa	Tibetan Buddhist monastery
Jannu	Go
Kani	Covered gateway decorated with scenes of local deities and Buddha
Kata	White ceremonial scarf presented to guests or lamas on special occasions
Lawa	Host for the Dumje celebration
Lungta	Wind horse—prayer flag
Madal	Small, cylindrical drum with skin on either end, played with both hands

Mandala	Sacred diagram in geometric shape representing the world
Mani	Tibetan Buddhist prayer inscribed in rock
Mikaru	"White eyes" term used to describe foreigners
Mendan	Long wall composed of mani stones
Momo	Pasta stuffed with meat or vegetables, similar to ravioli or pot stickers
Naamlo	Hemp tumpline of a doko
Nak	Female yak
Nagi	River spirit
Namaste	Traditional Nepalese greeting. "I salute the divine qualities in you."
Om mani padme hum	Mantra often used during meditation and prayer. "Hail to the jewel in the lotus."
Pak	Dough ball of tsampa, sugar, and nuts
Patni	Wife
Pem	Witch
Puja	Religious offering or prayer
Rai	A Nepalese tribes that lives south of the Khumbu
Rigi kur	Crispy potato pancakes served with a big lump of yak butter
Sarangi	Small, four-stringed instrument played with a horse-hair bow
Sem	Spirit of a dead person
Serac	An isolated block of ice that is formed where the glacier surface is fractured
Sirdar	Sherpa in charge of organizing and managing a trekking or climbing group
Sherpani	Female Sherpa
Shrindi	Malignant ghost that wanders restlessly, often causing human suffering
Sodene	Marriage proposal made by the father of the groom to the girls' parents
Sönam	Merit one accumulates over a lifetime to determine the next level of reincarnation
Sutra	A discourse of the Buddha
Sungdi	Thin braided string of red nylon blessed by a lama, protects the wearer
Thanka	Religious scroll painting usually of mandalas or deities
Thukpa	Sherpa stew

Toi ye	Damn
Torma	Conical flour cake decorated with colored butter to depict gods and demons
Tsampa	Roasted barley flour, staple food for Sherpas
Yersa	Temporary settlement used to pasture animals during the summer
Yeti	Nepal's abominable snowman
Zhum	Female crossbreed of yak and cow, used for milking
Zopkio	Male crossbreed of yak and cow, used for transport
Zendi	Final wedding ceremony

A NOTE ABOUT THE AUTHOR

Born in Denver, Colorado at the foot of the Rockies, Linda's love affair with mountains began as a young child. An adventure traveler to 35 countries on six continents, she first discovered the wonderful Nepalese people in 1986. Working with a group of Sherpas, she was a founder of the first hut-to-hut system in Nepal and helped establish 18 lodges in the Solo-Khumbu region. She began organizing and leading treks to the Everest Base Camp two years later. With a BA in literature and a Masters in Library Science, she combined her love of books, other cultures, and research skills to pen the first fiction written about Sherpas. High in the Himalayas during the worst storm in memory, she was appalled by world press coverage of the many foreigners who died but no mention of the Sherpas who also perished. She returned home to write their story.

**Give Beyond the Summit to your friends and colleagues.
Check your local bookstore or order here.**

❒ YES, I want ___copies of Beyond the Summit for $16.95 each.

❒ YES, I am interested in having Linda LeBlanc give a slide show on trekking in Nepal and the Sherpas of the Everest region to my company, association, school, library, or organization.

Include $3.95 shipping and handling for one book and $2.25 for each additional book.

My check or money order for $_____is enclosed.

Name. _____

Organization _____

Address _____

City/State/Zip _____

Phone _____ E-mail_____

Call (720) 232-7599 or
E-mail: mymingma@yahoo.com

Make your check payable and return to

Ama Dablam, Inc.
7122 Xavier Way
Westminster, CO 80030

www.beyondthesummit-novel.com